SKYLAR

THE MAGIC STOLEN FROM HIM

Copyright © 2021 Skylar A. Blevins

All rights reserved. No part of this book may be reproduced or used in any manner without the prior written permission of the copyright owner, except for the use of brief quotation in a book review.

To request permission, contact the author at:
skylarablevins@gmail.com

Hardcover: 978-1-7375256-2-2

Paperback: 978-1-7375256-0-8

Ebook: 978-1-7375256-1-5

First paperback edition October 2021

Edited by Jamie Powell

Cover art by Kelly Ritchie

To the man in the moon, the one whom I've told all of my secrets to, the one that never judged, the one I've loved all along.

Prologue

At the dawn of civilization, the world was created. Six gods shaped the planet into their liking, yet one wanted to create man while the others sought to create beings much more powerful. With it being decided that humans and magical beings are unable to live in harmony, the God took his humans to his portion of the planet, while the other gods sealed their portion off, allowing no humans to enter into their sacred land.

Half is called The Court of Dwimmér, the other is Masenia, and both started their rule in harmony. Dwimmér is ruled by a king and queen of each major beings: Lycan, Warlock, Witch, Faerie, and Demon. Since none are stronger than the others, it was decided they would rule as equals until a stronger being emerges.

Masenia is governed quite differently. A high-level demon named Whitehorn rules a land broken into factions, each one having a sole purpose—run his kingdom. Yet, even though Whitehorn had thousands under his rule, that power wasn't enough.

Whitehorn learned of a young boy tribrid that is both blessed and cursed by the gods. His blessing came first, the ability to harness mass power; the God who blessed him gave a portion of himself to the boy through a slice in his palm as a babe. This allowed him to be a true tribrid. Part Lycan, part Warlock, and part God. The curse on the boy followed suit. The beings in Dwimmér grew nervous over his abilities, knowing he would be strong enough to rule all once he was older. The other creatures called out to their creators and asked them to curse the boy, yet the prince's father was involved. With the threat of Whitehorn coming after his heir, King Silas offered his own powers up to seal the curse into his son.

The curse turned the prince's god like abilities dormant but brought out his Lycan side, demanding him to shift into a wolf every full moon. This is something that hadn't happened since the first true Lycan. He would be bound to the moon with only a few magical abilities until his mate would come and return the magic stolen from him.

The key to unlocking the curse would be the last Nightlighter, one born from a mother witch and father warlock. She would be born as the strongest of her kind and an equal for the god like king.

Young Prince Reznor was the strongest creation ever made, with the future of having a mate equally as strong. Whitehorn was threatened, and he sought to solve it by launching a war against the Court of Dwimmér, bringing magical beasts and soldiers to fight the court. Yet, after a year of fighting, Whitehorn was forced home to return to his land. King Silas defeated him but lost his life in battle. His wife followed a few months later due to a sudden illness, leaving the young price alone.

At the tender age of nine, Reznor was forced to become king; his lands were divided by the court but due to his foreseen power, the court feared to take much. He was able to keep his childhood home, but as the years passed some pushed in, trying to take what was his. After refusing to allow anyone to take his home, he was forced to send troops out at a young age. His reign as king was recured in a mass bloodshed.

    Beings and creatures flocked to Nightsend in seek of refuge to live freely amongst his lands. In the coming years, one particular witch sought the king out for a different reason. Scorned by Reznor, the rejected woman was filled with an all-consuming rage. The young witch went out and intentionally broke her species most sacred rule, forbidding any witch with laying with a warlock. The rule was in place to prevent the birth of a Nightlighter, the one and only thing that could fulfill Reznor's prophecy of unlimited power by joining him with his one true mate. Her rebellious tryst created the last Nightlighter, the mate to the tribrid king. Without ever telling Reznor, she fled to the mortal world to raise the child hidden amongst the humans. Yet the day the Nightlighter was born, the sky crackled with lightning and rolled with thunder. He caught her scent on a phantom wind. Ever since that day, Reznor has been scouring the planet in search of his mate, and nothing will keep him from her.

Chapter One: Birthday Surprise

Just after midnight, a storm rolls in over the mountains. The sky turns black and grey with a storm raging on. Rain and hail crashes to the ground, wind shakes the trees, and lightening is the only thing that can break the darkness. The sun is nowhere to be found amongst the dark sky, and it has been like this for hours. The power went out across the town of Somerstone Valley late last night, and the scared people flocked to the hospital.

What am I doing in the midst of this massive storm? I'm stuck at the hospital, working a shift I shouldn't have picked up. With my shift ending, I'm supposed to be leaving the hospital and heading home, but this weather makes me wary. I've been standing here in the doorway, contemplating if I'm going to risk driving home or go find a chair to sleep on. Honestly, at this point, finding a chair to climb into and sleep for hours is tempting, but I need to check on my mom.

My mom, she can get a little…crazy at times. Last night we had gotten into a fight because I'd picked up an extra shift. She kept making excuses telling me I needed to stay home because it would be my birthday at midnight, but that wasn't a valid excuse, and she knew it. So, I went to work, and she pouted about it. Now I kind of wished I had listened and stayed home, then I wouldn't be contemplating driving in the storm, or sleeping in a chair right now. The last thing I'd do is tell that woman she's right. Great, guess I'm driving home in the storm from hell.

Clutching my bag over my head, I dart out into the storm only to stop a few paces later as the sky goes quiet. It seems time has frozen as the world around me turns silent. Rain stops falling, the wind stops blowing, lightning doesn't strike, and thunder doesn't roll. It is completely and utterly quiet…then *boom*.

The storm gets harder, the wind nearly knocking me from my feet as I dashed the final stretch to my car before practically flinging myself inside. Maybe I'm in the eye of the storm, and if so, I need to get the hell out of dodge. It's bad enough I'm about to drive up the side of a mountain.

My mom and I live on the flat side of the mountain, which is almost perfect, except for the steep drive. Even now, I'm silently praying that my car will make it up against the beating of the weather. With a final groan from my car, I manage to clear the peak and park inside the garage. I need to get a new car, but that's on the list for things to deal with later because right now, all I'm thinking about is a shower, then my soft, fluffy bed.

Operating on autopilot as I wander into the house, I'm nearly halfway through the living room before my dazed brain realizes what a mess I've walked into. The living room is trashed, pictures are off the walls, the couch is turned over, and muddy footprints are all over the white carpet.

"Mom?"

"In the kitchen!" she shouts back. I meander through the trashed living room and find my mother cooking *something* on the stove.

"Why is the house a mess?" She hardly seems to register my presence as she frantically runs about the kitchen, adding things to the pot on the stove. Peeking at the concoction, I bite back a gag as the scent of sulfur hits my nose.

"Well, I lost something last night, and I couldn't sleep anyway, so I tore the house apart until I found it." She shakes something else into her creation.

"What did you lose?"

She glances up at me, narrowing her eyes slightly. "It doesn't matter now; I found it. That reminds me, happy twenty-first birthday!" She hurries around the corner and pats me on the shoulder. "Go get some sleep. We will celebrate tonight."

We're not exactly an affectionate kind of family, and even less so when she acts like this. Sometimes she trashes the house, muttering incoherent words and utter nonsense. When it happens, I do my best to ignore it, but occasionally she can get rather belligerent until I comply with what she wants. I'm starting to think she has a mental disorder and have contemplated pink slipping her by calling the cops once or twice, but every time I trick her into a doctor's appointment, she's magically *normal*. This behavior is practically her baseline and therefore, I'm going to proceed with my original plan.

A quick shower helps wash away the grime from last night's busy shift. The hot water was supposed to relax me, but it's hard to relax when the house is shaking from the storm. Drying off in the darkness, a stinging starts at the back of my neck. Reaching a hand back, I trace a finger along the area where the pain is radiating from. I try to find the source of the pain but come up empty.

I must have pulled something last night. Lately work has been harder on me—bags forming under my eyes, tiring easier and more frequently lately. Glancing in the mirror I'm not surprised to see the bags are growing darker. Even my light blue eyes seem a bit dull with my pale skin. My face is slightly rounded with high cheekbones, a nose I've always referred to as small (thank god) and brows that I hate most days. It's a struggle to keep up with them, but if I don't, I fear they'd crawl off my face. Lately, I've hardly kept up on them with my constant tiredness. Even now, I'm not bothering to put on clothes before I climb into the bed naked. I'm not sure if my head hits the pillow before I fall asleep.

Come to me...

Come to me...

Come to me...

Come to me...

A male voice speaks softly to me, feeling like a whisper against my ear. It's enticing, drawing me in and attempting to rouse me from sleep.

Liara!

With the shout of my name, I startle awake in a panic. Sitting up in the bed, I search for the source of the voice, but no one's in my room but me. My arms are covered in goosebumps and there is a strange pulling in my chest.

The stinging in my neck suddenly returns, this time more forceful. Again, I grasp the back of my neck, trying to find the source of the pain, but the only thing I find is my skin being freakishly hot. Then, as quickly as the pain started, it stops.

What the hell?

Annoyed at being woken up, I snatch my phone to check the time. It's only noon. I've hardly slept at all, but the adrenaline from my dream will not allow me to sleep anytime soon.

Abandoning my room after quickly throwing on some clothes, I'm pleasantly surprised to see the house is back in order. The outside of the house however does not look so good; the storm's still going, and we had a tree come down at some point. It's now leaning off the side of the porch, but hey, at least it didn't break it.

"Did you get some sleep?" my mom asks from her spot on the couch. She's lounging in sweats with her blonde hair now combed. Her peculiar purple eyes appear darker in the soft light, though her new wrinkles are becoming more prominent. She curses them every day, but no one can stop the aging process.

"Not really, I had a weird dream that woke me." I reply, shaking off the sensation that starts crawling up my spine.

"What was it about?"

Taking the seat next to her, I gaze out the window. "Just a voice, shouting my name."

She shoots me a concerning glance. "Hey, will you go check on Grandma since you're up? I'm worried about her. I haven't been able to get her on the phone today. While you're gone, I'll start working on your cake."

"Sure, just let me get dressed properly. I still feel like I'm half asleep."

Grams lives forty minutes away and up the other side of the mountain. I've driven there a million times, but this time, it's different. I feel like I'm being watched as I roll down the driveway. The feeling only stops once I reach town… that or I'm too focused on this phantom pain haunting my neck that won't stop. It seems the further I get away from the house, the worse the pain gets.

Groaning, I grab at my neck as a feverish sweat breaks out across my forehead. This pain is becoming uncomfortable quickly, and this definitely isn't a strain. Cranking the air up, I receive some relief as the cold air blasts my face through the vents, eliminating the heat that had swept over my body.

I finally reach Gram's house after a drive that was longer than usual thanks to the lovely storm. I practically run up her porch then strut through the door without knocking. "Grams?" I holler into the house.

"Liara?" she calls out she's sits in her study, writing in her journal. Much like my mom, she too has the special purple eyes. I was not lucky enough to receive that gene—nope. I got stuck with light blue. "Not that it's not a nice surprise, but what are you doing here?"

"Mom asked me to stop by and check in on you since she couldn't get you on the phone."

"What are you talking about? I just got off the phone with your mom."

It's my turn to be confused. "Then why did she have me drive all the way out here? Grams, mom's been acting worse than usual."

"How so?"

"She's been running around the house and trashing it more than usual; this morning she was boiling something that looked like lake water and smelled like sulfur."

Her face contorts for a moment before composing herself once again. "Maybe I should go check on your mom. It's your birthday; we can use that as an excuse."

"Thank you, Grams. I'm just worried about her."

She smiles, then rises from her chair. "I understand. Let me grab your present and change really quick. Then we can go."

Lightning strikes in the distance, lighting up the room. Grams eyes the storm before leaving quickly. Gazing out the window, watching the storm, I'm captivated by its beauty and power. It's rare we get a storm this bad, but I've always had a love for thunderstorms.

"It's a bad storm, isn't it?" Grams reappears in a pink sweater, jeans, and matching rain boots. Her white, blonde hair is tucked beneath a scarf tied around her head. Fashion is one of her favorite things. She'll never be caught looking 'dreary.' Her words, not mine.

"Yes, but it's beautiful. The strangest thing happened this morning when I was leaving work; it was almost as if the storm paused the second I walked outside. After a moment or two, a massive strike of lightning hit, and it all picked up again."

Grams drops her pink umbrella. "What do you mean it paused?"

"The rain stopped; the wind stopped. It was like everything went still for a few moments, then *boom*, it came down harder than ever."

Grams face drains of color. "Let's go check on your mom." She rushes me out of the door and doesn't speak again till we're nearly back to town. "What is it?"

My neck is throbbing again, the sensation coming in waves. "The back of my neck hurts." I've been clutching my hand to my nape for some time now, but the pressure isn't helping.

"Here, let me take a look."

I turn my head slightly away from her but straight enough that I could still watch the road, not that it matters much. Nobody is out in this storm. Grams traces something on the back of my neck, drawing my attention back to her.

"Is there something there?"

"Yes, but don't worry. You can look at it when we get to the house." Her calmness is a far cry compared to the look on her face. She then turns silent for the rest of the ride back to the house.

It's déjà vu when we enter the house; the living room is destroyed, but this time, things are broken, and blood and dark green slime is smeared along the floor. Great, now she's injured and tracking her green creation from this morning across the floor.

"Mom?" I call out.

No response.

I wander through the house searching for her, but she is nowhere to be found. The house is trashed in every room; even my bedroom has now been destroyed.

"Liara, come here!" Grams shouts from somewhere in the house.

I find Grams waiting by the basement door. "What is it?"

"She's down there. Come on, hun."

We creep down the stairs slowly. Standing in the middle of the basement is my mother with a man tied up in ropes. He has blood coming from his nose, eyebrow, mouth, and a vertical slice on his chest. Despite all the blood, I focus on the man's yellow eyes. It's a piercing shade that stands out against his coffee-colored skin...well, that and the blood.

"Mom! What the hell did you do?" I screech as I attempt to step forward, only to have Grams stop me by placing a hand on my shoulder.

My mother stands with a knife in her hand, engravings lining the handle and green slime coating the blade. "Liara, leave, this doesn't concern you."

"Maura, she already has the crest; it's too late." Grams reaches for the knife in her hand, slowly taking it away.

"She has the crest already?" She gapes in disbelief. "Where?"

"On the back of her neck. Liara, lift your hair up and turn around."

Doing as she says, I turn around, but not before speaking. "Can one of you explain what is going on?"

Grams steps forward with her phone in her hands and snaps a picture of my neck before handing it to me. A crescent moon with three small stars near the bottom now mark the back of my neck. "What is that?" I squawk at my new tattoo. My hands fly instantly to my nape, but it still feels the same.

"It's your crest. Your powers came in today." Grams coos with a soothing voice; she's trying to keep me calm, and it's not working.

"What are you talking about?" Maybe they're both crazy; then again, I am the one with a tattoo that seemingly appeared out of thin air.

"You need to tell her." Grams looks over the tied-up man who is staring at me with an assessing gaze.

"You have powers," my mother says blankly.

"Gods, Maura, start from the beginning… tell her about the curse. Tell her about *him*." Grams no longer has the soothing tone as she glares at her.

"Well, this isn't what I had planned for your birthday surprise."

Chapter Two: The curse

I just stare at them. This is nuts. The only reason I snap out of my daze is because the bleeding man speaks up and drags me back to reality.

"She doesn't know anything about the curse?" the man asks calmly, even though he's tied up in my basement. I still don't know what part of this he is playing.

Grams swats the man on the back of the head. "Hush, this doesn't involve you."

Staring at the man, I realize he doesn't look much older than me. His black hair is trimmed close to his head, an angular jaw with a dusting of facial hair, and of course his yellow eyes I keep looking at. I've never seen anything like it.

"Someone needs to explain, or I swear I'm walking out that door and calling the psych wagon," I mutter, running my hands through my hair nervously.

"Let's talk upstairs away from him." Mom nods her head in the direction of the man.

We migrate to the destroyed living room. I pace in front of the couch waiting for someone to start talking. Grams and mom are having a silent conversation with their eyes, and Grams seems on the brink of losing it and attacking her.

"Maura, hop to it," she says sternly.

Mom sighs deeply, rubbing her squinted eyes. "Liara, you have to understand one thing before we begin… everything I did was to protect us."

Then she told me about the curse.

"So, what does the curse have to do with me?" It's a fascinating little story, but I don't understand how it explains the sudden tattoo or the tied-up man.

"You're the baby girl destined to mate with the tribrid. When your father and I met, I had no idea he was working for Reznor. I had fallen in love with him. I didn't know until after I found out I was pregnant with you. Then I fled, but it was too late. Reznor already knew you were a girl; he knew what it meant.

"Since I'm a witch, I completed that part of the curse; I knew the punishment would come soon enough for you being conceived. I packed a bag, and I ran. Grams came with me to help raise you. We have been hidden ever since. You technically should have gotten your crest on your sixteenth birthday, but I was able to suppress it till now. Reznor must have figured out what I was doing because at the stroke of midnight last night, the storm began, and his warrior showed up when I sent you off to get Grams. He knows you have the mark now, and where you are; we have to run before he can get to you."

"Why do I have to run? I don't plan on spending my entire life running from some man." I scoff at the idea of being on the run. I have a life here… but not a good one. She expects me to stay here and be a nurse when I could go to a magical land…uh I'm going to choose magic over running for the rest of my life. Plus, having powers is like a dream come true; who wouldn't want to have powers?

"You have to, Liara. He is evil…the things he has done." My mother glances off into the distance, her face, angered.

"What kind of life is it going to be if I spend the next fifty years of it running?"

"It's better than being enslaved to that man." Mom's voice becomes snarkier the longer the conversation goes on.

"Who said he would enslave her?" The man from downstairs now stood against the doorway, wiping his hands clean of blood. It's this moment that I realize how tall he is; how mom got him tied up, I don't know. I catch sight of a tattoo marking on his exposed upper arm—a wolf howling at a crescent moon.

"How did you get out?" Grams asks as she takes a step back.

The man laughs and raises his hands in a show of good faith. "I have my ways." He turns to me. "I'm not here to hurt you, contrary to Maura's beliefs. Reznor sent me to get you. He knew if it was that easy for him to find you, then it would be just as easy for everyone else. That's what the storm is for, to stop them from finding you so easily."

"Don't feed her lies, Emanuel," Mom snorts.

"Maura, you are the one feeding her lies. You ran. You didn't want to give Reznor a chance. Instead, you ran away with the only thing in his life that he has ever needed," Emanuel spat back harshly. "Reznor could have come himself, but he didn't because he knew you would do something like this."

"She isn't going anywhere with you." My mom moves to stand in front of me protectively, snatching the blade from Grams hand.

"The others don't know he is here for her. There is still time for her to come back without anyone knowing." Emanuel stops looking at my mother, his gaze transferring to Grams. "Come to Reznor's land where you will come under no harm for your treason, or take your chances with those who still hate you. We both know she is safest with him."

Mom scoffs and jabs the knife in his direction. "We will do no such thing; she will stay here."

"For how long do you think that will work? You seem to forget that she is going to need him. Her body will break down the longer she is away from him in the mortal world. You seem to have left out that part of the curse to her." Emanuel takes a careful step forward.

"It's a myth—"

"What else is there?" I ask, cutting her off.

"It is told that once you come into your powers, you are on a timeline to complete the bond with Reznor. It's a safety net that was put into place. You have a little over three months before your body is broken down and brittle if you don't get to him. The gods made it that way, so if you ever were created, he could never have his powers if he didn't find you first. You are the key to the last lock. Once Reznor has his powers, he will be King of All, just like he has been destined to be from the start." Emanuel tells.

"There is no proof of that, Liara." Mom takes another small step toward me.

Emanuel does the same. "It's true. Reznor's abilities have been decaying a lot faster here lately. You just hoped he would be too weak to find her."

"Mercy," Grams gasps, shaking her head.

"It's what that monster deserves!" Mom shouts suddenly.

"She needs to come with me, regardless of your past with Reznor. She needs to be with him."

I hold up a hand. "Wait, what past with him?"

Mom is having none of that. "No! She doesn't get to have him; she doesn't deserve him!"

That's when an eerie feeling crawls in. She doesn't want me with him for other reasons that she isn't expressing. It makes sense for her to send me to Grams while she dealt with Emanuel if she intended to keep me from this 'Reznor' guy all along.

"She will die, Maura!" Grams snaps as she and Emanuel drawl closer to me.

"Then, so be it!" My mother turns to me with wild eyes.

Oh, this isn't good.

"Maura!" Grams cries. I freeze in place, stunned, staring at the three people before me.

Come to me, Liara... I will protect you... come to me. The voice calls out in my head again. A choice needs to be made, and very soon. Mom looks as if she is about to snap at any moment.

"How bad has he decayed?" Grams asks.

"Physically not much, but he can't do much other than shift. She won't complete the bond right away, but if she goes to him, they both will be stronger together." Emanuel takes another careful step toward me, although my mother still remains between us.

"How is he?" Grams voice falters; it seems she also cares for Reznor. Everyone seems to know of this man but me, and I'm the one going to be freaking mated to him…maybe…probably. Frankly, I'm too stunned to process any of this, I'm sure I'll have a mental breakdown about it later.

"He is himself as you know. The hate you speak of, yes, he still has it, but can you blame him? He has been betrayed so much that he doesn't trust anyone. He said you could come back, Misty. He truly wants to protect her." Emanuel stops his advances toward me as mom starts another outburst.

"Mom, don't buy it!" Mom screams at her.

"Maura, I understand that you might not want to go, but if he will forgive me and allow me to go home, then I will."

"I won't go, and neither will Liara."

"Actually, I want to go; I don't want to run my entire life." Three heads snap in my direction as the words leave my mouth.

"Liara, you don't know what you're agreeing to," Mom argues.

"I may not, but I don't want to live in fear here." She turns her back to me as she breathes in deeply. "Mom…" I call hesitantly.

She whips back around, pointing the knife at me. "I won't let him win!" she shouts, lunging at me with the blade, but Emanuel is faster and tackles her to the ground.

"Run, Liara! Listen to him and he will tell you what to do!" he shouts as he fights with my mom on the floor. His eyes seem to get brighter as his hands start to morph, turning into…paws? Sharp nails elongate and fur sprouts to cover the clawed hands. Just as hair starts to grow on his face, Grams hauls me out of the house by my arm. She places me in the passenger side of the car before darting to the driver's seat and tearing down the drive.

"Grams, do I go to him?" I ask as we speed through the storm. After mom's display, I'm not sure what to think.

She starts with that soft voice again. "Honey, I think you should, but I understand if you don't want to. Reznor is a hard man to handle, his past is filled with betrayal, there's still so much you don't know. It'll be hard work sweetie, and even then, more awaits you." She breaks off for a moment, "Have you been hearing his voice in your head?"

"Yeah, today was the first time," I say as I ran a frantic hand through my hair.

"Try and call out to him."

"What do you mean?" I had never experienced anything like this. I was an average adult a few hours ago. Magic wasn't real, and a man certainly couldn't grow paw hands, or whatever the hell he just did! My brain is reeling over and over, thinking about a human 'shifting' into something covered in fur.

"Say his name in your head and focus on it hard, lay back, and concentrate."

I lean the seat back and close my eyes, concentrating like she suggested. Even though I feel like this is some twisted dream, I call out to him. Here goes nothing.

Reznor, I called out his name again, *Reznor?*

Liara, come to me. His voice sounds relieved when he says my name.

I soon feel chills shudder across my skin, the tugging in my chest returning. *How?*

Are you with Emanuel?

Emanuel tackling my mother flashed through my brain. *No, he is dealing with my mom.*

Get to the docks. I'll meet you there.

I tell Grams what he says as I open my eyes again.

"He's here?" she asks, clearly surprised, then quickly combs through her hair.

"I guess so."

She drives quickly, heading toward the docks.

This was a lot for me to take in at once. I try not to reflect on the fact my mother tried to kill me and has lied to me for twenty-one years of my life. I guess a magical betrothal showing up is just icing on the cake.

Trying to calm my erratic thoughts and worries, I focus on the rain falling. Yet, my thoughts keep drifting. A life of magic and mythical creatures is something I had never dreamt of being humanly possible, but here I am, sitting in a car, driving to the bay to meet a supposed mate. I have learned so much today, yet still feel like I know absolutely nothing. Being a part of a curse and a prophecy seems unreal. It's like in a moment, I will wake up from this dream... part of me wants to.

The docks are getting closer and with the feeling of a tugging in my chest, all my other thoughts slide away. Invisible strings are pulling me toward something, my heart beating faster as we approach.

At first, I don't see anything amongst the boats, but the pulling takes me toward one area in particular. Trying to sort through the billowy scent coming off the water, along with the sound of the waves crashing against the boats, there is one single thing that isn't moving. Standing at the end of the dock in black slacks and a black button-down shirt is a silhouette of a man. In this moment, I know it's Reznor; I can sense him even being that far away, the internal need pointing directly to him.

The storm rages around as I trek across the rickety dock. The rain pelts my face and is soaking Reznor the same. He has raven colored hair that is longer on top than on sides. The long strands are styled neatly atop his head even as the rain batters him. He watches me closely as I approach him, but he doesn't move or speak; he just observes. It's a little unnerving.

Lightning shoots across the sky as if the storm grows stronger the closer, I get to him. The water rocks and splashes up toward the sky, the wind blowing my hair into a dance. Boats hit the dock, birds squawk in the sky as they fly away, yet all of it is background noise.

I stop a short distance from him, taking in his towering appearance. Set brows rest above his dark blue eyes, a sharp nose leads to full lips, and he has a clean shaved defined jawline. Broad shoulders that are ramrod straight, his hands are tucked deep into his pockets. His stance is wide, making him seem that much larger, but even covered by the shirt, the muscular evidence is prominent. He's intimidating, but that doesn't stop me from soaking in every feature he has, and my God, he is beautiful. He reaches out suddenly and tucks a piece of hair behind my ear. The moment his calloused finger touches my cheek, everything begins to spin. I fall, but I never hit the ground; he scoops me into his arms. That's when everything goes black.

Chapter Three: Not What I Expected

I love it when I sleep so hard that I wake up delirious. I had such a strange dream too—magic, some man named Reznor, my mom trying to kill me. It all was very comical…wait, my ceiling isn't grey. "Oh shit, it was real," I say to myself as I sit up in the middle of a four-poster bed. That's nice, I've always wanted one, but I'm feeling a bit panicky.

I'm sprawled out on a bed that's not mine, in what appears to be an apartment? The walls are a light grey that stand out against the dark wooded floor. The bare walls keep the room simple, yet with the luxurious silk fabric on the bed, and the heavily upholstered couch, a table set with white roses give the room decorative aspects. To the right of the bed is a set of double doors leading to a balcony. Climbing from the bed, I peek out the doors. The balcony faces a large, open field with roaming hills near a lake in the distance, with mountains further out. On either side of the field stands a dense forest, towering green trees standing proudly in the sunlight. The land is breathtaking, and of what I can make out from the balcony, so is the large manor I'm staying in. Peeking down, I find guards standing at different parts of the manor below, some chatting, others standing silently and watching for threats. From what I can see, the manor is Greystone with black trim outside the many windows and doors. The swirls and fans of masonry work give life to otherwise plain walls. My perch is high in the air; my estimate is six or seven stories. I think I'm in a tower of sorts, but I could be wrong. It's hard to tell from this angle; my primary view is down on the land before me.

I find the kitchen to be fully stocked, along with a walk-in closet filled with clothes in my size. There are gowns, dresses, pants, shirts, sleeping sets. If it's a type of clothing, it's in there. Running my hand along the elegant fabrics, I pad through the closet, which leads an attached bathroom. The bathroom consists of a deep tub that faces a window, giving way to another breathless view of a garden of flowers with more of the forest behind. A shower with a large glass door stands out against the black tile floor, a toilet and sink sitting on the opposite wall. This bathroom is as large as my room back home...wait, home.

All the things I have been avoiding come rushing back to me: my mother, the crest on my neck, Reznor. It's as if the flood gates are open again in my mind. Wanting to see the mark, I turn my back toward the mirror and peer over the back of my shoulder, straining to see the crest. The art is on full display now with my hair to the side. The black ink that appeared so suddenly earlier in the day sits proudly as if it has been there my whole life. Tracing the crest over and over, my thoughts drift to the most logical solution.

I'm having a mental breakdown.

Magic isn't supposed to be real; it's only supposed to be in children's stories and in the mind of the wishful...but this all feels very real. I pinch myself just to be sure, but nothing happens; I'm still standing in the bathroom, in the home of a stranger.

Reznor. How is this was going to work? For such a monster, his home seems to reflect that he lives in luxury. I wonder what he's like, although I don't have high hopes for him, considering he must have drugged me to get me here. I'm assuming he doesn't trust me, seeing as he didn't want me knowing how we got here... probably so I wouldn't know how to leave. This is me automatically thinking the worst, but I had no other words for why else he would have done it. It's never been my style to be an optimist. My glass has a hole it, with all the liquid spilling out.

Before I could fall down the rabbit hole of worst-case scenarios, a door opens and closes. Hurrying out of the bathroom, I find a woman in a grey dress looking at the empty bed with a panicked expression. Just as I am about to speak, her head snaps in my direction as I step on a squeaky board.

"Ah, Miss Liara, there you are! I'm here to see you dressed for dinner with King Nighterious."

"I'm sorry, who are you?" I ask, confused.

Her appearance is elegant, fair skin that resembles porcelain, soft features and mix between blue and grey eyes. Her blonde hair is up in a pristine bun at the back of her head. The grey dress is clean and ironed, going to the tops of her ankles with a white apron tied around the front and white cuffs at the end of the sleeves.

"My name is Anisa. I'm your personal maiden." She smiles brightly, but only to fix her gaze on the floor once more. That's not going to work for me.

"I have two questions."

She looks up and nods for me to continue.

"One, can you just call me Liara? Two, I'm no one special so can we avoid the floor staring? I like to look at people when I'm speaking to them."

Anisa gives me a shy smile. "Very well Liara, shall we get you changed?"

Anisa leads the way to the bathroom, moving through the room with ease as she pulls towels out of the closet and slings them on the rail of the shower. She turns it on and leaves the door open before retreating to the closet. Quickly undressing, I step into the shower and try to contain my excitement when I find the soaps to smell like roses and honey, my favorite scent. I'm not going to ask how they knew it was my favorite; I'm simply going to enjoy it because I've had enough for today.

When I step out of the shower, Anisa is waiting and hands me anther towel. I already had one secured around my body, and I wrap this one around my hair. She gestures to a black blouse and matching slacks. It's a…new experience to have Anisa assist me in dressing but hey, I'm not very shy. If you haven't seen it, now's your chance.

The top flows with hanging sleeves and small slits that go up the arm showing some skin. The pants are doing wonders for my curves, making my ass pop, and slimming my thighs. Black has always been my color. Anisa instructed me to sit on a bench where she brushed and dried my hair, then fasted half up leaving the rest to flow down my back.

"Can I ask a question?" I ask as I step into the black heels she set before me.

"Anything, Miss." Her cheeks quickly blush, "I mean anything Liara," she amends.

I have about a million questions, but the least important one falls from my mouth. "Why all the black?"

"Whenever meeting with King Nighterious, you must always wear black unless instructed otherwise. All of the other kingdoms have assigned colors that resemble their flag. Our flag has three colors, but King Nighterious chose black as our official color." Anisa reminds me of a mouse with how quiet and swift she moves. I thank her for her answer. I'll wait till later to banter her with questions. Perhaps Reznor can answer some fore me also.

Checking her watch, she whisks me out of the room. We leave my room, and I notice the only other thing in the short hall is a staircase to my right. Anisa paves the way as she takes me down into my first glimpse at the manor. We go down four flights of stairs before we stop inside a kitchen. The walls are plain and simple, not wowing me like I had hoped. From there, she guides me through the kitchen to a hallway. The floors are mahogany, and the interior of the manor is dark with decorations of plum, charcoal grey, emerald, green in other places, and of course, black. Elegant paintings and black trim line the wall baseboards while silver chandeliers are at each hallway junction. We didn't get to stop anywhere long enough for me to take in the grand halls. Anisa did however explain what doors lead outside and where the pantry, pool and training rooms were, along with which rooms were off limits. Which apparently, for me, was the entire east wing of the manor.

    We come to a stop outside a set of black double doors. After knocking, Anisa goes in first, and I follow behind when a deep male voice beckons us inside. The room holds a large dining table that runs the length of the room. The grey wallpaper has a Grimmett pattern while a black chandelier hangs from the ceiling. The room is wide with towering windows at the back, letting the soft light from outside shine into the room, brightening the area. At the head of the table sits Reznor with a glass of wine in his hand, staring rather intently at it.

    "Shall I set her a place?" Anisa asks with a soft tone, but her *hopefulness* can be heard.

    "No, tell them she will be dining in her quarters, leave us." Reznor dismisses her with a flick of his finger. There is a hint of annoyance in his voice, and I presume it's not directed at Anisa. Like I said, not off to a great start.

Reznor waits until Anisa is gone before meeting my gaze. I stand six chairs down from him, but he acts like he wishes I were further. "Liara, you will begin training with Charles tomorrow morning at dawn to work on your powers. You will train every day till you get a handle on them. I don't care what you do here, but we have some rules." He pauses, pushing his wine glass aside.

"You will eat in your room or in the dining room at the same dining time as the servants. You are to use their exits, and their part of the manor. Do as you please in your part of the manor. Roam the grounds as you wish, but if you leave this house, you must tell a guard. Try not to bother Serena as she is already not a fan of your arrival, and I do not wish to deal with anymore of her bullshit. We have three months until I must mark you, and I plan to wait until the last minute to do so." He stares at me as I remain silent. "That's it. You can leave."

I give an annoyed chuckle as I turn toward the door.

"What's so funny?" he calls after me.

"Other than that whole speech? I'm starting to realize I have made a mistake in coming here already. Perhaps my mother was right." I turn to look at Reznor, speaking briefly before continuing toward the door. "You're just using me so you can get your powers, aren't you?" I ask with my back still to him.

In the next second, Reznor is before me, blocking my path. "Watch your mouth, Liara. I never asked for a mate. I never asked for any of this. Be grateful that I don't mark you, then kill you." He growls, towering over me. His piercing blue eyes hold such disgust and anger that I didn't know was possible for a stranger.

"You know what, why don't you just do that because I'm not going to spend my life a prisoner to a bastard who doesn't deserve me. You have no idea who I am, Reznor." His eyes flare with his rage. If looks could kill… then I would be dead.

"I am being pleasant with you; don't make me regret it. Get out," he snaps as he prowls back toward his seat.

"With pleasure."

I slam the door behind me, and Reznor's response is the crash of a glass from the other side. A coolness races over my skin that seems to seep into my bones. I shiver, shaking it off before heading back up to my room. I'd made a mistake, and I'm already regretting coming. I've traded one secret monster for another. I had come with the notion that things would be different, but I never once thought that I would instantly regret leaving the mortal world.

A tray of food is waiting for me in the kitchenette, but I have no interest in eating. Tossing my heels by the balcony door, I step into the fresh air and nestle into the couch to watch the sun set. While staring at the mountains, I realize this is not what I pictured twenty-one to be like. I should have been getting drunk and partying, yet here I am, sitting in a freaking castle and watching the sun set.

The couch on the balcony is where I spend the rest of the evening until the sky turns black. When sleep starts beckoning me, I lock the balcony door then change into some pajamas before climbing into the soft bed. It'll be better tomorrow.

Maybe.

"Liara. Liara, it's time to wake up." Anisa's voice wakes me in the early hours of the morning. I groan and roll over to the other side of the bed, burying my face in the pillows. "Liara, it's time for your training with Charles." She shakes me again until I give in.

"Okay, okay, I'm up." I nearly crawl back into the bed when I see the sun is barely up.

Anisa seems to sense it because she quickly ushers me into black training clothes, then forces me to sit at the table. "Eat up, you can't be late."

Breakfast is simple: toast, eggs, and some fruit, but after not eating last night, I'm ravenous.

"You didn't eat last night; did you not like it?" Her concern is evident as she braids my hair from behind me.

"Wasn't hungry, Reznor turned my stomach sour."

Anisa gives a disappointed sigh. "Is there anything I can get you for your room today? Make it more like home?"

"I love to read. Do you think you could get me some books?"

Anisa nods eagerly but a knock on the door ends our conversation. Emanuel enters and chuckles at Anisa braiding my hair.

"Liara, I'm here to escort you to Charles," Emanuel says as strolls over to me. "It's going to be a long one today, fair warning." He smiles encouragingly, but I don't return it.

Great.

Emanuel is quiet as he takes me through the manor then across the dewy grass. We near the edge of the forest where a man with soft red hair is speaking with Reznor. The man looks over his shoulder as we approach and gives me a wild grin.

"You must be Liara, I'm Charles." He sticks his hand out for me to shake, I grasp his hand and return the gesture.

"Unfortunately, so." I smile to lessen the spiteful comment. Reznor won't look at me, and his mere presence is worsening my mood.

Emanuel tries to hide his chuckle from beside me, but Charles laughs wholeheartedly. "I like this one." Charles smiles brightly at me, and I'm suddenly worried if his chipper attitude will clash with my hate of getting up early. He just seems like a happy guy, and I'm the complete opposite; this should be interesting.

Our group falls into an awkward silence as Reznor continues to ignore me. Cool, I only fled the human world for him, but obviously that doesn't matter.

Charles however isn't accepting of my current predicament. "Well, Reznor, at least she's hot." Emanuel and Charles could hardly contain their laughter as Reznor growls then moves to stand in front of me.

"Are we done with the pissing contest?" I step out from behind Reznor only to be met with his roaming eyes as they rake my body. He huffs a breath then strides away, but his anger is still lingering. I find his sudden mood very pleasing; now we're even for how he treated me last night.

"You'll be good for him," Charles says, watching Reznor walk away, "well, if you don't kill each other first."

I shrug in agreement; this only encouraged their laughter. I have an overwhelming urge to be violent toward that man, but I keep that thought to myself. Afterward, the pair continued with jokes for a few more moments, but the fun came to an end as they led me to a trail.

"This trail will loop back to here. We are going to run this once together, then tonight you will rerun it." Then, without warning, Charles takes off running into the trees. I scramble after him but catch up quickly.

After about three minutes, Charles breaks the silence. "So, tell me about yourself."

"What do you want to know?" I ask between breaths as we round a bend.

"Anything you're willing to share. From what I hear, your welcome to Reznor's land was not a pleasant one."

This time it was I who laugh. "Well, seeing as he magically drugged me to get me here, and has been a dick to me since I met him, you could say it's been a rough start."

Charles leaps over a fallen log that comes into the path while I jog around it. "Yeah, Reznor can be a big brute, but he is a good guy once you get to know him, contrary to what the legends say about him." Charles is defending his friend, and he might be right, but so far, he seems like a prick. My mother had made it seem like his people lived in terror of him, and that he was this monster killing people left and right. The only person he has been rude to so far is me.

"Well, I don't know much about anything. Plus, my opinion doesn't really matter; he's made it clear where I stand."

Charles laughs again, his smile beaming. He's an attractive man with pearly white teeth and broad shoulders. A cluster of freckles covers his cheeks, nose, and his ears. "He will come around, don't worry. Every cell in both of your bodies craves the other's. It's inevitable."

"I'm okay with keeping my distance."

"Oh, come on. Don't give up on him that easily." I roll my eyes even though he can't see it. "Give it time," he says again. I just hum in response. I will be the decider of Reznor and so far, he is not doing well.

For the remainder of the run, we make small talk about my life before I came here, but toward the end of the run, I'm a panting mess. Charles never slowed down, running the rough trail as if it were nothing. I ran every day when I lived at home, but that was on a treadmill, not in the woods going up and down hills. After what felt like forever, we reached the end of the trail. Charles had hardly broken a sweat, whereas I feel gross; I'm a mid to plus size girl, and I always sweat. It's nasty.

"That was the warmup. Using magic feels like a full-body workout once you first start. The more you practice, the more natural it will come and feel, and that's why we are starting out with baby steps." Charles crosses to a large, grey bag sitting on the ground and pulls out a small satchel.

"Can you explain to me what I will be able to do?" Charles motions for me to sit on the ground across from him. I oblige and copy his stance, crossing my legs as we sit under the morning sun.

"A Nightlighter gets most of their power from the moon, which they can channel positively or negatively. Light and dark. However, both powers are strong on their own, but out of the five Nightlighters, none of them have been able to use both. It's one or the other. The Nightlighter is stronger than a witch or warlock, their raw, natural power coming directly from the moon. The power they have can vary from healing to telekinesis, protection… that's mainly the light magic. Not much is known about the dark magic of a Nightlighter. There has only ever been one dark Nightlighter, and she lived in the mountains, hidden from the Council."

"Why did she hide from the Council?"

"They wanted to use her in the war against Whitehorn. Now, your magic is going to be stronger because your instincts are greatly affected by your bond to Reznor. Your powers will feed off each other; you both are half to one whole. That's why some days, we will be practicing with Reznor once we get your abilities to reveal themselves. The best way to test them is with him, but first, we need to provoke them." Without warning, he throws a pebble at my face, hitting me in the center of my forehead with a small thud. "Try to stop it. I'm not going to stop throwing them until you stop one, or I run out of pebbles."

"How am I supposed to stop—" He cuts me off by another small grey pebble being gently thrown against my head. Charles, pleased with himself, tosses another. I smack the next stone down. "If you don't give me instructions, then how I am supposed to stop them?"

"That's for you to figure out. You need to muster up your powers; I can't force them to show up." He throws another pebble. I glare at him with annoyance, already I want to slap that cheeky grin off his face. After a few more stones, he sighs, "You're not trying. You need to focus on the pebble itself. You must want to control the pebble, want to stop it from hitting you. Close your eyes and try again."

I try to think about the pebble, about controlling it. That doesn't work, so I try it my way. Closing my eyes, I listen to the sounds around me. *Stop*, I speak in my mind. The pebble thuds my nose this time. *Stop*, I call again, this time with more force but, again nothing. I wait and listen again, trying to focus more on when it would make contact, and that's when I feel it. It almost feels like a warning sign lights up within my head, but in the form of sudden chills. *Stop*, I repeat a final time. At some point, I had created a fist without realizing, but I fear opening it until I'm positive the stone has been stopped. Cracking an eye open, I see the pebble has stopped a few meters from my face, suspended in the air.

Charles beams with pride as the small rock remains afloat. "Now drop it." I open my fist, and the pebble thumps to the ground. "Good, let's do it again."

Each time it gets easier; by the time we had gone through all the pebbles, I didn't need to verbally stop the stone. I could use my hands, or just think about stopping it. Near the end, I was even able to launch one back at Charles; it smacked him right between the eyebrows.

Emanuel roars with laughter, "Oh, this is going to be so fun!" It, however, is short-lived as I shoot one at him next.

The two boys bicker and laugh as I launch stones at them, then they also start throwing them at each other. Our fun didn't last because Reznor calls Emanuel away and instead, another guard comes to watch us...well me.

Charles insists he joins me for lunch, and we eat in the back gardens that I hadn't been able to see from my window. Two servants bring out sandwiches, fruits, and veggies assorted on each plate and set them before us. We both eat in silence at first. I'm enjoying the birds that are flying overhead and the beautiful flowers surrounding us, that, and the new glimpse of the manor from this angle The same brownstone with black fixatures line every set of tall, stained windows. From this side, it's difficult to make out what's behind the glass.

"You have to try these." Charles startles me as he snags a handful of what appears to be black berries from a bush next to the table. After dunking them in the bowl of water on the table, he places three on my plate.

"What are they?"

"Night Berries. The sprites have grown them ever since Reznor took over these lands. They're his favorite."

I pop the berry into my mouth and am hit with a flavor that reminds me of a wild berry but with a hint of a melon. It's surprisingly wonderful.

"You must have some questions?" Charles asks as he tosses a berry into his mouth.

"Where the hell is my grandma?" I blurt out immediately.

"Ask Reznor, now next question, I know you have others."

It's true, I do have questions; I just didn't know which ones to ask. Then I knew; Reznor's conversation with me from last night flashed into my mind. "Who is Serena, and why do I need to avoid her? Reznor brought her up but didn't give me any explanations."

He scratches the back of his head, immediately starting to look uncomfortable. "Of course, that's the first question you ask. Serena is someone who has been here a while. She's a firecracker. That's all I'm going to say on that topic, but what else?"

"Can you explain what I really have to do with all of this? The version of the curse I was given was very vague."

"That's because every person has a different version of the curse, but considering I was around when it was forged, I can enlighten you on the truth."

I'm taken aback; they had made it seem like it was thousands of years ago. "I would like that, but first, how old are you?"

"In human age, I'm thirty, but here we age differently... I'll explain that later. Can't give away all of our secrets at once." He pauses and glances at me briefly before standing up abruptly. "Walk with me, and I'll explain." We stroll through the gardens and begin making our way toward the lake, a guard in tow behind us.

"The majority of the curse you were told about is true; your part in it is the Nightlighter. Only five have ever existed as I have told you before, but it is said you are to be the last. Your role in all of this is you were created to be his equal, but not *only* his equal. The way they created the curse was to make you a weakness for Reznor. They thought if they created something that was designed especially for him, they could weaken him by threatening you. Once the mate bond kicks in, it will change everything from here on out. There is a reason there aren't mates anymore.

"Mates would do anything, and I mean *anything*, to protect each other. By doing this, they didn't realize that when mates are together, they are the strongest they will ever be. You are each other's rise, and downfall. You have to understand that Reznor isn't what everyone thinks he is. He is a good man, and he takes care of his people, yet people hate him. They are going to hate you also for the mere fact that you will be his bride, queen, mate, and equal. It's not because he's evil. It's because that type of power has never existed. The court is only ruled equally because no members are stronger than the other right now. When you two complete the mating bond, and process, then he will be the strongest there ever was.

"The Nightlighters' type of magic came from the gods alone. They decided who the Nightlighters would be at the start of time. Right before they left, they stopped creating mate bonds except for you two. When they died, or left as some say, they took that power with them, and that scares people. The fear someone is going to be as strong as one of the gods yet again, is why everyone fears him. The curse is made out to be a lot worse than it is, but it is called a curse for a reason. You both have different consequences if the bond is violated. That's what the curse truly is. The rest is actually a prophecy; the matrimony of you two is supposed to be the change of times for our world."

"So that's why everyone makes it sound so bad? They don't want to be united under one king?" Thinking about it, this really does make sense. Still, it also set things up to look differently, but whatever he's told me doesn't change Reznor's action since my arrival.

"That's exactly why, the other creature that wanted to be king, Whitehorn, we haven't heard from him since we won the war." He stops us in front of the lake and sits down, crossing his legs underneath him. "Enough chatter, time to learn."

Next, we meditated for hours, and I do mean hours. Breathing, stretching, taking in the surroundings. He would occasionally throw things at me without me knowing, and I would stop them without hesitation. We practiced until he decided it was time to do some strenuous workouts, and this was probably the worst part of my entire day. It was worse than any exercise I had ever done before as it was extremely physically demanding. We did self-defense training, where he threw me to the ground multiple times.

Standing in my strike stance, I finally land a blow on his forearm. He only falters for a moment then flips me to the ground again. "That's it. I'm not getting back up this time," I groan.

Charles laughs at me for what feels like the hundredth time today. "You actually did really good. No human would have even been able to have lasted as long as you have. You may not notice it yet, but your body is changing, learning to live with these powers, and what they can do for your body. Just wait, in a couple weeks you'll be able to beat anyone's ass. You do have to get up though. Run the trail then you're done for the day."

I ache as I allow him to pull me to my feet, taking my time to walk back to the trail I had run this morning. This time, Charles lingers by the entrance, leaving me to run it on my own. It's a blessing, truly, because I doubt I'd be able to keep up with him right now.

I use the free time to think about what has happened over the last two days and decide how I want to live my new life here. I'm already annoyed with Reznor, but Charles had made it clear I won't be going anywhere, and this is to be my forever home. It's an alarming thought, but the manor is big enough I can avoid Reznor if I need to. The land is gorgeous and everyone besides Reznor has been kind to me. I haven't spoken to him enough to form my own opinion yet. That will take some time, because if someone asked me now, I would say he's a temperamental king with fat mouth.

The run burns my already sore legs as I pound down the path, trying to take long strides to finish faster. The end of the trail is in sight when a branch is launched at me. I skid to a stop, throwing my hands out in front of me to stop it. Clenching my eyes shut, I wait for impact, but it never comes. When I open my eyes, the massive branch is floating in the air. Behind it stands Charles, and Emanuel with matching smirks. I don't know when Emanuel returned to guard us, but judging by the look on his face, he is pleased to be back.

"You assholes!" I toss the branch back at them, but I still laugh at their giddy reactions. They seem easy enough to please, and I've decided I like them already.

"Good job today. Same time tomorrow, get some sleep. You're going to need it," Charles says as he pats me on the shoulder.

We walk back to the manor together while the boys hold the conversation. I just listen to them talk of duties in this new land that's still foreign to me. Our polite conversation comes to a halt as Reznor and a red-haired woman step into our path. She's shorter than me by a solid six inches, slim with a small waist and petite stature. She has grey eyes and harsh features, her cheeks looking a little too sharp, and lips a little too full. Reznor shoots daggers at when he notices me standing between the two men, and I do the same to the woman who has her arm around Reznor's.

Who's this bitch? And why is she all over my man?

Wow that came out of nowhere. I've always been a stupidly jealous person, and this is a brutal reminder.

"So, this must be Liara," she sneers at me.

I nod my head, not trusting my mouth. By the look on Reznor's face, he's twice as annoyed as I am, and that alone almost makes me smile.

"We're going out. Emanuel, you're coming with us," Reznor states even though he's still staring at me. He remains that way till the red head whines like a child. Only then does he walk off with Emanuel in tow.

"Well, that was interesting..." Charles cringes while scratching his head.

I chance a glance at where they're walking and catch Reznor throwing me a distasteful look. Our eyes are still locked when I ask my question. "I take it that's Serena?"

"Yes, like I said, she's a firecracker." I register his words, but I'm more focused on Reznor's hateful glare. Tearing my eyes from his, I decide to let it roll off my shoulders and walk to the servants' entrance.

"Don't worry, I will tell him to stop being such an uptight ass," Charles calls after me. I thank him but decline the offer because I can handle Reznor. I would rather him tell Reznor to keep Serena away from me, but that would show my jealously, and that's something I'm not willing to reveal yet.

Not wanting to talk about Serena or Reznor any longer, I enter the servant entrance quickly, then climb the stairs at a painfully slow rate. My legs are jelly, and it only gets worse in the shower. The easiest part of my evening routine is throwing on a nightgown because I'm not lifting my legs more than necessary.

I've barely climbed into bed when Anisa enters with a silver tray and a bound leather book. I flip through the pages to become familiar with the court of Dwimmer. Images flash across each pages of creatures that I never could have dreamed existed. "All of these creatures live here?" I ask as my eyes scan the drawing of an elf. Supposedly elves live in the gardens and care for them year-round. They are responsible for all the life in each garden.

"Yes, and no. All those creatures have lived at one time or another, all across our world. It's best you focus on the breeds that live in our lands."

"And what kind of breeds live in our lands?"

"We have all kinds of people, creatures, and beings in these lands. King Reznor houses all kinds of species, but primarily there are Witches, Lycans, Demons, and Wizards."

"Most species are identified by their eyes?" I ask, reading down the page, not once taking my eyes from the words.

"Yes, but some can be labeled by symbols on their skin. You, for example, have the Nightlighter crest." Anisa strolls forward, taking the book out of my hands. "Enough reading; you have training in the morning. It's time for dinner. Where would you like it?" she asks, standing near the end of my bed.

"Anisa, I'm really not hungry," I say quietly, as I bask in the comfort of the bed.

"You need to eat. Your training is only going to get harder." She crosses to the bed and sets the tray down next to me. "If you don't like it, we can make something else."

I raise a hand to stop her. "Whatever it is, I will eat it, I promise…if you tell me what you are. Your eyes are different then everyone else's." I gasp instantly. "I apologize if that was rude! I didn't think!"

Anisa laughs, gripping my hand. "My family comes from a long line of dormant wizards, well until a great aunt had a fling with a demon." She taps her temple. "I have no powers nor abilities; I'm simply Anisa."

"That doesn't mean you're not special. In the human world, we're all simply people unless you have money or do things to draw attention to yourself and make you memorable. You're special for who you are, not *what* you are."

Anisa's cheeks brighten as she nods, but I can just make out the glossiness in her eyes as she rises from the bed. Quickly, she bids me goodnight then leaves the room. I can only hope I didn't offend her; I truly didn't meant to.

I'm glad to be alone. My dinner consists of something that reminds me of pasta, and a salad. I eat half of it, and even that is a challenge due to the exhaustion kicking in. I take the tray to the table then dive back into bed.

Chapter Four: Only So Many Chances

For the next few weeks, I'm up and running on the trail before the sun rises over the mountains. Charles continues to throw things at me as I run, and the more he throws, the easier it becomes. It's almost effortless now. Charles and I had just started our combat training when Reznor approaches with Emanuel. The pair talk off to the side and watch as Charles fights with me.

Charles is right. My power has been growing by the day. Fighting had been a challenge, but it's easier now. I use the magic to feel when a blow is coming, and along with this power comes a strength that can be called upon. It's the magic that's keeping my sense on high alert today.

I had just gotten used to Reznor's presence when something shoots through the sky toward him at lightning speed. Blocking Charles with one hand, I shoot my other hand out at Reznor. The arrow stops inches from his chest. All three of them are unalarmed by the arrow. With a flick of my wrist, I plant it into a nearby tree, then flip Charles onto his back.

"That's fighting dirty; I can't help those instincts," I tell Charles as he rises from the ground.

Charles jumps to attack me but is thrown to the ground before he even has the chance to touch me. Reznor had smashed Charles to the hard soil and moved across the field to stand in front of me in a matter of seconds. Clearly his reflexes are faster than mine because I'm still trying to dissect how he moved so quickly.

"Neither can he." Charles smiles proudly and clambers up again, this time holding his hands up in surrender.

Reznor glares at him as he steps to my side. This is the closest he has been to me since we met. His towering height is still something I'm trying to get used to. I had never been short, and now I feel small…I kind of like it.

"We need to start training with the both of you, but for that part, it requires you two getting to know each other. So, while you two are walking around the grounds talking and going about your business, we will be lurking to 'attack' one of you." He uses air quotations as he says 'attack'. I think he did so more for Reznor's benefit than my own. Reznor, and I both exchange glances before he sighs and turns his glare to Charles. His annoyance with this entire scene is blatantly obvious, but the peppy man doesn't seem to care; Charles smiles at Reznor boldly.

Without warning, Emanuel and Charles lunge for the both of us at the same time. I don't even get to try to help before Reznor grips both by the chest and slams them into the ground.

"You chose a shitty time for this. The full moon is two days away," he growls.

"The ceremony is in two months, which isn't that far away. She needs to be able to control her powers during the ritual, and so do you," Charles says from the ground, patting Reznor's hand.

Reznor releases them both abruptly then stalks over to me. "Fine, we can do this till sunset, but after that, I have arrangements to make, and she can't exactly be there for those."

I don't even want to question what those arrangements are. Instead, I want to know if this is going to be a pleasant afternoon filled with awkward silence, or another bickering fight. I don't know if I'm lucky because we both seem resistant to the task or what that means for us in general. We're supposed to be completing this bond in two months, and I've hardly spoken to the man.

Charles and Emanuel both stand up slowly, Reznor watching them like hawks. "Well, hop to it," Charles says, shooing us.

With hesitant steps, I follow Reznor, who has already turned around and is walking away. There is a rustle behind me, and I'm not entirely surprised to see Charles lunging for Reznor. Using my telekinesis, I slam him face first into the ground before he can take a step further.

Reznor smirks, looking at his friend who just ate a mouth full of grass. "Good one," he compliments before he walking on.

The boys wander into the tree line, leaving Reznor and I alone. I try to stay a few steps behind him, but I'm still not entirely sure what to do with him. It seems Reznor thinks the same as he stalks ahead in silence. For an hour we both say nothing. He only breaks the silence as we approach the lake, and that is to tell me to watch my step as we come down a steep hill. He lurks a few feet from the lake, standing on the sandy shores. I choose to sit on the grass, taking in the view; I don't know if King Moody wants his space or not.

The lake glistens blue, lilac flowers float around the water, while a white swan swims in between them. Reznor eventually comes to sit next to me on the grass. It seemed like we were going to sit in silence for an eternity until he finally speaks up.

"How is the training with Charles?" he asks softly. For a big brute, he seems to be a little shy with me.

"Good. It's a little strange having magic." Reznor won't look at me; mimicking his actions, I, too, focus on the lake.

"What powers have developed so far?" he asks as I catch him looking at me out of the corner of my eye.

"Telekinesis and a force field of some sort. Charles said he has never heard of a Nightlighter having it before." He nods in response, but yet again, we fall silent.

"Can I ask you a question?" Boldly, I peer at him instead of sneaking glances.

"Yes, but I can't promise I'll answer it." He rolls up his sleeves, and I momentarily get distracted by the action.

Shaking the thoughts from my head, I avert my attention back to my question. "Where are all the people?"

He is silent for so long, I think he isn't going to answer, but then he sighs softly. "The closest live about forty minutes from my manor. There are a few towns, and then some live in the countryside. Why do you ask?"

"I was just curious because I didn't know if the people in the manor were the only ones who lived out here."

"I live on the edge of my territory; this is just part of it."

Another question shoots to my mind. "Where is my Grandma? I haven't seen her since I got here, and Charles keeps telling me to ask you. Seeing how this is our first conversation, I would like to know where she is." The words fall from my mouth with more bite than I intend, but it's well deserved.

"This isn't our first conversation." Reznor mocks with a cocked brow.

I roll my eyes. "I don't count our encounters before this, so yes, this is our first *actual* conversation that is civilized."

He eyes me a moment before speaking again. "She was sent for questioning at the furthest part of my territory. From what I've been told, she is rather enjoying being back in Dwimmér."

A laugh falls from my mouth. "Why didn't he tell me that?"

Reznor develops a small grin on his face that he is trying to hide. "I'm unsure because I gave no such orders to restrict that information from you. I think he was trying to push you to speak to me."

Bitches.

I fiddle with the grass as we sit in silence for a few seconds. It's not an awkward silence, just peaceful. My thoughts come back to the statement he had made earlier. "What happens on the full moon?"

Reznor stiffens. "On a full moon, I shift into my beast form. The days leading up to it, the power from that form leaks over more into this one. You will have to stay in town that night. The scents of the townspeople are the best chance of covering yours."

I whirl at him, appalled. "What do you mean *scent*?"

He chuckles at my mortification. "Yes, you have a scent."

"Does it smell bad?" I ask, horrified.

This earns another chuckle to fall from his lips. "No, it smells like Roses and honey."

Well, that's good at the very least. "So, how does this scent thing work?"

He studies me as if it were a stupid question, yet he still explains it to me. "Every person, creature, and animal has a scent, but for us, it works differently. Your scent is stronger and sweeter than everyone else's. The scent everyone else smells is different than the one I smell for you. It's because of the mate bond. The more it kicks in, the stronger your scent gets. Only certain creatures can smell your natural scent, just like you can't smell my scent."

I pay close attention or try too at least. His voice is something that I could listen to all day. I find myself asking him anything and everything just to keep him talking. The conversation really piques my interest when he starts to tell me about this world. Apparently, Earth and the magic world are on the same planet. The Council put a spell on the humans to make them think they knew all of the earth's surface, and there was no more to explore on Earth. The side that the humans know as Earth is actually just a little under half of the planet we live on. The ecosystems are the same for the most part, but further into this world, the more magical it gets. We have the same moon and sun that rotates around this side of the planet. The humans have suspicions of magic but no actual proof because magic can't be used in the mortal world except for elemental magic.

"Is that why you couldn't find me for so long? Because I was a human until my powers came in?"

His back goes as straight as a rod, then he shifts his position, crossing his legs at his ankles in front of him. "At first, I hunted for you everywhere, but as the years passed, I stopped looking, I stopped caring." He clenches his fists at his side. "After that many years, I didn't care. Hell, I didn't want to come to get you now, but I had no other choice."

He says it so casually that I hadn't realized how much it hurt until a moment later. I mutter an 'oh,' but that's it. I don't like the fact a man I just met a couple weeks ago is hurting my feelings. It shouldn't be this easy, but at least he is honest about it. It explains his blatant disinterest.

"How is this going to work once the bond is complete?" I don't really want to know the answer, but perhaps he doesn't either.

"I honestly don't know; we will have to wait and see," Reznor states, tearing his eyes from me.

"Ha! That's promising," I add snidely.

"Listen, I'm a lot older than you, and you have to realize that. A year in your world is one hundred years here, and we age differently because of it. Since I was nine years old, I have been cursed with you. I waited and waited and waited, all the while knowing the Warlocks, and Witches wouldn't allow you to be conceived. When your mom got pregnant and fled, it was the last straw, and I gave up. For all I knew, she could have terminated the pregnancy so you wouldn't be born. So, I went about my life. I had multiple women and lived my life how I wanted. Then, I felt the day you were born and knew you actually existed. That's why when the time came, I went and got you so we both didn't dwindle away until we died a painful death. I brought you back here for survival, and because my people need a ruler. Therefore whatever expectations you have, you should lower them."

The audacity of this arrogant man. "Did I ever say I expected that? I mean, a little conversation besides telling me to stay to my side of the manor and you not wanting to see my face would be nice. I had no expectations..." I pause, trying to find the right words before I continue. "Reznor, I'm not from the magical world; I didn't know how any of this worked. I was shocked that day. I had no idea what was going on or what was going to happen, but a pull in my chest brought me to you. Now I'm here, so you're going to have to figure out how you can get through each day without looking like you want to hurl every time you see me."

He makes a pinched expression. "I don't make a face when I look at you," he argues.

"Oh please, the second I walk into a room, you make a face, and you leave a second later."

"It's not you that causes the face. It's the bond that causes me to make a face." He looks ashamed as he throws a pebble into the lake. When it plops into the water, a lily pad appears...*magic*.

I freaking love magic.

"Why is the bond so strong for you?" I ask.

"Because I'm in tune with my powers, and you were literally created for me. When you walk into a room, your presence alone drowns out everything else. Your scent is carried to me on an invisible wind. I have been able to smell you since you were born. I would get little wisps of it across the world from you. If the wind hit your skin just right, it came flowing my way. It was torture." He drops his guard for a moment and seems genuinely pained thinking back to the memory.

"I'm sorry that it taunted you for so long. If I had known, I would have come sooner." I'm feeling guilty. I have been tormenting him for years, and I didn't even know it.

"It's alright. I've been living with the possibility of you since I was nine years old. Well, technically nine hundred years old," he shrugs.

"How old are you?" Their concept of time still throws me off.

"Darling, I have been around twenty-five hundred years. In your terms, I'm twenty-five."

"Well, then I'm definitely going to grow old before you do, then you'll be out of the woods for our problems."

He shakes his head, a slight smile on his face. "No, you won't. Once the ceremony and ritual are complete, you will age like I do."

Again, there it was. Talk of this ceremony, and ritual which I don't know anything about. The look on my face seems to ask the question for me.

Reznor grimaces then pulls a ring out of his pocket and hands it over to me.

Reznor grimaces and then pulls out a ring, handing it over to me. A large pear-shaped amethyst set upon the center, surrounded by small black diamonds. I inspect the ring, taking in all its beauty before noticing an engravement of the moon that is etched into the back of my neck. I have no doubt the beautiful ring is humming as I hold it in my hand. "It's beautiful…is it for Serena?" I ask because I have to know; if it is, then I'm leaving tonight.

Reznor's eyes widen. "No," he snarls. "The ceremony and ritual will take place over two days leading up to the last full moon of the month. The first day, you and I will attend a party that will be held at the manor, then when the full moon is at its highest point in the sky, you and I, along with the priests, will anoint you under the moonlight. The final day will be our wedding and your coronation as you will become queen once we are married. That night, I will mark you." He speaks tensely, his neck visibly straining to get the words out. Once again, he won't look at me, only focusing on the Lilly pad before him.

Oh, so the ring's for me? It's probably bad that I have a little bit of pride in knowing the ring isn't for Serena. Something about that woman just rubs me the wrong way, and it's not just because I can be jealous. She's bad; I just don't know in what way yet.

"Won't you be in your wolf form?" I carefully choose not to call him a beast.

He looks surprised at my word choice but doesn't question it. "The ceremony's power will suppress me needing to change. All the sensations of that form will still be there, but it's the only way. You're not going to try and fight it…the ceremony?" Again, he won't look at me, his jaw tight, and his face tense with his eyebrows drawn. He is a beautiful man even when his face is burdened with his emotions.

"You've been waiting a long time." I rise suddenly, wanting my back to him as I stride toward the lake. I'm not sure if I can control my face when I tell him my answer. "I'm not going to make you wait any longer." To my surprise, Reznor follows me to the water. He stands close enough for me to sense him, but not close enough to touch.

"You're not what I expected," he says softly.

"Trust me, you're going to have your hands full with me. You just caught me on a good day."

He laughs the first genuine laugh I've heard out of him since I met him. "Good to know. Well, as you already—" He suddenly pulls me into his body in one swift motion as an arrow shoots past me. He has me pressed against him with one hand firmly at my back, pushing me into him further. I can't ignore the electricity that shot through my body when we first touched.

Over his shoulder, a black fog figure starts coming from behind, and I demolish it with a simple fist while still being pressed against him. I have the pressing urge to protect him, but being this close to him, he's right—it's distracting.

Suddenly, a soft clap sounds in the distance. Turning my head toward the sound, I'm met with Charles walking down the hill. "See, the bonding helps; she can sense fog creatures now."

Reznor glances down at me, still holding me against him. Feeling Charles eyes on us, I try to move out of his grasp, but his hold tightens.

"Charles be careful doing this. We wouldn't want you to get hurt," Reznor says with a snarl.

"Hey, you're lucky I left you alone this long. Its nearly sunset. I could have attacked you both fifty times by now… but I see my decision to let you talk worked out better. Meet us on the training field at the usual time, Reznor. Tomorrow will be fun." He smiles cunningly then returns the way he came.

I gasp as I'm suddenly pulled flush to Reznor by both his hands. He slides one hand up to my face and grips my chin, angling it up, forcing me to meet his eyes. "Don't ever try to pull out of my grasp again." His fierce stare meets mine, his deep, blue, ocean eyes flaring with anger. He abruptly releases me and stalks away. "Keep the ring," he yells over his shoulder, "consider this the start of our engagement."

Peering down, I find the ring nestled on my finger. I hadn't even realized he'd put it on, nor noticed that it's a perfect fit. My brain is too preoccupied with the aching emptiness that I feel as he walks away.

"I need to go for a run," I chastise myself, then take off for the forest trail. I run the trail until I'm not thinking about him or the encounter; only thing I'm focusing on now is the stinging of my muscles. Thank the gods.

The relief is short lived as a short while later I stare at the ring, the moonlight hitting it perfectly from my place on the balcony. Its then that I realize this ring was created for me, and by the looks of it, it had been made a long time ago. He has waited hundreds of years for me. He is blessed by a god, then cursed by another, and I am a part of both. My role in it, is to be his bride.

Chapter Five: Too Far

Charles, Emanuel, and Reznor are chatting on the training field while the sky slowly brightens. I had already run the trail as it has quickly become part of my morning routine. At first, the trio didn't notice my arrival, but when Reznor snaps his head in my direction, it brings the attention of the others.

"You're late," Charles calls out.

I roll my eyes but continue advancing toward them. "I was running the trails like I always do. You're just on time for once, and I'm assuming that's because Reznor is here," I snark; I'm still not a morning person. Not even for happy going Charles.

Emanuel laughs and playfully shoves Charles' shoulder. "She has a point."

Charles just snorts in response.

I peer at Reznor, who makes a different face this time. He still seems annoyed, but this time, I think it's due to my clothing. It has been oddly hot these last two days. Today, I chose to wear black shorts and a matching tank top for practice. It's a lot of skin and Reznor doesn't seem pleased that so much of it was on display. It also seems like a personal problem he is going to need to learn to live with.

I walk to stand next to Charles, but Reznor gives me a look that makes me question my decision. Reluctantly, I go and stand next to him instead. His shoulders relax a fraction, but not much. This territorial mate thing will take some getting used to.

"Today we will be doing strike training. We will pair off then switch. Reznor, you're with Emanuel, and Liara, you're with me."

Reznor is not pleased. I can feel the anger radiating from him as I cross in front of Charles. Thinking back to his *wolf* form, I begin to wonder if this practice is a good idea. The boys might be getting in a little too deep; they've never tested his control with so much of his power seeping through him.

Standing before Charles, we begin sparring. He makes fewer blows than he ever has as I duck and hastily avoid the impacts. Charles seems pleasantly surprised with my improvement, but even though I have gotten better, he is still able to pick me up then pin me against the ground. He is atop me for one second, then ripped from me the next. Reznor launches Charles halfway across the training field with little effort on his part.

Without taking his eyes from Charles, Reznor sticks his hand down to me and pulls me up from the ground. When our skin touches, a tingling sensation spreads all the way up my arm. Goosebumps rise across my skin. Reznor stares down where his hand still remains in mine, then let's go. I back up a step, trying to clear my mind and force the chill to leave my body. The bond is strong today.

Across the way, Charles groans as he gets back to his feet, strutting back over to where we stand. He seems in good spirits, winking at Reznor as he passes us.

"You want to throw her around, do it when I'm not here and when it's not the day of a full moon!" Reznor shouts the last part, unable to keep his temper in check. Without realizing, I take a step forward at his sudden outburst, the need to calm him washing over me like cool water. Okay, maybe the full moon affects the bond also.

"Maybe it's best if we switch now," Emanuel adds, his speculating eyes scanning over Reznor and me. The dawn of *something* flashes in his eyes, but I can't be sure what it was. Charles seems to notice it too because he nods in agreement.

"Liara's with me," Reznor states as he narrows his gaze on Charles once again.

I catch Emanuel smirking as I turn to spar with Reznor and quickly realize why we switched. Reznor is *furious*. The anger radiating from him has only grown, yet no matter how mad he is, he is not willing to spar with the boys. Even though it would surely help him get out his rage. I oddly find myself pleased with this because he doesn't trust them not to hurt me while fighting. At least that's what I'm telling myself.

"Ready?" I ask Reznor.

He lays his eyes on me reluctantly, nodding while still watching the boys from the corner of his eyes. Positioning myself between Reznor and them, I bring his attention back to me. Throwing a punch out, Reznor effortlessly deflects it, and the second he pushes my hands away, the tingles drift up my fist. It feels like butterfly kisses on my knuckle and wrist. Each blow has this effect. Reznor's tension in his shoulders lesson as he appears to calm down, and I think it's due to *my touch*.

At some point, the boys had stopped sparring and watch us spar instead. We're graceful, like we're preforming a dance. The way we fight against each other with no strain or question makes it seem as if we'd done it a thousand times. A sense of ease seems to fall over us.

However, it's up to Charles to ruin the moment. He launches himself at us, but I'm too focused on how Reznor is holding me in his arms as he pulls me toward him and away from Charles. I didn't even notice the force field I had thrown up to protect us. Reznor realizes Charles can't get any closer and releases me. The second he does, I drop the shield, suddenly feeling drained. It's like someone ripped out my battery.

Charles uses that moment to strike. He throws me over his shoulder then takes off running across the field. "Catch us if you can, Reznor," he shouts tauntingly. Sprinting across the field at an unnatural pace, I cling to his shoulder, hoping I don't end up face down in the grass.

A growl that shakes me to my core roars across the open space behind us. Reznor is nowhere to be seen from behind, but a mere moment passes. Then, I'm airborne.

I shriek and squeeze my eyes shut, waiting for impact, but it doesn't come. I land in a pair of strong arms and as a tingling sensation runs through my body, I know who cradles me against their chest.

"That's enough for today," Reznor snaps. Without another word, he carries me all the way to the manor. "Come with me."

The moment Reznor sets me down, he looks me over then turns and starts through the manor. It's the first time to see this part of his home. He shows me through a hallway lined with painted images. Some are creatures, others are flowers and a variety of other magical paintings. The floor is a darkened marble and causes the life like paintings to appear brighter. The walls change from dark to light with each turn, but through the manor, a theme remains. It's dark but elegant, the lightest color being the gold that trims the frames.

We travel up a grand staircase lined with gold flecks engraved in the swirls in the wood. Walking behind Reznor, I find that his hair looks somewhat disheveled. This training seems to have unnerved him more than I thought. I don't quite understand the territorial needs he has, but I'm not a tribrid, nor am I going to turn into a wolf tonight.

He stops outside a dark wooden door, then motions for me to go through first. I step into what appears to be his study. Books fill the floor to ceiling shelves on either wall. Two large windows show a view of the forest. A grey couch sits by the fireplace with a plush blanket folded neatly on the back. A large desk with two chairs sitting before it, a table set with maps neatly placed is to the left of his desk. The room is not what I anticipated. I expected something darker, seeing as the king enjoys dark colors, but this all feels rather cozy.

"You should wear more clothes next time we practice," he says coldly over his shoulder as he sulks to his desk.

I scoff, "That's why you dragged me in here?"

"It's not my fault you can't dress properly for training," he says more harshly, this time, whipping his head around.

"You should learn to control yourself around me, then maybe it wouldn't be such an issue."

Within seconds, he crosses the room. Gripping the back of my neck, I should have been startled or scared, but though his hold is firm, he's gentle as he forces me to look up at him. When I meet his stare, I find his blue eyes are now red, taking on an animalistic nature.

"Don't test me, Liara," he says dangerously slow. "Go to your room and spend the rest of the day there." He still has a firm hold on me while he gazes into my eyes. Though his words tell me to go, his actions seem reluctant to do so. Then as quickly as he had grabbed me, he releases his hold and stalks to the window, giving me a clear dismissal.

"You should come with a warning label, or list of instructions on how to handle your ass!" I snark then turn away from him.

Without looking back, I leave the study, slamming the door in the process. I storm through the manor, muttering all the spiteful comments I wanted to say to him but didn't. Releasing a heavy breath, I lean against my closed bedroom door. Reznor is intense, and the confusion of the bond is clouding my judgment. I just can't get a good read on him and just when I start to enjoy him, he reminds me of why I shouldn't.

The moments we have had together reel through my head like a movie. He's hot, then he's cold. He opens up a little, then closes off tightly. I don't understand this man, and it has nothing to do with the fact that he's a magical creature. I'm supposed to marry him in two months, and I don't even know his full name.

Anisa arrives a couple hours later with a tray for lunch. She laughs at my lounged position on the couch. "Lunch is ready."

I nod but make no moves to get up. She goes to leave, but I stop her. I need a little conversation before I can stew any longer. "Will you sit with me, Anisa?" I ask while staring off into the distance.

"Of course." She sits in the chair opposite of the couch.

"Do you like it here?"

"Yes, King Reznor treats us all very well here. He will take good care of you, Liara. He is a good man."

Shaking my head, I shuffle into a sitting position. "He just makes me angry, you know," I say in a rush. I understand his reasoning, but I would prefer he treated me differently. King or not, I refuse to be treated like this. I have been a taunt to him for years, and he has a lot of resentment, but I'm still a person. I left everything I knew for him, the least he could do is be civil, and less cave man carrying me over his shoulder and whatnot.

"He means well. He is someone you have to get used to."

This earns a laugh. "You're the second person to tell me that."

Anisa smiles softly at me. "Then maybe you should listen to us. You must have upset him because he made quite the mess."

"What do you mean?"

"He trashed the study and has been out of the house ever since. He even yelled at Serena, and he never does that."

Ah Serena, she seems like such a hateful woman. "What is Serena to him?"

She instantly averts her eyes and wrings her hands. "Are you sure you want to know the answer?"

"Not really, but I would like it if you told me anyhow."

"Serena is his lover. They have known each other since they were sixteen and have been sharing a bed for the last year." So, she actually means they have been together for the last hundred years. But one-year mortal time.

"Why don't you just say they're dating?"

She laughs. "That's because they aren't dating; they only share a bed. They don't spend time together for anything other than recreational visits. He does nothing romantic for her."

Her statement makes me cringe, and the jealousy returns. These irrational feelings are the least of my problems. The fact that my fiancé has a lover is what's bothering me the most. Yet, this feels like an arranged marriage, and I shouldn't be too surprised about his lover since he didn't want to bring me to Dwimmér anyhow, but it's still sticking with me.

Anisa must have sensed my displeasure because she quickly changes the subject and asks how I like it here so far.

"It's definitely a new experience, but I love learning how to use my powers. I miss mom and Grams. Sometimes I miss how my life was. I was almost done with nursing school before I left, but now I train and have magic. I do like it here, and even though it isn't what I expected, I'm still glad I came."

She nods her head knowingly. "I left my family to come here and be with Emanuel. They disowned me for coming to work for King Reznor."

"You're dating Emanuel?" I squawk.

"Yes," she smiles brightly, "we've been dating for three years. He is a sweet, sweet man."

I realize that they refer to their years in a sense where they count a hundred years as one. "I'm happy for you. I'll have to tease him next time for not telling me."

"I told him not to. I didn't want you to think less of him for dating a servant," she says shyly.

"Anisa, I would never think that. You're a sweet woman, and he is a great guy! I bet you guys are an amazing couple."

For the next few hours, we talked about everything. I told her about the mortal world, and she told me about the magic world. For the first time being here, I honestly felt like I had a friend. We only stopped talking long enough to pack a bag.

I had almost forgotten about going to the village until Anisa reminded me. Even now we're rushing to the front of the manor since we're due to leave in a few minutes.

I wasn't expecting Reznor to make an appearance, but he approaches me just as I start for the waiting car. His hair is still disheveled, and he's in the same clothes from earlier. The second Reznor hits the last stair, Anisa and Emanuel suddenly disappear.

"You're staying with a family friend of mine. She owns the inn in town," Reznor states as he shoves his hands deep into his pockets. When I nod and try to step toward the car again, he gently clasps my elbow. "Be careful, Liara; it's still dangerous until you're marked."

I frown slightly. "I will, but you're the one that should be careful. I'm just hiding out in the village," I tease and step closer to Reznor as a guard takes my bag.

His thumb strokes my elbow where he still holds it. "I'm sorry about earlier—"

"Don't worry about it. I know everything is magnified with the moon."

He huffs a laugh. "Honestly, I probably would have been mad, full moon or not."

I join in on his laughter because he's probably right.

"We're ready for her," Charles says before climbing into the front of the car.

Reznor gives a jerk of his head, but still doesn't release my elbow. He clears his throat as he reluctantly lets me go. "Don't want to keep them waiting."

Gazing up at him, I smile, then place a soft kiss on his cheek. The action surprises both of us, but I refuse to lose my nerve. "Thank you for the apology, but I'm never going to stop wearing shorts, so you may have to get used to that," I whisper into his ear before getting into the car.

He smirks at me as he steps closer, "We'll see about that."

Chapter Six: The Full Moon

My first glimpse of the village feels like something out of a fairytale. The small town is filled with shops, cottages lining the roads, carts filled with goods, and lots of smiling faces. The only vehicles in the whole village are our car and the one behind us. A tri-colored flag with purple, black, and blue with a crescent moon, a wolf head, and flames, hang from every other light post.

The wolf matches the tattoo Emanuel and Charles have on their arms. They told me the story about how they got them after fighting in their first war for Reznor. It was a sign of their dedication and honor to fight for King Nighterious. Apparently Reznor hates them, and the boys love to tease him for it.

The town's people also seem to celebrate Reznor because many of them have the flag flying over their cottages. The people are smiling and bustling across the square. Most of the villagers are dressed in seemingly normal clothes, but some wear bright gowns, their hair in strange styles. One woman's hair is standing straight up. The entire town fascinates me, and I wish we could get out and see more of it, but I know that's not part of the plan.

Continuing on, we stop outside a four-story brick inn with white railings and roses growing up the sides. A woman sits on the porch in a rocking chair but leaps from her seat the moment the car stops. She hurries over and hugs Charles the instant he's out of the car. Anisa motions for me to follow her, and I'm not entirely surprised to see him smirking and joking with the woman. She wears a dark purple dress and stands slightly hunched over, a walking stick in her hand, black hair with streaks of grey running through it.

The woman gazes at me with yellow eyes and a bright smile. "Ah, you must be Liara." She reaches up and pulls me into a tight embrace before smacking a kiss on my cheek. "I've been waiting many years to meet you."

"Nice to meet you." I find myself mirroring her smile, her happiness being rather contagious.

"My name is Morana. If you need anything at all, dear, let me know," she says before moving to Anisa and Emanuel to envelope them both into a hug.

The second Morana releases him, Emanuel glances at me. "We should get her inside. The town folk still don't know he found her," Emanuel whispers as he peers at some towns people walking down the street in our direction.

I'm quickly ushered inside where Morana takes me to a room on the top floor. The room is large with a bed sat against the far wall. Floral wallpaper lines the walls, and the mattress is covered in a light pink duvet with matching pillows. Windows on the far wall show views of the town below, and already I want to migrate there to people watch.

"I hope this is okay."

Turning, I smile at Morana. "It's perfect. Thank you for your kindness."

Morana approaches me and touches a strand of my long brown hair. "I remember when I was as young and beautiful as you. My people have waited for you most of their lives; they will be so excited to learn you are here. Finally, a queen for our king."

I smile, even though the weight of her words are settling heavily, and I can't do or say much else. Anisa is a saving grace as she enters with my bag. Morana leaves, telling us dinner will be ready soon, then hurries out.

Anisa chuckles as she catches me peering out the window as I study at the town. "What do you think of the town?"

My smile widens. "Its beautiful here."

"I thought you would like it. Once the town knows you're here, the king will have to bring you back and show you around properly."

"Why don't they know I'm here?"

Anisa pats the spot on the bed next to her, motioning for me to sit. "It's for your protection. The king has many enemies, and if they learned you were here, that would put a target on your back instantly."

I nod knowingly; Reznor has mentioned it before.

"Since we aren't at the palace, the king requested I sleep in here with you. I can have them bring in a stowaway bed."

"There's no need for that. The bed is big enough for you and me to share." I'm not anyone special, and this all seems to be a big fuss over something so small. Plus, a sleepover would be nice; I've been spending a lot of alone time lately.

"The king wouldn't like that," Anisa says in a rushed voice.

"Well, it's a good thing the king isn't here." I wiggle my eyebrows, and Anisa loses it in a fit of laughter.

Anisa leaves me to gather her things from downstairs and when she steps out, I see another guard lurking outside. They have this house locked down. I'm the only occupant, and Reznor still sent six guards and Anisa to keep me company. Apparently, he isn't a fan of me traveling alone with only men. I would expect nothing less from the brooding man.

As the sun sets, we eat dinner in the small dining room where Morana tells stories of a young Reznor. Apparently, she used to be his nanny after his mother died; It's devastating to learn he's an orphan. I knew his father had been murdered, but she said he would have to tell me how his mother died, even though I hadn't asked in the first place. Death is a personal thing, no matter how many people it affects.

"He was a rotten little boy full of spunk and energy. He would play for hours, running through the palace and hiding from me. I would have to turn the entire manor upside down looking for him." She wears a smile while talking about the "little menace" as she called him. She had raised Reznor as her own.

When everyone else left the room, she turns to me and grabs my hand, holding it lightly. "He may appear tough and hateful, but that man has a heart of gold. You just have to allow him to show you that side of him. If you show him, he can trust you, and get him to let you in, you will see he is worthy to rule all the lands rather than being seen as a monster."

Her words yet again stow a weight on my shoulder and once again, I'm not entirely sure what to say, so instead, I make an excuse and took to hiding out in the bath. It's strange to learn so much about Reznor without hearing any of it from him. He had a rough childhood and is cursed. They wanted him to be hated, but it seems that didn't work because his people love him.

Learning more about him does make me want to talk to him, get to know him better. I want to know everything I possibly can, yet I know we aren't to that level of intimacy when it comes to that.

Thoughts of Reznor and well, *our* future, keep me in the tub till the water turns cold, and my skin resembles a prune. The only thing these kind of thoughts do is make me more confused and give me a headache.

The room is empty when I emerge out of the bathroom, but I'm silently thankful. I still want time to calm my thoughts. Some people watching would help that. Curling on the couch, I stare outside, looking at the night sky and the town below.

People are dancing and singing. Even on the other side of town, the music carries to my ears. Drums beating, guitars strumming, people cheering. The music sounds so happy. I could picture the smiles and the laughter they would be sharing. Pushing the window open, the soft melody floods the room.

The only thing to drown out the music a short time later is a howl that sent shivers up my spine. I waited up as long as I could, waiting for another howl, but sleep beckoned me. I curled up to sleep before Anisa returned.

Thump...

...Thump

...Crash!

I startle awake and flounder in the bed a moment as a crash comes from down the hall. Anisa is already reaching for the light when another crash comes. We exchange a questioning look before we creep toward the door. It suddenly bursts open to reveal Charles and Emanuel. Anisa and I both jump back, grabbing at each other.

"Come on girls, we have to go now!" Charles whispers as he throws our bags onto the bed.

Anisa hands me a sweater to slide over my nightgown, before she does the same. "What's going on?" I whisper as another crash comes from down the hall.

"Someone broke in. They're trashing all the rooms looking for you. We need to go before they find you." Emanuel peaks out the window, looking below.

I quickly shove my feet into my shoes and toss my bag over my shoulder. Charles shoves his head out the door then motions for us to follow.

I snatch him by the arm. "What about Morana?"

"She will be fine. Our priority is to keep you safe." Charles pulls out of my grasp before leading us down the hall where we meet two other guards. The men close in ranks around Anisa and me before we start down the stairs. We all are creeping along trying not to make a sound, but even the group's calmness couldn't stop the shaking of my hands, nor the spike of my heart rate.

The stairs take us to the kitchen, and we barely reach the floor before masked men start firing guns at us. I don't get down fast enough, and a bullet pierces my upper arm. I barely register the pain as I conjure up a shield to protect us, then throw out both hands, sending the men flying. One flies and hits a wall while the other two crash into the China cabinet that sends glass shards everywhere.

"Are you okay?" Charles asks while looking at my arm, blood pooling from it.

"I'll be fine, let's get out of here." I gasp as I apply pressure to the wound.

Emanuel is trying to take me from the kitchen when I see Charles kneel next to one of men and pull off one of their masks off. On his neck is a tattoo of a pine tree.

"What does that tattoo mean?" I ask, peering at the man who lies unconscious.

"Nothing good," Emanuel bites out. "Let's keep going."

Our group is almost out of the inn when I hear a cry of pain coming from Morana's room.

"We have to help her!"

"No, Reznor will have my ass if you get injured any further," Charles hisses.

"Either we help her, or I'm not leaving," I say sternly.

With a sigh of defeat, Charles cautiously opens the door, crossing the threshold after instructing me to leave with Emanuel. I, of course, ignore him and follow him into the room. Morana's bedroom is trashed, and she lies beaten on the floor. Dropping to my knees next to her, I assess her injuries.

"I'm sorry, I don't know how they figured out you were here. I couldn't stop them," she cries as she clutches my hand. Morana is marked with a large gash across her forehead, a bulging black eye, broken nose, then two large slashes across her abdomen and lower leg. There is blood seemingly coming from everywhere and if she doesn't get medical attention soon, she's going to die from blood loss.

"Don't be sorry, you did everything you could," I coo, in an attempt to ease her worries.

She tries to smile but ends up wincing instead. I need to help her. Gripping her hand tighter I focus on healing her. *Healing her, repairing the damage that was inflicted upon her.*

My eyes flutter open as a gasp erupts from somewhere in the room. A golden light is flowing from my hand and drifting across Morana's body. Every part of her body the light touches begins to heal. The wound on her face starts closing along with the rest of her injuries. Her skin mends itself as if the injury had never appeared in the first place.

"You healed me," she gasps in disbelief. With some assistance, she rises to her feet. I resist yelping as she tugs on my injured arm.

Charles surges forward. "We have to go. Now."

Stomping from further in the house sends our small group fleeing into the waiting vehicles. I'm lodged between Anisa and Morana with Charles and Emanuel at the front of the car both looking worried as we tear through the sleeping town.

"Wrap her arm in something so she doesn't bleed out. It's been long enough that Reznor should be in his human form; we're going back to the palace," Charles shouts as he presses on the gas harder. So much for the easy-going Charles.

Anisa takes a shirt out of her bag then ties it tightly around my upper arm. I force myself not to groan as she twists the fabric, creating a makeshift tourniquet. "I'll dress it when we get back to the manor." She starts to look worried at the amount of blood that's all over the right side of my body from the gunshot wound.

"It just nicked me; I'll be fine."

Anisa doesn't argue with me, but every few minutes she looks back down at my arm and then checks my complexion. She goes as far as checking my forehead with the back of her hand then checking my pulse.

"Morana, do you want us to drop you off at your daughter's? It's on the way," Charles asks.

"Yes, please, if it's not a hassle," Morana beams. She's still smiling brightly even after what just happened. We drop her off at a small cottage on the outskirts of town. She kisses my cheek again and thanks me before disappearing into the house with her frantic daughter.

The remainder of the car ride is silent. The clock on the dash reads five-thirty by the time we arrive back at the palace. I begin feeling dizzy as I trudge up the stairs. Blood is dripping down my arm and marking the concrete with each step. Charles quickly ushers me through the door, only to try and stop me by accidently grabbing my injured arm. I yelp, but it isn't just because of the pain, it is partially because I'm startled by what is happening on the foyer table.

Reznor stands behind Serena, thrusting harshly against her. They both are completely naked, Serena laying with her chest pressed into the table. Reznor's sculpted body glistens in the soft light coming from the moon shining through the large windows. Serena looks up and shoots me a sinful grin as she moans his name loudly. Reznor's hips never falter, and he seems completely unaware of our presence, until he hears me cry out as Charles tries to tug me out of the room by my injured arm.

I swat his hand away. "I'm going to take care of this before I pass out from blood loss."

Reznor's eyes jerk to me as I breeze past him like nothing is happening. I put one foot in front of the other, trying to ignore the sounds of Serena moaning. I don't miss the fact Reznor's red eyes track my every step before I disappear down the hall. A cold, dark feeling strikes my chest as they *continue*. Not even my scent seemed to deter him, and that alone made me nauseous. I think I might vomit, but I force the feeling down until I'm safe in my room.

I'm not as lucky when I barge through the door. Sprinting to the toilet, I barely make it before I empty the contents of my stomach. I hurl violently until I'm left dry heaving as my vision blurs a little; there's a fierce pounding in my head and my arm beats in tempo with it.

"Liara?" Anisa calls out hesitantly.

I barely pull my head from the cold bowl. "Maybe I'm bleeding more than I thought."

Her hands flutter over my forehead before she helps me up from the ground. "Let's get you cleaned up." she says sadly. Her face is blanched of color, but I can see the pity in her eyes.

Her reaction to my state sends the words tumbling from my mouth. "It's okay. I can handle it."

"At least let me wrap it for you." she begs with a need in her voice that makes me cave to her wishes.

She carefully takes my arm, removing the shirt that was wrapped around it, then helps me out of the sweater. The bullet tore through the side of my arm, leaving ragged edges that would need stiches to heal properly. The wound itself looks rather nasty. It had been gushing earlier but now it only oozes. With careful movements, Anisa cleans then packs the wound before skillfully wrapping my arm.

"Can I heal myself?" I ask, even though I think I already know the answer.

She visibly grimaces. "No, only certain species have advanced healing and if one has the gift of true healing, it can only be used outward."

"Great."

She helps me clean the blood from my body and change into a fresh night set before she leaves the room to get some pain medications. With her gone, I tug down my top to look at the bruise I had caught sight of earlier. A black mark rests right above my heart. It doesn't feel tender, but it certainly hadn't been there when I was in the bath. I make a mental note to check on it again tomorrow, but right now, I'm absolutely drained.

Clinging to the wall, I make my way to bed very slowly. Flashes of dizziness wash over, but I force myself to climb into bed then take the pills from Anisa. She casts me a final saddened look before holding my cold hand. "I'll make sure no one bothers you today…you'll need to rest. The pills might cause you to sleep *awhile*."

"Thanks, Anisa, I'm going to try and sleep off my gunshot now." I try to joke but it's halfhearted. Anisa knows it too. She shuts the curtains and turns off all the lights before she leaves, but the moment she's gone, I let out a breath I didn't know I'd been holding.

I'm not sure how I feel about anything that happened tonight, but I know I'm blaming everything on the blood loss. The vomiting, the sickening feeling, the sense of betrayal…well the latter I can't exactly blame on the wound, but I'm going to anyways. I'll feel better after some sleep. I'm totally not going to be pissed in a few hours about walking in on Reznor screwing his lover. I'm not going to be furious that he didn't stop, or even notice that I was bleeding right in front of his eyes. Nope. I'm going to shove it to the back of mind like he did with my existence for years. Maybe then I won't want to slap him next time I see him.

Chapter Seven: Running With No Destination

Anisa kept true to her promise; no one bothered me at all yesterday. I spent the entire day in bed sleeping off and on. I only woke to take the pain medication and to let Anisa re-wrap my arm. She refused to let me do it, and I was too drugged to fight her.

My good luck has run out it seems because I wake to Reznor's voice seeping through my door.

"Let me in to see her," he growls.

"I'm sorry, your Majesty. She is sleeping, and needs her rest," Anisa replies quietly.

"Then come get me the moment she wakes up."

I try not to laugh at his words; he only wants to talk to me because I caught him banging his woman. I have no interest in speaking about it, and he's just going to have to get over that.

I tense when the door creaks open but relax when I realize its Anisa crossing the room. "You can't avoid him forever, Liara," Anisa states as she rips the curtains open.

I groan, shielding my eyes. "It's been one day—"

"Ah, ah, ah, it's day two," Anisa corrects.

"That hardly counts. I was drugged for those twenty-four hours."

"You're lucky he didn't barge through the door and just come in. He knows what you saw…" Anisa's gaze drops to the ground. Her face drains of color as she takes on a somber expression.

No, we are not talking about this. I vowed to shove it away into a corner, and that's what I plan on doing.

"I was shot. I feel like I am allowed to have some 'me' time, and some space away from people." I intentionally change the subject. I'm not going to address his *activities* with Serena. Not my business, or at least that's what I keep telling myself.

"Liara, we can talk about it, if you want to. I know you two aren't very close, but—"

"I'm good. He doesn't owe me an explanation. It's his life. I'm just living in it."

Anisa opens her mouth as if she wants to say more, then she quickly clamps it shut. Instead, she wanders to my closet and pulls out a sundress and some sandals. "If you won't talk to him, you might as well avoid him. I'll take you for a walk on the grounds. I can't promise anything, the guards might alert him that you're awake."

It's as good a plan as any. Reznor might not try to bring it up if I'm with Anisa. Plus, I'm already going stir crazy.

I pull on the blue sundress with a pattern of white flowers and long flowing sleeves. Anisa undoes my braids from yesterday, allowing my hair to fall in waves down my back. Unfortunately, I struggle a bit with the shoes because I can't strap them up properly without straining my arm. She brushes my hands away then kneels by my feet to fix them for me.

I feel a little bit like a child, especially when she sends me to the bathroom to brush my teeth while she makes my bed. Checking the spot on my chest while scrubbing my teeth, the bruise hasn't spread and still doesn't feel tender. Huh, I don't know what it is.

Anisa is beaming with excitement when I leave the bathroom. "Ready?"

"Let's do it."

Linking my good arm with hers, Anisa and I sneak out of the manor, taking a secret exit only the servants know about. Reznor's ploy to keep me near the servants' quarters has backfired because now I know how to sneak around. Our stealth however is pointless because we'd gotten fifty feet from the house when Charles and Emanuel step in front of us.

"Gods, are you trying to piss Reznor off?" Charles is trying to block us from walking any further.

Tugging on Anisa's looped arm, I steer her around the boys. "We're just going for a walk, Charles."

"Well, we might as well come with you, so you're protected," Emanuel pipes in, falling in step with us. "How's the arm?"

"Sore, but it stopped bleeding mostly. The herbs Anisa put on it really helped."

"Liara is stubborn and won't take any more of the pain medicine I offer," she criticizes.

"It makes me feel loopy and then I pass out for hours. I'd like to be somewhat conscious to what's going on around me."

"She's tough, I'll give her that," Emanuel jokes from beside Anisa, his hand gripping hers. I make sure to shoot Anisa a wink as I bump her with my hip.

"I feel left out," Charles complains, then snatches Emanuel's free hand. "There we go, that's better." We all fell into laughter and just like that, the tension from earlier dissipates.

Anisa takes us to a wildflower garden. We have to track through the woods to get here, but it's worth it. The meadow is filled beautifully with flowers in various colors: red, blue, green, yellow, pink, and purple. They sit in an oval like clearing in the middle of the woods. It contains all different kinds of flowers and even some of the Night berries.

I find a spot to sit in between flower patches. Taking my shoes off, I lay on the ground with my eyes closed and drape my injured arm across my stomach. Laying here listening to the sounds of birds chirping, and singing to each other, the sensation of heat seeping into my skin is just what I needed. The tension that's built up in my shoulders over the last two days starts to slowly dissipate. Anisa, Emanuel, and Charles are laughing off in the distance, allowing me to enjoy time to myself.

After some time, the sound of footsteps approaches, followed by the rustle in the grass as someone sits next to me.

"When are you going to talk to him?" Charles questions, his voice hesitant even though he is boldly addressing the topic.

I carefully sit up as I process how I want to answer his question. "Why do I need to talk to him? I know he's been sleeping with her. It's nothing new."

"How'd you figure that out?"

I give him a pointed stare. "Them fucking like bunnies in the foyer yesterday didn't give it away?" Charles' face blanches as I continue, "But I knew before that. He didn't exactly hide it from me."

"Well, he obviously wants to talk about it."

"I will tell him the same thing I told you. There is nothing to talk about."

Charles laughs, "We'll all have something to talk to Reznor about when he finds out we purposely allowed you to avoid him."

"If he wishes to stay in my good graces, then he will leave you all alone." I eye Charles from beside me. Anisa, Emanuel, and Charles, all put themselves in a vulnerable position by being here with me. They risk his wrath to let me sit in the sun, and yet I still resent him a little for what comes out of his mouth next.

"He just wants to protect you."

I laugh, rolling my eyes at his remark.

"Well, this is interesting," Reznor steps out of the woods, leisurely strolling toward us. He looks a little disheveled, his deep red button-down shirt is wrinkled, the charcoal slacks have creases in them as if he's slept in his clothes.

"Sir, I can explain—" Charles starts, but Reznor put up a hand up.

"Get Anisa and Emanuel and get back to the manor. Liara, and I are going to have a chat," Reznor declares.

Closing my eyes, I lay back down on the ground, waiting for him to speak. Reznor waits till the three leave the area. "You're avoiding me."

"No, I'm sunbathing," I retort, keeping my eyes shut. I can feel the glare he shoots at me through my closed lids, yet even then I can't bring myself to look at him.

"You were awake both times I attempted to talk to you, and yet you had Anisa send me away." I snap my eyes open, startled by his knowing. He simply raises a brow then continues. "I could hear your heartbeat and breathing."

Coming up with a lie quickly. "I didn't want to talk about the shooting; it's over with." I sit up abruptly after he's ruined my good mood.

Reznor flinches out of the corner of my eye. "You're bleeding again."

"No, I'm not—" but seconds later, blood starts soaking through my dress. "Well shit."

Reznor hauls me to my feet, but his touch nearly sends me to the ground again. What used to feel like soft flutters now feels like jolts across my skin. Startled, I freeze in his arms.

"Are you alright?" He guides me closer, the sensation increasing with our nearness.

Jerking out of his grasp, I take a step back to clear my head. "Yeah, I'm fine, just lightheaded is all."

He sets his jaw, and I force myself not to laugh when I realize what I've done. Considering he is already pissed, I take this moment to turn around and walk back to the manor. To my surprise, he doesn't follow me.

"What did he say? What did you say? What did he do? Was he mad?" Anisa quizzes rapidly, not allowing me to answer once. She continues to grill me as she redresses my arm in the safety of my bathroom.

"Nothing. He noticed I was bleeding, then let me go."

"Oh, that's all?" She is obviously disappointed.

"Yeah, nothing exciting."

Anisa starts repacking the kit she keeps her medical supplies in. "Well, I'm going to have to run. The king is meeting with some important people today; I won't be around much, and neither will most of the staff. I'll leave some bandages and your medicine. Then check on you after the dinner is over."

"Who's coming?"

"I don't know, but I'm assuming it has to do with the people who attacked us." Anisa doesn't have time to say anything else before waving goodbye and darting out the door.

The rest of the day, I hold up in my room reading the books Anisa brought for me, yet even they can't keep me entertained. As the sun just starts to set, I decide I can't stand the boredom any longer. Deciding on going for a run, I quickly change and make sure my arm isn't bleeding before I find my useless phone. Anisa had charged it for me when she brought my purse this morning. Grams had given it to Reznor when he brought me here; she knew we used phones in the human world but not many are used here. In fact, though they have most of the same technology we have, they choose not to utilize it due to seeing how it's tainted the humans and what negativity comes with it. Dwimmér only uses landlines, their own unique form of electricity, vehicles that run on magic, running water, and a few other types of luxuries.

Slipping out of my room and down the many flights of stairs, I'm surprised that I don't pass a single servant or guard. They must be swamped. The guards that are usually stationed outside are also absent; I had planned on informing *someone* of my whereabouts, but it seems that won't be happening. Popping in my earbuds, I start at a slow run across the field toward the usual trail.

My arm stings at first, but the more I run, the less pain I feel. I loop the trail, but quickly grow bored of it. I feel restless about a number of things today apparently. Branching out, I explore parts of the neighboring forest. I'm deep in the towering woods when I realize my light is quickly fading.

I've been too caught up in the scenery to notice the time or location of the sun. Everything is tranquil here and easily distracts me. Even the mushrooms look like each and every one has been hand-painted and crafted to its perfect state.

I make stops along the way, using precious time to capture some pictures. I don't stop long because when I do, my arm begins to ache again.

Gazing at the retreating sun, I veer back toward the manor. Hopefully, I will be able to find my way back. Weaving through the trail, trying to beat the sun, seems useless because it's winning. The light fades faster and faster, and I know the sun will be down before I'm out of the woods.

I'm momentarily trying to recognize my surroundings in the fleeting light when I'm jerked from the path. It happens so fast I don't know who, or what grabs me until I hear the voice.

"Where have you been?" Reznor bellows. He has me in an iron grasp; I would have fallen had he not been so strong. I'm pressed against him so tightly I couldn't move if I wanted to. Still taken aback by him scaring me half to death, it takes me a moment to regain my composure and answer him. I pry my arm free from his and yank out my earbuds.

"Are you crazy?" I shout back, only to regret my decision immediately. At this moment, it looked like he wanted to kill me. If he did, that would solve a lot of my problems, well some of his too. Oof, I need to cool it with the dark humor, even if it's in my own head.

"What were you thinking?" he asks through gritted teeth, towering over me again as he invades my space.

"I went for a run. I was on my way back!" I flare my one free arm. "You act like I was running away or something! I was going to tell a guard, but I couldn't find anyone."

His eyes flash with a flair of pain before the anger takes hold. "Everyone has been looking for you! You were attacked yesterday! I thought someone had taken you! How inconsiderate can you be?" he roars in my face.

I don't know what comes over me, but I slap him right across the face. Reznor's face starts to contort as he clenches his eyes and strains hard, trying to keep *something* at bay. My heart's pounding in my ears as I helplessly watch his eyes turn bright red. "Rez—" I start only to be thrown over his shoulder.

"Put me down!" I scream while slapping him on the back. He growls in response and keeps strolling through the forest.

Eventually, I give up and lay there as he carries me out of the woods. He proceeds to take me all the way to my room, where he flings me onto the bed. My now very sore arm collides with the bed, causing me to hiss out in pain as I crush it into the mattress.

With his eyes still red, he snarls, "Stay in this room!" He growls so loud it rattles the windows as he stalks to the door before adding over his shoulder, "And clean your fucking arm up!"

I lay there in shock for a few minutes then force myself from the bed. My arm is what causes me to move, that and the blood dripping down my skin. Great.

The scalding water is welcoming as I slide to the floor of the shower, sitting directly under the stream. Dried specks of blood and fresh blood mixes with the water before running down the drain. My arm craves relief from the heat, but I refuse to move from the floor. I disassociate as my thoughts try to press in.

"Are you going to get out of the shower anytime soon?" Anisa calls out as she opens the shower door, letting the steam roll out like a wave.

"How long have I been in here?" I ponder, only now realizing I've lost track of time.

"About an hour or so."

I linger a few more moments, contemplating if I truly want to get out or not, but eventually, I climb to my feet. Immediately, I cry out in pain as I move my arm. Running probably wasn't the best idea, I now realize for numerous reasons. Shutting the water off, I take the towel from Anisa.

"My Gods, look at your arm!" she shrieks.

Carefully wrapping the towel around my body, I emerge from the shower, and the moment I do, Anisa is cradling my arm in her soft hands. The skin is red and irritated, but the wound itself has reopened, looking worse than when I first got shot.

"It's fine. We can deal with it after I get dressed." I carefully move out of her grasp.

She follows behind me as I yank a random nightgown from the closet. The entire selection of nightclothes they have here are all rather revealing At first, it had bothered me, but now I can't seem to care. Opening another door, I take out a pair of underwear when a flare of pain strikes my chest, causing me to gasp for air. Grasping at my chest, I try to force air into my lungs as I crash to the floor. The pain is like nothing I've ever felt before, worse than being shot.

Anisa rushes to my side. "Are you alright?" When she realizes I can't respond due to gasping like a fish out of water, she darts to her feet. "I'll go get help!"

I try to stop her, but I'm barely getting air in, let alone words out. Clinging to my towel, I try to force myself to breathe through the pain, but nothing is working. The time seems to pass by painfully slow as I thrash on the floor.

"I sent Charles to get Reznor; what do we do?" Anisa asks Emanuel as they both reach my spot on the floor.

"What happened?" Emanuel kneels next to me as he and Anisa try to help me in any way they can.

I frantically shake my head. I don't know what this or why it's happening. The sensation feels like if someone is stabbing me in the heart, crushing my lungs. Just as I feel like I might pass out, it suddenly stops. Taking a large lungful of air, I try to calm my frantic heart. "What…was…that?" I gasp out in between heaving breaths.

Emanuel and Anisa's shoulders both sink with relief.

"I have no idea," Emanuel states as they help me to my feet. Anisa carefully ensures my towel is secure while I focus on not falling over, my dancing vision making it difficult. "Did something happen?"

I'm just getting over a wave of dizziness when an out of breath Charles enters the room along with a shirtless, and disordered Reznor. I'm still seeing stars, blinking rapidly, and trying to regain my breath while Anisa and Emanuel hold me steady. I should have realized sooner that they called him, but it's too late to fake wellness now.

"What happened?" Reznor asks frantically. Stepping forward, he takes me into his arms and out of the others' grasp.

"I don't know. I had just gotten out of the shower when it felt like someone stabbed me in the chest," I speak slowly, still dizzy from the lack of air. "I couldn't breathe." My nervous hand flutters to my throat, trying to calm my own panic. Reznor strokes my back, his touch on my skin instantly calming the lingering pain and soothing my rapid heart. That's odd.

"Are you okay now?"

"I think so."

Reznor takes in the room, and the men seem to get the hint because they clear out the second Reznor raises an eyebrow. "Anisa, help her get dressed, then get me once you're done. I'll put her in bed."

Anisa replaces his grasp as he slowly removes his hands from my body. Lingering a moment, he watches to see if Anisa can keep me up on her own. I don't take offense to it; I'm voluptuous whereas Anisa is very tiny.

With Reznor a few steps away from me, I'm able to take in his appearance better. He has sweat glistening off his body, his hair looks as if *someone* has tugged through it. Then when he turns to leave the room, it all clicks as I see the faint nail markings down his back.

"Shocked he was able to make it," I say dryly.

"Let's just get you dress—" Anisa stops as she removes my towel and gaps at the sight of my chest. What was once a faint black mark, now runs along the pathway of my veins, starting at the bottom of my left breast and creeping toward my navel.

"Don't tell him," I breathe out, trying to cover myself.

"What is that, Liara?" She slides the nightgown over my head, and I pitifully help pull it down. Even this is exhausting me.

"I don't know, but you can't tell him. Not yet." Carefully, I pull up my underwear, thanking god...or gods that I didn't fall over in the process.

Anisa glares as she wraps my arm in silence. I feel so unbelievably weak. I honestly think if I try to take a step, I'll probably fall.

"You better explain to me what's going on if I'm going to lie to my *king* for you," she bites as she slams the drawer, which is the biggest outburst I've ever seen from her.

"I don't know what's happening, but I have a theory. I just can't tell it to you now."

"I'll go get Reznor." Anisa starts for the closet door then freezes when we hear the commotion coming from my room.

"She faked it just to get attention from you, Reznor! Why don't you see that?" a high-pitched female voice calls out.

"Not now, Serena," Reznor groans.

"You, and I were in the middle of—"

"Not now, Serena!" he bellows, cutting Serena off from finishing her words.

"No, we are going to do this now because I'm not *finished*!"

Blind with rage, I step forward without grabbing onto Anisa, even as my legs want to protest and wobble. I steel them off and focus on emerging from the room. Anisa however snatches my good arm as I wobble on the second step. She casts me a warning glance as we exit the closet, and her grip immediately tightens.

"See, she's fine." The hateful redhead sneers, standing in the doorway of my bedroom.

"I told you to get me," Reznor moans in annoyance as he reaches for me, but I stop him.

"Like Serena said, I'm fine. Go *finish* your business, or hers, whichever suits you." I exaggerate the word as I give Reznor a disgusted look.

"Rezzie—" Serena starts again, but he cuts her off by shouting again.

"Out now!"

Serena visibly flinches from the doorway then stomps away, but not before throwing me a hateful look. I smile smugly while flipping her off. Anisa looks mortified, but Charles is choking on his laughter. That earns a swat from Emanuel while Reznor runs a hand down his face.

Reznor's eyes are threatening to turn red, but he manages to stop them before clearing his throat. I don't let the pain show as my body protests every movement I make while climbing into the bed. Anisa returns with two white pills that I know will knock me out for hours. I down them while avoiding eye contact with Reznor.

"Anisa, thank you. You're dismissed, along with the rest of you," Reznor glowers as he crosses his arms over his chest. Anisa casts me a hesitant look, but she leaves the room with the rest of them.

Reznor watches me momentarily while I simply wait for him to yell at me again. Really, I wait for him to say anything at all but instead, he leaves and slams the door behind him. It's probably for the best that he didn't linger because I was moments away from telling him to go fuck himself and high tailing it back to the mortal world.

My plans to sleep that night get ruined due to crying out in pain each time they are *together*. It just got longer and longer, and each time, it felt like someone was stabbing me. In the beginning, it hurt so bad that I cried, but toward the end, I didn't have the energy to fight against the pain. My heart aches along with the rest of my body. Both throbbing from the stabbing, pulsating pain radiates through me.

When they stopped the first time, I was so thankful, but it only started again a few moments later. There were two hours where I was able to sleep before being awoken again. I'm glistening with sweat from thrashing around, trying to ease the pain in any way I can, but nothing helps.

    The sun just started to crest the sky when my heavy eyelids begin to close. I'm not sure if it's because they have finally stopped, or because my body can't fight to stay awake any longer. The sound of shuffling rouses me slightly, and just before sleep captures me, I catch Reznor sit down in the chair next to my bed.

We lock eyes, and I want to shout at him, but I'm too tired. I want to tell him to hold me, so the pain would stop, but I don't, because I'm stronger than that. It's twisted that his touch can take away the pain that he causes, so instead of being tempted further, I give into the blackness, and fall asleep with Reznor watching me.

Chapter Eight: Try Harder

Waking up, I'm thrilled to find that Reznor is gone, but in his place is a demanding Anisa who marches around the room hastily.

With an unnecessarily aggressive toss of my training clothes, Anisa finally speaks up. "Reznor healed your arm by the way." She yanks back the covers and gestures to my exposed arm. Where had once been a gunshot wound, an injury that should have led to scar, now has perfectly healed skin. There isn't a single mark on my arm.

"He would have healed it sooner had you spoken to him like he requested."

"Anisa—"

"No, you're going to explain this minute, or I'm getting Reznor." She crosses her arms over her chest, glaring at me.

"If you would stop being so dramatic and sit down, I'll tell you."

She plops down in the chair near my bed, her eyes analyzing me as I climb out of the bed, and to my surprise, I'm not aching.

"Huh, that's weird."

"What's weird? Are you trying to distract me?"

Rolling my eyes, I launch into my explanation. "The night of the full moon, when we came to the manor and...saw Reznor and Serena frolicking, I felt this crushing weight prick my chest. It's what caused me to get so sick, not the blood loss unfortunately."

Anisa makes an exasperated sound, and I pointedly ignore it, wanting to get through this as fast as possible.

"After you left, I found a small black mark over my heart which I thought was a bruise. Well, I thought it was a bruise until last night. When Reznor is *with* Serena, the pain starts, and only stops when they *finish*." A look of horror crosses Anisa's face as she digests my phrasing.

"Last night they went at it again and again. I was up for hours because the pain wouldn't stop. It was the worst pain I've ever felt, and it only got worse when Reznor came into my room this morning and watched me sleep. I wanted to yell at him, cuss him out maybe, but I didn't have the energy because I was so spent. I also can't bring this to him because he will resent me even more than he already does; he wants his time with her before he's tied to me.

"This is the curse portion. Since the mate bond is being violated on his part, it's punishing me, in what I'm guessing is a way to hurt him by torturing me. It almost feels like the bond is trying to force us together now; when he touches me, it soothes the pain. It's like it's begging me to be near him, to be touched by him. To top it all off I can't decide if I'm pleased with him for healing me because it took the pain from last night away, or furious he had the audacity to come seek me out after he nailed her through the night."

Anisa sags into her chair. "Liara you're going to have to tell him at some point. You can't put up with this for two more months!"

"I can and I will, but I don't need him to have another reason to resent me by taking his precious time away. I also don't want him to treat me any worse because he can't be with his lover." My first conversation with Reznor flashes through my mind, his demand for time. He can have it, but the cost of it might not be worth it in the end.

"How does it look now?"

I hadn't checked on it myself, and now is as good a time as any. Lifting my nightgown to just beneath my breast, Anisa gapes at the sight. The blackness has spread further down my stomach and branches toward my sides.

"Liara, I don't think you understand," she pauses, faltering her words as she continues. "With how, uhm, active they are, you physically won't make it."

Her words make my skin crawl and stoke more anger from me. Jerking my gown back into place, I assure, "Then I'll hold out as long as I can. When I can't handle it anymore, we'll tell him."

"This isn't a good idea; you two are supposed to be getting closer…this is just going to push you apart."

I laugh at her. "Anisa, we don't get along because we are very different Just because our bodies are physically attracted to each other doesn't mean that our minds ever will be. She frowns and stands suddenly. "You need to try anyway for both of your sakes. Reznor deserves to be loved. He is a good man no matter what you think." Anisa rushes toward the door, suddenly angered.

"Anisa, I didn't mean it like that," I try to explain, but she won't hear me out.

"You might not have, but you're not trying very hard either. The mate bond is overwhelmingly strong for him; it literally drives him mad. After that stunt you pulled last night, he went postal for an hour before he went to bed with her. He would have stayed with you all night had you asked him to. Hell, if you had even talked to him, he never would have gone to bed with her. *Your* actions drove him right into her bed!" She flings the door open. "Try harder, Liara. It's not just you that will be affected by this. The mate bond can kill both of you. He already cares for you, whether you see it or not."

Oh, now I'm pissed. I snap at her words and take an angry step forward. "Don't you dare act like this is my fault! I had been here over a month before he even agreed to have a civilized conversation with me. I have been trying! I'm sorry if I don't know how to deal with him. I never planned on my relationship to be counted on by all of his followers, or for me to be the missing piece in some thousand-year-old puzzle!"

Anisa is taken aback by my outburst before she glares at me. "Do you need anything else *Miss*?"

I stare at her blankly, Anisa taking on a smug look before exiting the room. Heaving in a breath, I try to will the anger down as I snatch the training clothes and change. Hopefully training can calm me down, but my hopes dwindle when I get a new shadow.

A guard trails me from the moment I step out of the house until Emanuel *verbally* states that I am now under his watch. The guard gives a jerky nod before strolling back toward the manor.

"Look, sleeping beauty is finally awake," Charles teases.

I only glare at him. I'm really not in the mood.

"Are you feeling better?" Emanuel questions.

"I'm fine."

The boys exchange a look before refocusing on me. Charles clears his throat "You want to talk about what happened last night?"

"No, I want to punch something." I emphasize my words by cracking my knuckles.

Charles smiles enthusiastically at Emanuel. "Get the wraps! The last thing we need is you getting hurt again."

I ignore the little dig but stew on the comment while he wraps my hands. Once it's time to fight, I nail him in the jaw. "Oops, I wouldn't want to get hurt again."

Charles just laughs before we launch into training. We fight back and forth, landing blows on each other occasionally. It's getting easier to keep up with him now that I'm mad. We go rounds before he makes me take a break after he accidentally hit me harder than he should have.

"Charles, you hit like a girl. I'm fine." I flex my fingers, trying to get him to continue boxing with me, but he isn't budging.

"Sit your ass down, Liara, and take a break," Charles snaps.

Pouting, I slide down the bark and sit between the boys at a nearby tree. We all are sweating, and the trees is a welcoming escape from the scorching sun. Luckily fall should be coming soon, and that means practices will get a lot cooler.

"Reznor is going to train with us once he is done with his meeting," Emanuel says, nudging my shoulder slightly.

"Oh joy."

Charles frowns. "I thought things were going well with you guys."

"Well, him screwing Serena on the table can change a few things," I mumble as I close my eyes, leaning my head back against the tree. Things with Reznor have been decent; sometimes we can tolerate each other, then others I'm slapping him across the face, then he's throwing me over his shoulder. It's like a merry-go-round, and I can't get off it because some God decided I'm his.

"I understand that. I would be livid if I saw Anisa doing what Reznor was." Emanuel starts shaking his head as if he's trying to get the image out.

The mention of Anisa triggers the anger from this morning's conversation all over again. "According to your girlfriend, I'm not doing enough, or giving him the benefit of the doubt." Once the words are out of my mouth, I realize they sounded more bitter than I intended.

Emanuel looks surprised and is opening his mouth to speak, but Charles beats him to it. "That's not fair; you're both emotional, it's not going to be easy. It would be easier to tame a troll."

That little comment sends all three of us into a fit of laughter. It's the ice breaker I didn't know I needed. I cool down quickly enough and continue to laugh as they cheer me up with witty comments. Emanuel and Charles aren't judgmental, and that is something I need right now.

"You sure you don't want to talk about it?" Emanuel presses one final time; he's smart and waited till they got me back to my neutral baseline.

"So, what, he fucked some chick in the foyer? He did the same thing last night...the entire night." I grimace. "He and I aren't together. That has been made abundantly clear since I got here. What he does is not my problem. If he wants to ruin whatever progress we were making, that's on him."

"Wait, how did you know about yesterday?" Charles looks instantly uncomfortable.

"He had nail marks down his back and was sweating. Hell, he practically smelled of sex," I bite out, once again disgusted with his behavior. Thinking back on it still makes me nauseous, and there it is again—the bubbling anger that comes with it. I had just calmed down too, damnit.

"But how do you know they had sex all night?" Emanuel asks, though he looks like he'd rather not ask that question.

"I could hear it," I lie casually. Both of the boys cringe slightly.

"You're really not mad?" Emanuel prods again, but he is going to get the same answer.

"Hard to care when there's nothing to care about. The bond is compelling us together; it's not actually something he wants. Makes sense he has a side piece because he is *not* getting anywhere with me." I try to believe my words, but I know they aren't truthful. He is disrespecting me, the woman that was created for him. It's gotten old quickly, not to mention he makes me feel like I'm the problem. He's the one parading around with another woman while his engagement ring is on my finger. If he put half as much time into us as he did sleeping with Serena, this might be an entirely different situation.

"Well, that's enough of this conversation because here he comes," Charles says in a rushed voice and scoots a few inches away from me. I cast him a confused look, but he won't meet my eyes.

Reznor strolls up casually, and for the first time since meeting him, it's like my body is calling out for him. I'm aching to be near him, to smell him, to be touched by him. It has to be part of the curse; it's trying to force us together, because being next to him is the last thing I *want* to do.

Reznor is dressed in his usual training attire, his hands stuffed into his pockets. Nothing appears to be different, but the bond feels different. Charles leaps up and waltz over to him. They exchange words in hushed voices just soft enough for me not to hear. Reznor keeps glancing between Charles and me, yet he doesn't come any closer.

Emanuel snaps my attention away from analyzing Reznor. "Did you, and Anisa clear things up?"

Ah yes, his lovely girlfriend, another one of my problems. "I don't think so. She called me 'Miss,' and she knows how I feel about that. I don't understand why she is so mad at me."

"I think she's just worried more than mad. You scared her half to death last night. She was up all night worrying about you." Of course he'd defend Anisa, but it doesn't change what she said.

"But to say I'm not trying? There isn't much for me to do. He said to give him space and avoid him till the ceremony, so that's what I'm doing." The ground quickly becomes more interesting; if I play with the grass at least then I won't be tempted to look at Reznor.

"I don't think he wants you to avoid him. I think you two just don't know how to approach each other. There is so much…pressure on your relationship. It's taken a lot out of both of you. You got attacked, and now we think there is an internal leak. Then what happened last night and ruling the lands, it has taken a lot out of him. He isn't usually like this, but you also make his inner beast come out more because of the bond. Then in your defense, you have this man whom you've never met and are thrown into this unknown world with basically the biggest decision of your life spelled out for you. Both of you are in a stressful situation, but if you could find a way to work together rather than apart, maybe that's the next step to take." Emanuel's defending both parties the best he can, but it doesn't make things any easier.

While Charles and Reznor are still talking, Emanuel helps me take the wraps off my hands and wrists. Reznor's watchful eyes are trained on Emanuel as he works. Emanuel is taking extra caution, trying not to jerk them while also keeping a respectful distance.

Emanuel glances nervously as Reznor approaches, then he averts his eyes as he moves faster than before.

"Are you feeling better?" Reznor asks, attempting to use a casual voice.

"Yes, thank you."

It's uncomfortable now since we all knew what happened, and yet we all were avoiding the elephant in the room. The second Emanuel is finished unwrapping my hand, he is off the ground and away from me. I cast him a hateful look. Still, he just mouths 'I'm sorry' as he moves further away from us.

Reznor sticks out both of his hands, offering to help me up from the ground. I hesitate, but eventually grasp his, and stand up. I ignore that the second he touches me, the anger dissipates, but I can't ignore the stare he casts at me with furrowed brows. When we touch this time, it feels different. It seems more urgent, and now that we have contact, it demands that I stay in his grasp. Shivers erupt over my body as our hands linger in each other's.

Dazed, I'm soaking in the feeling when Charles clears his throat. Reznor practically throws my hands from his and shuffles back slowly. I brush off the pang that strikes my gut at the loss of his contact but, watching him step away causes the pain to stir deeper. It feels like my bones are sad. If that is even possible. I'm growing tired of this already; I don't like depending on people. To remind myself that I am indeed still angry at him, I step away from Reznor also. I need a clear head and being near him won't help that.

"Today we need to work on Liara throwing her shield up over not only herself, but for Reznor as well. One of us will fight with Reznor, and she has to try and shield him while fighting on her own." Charles pulls out a gun. The pure surprise on my face amuses him as he breaks into a toothy grin.

He fires the weapon at Reznor, but the bullet never gets near him as it repels off an invisible shield and falls to the ground with a thud. They all appear surprised, but Charles is pleased.

"How does that keep happening? I wasn't even thinking about the shield." I question while crossing my arms over my chest.

"It's the bond. Your body wants to protect him on instinct. Just like if I try to shoot you—" Before he could finish his sentence, he is flung through the air, landing twenty feet away.

Reznor holds a blank expression as he stuffs his hands back into his pockets, then retreats away from me…again. "I warned you not to do that, Charles."

Rolling my eyes, I cross over to Charles then help him off the ground. Charles is unharmed; he is just a bit dramatic at times…well, most of the time.

"With today's training, you're going to have to keep that at bay because she needs to focus on protecting you and herself at the same time, and I can't do my job if you keep tossing me across the field." Charles dramatically points his arms in the direction he had just been thrown. "Since I seem to be a trigger, let's try it with the gentle giant. Emanuel, you're with her first, and I'll be with our lovely king." Charles bows to Reznor, which only earns a small chuckle from him.

Emanuel draws his sword; it's by far the weapon he's best with. In our training, we have used various weapons. Still, a sword is the hardest one for me to yield, and unfortunately, very common here.

"Come on, I suck at using a sword. I almost get stabbed every time. Shit, I almost stabbed Charles last time." I look at him apologetically.

"That's why we are going to keep using them till you get the hang of it." Charles states, putting the gun in a holster at his hip before he tosses Reznor a sword. Reznor twirls the sword in his hand with ease, seeming pleased to be holding one. Guess he doesn't get out of the office much.

Emanuel passes me a sword the same size as his. I think that's the problem; all of the men here are ridiculously tall, especially Reznor, and the blades are just as large. The sword in my hand is the length of my arm at least.

"Do you have any smaller ones?" They all laugh at me. "Piss off," I snark.

Emanuel nods to me before he swings; he is giving me a warning. The two others are still laughing, but Emanuel is focused and watches me swing the sword toward him before deflecting it easily. We strike back and forth while Charles and Reznor observe for a few moments before starting themselves. Emanuel draws back before swinging his arm quickly, while I jump back to prevent myself from being impaled. It earns a low growl from Reznor, but I dismiss it and strike back harder, then twist my wrist, flipping the sword out of Emanuel's hand. Everyone halts, and all look at me surprised. I'm even a bit shocked that I managed to disarm him.

Emanuel smiles as he bends down to pick it up. "That's really good, Liara," he praises while getting into his fighting stance again. Emanuel never holds back with me but is always conscious of every move he makes. We start fighting again, swinging against each other, steel crashing against steel. Remembering I'm supposed to be protecting Reznor, I decide to play a little game. I'm going to protect Charles instead.

Trying to focus on both fights is difficult, but I manage to block Emanuel in enough time to see Reznor swinging at Charles, and I throw up a shield blocking his swing. His sword skids to a halt on the shield before his gaze jerks to me. I toss up another shield to block Emanuel as I shuffle to the right, quickly avoiding the edge of the blade. Charles laughs obnoxiously and goes to strike Reznor, but it's blocked with ease.

Reznor keeps stealing glancing in my direction as Emanuel and me fight, but then his and Emanuel's eyes both go glossy for a moment. Emanuel suddenly flicks my sword out of my hand the same time Reznor attempts to strike Charles. I jump for my sword while slamming up a shield. This time I had just barely stopped Reznor from striking Charles in the side. I fall to my back, using my blade to block the blow that Emanuel bestows down at me. Launching Emanuel back with my mind, I send him flying toward Reznor and Charles.

Moving to my feet, I breathe out, "You fucker."

Reznor and Emanuel both think it's quite amusing. Annoyed, I trip Reznor, causing him to falter and allowing Charles the opportunity to swing at him. Reznor still blocks it then slings him to the grass.

"Okay, I think it's time to switch," Charles groans from his back.

"Good idea."

Charles gestures to Reznor, "Can you actually try and shield him this time?"

"Why? He doesn't need it. He literally just kicked your ass." The point of the whole exercise confused me; I already have a natural instinct to protect Reznor, and it actually took more effort to defend Charles than it did him.

Reznor laughs deeply with Emanuel joining in on it, but it stops when Charles speaks. "Fine, I have an idea. Let's call Serena out here, and let's see if you can focus on fighting us, with her and Reznor together."

I square up with him moving closer. I smile up at him in a predatory manner. That comment is supposed to be a dig, and I'm going to prove him wrong. "Go for it," I say, raising both arms.

"No," Reznor snaps.

"I don't think that's a good idea," Emanuel adds.

Charles goes through with it anyway.

Serena comes sauntering across the field in a skimpy orange dress that clung to her body like wet clothes. The fabric was cut to her midthigh and had a plunging cut in the dress that reached just above her navel. Her fire hair is pulled up, revealing the mass number of hickeys covering her neck. Gross, what are they, teenagers?

She struts over to Reznor and kisses him on the cheek. I suppress the rage that blossoms at the sight. Keeping my demeanor calm, a sting starts in my chest, but I push that down too. I need to focus. I won't mess this up, not with so much on the line. If I lost, Charles would torment me forever, plus, now Serena can see who she is messing with. Maybe then she'd learn to keep her hands off things that aren't hers, yet I doubt it.

"Try to distract her…gradually," Charles emphasizes the last word. He then motions for Emanuel to come over. "We both are going to fight you. Let's see if you can *kick our asses*."

I smile while readying myself with my sword. "Gladly, you'd probably fight better if you didn't let your ego get in the way."

That launches the fight; Charles lunged at me first, and I manage to block him. Emanuel waits, assessing the fight, then moving in behind me slowly. Serena is reaching toward Reznor, but I can't focus on that, or I'll end up with a sword at my back.

Pushing Charles back with a blow from my sword, Emanuel strikes at me from the other side. When I block Emanuel, it pushes me a step closer to Charles. Throwing up a shield I stop Charles and use my sword to force Emanuel back. Just as I'm getting the upper hand, the sting in my chest starts spreading.

I risk a glance in Reznor's direction and find him watching Serena as her hands roam his body. The anger I had before is increasing quickly. Not only is he allowing this, but he also seems to be enjoying himself. Yeah, that stings my pride a bit.

Time to end this fight before my mind gets lost in the anger.

Dropping my shield allows Charles to swing for me again. I block him then maneuver around him to use his body as shield against Emanuel. It works for a moment, but then they are circling me again. The two fight relentlessly, strike after strike and blow after blow, all the while the pain keeps building.

It isn't just the pain that bothers me now. No. It's the fact that Reznor is watching me as his lover strokes him. Though he seems more focused on me than her, the action still makes my skin crawl. I'm gradually losing the fight while being closed in by both boys.

Fight them, they're tricking you, Reznor says down the bond.

Focus on your girlfriend, I can handle myself. I spit back, and even though I shouldn't, I meet his eye.

Reznor glances my way one more time before Serena captures his attention. She brings his mouth to hers and kisses him as the static starts to build arounds us.

I'm trying to focus on the fight but between the pain, the bond, and those two kissing, my brain is getting overwhelmed. Forcing Emanuel back by shoving my shoulder into him, I swing out at Charles, forcing him back also.

Reznor's eyes find mine as Serena pulls him closer and moves one of his hands to her chest, encouraging him to touch her…and then he is focusing on her as his hand roams her body. It's the last straw.

As Charles and Emanuel both lunge for me at the same time, lightning flares across the sky as I cast both men in the opposite directions. A cracking echoes around us as the men tumble through the air. I'm vaguely aware of the fact that Emanuel sliced my shoulder before I launched him away, but that is the least of my worries.

Panting heavily, I find all eyes on me; even Serena looks fearful as I toss the sword to the ground. Stepping over Charles' body, I storm for the trails. "I win. We're done for the day."

"Liara!" Charles calls after me.

I raised an arm over my head, waving him off. "I'm gonna go run the trail."

So much for keeping my cool.

No one else tries to stop me as I head deep into the woods. Taking off at a sprint, I give a silent thanks that no one noticed I'd been cut. Taking calming breaths, I relish in the fact the pain has stopped, meaning that Reznor and Serena are no longer touching. Good, now I can really focus on the run and not that disaster of a fight. A voice shouts my name, but it doesn't matter, I'm already running deeper into the forest. I said I was running *a* trail—I never said which one.

Being on the trail was supposed to be a good way to cool down after a day of training, but now I'm running because I need to take the edge off.

The anger edges away after my second loop around the trail, but I don't think the feeling is going to disappear anytime soon. Forcing myself from the woods, I'm surprised to find Emanuel waiting for me just outside the forest. He jumps to his feet when he sees me, his eyes drifting to my arm.

"I cut you."

"Emanuel, you barely nicked me. It stopped bleeding in the first half of my run." It is indeed a lie, but it should make him feel better. He has a black jacket with him, and I reach for it. "Give me that; I'll wear it inside, and no one will ever have to know. It'll be our secret."

"I didn't mean to—"

"I know, you're always careful. We all got a little carried away today." Taking the jacket, I zip it up over the white shirt that is tinted red down one side.

Emanuel won't look at me. "I'm sorry, Liara."

I grip his shoulder. "It's okay. You can make it up to me by making your girlfriend not be mad at me anymore." At the mention of Anisa, he smiles and agrees to talk to her for me. When his silence starts to overwhelm me, I ask him a question that I know will distract him. "So, what can a Lycan do? I saw you shift once when you were fighting with my mom, but you didn't turn into a full wolf."

Emanuel nods, scanning the area as we cross the field and head toward the manor. "Lycan's can only partially shift—teeth, claws, snout, and then the enhanced senses. It's why we only shift when truly fighting; we can get carried away sometimes. Reznor is the only one who can do a full shift."

I notice that he tries to bring up the man of the hour, but I'm leaving him out of this conversation. "It kind of startled me when you did it." I laugh softly. "I thought I was having a fever dream or something."

"See, in that moment, I was wondering if your mother was going gouge out my eyes or not." He gives me a teasing smile, but I had wondered that too.

Emanuel escorts me back to my room, giving me the bad news once we're safe inside. "I have to tell Reznor you're back from the run."

I take the jacket off, handing it back to him. "Oh, joy. What does he want now?" Veering for the kitchen, I hurriedly fill up a glass of water.

"He probably wants to talk to you about what happened today." He scratches the back of his head nervously.

"Nothing happened today; we trained. It's no big deal."

"Liara, you and I both know more happened on that field today than just that."

"Did I hurt you?" I keep thinking back to the lightning strike then the boys being flung away from me. I could have set the field on fire and wouldn't have noticed. That kind of rage isn't good for anyone to have.

"No, both of us are fine, but—"

"Then tell Reznor I went to bed. There's nothing to talk about."

Emanuel sighs in defeat. "You two are so similar, it's infuriating."

"What do you mean?"

"Nothing. I can't lie to him, so I suggest you clean up before he comes up here." He holds the doorknob, shooting me one last remorseful glance before leaving.

I down three glasses of water before I toss my shirt into the trash then head straight to the bathroom for a shower. Carefully washing my shoulder, I inspect the wound. The gash is maybe three inches long and not too deep.

The blackness on my abdomen appears the same as it did earlier, thankfully not spreading further after the little fiasco on the field. When the anger stirs up, I quickly exit the shower and focus on my arm instead.

I bandage the wound then cover it with a sweater. Poor Emanuel is so upset for such a small cut.

He's a good guy; the thought of him feeling bad for hurting me makes me sick. His comment about Reznor and I being similar still throws me off, but I'm not any closer to understanding Reznor. That man is a ball of problems, and it just keeps getting bigger.

A door closes and draws me from the closet, but nobody is there, just a silver domed tray holding my dinner. It seems Anisa's still pissed. Taking it with me on the balcony, I eat the meat and gravy dish half mindedly as I focus on the mountains. For some reason after everything that happened today, all I can think about is my mom.

Mom...

I miss her even though she probably doesn't miss me. I mean, she did try to kill me. The thought of her ruined my appetite. Since I have been here, everything has changed, and things just kept getting worse. I miss how easy things were at home, but this is the new normal, and I need to get used to it.

Just the thought of everything changing has me pushing the mostly eaten plate away. Focusing on the sunset, I curl my legs beneath me as the orange sky starts to turn pink toward the horizon. Even if Nightsend is the only part of Dwimmér that I've seen, I can't complain because everything here is so lively. This part of the world is utterly beautiful.

A prickling sensation covers my skin moments before the couch dips next to me. I don't have to look to know who it is—the bond tells me. Reznor makes himself comfortable by draping his arm across the back of the couch. He doesn't speak; he just settles in and watches the light fade from the sky with me.

When the only light left is the stars twinkling in the sky, I break the tranquil silence. "Is there a reason you've blessed me with your presence?"

He tracks his fingers through his hair. "Morana has been asking about you all day."

That was not the response I expected but it causes me to smile, nonetheless. "How is she?"

"She is doing very well. Thank you for healing her, Liara. Not many people have that gift."

I disregard his thanks; Morana deserved the help. "Morana is a lovely woman. She spoke very highly of you."

Reznor studies me tentatively. "Let me guess, she told you how much of a tyrant I was as a child, didn't she?"

"Yeah, that might have come up." I chuckle.

"Well, I guess I should be thankful she didn't go into detail about my teen years. I put that woman through hell." A blank expression takes over his face before he grimaces.

"I think most teenage boys do that," I say in an attempt to make him feel better although after today, I should be letting him stew in his thoughts.

"Were you a wild teen?"

I cackle before I could get any words out. "No, my mom kept me on a very tight leash. She tracked my phone and even put a tracking device in my car."

"That doesn't surprise me, knowing your mother. Morana hated it when Maura would follow me around the grounds."

"She used to follow you around the grounds?" I keep forgetting they knew each other before I was born.

"Yes, your mom has been obsessed with me for as long as I can remember." The thought repulses me, thinking about my mother and Reznor in that way. "She was about four years older than me. My mother had banned her from being anywhere near me for a while, but eventually, people forgot about it."

"My mom knew your mother?" I ask curiously.

"Maura was thirteen when my mom died. She had been my mother's apprentice of sorts, but when she saw how obsessed Maura became with me, my mother banned her from seeing me. Once my mom had been dead a few months, she started poking around again." His shoulders sagged as he speaks of his mother.

"Well, I guess we both got to witness Maura in her crazy phases." When he appears confused, I elaborate. "Ever since I was little, she would go through these phases where she would trash the house and mumble to herself. One night on my sixteenth birthday, she slit her wrist and painted these symbols on the walls in blood. She told me never to ask her about it if I wanted to live. She would just get belligerent and go crazy."

"I'm sorry she did that to you. You deserved to have a normal childhood."

I shrug. "It's alright. It sounds like neither of us had normal childhoods."

"That is very true. I've been a king since I was nine years old." He grits with a small shrug.

"How did that work out?"

"Well, both of my parents died in the same year, and I was the only one of my bloodline, so it fell to me. I had a lot of help along the way, but once I was sixteen, I took the kingdom over completely." He looks straight ahead, his face not showing any real emotion.

"What was it like being a king at nine?" Shifting in my seat, I angle my body toward his. I have become intrigued by this conversation along with soaking up any information he is willing to give. Maybe something in this conversation will make me dislike him less.

"At first, it was easy, but then the war started, and I had to make final decisions on where to send troops and how to protect my people. It was hard. There is a reason I'm known as a heartless leader because I will do anything to protect the ones that I care for, and at that point, I didn't care for anything other than them. I fought in the next war along with my warriors, and I slaughtered so many people that it became easy. I had to think about them, and I always chose to protect them. Then at the end of the day, I would come home to an empty manor filled with strangers who were here to take care of me." He glances at me occasionally, but mainly, he speaks while staring at the stars.

My heart aches for that nine-year-old little boy. No one should lose all their family, let alone be forced to rule at such a young age. Being forced to send soldiers to war when he was so young, he probably couldn't even grasp the concept.

"That's awful, Reznor. I'm sorry that happened to you. I haven't been here long, but it looks like you did a great job. Every person I have met has told me how wonderful you are."

He chuckles halfheartedly, "Well, some people would tell you differently."

"Everyone is entitled to their own opinion, but it doesn't always mean they are right."

He strums his thumb on the back of the couch as the silence begins again. "I'm sorry about what happened on the field today, it shouldn't have happened, or the other—"

Nope, not happening. I cut him off quickly as images flash into my brain, causing the pain to start. "It's fine, you had an existing life, now I'm just thrown into it. Although next time maybe don't shove it in my face." I snap the words to Reznor, hoping they make me feel better, but they don't. Standing impulsively, I try to put distance between us by grabbing the plate and heading back inside.

Reznor follows, lingering near me in the kitchen. "You've been in my life forever, but you just didn't know it."

Momentarily, I freeze, then place the dish in the sink before turning to face him. I note he avoids the topic of Serena, but I don't want to discuss her either. "Well, you're in mine now, and I would appreciate it if we could stop hating each other. I mean, we are stuck with each other."

"I never said I hated you." He strolls toward me slowly.

"Could have fooled me. The first time we had an actual conversation, you said you didn't want to have to look at me. I understand your resentment toward me; I was just another part of your life decided for you, but it would make things easier on both of us if the fighting stopped. Things like today, they can't happen again, or someone's going to end up hurt." I'm trying to maintain eye contact, but Reznor's gaze is too intense. He intimidates me and as I get hit with the urge to touch him. I try to move past him only to get snagged by his arm.

He carefully holds me back by placing his hand on my hip. "I don't resent you, Liara. It's harder for me to control the bond when you're around, and I can't think straight. Yes, you were solely created for me, but it doesn't mean that I'm not thankful that you're alive, and here." He says the words softly as he watches me. Sparks are dancing across my hip where his hand is placed.

Unable to stop myself, I reach up and cup the side of his face. My thumb absently swipes over his chin while we stare at each other and bask in the feeling of the bond. Everything in me wants to stay pressed up against him, and it hasn't always been this way.

"Why does it feel stronger now?" I ask while he pulls me closer to him, his other hand sneaking to the small of my back, drawing my body to his.

"You feel it, too," he hums, as he leans his head slightly into my hand. "I don't know why it changed. But I don't mind it either." I agree with him, almost entirely. The sparks I feel when we touch, it's intoxicating, though with the high comes the crash when we separate.

"You should go to bed," he says, suddenly coming to his senses.

I immediately drop my hands like I've been stung, stepping away from him to shut the balcony doors. His eyes are like a weight on my back as I cross through the room, shutting curtains and finding any excuse not to look his way again.

"Goodnight, Liara. I'm sorry about today. It won't happen again, I promise." Reznor calls softly before leaving the room.

I meant to reply but instead, I focus on the wall longer than I should have while thinking of his hands on my body and the apology he just gave me. Not only is he confusing me with his touches, but now with his words also.

Chapter Nine: Minding Bridges

Anisa wakes me up then leaves without a word—she's still mad. On the bright side, I wasn't awoken by a miserable pain. That alone puts a pip in my step as I take my breakfast on the balcony. I freeze when I catch what's happening on the lawn below. Even from up here, I can tell Reznor is not happy.

Charles and Reznor are arguing. It continues for a few minutes before Reznor turns and storms toward the manor. I attempt to mind my own business, sinking further into the couch with the hopes they hadn't seen me. Just when I think I'm in the clear and can sneak back to my room, Reznor appears in the doorway. He freezes, eyeing my outfit, but he doesn't comment on the shorts.

Smart man.

Eventually he rips his eyes from my body. "I won't be training with you today, but I will meet with you later."

"Oh, okay." Unable to keep my mouth shut, I take a chance and ask him what happened with Charles.

"A disagreement in training for you," he falters, then adds, "and us." Reznor steps to the ledge, gazing down at Charles, but doesn't elaborate any further.

Rising from the couch, Reznor of course follows me as I head to the kitchen. I've just barely turned from the sink when he traps me between his body and the counter. His arms cage me in as his hands rest on either side of my waist, shifting his weight onto the counter, the action putting us even closer.

"You know I really don't like it when you wear these shorts." His voice turns gravely, causing shivers to rise across my skin.

I slowly narrow my eyes at him. "Well, you bought them for me. Or would you rather I wear one of the short nightgowns you bought? Perhaps one of the lingerie sets would be more fitting."

He smirks; the look is something devastatingly handsome. Turning his head, he softly chuckles, his hand moving from the counter to rest on my hip, giving it a soft squeeze. After looking me over one final time, he steps back. "Touché." Striding toward the door, he cast me a devilish smirk. "Don't worry. There will be plenty of time for you to wear those short dresses and those lingerie sets for me." With a playful wink he ducks out the door.

I should be irked with him, but instead, I laugh. This is a stark contrast compared to how we usually act. I like this change. I like it so much I go to training with a grin on my face, only it doesn't last long.

Training this morning is brutal.

Charles is ruthless as he takes out his anger on me. We aren't even sparring with weapons; it's hand to hand combat. I've been slammed to the ground repeatedly. I'm bound to have a bruise on my ribs, and my arms and legs feel like jelly. Yet each time he takes me down, I get back up. I try to focus on blocking his blows, but he just keeps swinging and swinging. I'm weakening quickly and when he strikes me one too many times, I use my powers to send him flying backwards.

"Enough!" I shout before doubling over in a breathless mess. My stray hairs stick to my face, sweat rolling down my brow. Grass stains litter my arms, and I can just make out faint marks tainting my skin that will turn to bruises later.

Charles climbs back to his feet, swiping a hand across his forehead. "My apologies, I got a little carried away," he admits before pointing to a nearby tree. "Let's sit down for a moment."

I practically throw myself to the ground. "What happened with you and Reznor? And why are you taking it out on me?"

Charles pauses his drinking. "How do you know about this morning?"

"I saw you from my balcony, plus, Reznor came by my room earlier."

"We had a disagreement in training fundamentals. He wasn't a fan of what I had him do yesterday. I'm not trying to take it out on you…I'm just trying to get it out."

"He sure seemed fine with being all over Serena," I comment, my bitterness still fresh. Even though Reznor apologized, I'm still a bit unsettled about the incident. Although, I can say that I agree with Reznor when it comes to his talk with Charles. Yesterday was bad for me…really bad.

"They're not the topic I want to address. Are you mad about what I did?" Charles avoids meeting my eyes, choosing to adjust the strap on his water jug.

"No, it was a low blow, but I can handle it. I'm a big girl." I grin at him, trying to prove that yesterday hadn't bothered me at all.

"I just wanted to see if you could handle yourself." The guilt burns across his face.

"No, you were getting even."

If Charles had actually known what Serena and Reznor's touches do to me, he never would have suggested it. He probably would rip both of them a new one, then me for not telling him. I have an opportunity right now to tell him, but it still feels like I can't.

"Reznor's coming to your room now, huh?" He wiggles his eyebrows at me before laughing at himself. I shrug, unsure of how to answer; either way I respond, I'm sure to get teased. "No, no, I want details," he presses further. There is no stopping this conversation now.

"He came by last night and we talked for a bit, then he came by again this morning. That's it." I try to say it casually, though I feel my cheeks heating. Charles doesn't get to know about the counter situation.

He swirls his hand, asking for more information.

"That's it, really; there's nothing else to tell."

"Fine, since there isn't anything you want to *share*, let's get back to practice, Princess." I shoot him a glare but rise to my feet. I'm hoping the second time around he isn't going to hand me my ass on a platter.

Charles fights with a level head this time, but he still doesn't back down as we spar on the field. I had just gotten the upper hand when the pain starts building, a persistent stabbing in my chest. Not this again, the timing couldn't be worse. I struggle to keep a straight face as I swing a punch toward his face jaw.

The ache quickly climbs across my body; I'm not going to be able to keep this act up much longer. It's blazing across my skin like a wildfire; it's an effort not to scream out in agony. Black spots cloud my vision, causing me to stumble over my feet. It sends me falling into Charles just as he's aiming to hit me, but instead of blocking it, the blow lands on my side… hard. The force of the punch knocks me to the ground, but the pain from the bond keeps me there even as I try to scramble to my feet.

"Liara, I'm so sorry. Are you okay?" Charles frantically reaches down to help me. I grab his hand, but I'm little help as he hoists me from the ground.

"It's not your fault," I gasp out, clinging to him. "Will you take me to my room? I promise this isn't your fault." Charles wraps his arms around me, sweeping me up into the air. He strides quickly, taking me up to my room, while the burning keeps a relentless pace.

Charles kicks open the door before walking me over to my bed and carefully laying me down. "What is going on, Liara?"

I'm only able to groan as I chomp down on the inside of my cheek, the grip on the sheets is iron clad, and I doubt anything could pry me from them. "Give…me…a moment." I manage to get out.

"That's it. I'm getting Reznor."

"No, I'm okay. It will stop in a minute," I screech quickly.

Charles voices very loudly how stupid of a plan this is before taking a seat on the bed next to me. He watches me until the pain starts to subside a few minutes later. Now that I can breathe and think clearly, I needed to come up with a plan, or rather, a lie.

He peers down at me with suspicious eyes. "What was that?"

"Cramps," I say flatly.

This earns an eye roll from him. "That wasn't cramps—"

"Human cramps are different, Charles," I argue.

"You're not human!" He watches me skeptically, but he doesn't push the topic any further. "I will have to tell Reznor about this."

"No, don't, it's not a big deal. I'm good now."

Charles gives me an odd face, raising one eyebrow and squishing his mouth. "Why don't you want me to tell him?" he asks, raising his eyebrow higher.

"Because he will overreact. Plus, he doesn't need to be alarmed by my monthly cycle." Then I mumble under my breath, "Plus, I'm sure he's *busy*."

"Whatever he is doing isn't more important than you." Charles checks me over again. "If it gets worse, I'm telling him." Leaning back from his previously hunched state, he continues to sit on the bed. I try to thank him, but he just waves his hand in response. "Are you afraid of him?"

"No, why?" I'm trying to act like I'm offended by his question.

"You're very timid around him."

"I don't know him, Charles." I slap his arm. "If Reznor scared me, or if I wanted to leave, I would have broken out and ran already."

"That is very true, but trust me, you two will be a power couple. You both are—" He stops talking as Anisa enters the room with a large box in her arms.

She takes in the scene before her and raises her eyebrows analytically. She is critically silent while placing the box on the kitchen table.

"I'll leave you to it." He rises from the bed, shooting me an apology for hitting me one last time before leaving me with Anisa. I palm my face as Anisa sends daggers my way the moment he slips from the door.

"We will not be telling Reznor about this." Anisa adjusts her apron, smoothing it out in a downward motion.

"I already told Charles not to. I had an…" I pause, trying to think of the right word. "episode on the field today. He carried me to my room."

Anisa's face instantly softens. "Did you tell him about the marks? Are they as bad as the first ones?"

I shuffle up into a sitting position on the bed, wincing at my stiff muscles. "No, I told him it was cramps. They all feel the same, but if Reznor does it more than once, it gets worse the longer it goes on." The statement awkwardly falls from my mouth. It's uncomfortable even thinking about Reznor's personal life in this way, let alone having to discuss it with someone.

Anisa gives me a pitiful look then changes the subject. "Today, we start planning the ceremony and wedding. There isn't a lot you can plan for the ceremony, but Reznor has allowed you free reign on the wedding." She pulls out color palettes, a book that has pieces of ribbon falling from it, and stacks of more books. I'm suddenly wondering how she carried that box up numerous flights of stairs.

"Before we get any further, I need to apologize. Emanuel told me what you did for him. I'm just protective of Reznor, I'm sorry. I didn't mean to take it out on you."

"I appreciate the apology, but there's no need, consider it forgotten."

She smiles brightly as she arranges the books on the table. For the ceremony, I had to pick a dress out of a book, along with the flowers. The dress is being custom made, and a seamstress will be out closer to the ceremony to fit me for the dress. The preparation for the wedding is torturous. She has me selecting different shades of white when they all appear the same. I don't understand the fuss, but once I select a cream, she makes me do the same thing again with grey. Then it's the color of the runner, and then silverware. The list goes on, and on.

"Can't you just pick what you like?" I ask as I grow frustrated with the minor details.

"Are you sure?" Anisa is completely surprised, although her eyes hold a glint of excitement.

"Yes, please! If you want guidance on the bigger things, I'm willing to help, but I don't really care for all the minor details," I say eagerly. She nods slowly before packing some of the items up and placing them back in the box. "It's best if you plan this because I don't know the way weddings work here," I add, which earns a grin from her.

"Okay, I'll plan it according to your style, *but*" she emphasizes, "if you want to change anything, just tell me."

"Anisa, I trust that you won't let me down."

When she giggles, it's contagious, and I join in as I ease out of the chair and stretch.

"We should get you changed," she says once our laughing stops. The confused look on my face sends her smiling again. "Reznor told me he was coming by to collect you tonight." She wiggles her eyebrows while her smile turns to a smirk.

This throws me into a burst of hysterical laughter, but Anisa stops it quickly. Ushering me into the closet, she combs through my clothes. "Let's go casual because I don't know what you will be doing."

"Anisa, this isn't some big deal. He came by last night, and I was in pajamas." She whips her head in my direction with a slight grin. "My god, you all have your heads in the gutter!"

Anisa shrugs as she pulls some clothes from the racks but does nothing to deny my claims. "Liara, I have known the king for a long time, and let me tell you, his mind is always in the gutter, as you say." I must admit I'm intrigued, but I don't ask any questions. I'm still upset with him.

"The bond has gotten stronger lately; it's very intense. When he barely touches me, it makes me weak in the knees." I turn my back to her, moving toward the bathroom. I don't need to look to know she is grinning like a fool.

"Reznor spoke of the bond getting stronger to Emanuel and Charles last night. He's worried about it." She appears in the doorway as I turn on the water to the shower and quickly get in it.

"Why would he worry about the bond getting stronger? Isn't that a good thing?"

"For him, the bond is already magnified; that's part of his curse. With it gradually intensifying, it becomes harder for him to control himself around you. He has to wait until the ritual to mark you. It's the one thing that must go according to plan. It's something the Gods set in place all those years ago for the kings and queens. Other mates were able to mark their spouse when they felt like it, but royalty cannot."

"What exactly is marking? Is it just sex?"

Anisa laughs at my question. "No, Liara, he has to bite you and mark your skin. Set his claim on you."

I stop washing my hair and peek my head out of the shower door. "He has to do *what*?"

The look on her face is pure amusement. "It's not a big deal. You and him will be in front of maybe six people, he will mark you, and then you will complete the bond."

I shut the door and resume washing the soap from my hair. This wasn't part of any plan I was told about; it would have been nice to know before I got here. "That sounds like a big deal to me." The thought of strangers watching him bite me sounds like something out of a cult, a blood initiation of sorts.

"It will be over before you know it," she assures me.

"Will you be there?" Maybe that would make the ritual less awkward.

"No, but Reznor's servant will be, along with Emanuel, as his right hand." Like that will make anything less awkward. It sounds like it's going to be two days of hell.

I groan as I lather my shoulder in soap. I'm still sore from yesterday's sword training. "If they have guns in these lands, why are they making me wield a sword for twelve hours a day?"

"Not all creatures can be killed by a gun, with some, it only slows them down."

"What do you mean?" I ask bewildered. "Then why do they have guns here?"

"Sometimes a gun can be the only thing that can save you. It will slow them down and buy you enough time to be able to deliver the attack you need. Don't underestimate the power of a gun in our world; they've saved lives and…limbs on more than one occasion," Anisa states in a matter-of-fact tone.

"What would happen if I were to shoot Reznor?" I question out of blatant curiosity.

"Liara!"

"It's just a question!" I try to reason but fail miserably as a laugh falls from my lips at her shock.

"You two are going to be a problem couple, I can see it now," she mumbles.

"Probably…if we can even last that long."

Anisa doesn't respond to that, and I'm glad. I stew on my thought as I go through the motions of Anisa getting me ready. I dawn the red blouse with lace that trims the v-cut at my breasts. I shimmy myself into the tight black jeans, then zip up the heel booties. Anisa tames and dries my hair before tying half up in top knot.

"Try and enjoy tonight."

"Will do." I chuckle, taking a book from the stack she brought me and head for the balcony. I'm still attempting not to frown about the fact that Reznor slept with Serena earlier. I don't want to be angry right now, and the best way to distract myself is with a book. The novels here are rather interesting. Some tell stories of this world from when their gods roamed the Earth. It's incredible to see how the world has changed since then. I have been so focused on a battle scene in the book that I don't notice Reznor until he calls my name.

I glance up at him before shutting the book. "Sorry, it's a good book," I laugh, embarrassed at my lack of awareness.

"If you like that book, I have plenty more in my study you could go through."

"I'd like that," I admit, a soft grin creeping across my face. Dammit, I'm supposed to be mad at him.

He nods toward the door. "We will have to do that another time because right now, I feel like going for a walk."

Chapter Ten: Movement In The Woods

Reznor takes us along a path through the dense forest. We had barely gotten inside the tree line when he motions for me to walk closer to him. "Charles said you guys cut training a little early, did something happen?"

His question startles me, causing me to falter in my step. I end up brushing into him, sending sparks tickling up my arm. This sends my mind spiraling; it takes me a moment longer than it should to answer his question. "No, Anisa just wanted to start planning the ceremony and wedding. She realized I'm in over my head, so she is going to take over the planning."

I'm still mad about his earlier activities. The pain keeps flashing through my mind, stoking the anger, higher and higher. It's almost as if the bond wants me to forgive him because with another brush of his arm against mine, the bond tries to edge the feeling away.

"Anisa will plan something beautiful, I'm sure." He strolls closer, sending more shivers prickling along my skin. I enjoy his touch, but it also keeps distracting me from being displeased in his tactics with Serena.

"How was your meeting today, or were you busy with Serena?" I question as we walk around a bend.

Reznor practically groans. "I was with Serena for twenty minutes, and that was to shut her up. The meeting didn't go as planned, but I got what I needed out of it." He glances down at me, an odd expression on his face. "Do you know how long it's been since someone has asked me about my day?"

I don't believe his words about Serena, but he does look genuinely annoyed that I brought her up, giving me some joy. "How long?"

"It's been so long that I can't remember when."

"That sounds awful. I'll keep that in mind." Smiling lightly, I tilt my head away from his eyes as a light blush creeps up my cheeks.

"I used to walk this trail when I was younger whenever I wanted to clear my head." Reznor takes his hands out of his pockets and carefully grasps my arm, stopping me. Sliding his hand down to mine, he intertwines our finger before leading me over to a cluster of trees. Just behind them sits a small pond. Ducks swim on the water while fish dart beneath the surface. I never would have known there was a pond if he hadn't pointed it out.

Still holding my hand, Reznor takes us back onto the trail. The sensation of us touching is distracting, and I nearly forgot what I planned to ask him. "Did you need to clear your head today?" I feel his hand tense momentarily, but he relaxes it quickly as his thumb strokes the back of my hand.

"Yes, and no," he admits.

I don't pry for more information, but I also don't want us to fall into an awkward silence. "Are weddings here different than in the mortal world?"

"Well, I've never been to one in the mortal world, but I can tell you about weddings here." Of course, Liara. I want to groan in annoyance at my own stupidity.

"Weddings here, we stand in front of the guests, usually in mass halls, but since I'm king, ours will be in the throne room. We will repeat a scripture that has been around since the Gods were here, then I will crown you. We'll kiss, and then leave the hall," he states.

"That's similar to a human wedding, but it usually happens in a church. Where does this whole marking thing happen?" I ask, raising my eyebrows at him.

Reznor gives me a wolfish grin. "Ah, someone told you what marking is."

"Yeah, a warning would have been nice."

He chuckles and tugs on my hand, pulling me past the cluster of wildflowers we stopped at. "If you didn't know what it was, you wouldn't have any reason to be nervous. It's going to happen in a bedroom."

I snatch my hand out of his, pressing it into his chest as I step in front of him. "You want to *bite me* in front of other people in a bedroom?"

"Would you rather I mark you in front of the hundreds of people who will be at the wedding?" he challenges, raising a brow.

"No, but—"

"Trust me, you're going to want to be in the bedroom after I mark you. The urge will take over the second I do; it's better to do it there."

If I thought I was blushing before, I'm scalding now. I duck my head as I think of what the marking is going to be like. Hmm, now is not the time nor place for these thoughts.

Reznor steps forward, invading my space further. I put both hands up instinctively, but he grasps both with his own. "Are you worried about me marking you, Liara?" he throatily asks, leaning into me further.

I'm doing two things, and both are lies. One, I am indeed quite worrying about him marking me. Two, I am trying to show that his proximity, or touch isn't affecting me (which it very much is). I straighten my shoulders and peek up at him through my lashes. "No, just don't get blood on my dress." I smirk.

Instead, he releases my hands only to wrap his arm around me, pulling until I'm flush against him. "You'll be lucky if I let you wear a dress."

Two can play this game. I lean my head in closer, dragging my hands up onto his shoulders as I bit my lip. "You sure you want me naked in front of all of those men?"

I can feel his shoulders tense, his grip tightening on my waist. "It won't matter if it's my name that's falling from your lips."

I pull away and slip out of his grip before he can register what I'm doing. "We'll see about that," I call over my shoulder. "I don't think your girlfriend will like that," I mutter, then walk three steps total before he is behind me, wrapping his arms around my waist, keeping my back against his chest.

"Liara, you best be careful with talk like that," Reznor whispers, his lips brushing against my ear. He ignores my comment about Serena, or perhaps that is his answer...

"What are you going to do, *Rez*?" I ask softly, my smirk rising with each word.

"Wouldn't you like to know," he teases, releasing me from his hold. "You're a flirt."

"Well, I don't get out much anymore; who else am I supposed to flirt with?" I notice a hint of jealousy rolling off him. Payback is a bitch. Guess he shouldn't attempt to have a fiancé, and a girlfriend.

"No one. Your quirks are meant for no one, but me. If you feel you're being deprived of attention, I can change that." Reznor's tone is so cool and calm... it's almost scary, yet still alluring. I take this chance to brush against him, trying to get him to calm down. I bump my arm against his for a second time, and sure enough, the longer I'm against him, the quicker his anger simmers away.

I guess someone doesn't like to play games.

We do this for a while, exchanging small talk as we brush against each other. His hand against mine, my arm gliding against his, it's easy to get lost in the bond... that is until the forest around us goes silent.

Birds stop chirping, and bugs stop buzzing. It's silent for a few seconds, then the sound of guns firing fill the air. Reznor grabs me and jerks us behind a tree, using his body to block mine. As the guns continue to fire, I cast a shield around us. Reznor presses in tighter as the sound of rustling movement moves closer. I fist my hands in his shirt while keeping my eyes shut.

"Keep your shield up, I'm going to take them out." I don't even get the chance to try and stop Reznor because in the next moment, he's gone. Peeking around the tree, I watch Reznor tear through the men one by one. They can't see him; he moves too swiftly. He snaps their necks, ripping some of their limbs entirely off. He is so caught up in the fight, he doesn't notice one coming up from behind him.

"Rez!" I scream as I send the man through the air, crashing into a tree.

Reznor glances at me before he runs over to the man who is trying to get up. With a single punch, the man is knocked unconscious. Reznor quickly ties him up with his belt as his eyes gloss over. He jogs back over to me. "Are you okay?" His eyes rake over me, while his hands do the same, looking for injury of any kind.

"I'm fine, are you okay?" I mimic him, looking over him quickly, but he appears unharmed. There is blood on him, but it's not his.

"Yes, guards are coming; they'll be here in a moment." Reznor runs his hand along the side of my head. "You're sure you're not hurt?"

"Yes, I promise. You're the one who did the attacking; I hid behind the tree."

Rustling comes from behind us, and Reznor steps in front of me, blocking me from whoever is coming.

"What happened?" Charles calls out.

Reznor meets Charles and Emanuel halfway as the other guards start to monitor the area. They move through the forest, searching for others. Taking in the damage, there are twelve dead men. It's a horrid scene, but I'm more upset about the damage done to Reznor's trail rather than the bodies scattered around.

Reznor reapproached me, taking me by surprise as he wraps me in his arms. "Hug me back, and act as if everything is normal," he whispers in my ear. Doing as he says, I reach up and wrap my arms around him. "You're going to go back with Emanuel and Charles. Go up to your room and lock the door. I will be there once I'm done with things to explain what's going on. Walk back to the manor with your shield up, Liara." He kisses my cheek, then pulls away slowly.

Emanuel hurries me along, both he and Charles stand closer than they usually do as they usher me back toward the manor. I'm reluctant to leave, but there isn't much I can do. Charles doesn't even crack a joke; that is the only clue I need to keep me in line and hurry with them.

When we get to my room, Charles goes in while Emanuel and I wait out in the hall.

"Clear," Charles calls from inside.

"Can one of you tell me what's going on?" I snap when I notice Emanuel locking the door, and Charles doing the same with the balcony doors along with shutting the blinds after checking each window.

"I'm not sure. Reznor told us to bring you up here, and to wait for him. He has a theory and told us he would fill us in later."

"Well, that can't be good." I plop myself down onto the bed.

"You might want to change; you have blood on your shirt," Charles points out.

Blood is smeared across my chest from when I hugged Reznor. "Eh great, give me a moment."

Rushing, I change into a night set after Charles informs me that I will not be leaving this room tonight. I planned to ask them about it but when I enter the room, they still haven't moved from their spots. Both are tense and staring at one another with that glazed overlook as if their eyes are unfocused. It is exactly how Reznor's looked in the woods.

"Are you two alright? You're starting to freak me out."

Both boys' eyes refocus and Emanuel sighs. He tosses my comforter across my bare legs as I settle into the bed.

"Reznor has bigger issues than you guys seeing my legs."

Charles grins. "Yes, but it would be us seeing your legs that will set him off today."

"Reznor is feeling a little…protective," Emanuel amends.

"Oh, dear god, you two are killing me."

"How was your walk before the attack?" Charles presses with a lopsided grin. There is the typical Charles! I don't even mind the teasing; as long as he doesn't look freaked out, then things are good.

"It was decent."

"So, progress, I take it?"

"Yes, I suppose you could call it progress."

Emanuel joins Charles in laughing, but they both have hopeful grins. They grill me a bit longer but fall silent again. I try to read a book to distract myself, but I end up taking turns pacing with the boys as the hours pass.

Just after midnight, there is a knock on the door. Emanuel practically leaps over the coffee table to get to open it. Reznor enters, his gaze immediately searching the room for me, only relaxing when he finds me standing by the windows. He's changed and showered, then must have come straight here because his hair is still wet. He settles into the chair next to my bed, then motions for me to sit.

"We have a breach within these walls. Someone told them I was taking Liara out on the trail today. They were trying to kill her; that's why they had the guns. They knew it wouldn't harm me but would kill her. We need to announce her arrival and plan the ball immediately." He rakes a hand down his face. "It's the only way I can see where everyone stands with her arrival. We'll need to take a trip to visit my cousin. She and her husband might know something about the men that keep attacking. We will be gone for two days and leave in the morning." Reznor releases a breath, running his fingers through his damp hair.

"What are we going to tell them?" Charles asks.

"We are going to tell them nothing, just that we will be gone for two days. At this moment, the people in this room are the only ones who can know what the plan is besides Anisa." Reznor appears exhausted. "Go get your affairs in order. I'll stay here tonight; we can't take any chances." On Charles' way out, he throws me a smirk that Reznor can't see as they leave the room briskly.

"You should get some sleep," Reznor adds quietly as he settles into the chair.

I crawl beneath the sheets and turn my back to him. "You're not seriously going to sleep in that chair all night, are you?" I ask, but he doesn't respond, although I feel his eyes on me. "You can sleep in the bed if you want."

"Are you sure you're okay with that?"

"You saved my life today Rez; yes, I'm sure you can sleep in the bed." I don't hear Reznor move for a moment but then he shuts off the lights and climbs into bed with me.

Chapter Eleven: Meeting His Family

I startle awake by the sound of gasping. Anisa stands in the doorway with her mouth hanging open, clearly shocked at the sight of Reznor in bed with me. Reznor, however, is unimpressed as he waves Anisa closer. I'm firmly pressed against his chest like I have been for most of the night. It happened at some point shortly after I fell asleep and even when I woke up once, I didn't move from his arms. I know I should move now, but he's too comfortable to lay on, especially with his arms wrapped around me.

"We will be leaving for Greensboro at eight. Can you pack her a bag?" Reznor asks Anisa in a gruff morning voice.

"Yes, Your Majesty. How many days?"

"Two days. Make sure she has a travel outfit for when we come home but lay out something presentable for her to wear today. You will need to have the dresses for the ball ready on our return." I try not to laugh at his careful instructions for Anisa. Only once she has shuffled away does Reznor chuckle. "She acts like this should be surprising."

"Well, to her, this probably is surprising. She hardly sees us in the same room together, let alone you in my bed."

He shrugs his shoulders. "Well, she will have to get used to it. Especially if people keep trying to attack you."

"I don't think Serena will like that very well."

He frowns. "And what exactly do you know about Serena and me? You keep implying she is my girlfriend when she's not." He cocks an eyebrow at me.

I set my jaw. "Reznor, I saw you fuck her on the foyer table. I'm not stupid."

"I wondered when you would bring that up." He palms his face, grimacing slightly.

I scuff and roll over in bed, facing away from him. "I was just proving a point," I explain, closing my eyes once more.

He shuffles behind me, moving closer. "Mhm, no, you're mad," he murmurs as his head rests against mine. For a big bad wolf, he sure is cuddly.

I hate how comforting his touch is. "It doesn't matter if I was mad. It wouldn't stop you; you literally had sex with her yesterday." My anger gets the best of me as I spew the words.

He tenses behind me. "How do you know about that?"

I crinkle my face, contemplating if I should answer him or not. "I don't think we should be discussing this right now," I plead in an attempt to back track my words from earlier.

"Liara…" he presses on.

I groan, giving in. "I have my ways…"

Reznor grabs my waist, pulling me to face him. "How did you know?" he asks again, forcing me to look at him.

I curse. I guess we're up for the day. "Some servant was talking about it. I heard them talking about it when I came back in from training," I lie smoothly.

He stares at me for a while, I silently hope he believes the lie I told. "Sorry you had to hear that," he murmurs as he moves a strand of hair out of my face.

I swat his hand away. "No, you're not. You have an active sex life, own it. If you're going to act the way you do, you don't get to feel guilty about it." I attempt to roll back onto my side, but he stops me again.

"Liara, come on."

"Rez, I'm not mad. However, if you keep sleeping with her when we are actually married, I will beat her ass," I pause, "then yours."

"I won't, I promise." A grin creeps to his face. "So, it does make you mad."

"Yes, Reznor, it makes me mad. Just like it makes you mad that I wear shorts when I train."

He opens his mouth to respond, but I roll over before he can. He huffs as he lays back down, draping an arm over my waist. "You're ridiculous," he mumbles, still annoyed.

"I warned you. Plus, I'm not the sleeping with someone else." I don't feel bad about what I say, it's the truth. When Reznor scoots closer to me, I'm hit with a musky scent that is earthy like sandalwood. It's intoxicating. "Are you wearing cologne?" I ask abruptly.

He chuckles, his hot breath hitting my ear. "No, why?"

I take another deep breath, filling my lungs with his scent. "You smell *really* good, that's why."

He freezes behind me. "You smell me?"

"Well, when you say it like that, it sounds weird."

"You shouldn't be able to smell my scent…that's interesting. Everything about our bond is different. It's getting stronger."

I can't respond to that because I didn't know how. We both know the bond is evolving, and this is the least alarming part of it.

Neither of us go back to sleep, yet we both remain in bed. Reznor strokes my side while we lay in silence, only moving to hold me closer. I think yesterday scared him as bad as it scared me. Since then, we both have been rather clingy. When Anisa asks me to get up, both Reznor and I are reluctant to do so. He warns Anisa of the secrecy of what we're doing one more time before he brushes his hand against mine as he parts, but it still didn't stop my momentary panic with him leaving.

Anisa is absolutely beaming as she curls my hair with a bright smile on her face.

"Something bothering you, Anisa?"

"Oh, nothing. It just seems you and the king are getting rather close," she gushes with an excited little squeal.

"I think the bond has gotten stronger, and we both are giving into it."

Despite everything going on, we have been making compromises. He doesn't despise me anymore, but I still don't know how I feel about him. Last night doesn't change the things he's done in the past, but something has changed between us. Even I can't deny that.

Anisa pouts as she curls the last strand. "It's progress for you two, and you know it."

When I don't argue, Anisa smiles and continues to pin silver leaves into my hair, forming a crown around my head. For the first time since my arrival, my makeup is done with grey, and black shadowing my eyes. Diamond studs are placed in my ears, and a single onyx stone necklace is the only jewelry I wear...well besides my engagement ring.

The gown is my favorite part. The black fabric is covered in silver shimmers, like the stars in the sky. The bodice is fitted silk with triangle straps leaving my shoulders bare. There is a slit at the thigh between the tulling of the skirt, allowing more skin to peek through.

Anisa nods in approval after she straps on my black heels. Staring at the pumps, I realize even in these shoes, I won't reach Reznor's height. At least I'll get to feel dainty again; it seems to be happening more and more.

"Do you like it?" Anisa looks worried; she must have mistaken my silence.

"Yes, I love it."

"You need to represent the king's court today. Tomorrow, your dresses won't be as dark."

I run my hands along the tulling, smoothing it out. "I really like this dress. I actually don't mind wearing dark colors," I pause, "in fact, I *like* them."

Anisa snorts. "Of course, you two are mates. A brooding couple who like the dark."

"I'm going to take that as a compliment," I say as I watch myself in the mirror. I haven't looked this good in a while. Plus, all this training has helped me lose some weight.

"Of course, you are, and I suspect Reznor would say the same."

"Probably, now let's go show him. I feel a little payback is in order. I still dislike him being near Serena."

"Well, this dress will do the trick. Let's get you downstairs. It's nearly eight." Anisa grabs a bag that seems too large for a two-day trip.

Placing my hands on my hip, I eye her skeptically. "Are you sure I need that many clothes?"

"This is three dresses: one for tonight for dinner then, two for tomorrow, your travel outfit home, two-night gowns and undergarments. Plus, four pairs of shoes and accessories along with makeup. I will not have my future queen walking around another court looking like a mess." She's acting as if I insulted her as she drags the bag toward the door. "Well, are you coming?" she hollers over her shoulder.

I follow Anisa down the many flights of stairs and through the halls until we end up outside at a large concrete staircase in front of the manor. The daunting building stands behind us, towering high and wide, so wide I can't see the gardens and forest I know lurk behind. Black erns sit at each pillar at the front of the manor, large doors lead to the foyer inside, but the towering and pointed architecture of the palace is what always distracts me. Pointed arch windows are lined in black masonry work and stretch across the expanse of the long halls. A large square tower erects from the center of the manor, Reznor's flag flying high and proud.

Reznor, Emanuel, and Charles all stand in front of a black SUV talking amongst themselves. They don't notice our approach until Anisa thuds the bag down the stairs. I try to contain my cackle as I follow after her.

All the heads turn in our direction when my laughter finally breaks free as Anisa flexes her muscles at me. Reznor seems fascinated in the way I approach the group; not once does his eyes leave my being. Anisa smirks, knowing she chose wisely, even going as far to cast me a wink.

With an approving nod, Reznor tugs his bottom lip between his teeth. "Nice dress."

"You bought it; I would hope you like it."

His smile fades when he catches Charles smirking in our direction. Sliding a protective hand to my back, he steps closer. "Put her bag in the car," Reznor orders before guiding me to the back of the car.

"Gods, Anisa, did you pack enough clothes for two days?" Charles fumbles as he is handed the bag.

"I will not have her looking like a fool," Anisa says sharply before turning to Reznor. "For the love of the Gods, do not let them do her hair, or makeup unjustly."

"I can take care of myself," I chime in.

They both ignore me.

"Anisa, you're in charge of helping plan the ball. There isn't much time, but it doesn't have to be perfect. They sent out the invitations last night and the other servants are at your disposal," Reznor hands Anisa a packet.

"Yes, Your Majesty." She curtsies, then steps aside, moving to Emanuel to bid goodbyes.

Reznor opens my door and offers me a hand as I climb into the vehicle, he then sits in the back with me while Emanuel drives, and Charles sits up front.

"Alright, let's go see Tatiana," Reznor says with false enthusiasm.

The drive isn't what I expected. We passed cars every so often, but other than a car here and there, the streets are empty. Even the roads only look like smooth worn dirt; I swear we didn't hit a single pothole. That simple fact is magical on its own.

I spent the time gazing out the window, comparing Dwimmér to the mortal world. It resembles the human world mostly, except some flowers and trees seem to be different in this part of the world. There aren't big cities or highways. It is delightful to see such a world that is full of life and health.

Reznor and I talked some, but he even seems preoccupied. The boys have tried and failed to keep me engaged in the conversation. After a while, they realized the scenery was more interesting to me and began discussing battle techniques I needed to learn. That was the only thing that pulled Reznor from his stewing as they suggested one technique that he shut down so quickly the boys rumbled with laughter. I would have laughed had I known what the hell they were talking about.

Eventually, we come to a stop outside a large three-story manor with colossal, stoned archways. It reminds me of a castle and even with its mass size, it's still smaller than Reznor's manor (which he really should just call a castle). Multicolored flowers along with long vines climb the arches. There is an abundance of large orange flowers that litter the castle walls, lining each balcony and tracing each window. The manor is beautiful, and this is just the outside.

Exiting the car, I stand at Reznor's side with Emanuel and Charles, all four of us dressed in black from head to toe. We're a sore thumb sticking out against the bright colors of the palace before us.

Reznor leans down as he rests his hand on my waist. "Do not leave my side while we are here. If for some reason you need to go somewhere else, take Emanuel or Charles with you," he whispers quietly as a woman with black hair cut into a bob and a long flowing yellow dress approaches, smiling widely.

I subtly nod to him, letting him know I understood the order. I could have spoken to him, but I'm trying to digest all the *yellow* that is hurtling our way. I try to take in the rest of her appearance, but I'm transfixed by her glowing yellow eyes.

"Reznor!" She beams as she approaches, throwing her arms out and crushing her face against his chest.

Reznor doesn't allow for his grip on me to slip as he pats the woman's back with his one free hand. "Tatiana this—"

"You must be Liara!" She releases Reznor then hauls me into her arms. The air is forced from my lungs as she holds me tightly. "You're lucky you're mates,

Reznor, or I would have tried to swipe this beauty from you. She looks rather luscious."

Reznor growls behind us, and I'm thankful when he pries me from her arms because she was still compressing my lungs. "Tatiana," he warns.

"Oh hush, I mean no harm, and you know it. I'm just excited to meet the woman you've been waiting for." Tatiana turns on a dime, heading for the corridor. "Come, I've got lunch ready."

Reznor tightens his grip before we follow Tatiana through her home. He still seems annoyed with her initial display, but I wouldn't expect anything less from the possessive male. I shoot him an apologetic look and give his chest a little pat.

"I have so many questions," Tatiana gushes as she finally stops outside a seating area.

The room is decorated in a bright blue floral wallpaper, with two bright orange couches facing each other, a gold coffee table separating them.

Tatiana plants herself into one of the orange couches as she waves over a servant. "Take King Reznor and his fiancés bags up to his guest room." When she hurries away, Tatiana gestures to the coach. "Sit, sit."

Sitting opposite of her, Reznor drapes his arm across the back of the couch, but he sits so close that our sides are nearly flush. The goosebumps crawl across my skin instantly. I have to resist the urge to lean into him further. This bond won't be satisfied until I sit in his lap, but that isn't happening today.

Dressed in an all-black suit, Reznor leaves his jacket unbuttoned, giving off a calm appearance, but he's tense against my side. "Thank you for agreeing to meet with us, Tatiana."

"No problem, anything for family. Plus, it gives me an idea of who will be marrying into the family." Tatiana winks at me, and that causes Reznor to tense even further.

Knowing he is already on a short leash, I lean into his side a bit more to bring us closer together. "You'll like her, I'm sure of it." His voice is less strained as he brings his arm forward to rest on my shoulder.

"I will be the judge of that." She smiles slyly. "Arnold will be joining us later. Right now, he is training my guards. We'll discuss the matter you called about later in private once he returns. For now, I can get to know the Nightlighter."

While we dine in the sitting room, Tatiana spends the majority of the time grilling me about my life in the human world. By the time the meal is over, Reznor is beyond annoyed, and I feel like Tatiana knows more about my life than he does. The moment we're done eating, he practically carries me out of the room, seeming like he wants to get away from her as fast as possible.

Reznor treats me to a tour around her manor. He shows me the little details that explain who a majority of her people are and who she speaks for. Tatiana governs the Lycans as their queen, along with her husband, Arnold. The general idea is that there are five kings along with queens who rule each key breed. Each territory rules independently over their people, and if all of the royals need to meet, they will call a council meeting for all in the court of Dwimmér.

The territory Tatiana dictates used to be a part of Reznor's, but once his parents died, his lands were split; he was given his own territory to rule, and he got to keep his childhood home that we currently live in. Tatiana's lands are technically what was once the lower portion of what his parents used to rule.

"Were you upset when your lands were divided?" I ask Reznor as he moves to my side while pointing to another place on the map of the territories on the wall.

He gives me a cocky grin. "No, because even with this portion gone, I still have the largest portion of Dwimmér. I wanted to keep Nightsend and the manor; the rest didn't matter to me. The only reason I have as much as I do now is because they feared they would displease the God who blessed me."

I frown. "They shouldn't have taken anything from you. You lost your parents and got cursed. It's disgusting to steal from a grieving child."

He smiles then catches my hand. "It turned out better this way."

Reznor is taking all the precautions to keep us away from Tatiana until dinner. Yet the moment I see the golden themed room with bright floral wallpaper, I'm ready to leave it. We both cringe at the first assault of the clashing colors.

"Only Tatiana can make something this elegant look awful." He flinches. I half expected Reznor to leave once we got to the room, but he stays, even when I start getting ready for dinner.

I leave him in the bedroom while I change into a robe in the lavish bathroom. The servant arrives to get me ready and when she tries to shut the door, Reznor stops her. It's an odd request, but it's for safety, and it seems the big guy is still a little uneasy.

The servant sits me at the vanity and starts her work, yet Reznor continues to watch her from the bed as she re-curls bits of my hair. I shoot him a questioning look, but he shrugs as his eyes scan the servant again. The short, older woman redoes my makeup, wiping off the scarlet lip and dark shadow from before. It's replaced with a bronze color on my eyes, and a clear coat on my lip.

"Simplicity is key," she murmurs as she allows my hair to fall in simple waves. After I thank her, I dismiss her without getting dressed. I will do that later.

Reznor's lounging diagonally across the hideous orange, yellow, and gold bedspread as I walk around to sit on the other side of the bed. Reznor glances up at me quizzically as I adjust my grey silk robe. "Not getting dressed yet?"

A shake of my head. "Did you see how short that woman was? Even on the step stool she wouldn't be able to zip the back of my dress. Plus, dinner isn't for another thirty minutes." The real reason is so she won't see the black marks that now line my abdomen, lower back, and the very tops of my thighs.

"She was rather short," Reznor agrees. He cast his eyes up, staring at the ceiling where gold swirls dance across the plaster in no particular pattern. "My mom would have loved this room," he says suddenly, his face blank, giving away no emotion.

I shuffle next to him on the bed, mirroring his actions. "Did she like bright colors?"

"Yes, she did," he chuckles. "When I was younger, she dressed me in this hideous bright green suit. It was awful. I rolled in the mud just to ruin the outfit. It was a long time ago, so it was one of those puffy suits like in the times your people call the renaissance." He smiles, thinking back on the memory.

"I bet that was a sight for everyone."

He laughs at my comment but nods in agreement. "She made me promise her that I wouldn't wear dark colors for her funeral, so I wore a purple suit." He becomes somber as he stretches his hands out behind his head.

"Did she know she was dying?" I ask him, choosing to roll the dice to see if he would shut me out or not.

"I could never prove it, but she was murdered. Someone started slowly poisoning her after my father's death." I whip my head to look at him, but he continues to stare at the ceiling, thankfully not witnessing my horrible expression.

"She deteriorated right in front of me. It started to get worse. That's when she started asking me to make her promises: little things, big things. It helped distract her, so we did it every day," he pauses again. "She told me she was dying, but up until the moment she passed, she was the kindest and most loving woman I have ever known. She looked awful when she died. Her skin was grey, and her eyes turned black. That night, she cried out in pain so loud, it woke me up. I ran into her room, but she was already gone." Reznor tears his eyes from the ceiling to look at me.

I can't hide the sadness from my eyes as he peers at me. Reaching out, I cup his face with my hand. "I know people probably say it a lot, but I am truly sorry you had to go through that. Losing any family member is hard, but I can only imagine what it's like to lose a parent. I'm sure she would be very proud of you if she were here; you've completely changed your kingdom and thrived while doing so."

He takes my hand from his face, moving our hands to the mattress as he intertwines our fingers. "Thank you," he says quietly, returning his stare to the ceiling.

I shimmy down into the bed next to him, moving until I'm close enough to lean my head against his shoulder. We remain like this until a servant arrives to tell us dinner would be served soon. Reznor wears the same outfit, but I go to the bathroom to change into the lilac-colored dress Anisa had chosen. It's a spaghetti-strapped silk garment that runs to the floor. I manage to zip the dress a majority of the way, but I can't manage to finish it.

Creeping out of the bathroom, I keep the dress pressed against my chest. "Can you zip this?" I silently pray that he won't be able to see the ugly lines crossing my lower back.

Reznor nods, standing behind me and brushing my hair to the side. Carefully zipping the dress, he allows his finger to glide along my spine. Shivers run across my body immediately. He lingers behind me, tracing the moon that sits at the top of my spine. The touch gentle but causes all the air to evacuate my lungs.

When he removes his hand from my neck, I turn around to face him. "Ready?"

A small smirk brushes his lips, but he gestures to the door, motioning for me to go first. The moment I'm out of the door, Reznor falls into step beside me, placing his hand on my lower back for the millionth time today. My heels clink against the floor as we cross the hallway, but that seems to be the only sound that can be heard throughout the manor.

"Why is it so quiet?" I whisper.

"Because Tatiana isn't in the room." I cackle, and Reznor smiles from ear to ear.

Servants open the doors to a large dining room where Tatiana and—a man whom I assume to be Arnold— sits. Unlike Reznor's, this table is much shorter, and decorated in bright, colorful centerpieces. The walls are an aquamarine with gold light fixtures. It's the darkest room we have been in so far, and that says a lot.

Reznor takes a seat at the other head of the table, and I claim the seat to his right. I'm still not used to dining with him. I'm also painfully aware of how close we sit to each other. Once again, I start to feel overwhelmed by his presence.

Tatiana grins the moment I sit down. "I love that dress," she gushes from across the table. I politely thank her; Anisa will be thrilled to hear that her gowns are such a hit.

"Arnold, this is Liara," Tatiana boasts.

"It's a pleasure to meet you." Arnold takes my hand, placing a kiss on my knuckles.

"Arnold, I wouldn't do that again." Reznor threatens. I draw my hand from his grasp and lay it in my lap. I have to suppress an eyeroll and a snide comment. Reznor and his territorialism perplexes me sometimes.

"Oh, Reznor, how I love to mess with you," Arnold coos in a sing-song voice. He's rather ugly, but it's obvious Tatiana is smitten with him. His orange hair starts halfway down his head. He has matching yellow eyes and is heavy set unlike the other Lycans. Arnold prances back over to his chair then calls for the servants to bring in the food. Once a plate piled with meat, potatoes, salad, and a roll is placed before all of us, he then dismisses them. Small talk is exchanged till everyone is done eating. Arnold waits until the room is clear before bringing up the matter at hand.

"As much as I love to see you, Reznor, Tatiana tells me there is a reason for your arrival."

Reznor drinks from his wine before speaking. "Last month, during a full moon, a group of men attempted to attack Liara. Then, yesterday they attacked us again on a trail." Tatiana gasps, clasping her hand over her mouth. I try not to react to the pain that crawls beneath my skin at the thought of the last full moon and what happened in the foyer.

"They all bore a tattoo of a pine tree on their necks, and they aren't coming from the mortal world. The closest land they could be coming through is yours."

Tatiana's face contorts in anger. "We have had some issues ourselves with people bearing the same tattoo. They have been running through our lands and attacking some of our people."

"Do you know who is sending them, or who they are? Last time I saw these tattoos was in the war, but I haven't heard from them since." Reznor leans forward, refilling his glass.

"They are called the People of the Trees. That's all I really know about them. They had many friends during the war, but they have since isolated themselves.

I don't see why they would be targeting you now, or who would have sent them." Arnold appears confused to even be discussing this. "They tend to be peaceful; I truly don't understand any of their current actions."

"But what would they want with Liara?" Tatiana ponders.

Reznor huffs, "That's the question I've been asking myself since the attack in town." I glance at Reznor sideways. I hadn't realized the attacks have been bothering him to this extent.

"I don't even know where they live at the moment. They have been hidden for years; I just assumed they had died off after the war." Arnold's face morphs into worry. "If we had known, I would have told you!" He adds quickly.

Reznor tilts his glass to his lips. "I know, I came to you because I trust you."

"What do we do now?" Tatiana asks.

"We try to figure out what they want, set up precautions to keep them from entering our lands. Keep an eye out at the ball, we can identify them pretty easily. If you find out any information, let me know." Reznor says it in such a calm manner that it impresses me. He can be very composed when he wants to. Well, that is if I'm not involved.

"We should head to bed. We can take you to talk to the warriors, and some of our people might have some more information." Tatiana removes the napkin from her lap and stands. We all do the same, leaving the dining room in a cluster.

"Go with Emanuel and Charles, I'll be up later." Reznor watches me until I fall in step with the boys without a word.

Both make themselves comfortable while they wait for Reznor to return. The servant doesn't come back to the room, and I'm already feeling drained. I turn to Emanuel. "Can you unzip me?"

Charles. and Emanuel exchange glances, but neither move to help me.

"Can you get the servant from the hall?"

"Gladly, I would rather Reznor didn't kill me." Emanuel smiles politely, then turns on his heels, aiming for the door.

"I asked you because you're the one with a partner; it's the least threatening."

Charles snickers, "Tell Reznor that."

Well... he has a point.

The servant trails me into the bathroom only to be sent back out immediately after unzipping me. She doesn't need to witness the marks on my skin. Digging through my clothes to get dressed, I realize exactly what Anisa packed me. She picked some revealing underwear but decent nightgowns, although they are still rather short. "She needs a talking to," I mutter to myself as I grab a black nightgown with white trim. The silk material has quickly become one of my favorites to sleep in due to the coolness of the fabric.

When I exit the bathroom, Charles and Emanuel are still there, but Reznor has returned. His eyes snap to me as they rake down my body. The boys quickly avert their eyes when Reznor lets out a low growl. I merely shake my head in response and cross to the bed, slipping beneath the covers to appease him. He still appears displeased as he trudges to the shower, not bothering to shut the bathroom door.

What is with him and leaving the bathroom door open?

Both boys linger with me until Reznor is out of the shower, striding back into the room in nothing but a towel. I check him out over the top of my book, but quickly avert my eyes, so no one catches me.

"You two can go. Be ready to go with us to town in the morning." Reznor digs through his bag until he finds what he's looking for, then disappears back into the bathroom.

Charles winks at me.

I flip him off before returning to my book. Reznor's still changing in the bathroom with the door wide open. I keep my eyes glued to the page, though I've reread the line six times now. I'm not going to look, or rather I'm trying really hard not to. But then he emerges from the bathroom in silk black pajama pants looking like a god, and I can't help but peek at the masterpiece before me.

"Who unzipped your dress?" Reznor asks as he settles himself into the mattress, his bare chest glinting in the soft light.

"A servant did, although I did ask Emanuel to."

Reznor growls. My head whips in his direction as he snatches the book from my hand. "You did what?" His eyes flash red for a moment; it happens so fast I almost miss it.

"I asked him to, I didn't know where you were. Plus, we all know he wouldn't try anything. Hell, those two are like my big brothers at this point." I reach for the book back, but he moves it out of my reach again.

"Don't ask another man to unzip your dress." His words are laced with venom, yet I can hear the lingering jealousy. Glaring at him, I open my mouth to say something about Serena, but I opt not to. Instead, I decided to take the conversation in another direction.

"Don't you think if I wanted to try and be with someone else, I would have done it by now?" I roll away from him, shutting off my light. I don't want to see his reaction to my question.

Reznor quickly pulls me back to him, my dress hitching up higher beneath the sheets. "We are not having this conversation," he growls, wrapping me in his arms.

"Why, can't admit that I'm right?"

"Liara," he warns.

His tense body relaxes behind me the second my bare skin comes into contact with his. He and I both freeze for a moment. The tingling sensation travels across my skin feeling like butterfly kisses, leaving goosebumps in their wake. Reznor hums in approval before he shuts off the other lights, then, surprisingly, he kisses my temple.

Chapter Twelve: Closer Than Before

"They look so cute."

"Maybe we should let them sleep longer."

"He looks like a little baby."

I hear Charles and Emanuel's voices from somewhere in the room, but I'm not going to open my eyes to look for them. I'm not ready to start the day, or leave this bed, or put on pants. Yeah, definitely no pants.

"You two are obnoxious," Reznor rasps in a sleepy voice, shifting in bed. He untangles himself from me, but I'm still laying on his arm.

"Tatiana sent us to wake you up. It's nearly nine," Emanuel whispers.

"I get the point, now get out," Reznor barks, pulling the blankets over me after he carefully slides his arm out from under my head. "I'll wake her up in a bit."

"So cute—" Charles starts, but Reznor cuts him off.

"Out!" he hisses. I try not to laugh at Charles' mockery. Finally, Reznor is able to receive some of the burden that is Charles' teasing.

Reznor moves around the room while leaving me in the bed for a bit longer. Yet it wasn't long enough because minutes later, his scent hits me as Reznor gently wakes me up, although I hadn't really been asleep.

"Liara, you need to get up."

My eyes flutter open, and the first thing I see is Reznor dressed and sitting next to me on the bed. "Once this whole ceremony thing is done, I'm not getting up early for a month."

He smirks. "Sounds like a plan." He huffs giving me one last look before rising from the bed. "I'm going to talk to Tatiana, meet me downstairs for breakfast." Before I've even gotten out of the bed, Charles and Emanuel return to the room as Reznor ducks out.

"Aw, look, sleeping beauty is awake," Charles coos.

I ignore him. I need to wake up more before I can deal with his obnoxiousness, or he's going to end up getting punched. I dismiss another one of his jokes as I trudge to the bathroom.

Today's dress is baby blue with lace quarter sleeves. The fabric clings to my body in all the right places until it flares at my calves. It's cut to reveal my mid-calf down to my feet, with shorter material in the front than in the back. Luckily, I don't have any recent bruises from training.

The same older servant from yesterday assists me today. She styles my hair with a chunk braided behind my head, leaving the rest flowing down. The outfit is rather feminine and whimsical, but it makes my eyes pop. After one look, I decide I like it, even if the silver strappy heels are a little uncomfortable.

"Took you long enough," Charles groans, standing from his chair the moment I emerge from the bathroom. "I'm starving, let's go!" He strides to the door, throwing it open and leaving Emanuel and me to trail behind him.

We're still in a fit of laughter when we enter the dining room. Reznor immediately looks annoyed with how close I stand between the two men. He even glares after them as I settle into my seat next to him. We are the only ones in the dining room after Charles and Emanuel dip into the kitchen through a swinging door.

"Tatiana is getting our rides prepared," Reznor states as he picks at invisible pieces of lint from his shoulder.

"When's the next full moon?" I question, raising an eyebrow at him.

"In four days, why?" he asks, almost defensively.

"I was just wondering what we were going to do since you can't send me to town." It's an honest question, but it's not the reason I asked. Reznor's been feeling all his emotions a lot more recently. Even his clinginess seems odd, along with his need to protect me rocketing through the roof. He knows Emanuel and Charles aren't a threat, but with the moon and his wolf form playing with his emotions, it's overwhelming him. It's easier for me to notice it, and now that I do, I want to help.

"I'm not sure yet, but we'll figure it out." He averts his eyes.

Tatiana arrives not a moment too soon, although when she enters, I wanted to shield my eyes. Her green dress is so bright, it seems like it's glowing. "Sorry I'm so late. Let's eat," she calls dramatically.

I only pick at my food, my thoughts keeping me too preoccupied to even think about eating. Plus, Reznor is watching me way more than he should be it makes me a little wiggly. I shudder a breath of relief when we leave the dining room and walk along the outside corridor.

"You didn't eat much," Reznor states, not leaving room for it to be a question.

"I wasn't hungry." I smile at him, amused, but he doesn't seem to find it funny.

"Are you eating the proper amount of food at the manor?" He blocks me from taking another step.

I stroll around him. "Yes, Rez, ask Anisa, she sits with me for almost every meal."

He catches up to me quickly, taking my hand with his. "We're going to have to start dining together if you don't start eating properly.

I swat his chest with my free hand. "Or you could just have dinner with me to spend time with me."

"Fine."

I eye him. "That's what you have to say to that? Fine?"

He opens the car door. "Yes, at least then Anisa can stop lugging a tray across the manor." I swat his chest again, but when he laughs, I realize he is actually teasing me. It's a pleasant change. Maybe we are getting closer.

The town of Greensboro looks to be just as lively as Reznor's. The people are out walking amongst the town on this warm sunny day. We stop outside of a shop with a sun painted onto the small sign above the door.

"This is where we had our first incident with the Tree People," Tatiana calls before she opens the door.

"Queen T!" a young man gushes as we all pile into the small store front.

"Hello, love, I've come with a dear friend of mine. We have some questions about the break-in you had a few weeks ago." Tatiana cuts right to the point.

The young man rounds the corner. His blond hair is shaved close to the skin, and just like most townspeople, he has yellow eyes. The man's eyes immediately go to Reznor then fall to me. Reznor tenses next to me as the shop keeper's stare lingers on me for too long. Reznor cocks his head in a challenging fashion, his grip on my hand tightening.

The shop owner visibly swallows. "What do you want to know, King Nighterious?" He nods to a small table surrounded by a sea of candles. In fact, candles line every space on the walls of the shop.

"Explain to us what happened in detail." Reznor probes while he glances around the room.

"I had just finished crafting some candles when I heard a crash from the front of the shop. I ran out here and these men with a tattoo on their necks were stealing some of my candles. I tried to stop them, but one knocked me out before I could call for help."

"Have you seen these men since?" The man shakes his head no. Reznor glances at the candles. "Did they take any of your enchanted candles?"

"No, they stole my cheapest candle, actually. It's just wax and a wick."

Reznor thanks the man then we're off again, the next stop is a grocery store. With all five of the remaining stores, the story remains the same. Each store was robbed, but just of the cheapest materials. The tattooed men took the bare minimum, then they were gone.

The robberies only turned violent if there was a witness that had actively tried to stop them. They had very few injuries or losses, yet in Reznor's lands, they're trying to kill me. It seems we really got the short end of the stick.

By the time we leave the last shop, Reznor is annoyed by the lack of answers. Or rather the fact all we have received are useless answers. While he is feeling prickly, I'm just glad to be around new people and out in the world again. It initially had been easy to ignore his foul mood, but with each shop, he only gets angrier, and I'm tired of it.

I veer from the group, pulling Reznor with me. He's visibly confused but follows after me anyways. Charles and Emanuel try to follow, but Reznor waves them away, ignoring their protests like I did.

We stop near a fountain where I turn to him, crossing my arms over my chest. "What gives?"

"What do you mean?" He still seems confused. It's kind of cute that he thinks I'm not paying attention to his mood swings.

"You have been getting more agitated at each stop."

Reznor eyes me as he puts his hands on his hips. "If we can't figure out what they want or what they are planning, I can't keep you safe. I've waited over a thousand years for you, Liara, I'm not going to lose you now," he says defensively.

"Snapping at them isn't going to help you get any answers."

"I didn't get any answers anyways," he grumbles.

"Gosh, I wonder why?" I huff, then wrap my arms around him.

"What are you doing?" he asks, laughing slightly, but he doesn't attempt to pull out of my embrace.

"Hug me, it will calm you down, so you don't snap any of the warriors' heads off." I continue to hold on to him, yet Reznor still doesn't reciprocate the act. "Don't suddenly be afraid to touch me now—"

His hands dart to my waist. "I'm never afraid to touch you." He leans down, wrapping his arms around me. "I just don't trust what you do to me."

I don't think he meant to say those words, but either way, I feel the same. I don't trust what he does to me, but I shouldn't be thinking about that now. Not when we're communicating decently well, and he's starting to admit some of what he's thinking and feeling.

I keep a hold of him until I feel like he's calm enough to talk to the soldiers. Reznor doesn't seem to mind that we stood there like a couple of loons in front of a fountain, hugging for fifteen minutes. Nope, the tribrid king held me with a smile on his face, but because the smile is there, I doubt they would recognized him.

We stroll back to the car hand in hand, ignoring the smirk Charles shoots at us as we get in. Reznor doesn't let my hand go; he only releases it when we parts ways as he goes to talk to the soldiers. I figure my presence around that many men would enrage Reznor further, and he just mellowed out. He needs information about the attacks, and me being there will only distract him.

I hadn't realized how much these attacks had been affecting Reznor. He's torn up over the incident on the trail specifically. I knew he was upset, but I had presumed it was due to people invading his lands, not because it was a direct threat to me. Reznor's been waiting all this time for me, and these people are threatening to take that away.

"You know how to calm him down." Tatiana's comment draws me out of my daze.

I had been so focused on Reznor I hadn't noticed where she's taking me on this stroll. "No, the mate bond knows how to calm him down," I say dismissively. I just used my body to my advantage… and I suppose his.

"No, you saw his anger spiking, and you calmed him down. Give yourself some credit." Tatiana stops near a bench that sat atop a hill looking out over the training field. We sat together as she continued, "Is he still seeing that hateful woman, Serena?"

The mention of her name sends a bolt of anger through me. "Yes, he is." I hadn't realized how much hatred would come out when I spoke those three words, but I'm not entirely surprised.

"I've hated that woman for so long. She is a terrible influence," she sneers.

"Yes, she is. He says he'll stop seeing her when the bond is complete, but knowing her… I don't know if I see that happening." As if I wasn't already worried about it, Tatiana nods her head in agreement.

"I don't say this to hurt you, but she will not give him up easily. I can promise you that." Tatiana frowns and gives me a look of sympathy. "How are you and Reznor getting along so far?" She changes the subject, but still, I don't find this one much better.

"It started out bumpy, but things have improved." I'm going to be with this man for the rest of my life. I need to remain hopeful, even though that's hard for me.

"He is a good man, you—"

I raise a hand to cut her off. "I just need to give him a chance and not give up on him?"

Tatiana starts laughing so hard she has to hold her stomach. "Can you blame so many people for trying to push you two together?"

"No, I understand, but it gets old. I'm trying. Hell, Charles can vouch for that." This time Tatiana and I laugh together, but looking behind me, I find Charles smiling as he eagerly nods.

"They fight without screaming at each other now, it's quite nice."

Tatiana grins, "You will be a great addition to the family. Hopefully, you can simmer him out. Just don't let this world fool you. There are some people out there who do not want you and Reznor together."

"I guess you'll have to help guide me. I don't know much about ruling anyone or anything. I was going to be a nurse."

"You like to take care of people, so take care of your people. The best person to guide you will be Reznor. I'm older than him, but he has been ruling longer than anyone in this kingdom."

"How do they treat him?" Reznor has spoken of many enemies, but never explains who and why.

"Many tried to take advantage of him, but as he got older, he learned how to keep them from pressing in on his lands. Most of the territories in Dwimmér treat him with respect and often go to him for help, but others have been out for his throne since he got it." Tatiana gazes at the field filled with soldiers and gives a shake of her head.

"It seems greed for power is something that lives in both worlds."

"Ah, yes, humans. What joyous creatures." she says facetiously.

I can't say she's wrong. I lived as a human once, and they did some awful things. But I suppose all species have their issues.

The rest of the day passes in a blur. I practically crawl to the room. The moment I enter the space, I hurry to get my shoes off; my feet are killing me. I can worry about changing later, right now I just need to be off my feet. Charles and Emanuel cackle as I chuck my shoes across the room.

"Remind me to tell Anisa that I *cannot* wear those shoes all day again," I whine while rubbing my sore toes.

"Not the best touring shoes?" Charles teases.

"Let's see you walk miles in small strappy shoes." Charles' face lights up and goes to grab my shoes. "Don't you dare, Anisa will throw a fit!"

Charles turns, preparing to make a witty comeback when his eyes un-focus, a quick glance to Emanuel showing the same. In the next fleeting moment, they are darting out of the room without an explanation, but they don't need to tell me something's wrong. Cautiously, I climb off the bed and creep toward the open door. I hadn't even stepped out of the room before Reznor's voice rings out in my head.

Stay in the room.

I jump slightly; I'm still not used to communicating this way with him. *What's going on?*

Just stay in the room, I'll explain later.

Quickly shutting the door, I began pacing the room as more and more time passes. Something's happened, and it must be bad if Charles *and* Emanuel leave me alone. That also means Reznor is in danger…

With the second hour approaching, I'm moments away from leaving the room when Emanuel returns in fresh clothes and a grim expression on his face. It falls further when he sees I've been preparing to leave.

"If I were you, I would stay here," Emanuel warns, sinking down into the chair and resting his head against the upholstery.

"What happened?"

"The tree people; they were here on the property. They ambushed Reznor and Arnold while talking with another soldier."

"Is he hurt?"

Emanuel is silent for a moment. "He took a hit or two," then quickly adds, "he should heal before the night's up."

"What do you classify as a hit or two?"

"Liara, he's fine. He'll return later, but they're interrogating one of the men they captured. He told me to tell you not to wait; it's going to be a while."

"Of course, he freaking did." I whirl on Emanuel. "Does he think I'm stupid, because even I know you two wouldn't have been pulled off guarding me if it wasn't serious."

He palms his face. "He doesn't want you to worry. It's all going to be okay."

"Why wouldn't I worry? He got ambushed! Oh, that man is going to drive me insane."

"I think the feeling's mutual." Emanuel grins, then points to the bed. "Get some rest. Reznor's not coming up anytime soon."

I tried to sleep, I truly did, but my mind is swimming with questions. I'm worried about Reznor; I'm scared because now they're trying to kill him too. They have been mostly peaceful in Tatiana's land. We're here two days, and all hell's breaking loose. We're still not any closer to answers than we were. They want me and Reznor, and all the reasons I can think of only lead to more problems.

A while later, Reznor comes through the door, only to freeze in the doorway when he sees me sitting up in bed. "You're awake."

"Yes, are you staying or going back out?" I cross my arms over my chest, waiting for an answer while both men gawk at me.

"I'm staying."

"Good, Emanuel please leave." Emanuel doesn't even look to Reznor for confirmation before darting for the door to make a speedy exit.

"Are you okay?" Reznor's black shirt doesn't show any wounds, but parts of his neck and exposed forearms have dried blood marking his skin.

Reznor strides to the trash bin, unbuttoning his shirt along the way. When the last button is undone, he takes off the shirt, dropping it into the bin. The moment I see his back, I gasp and jump off the bed. A closing bullet wound on his shoulder, a large slash across his back, a stab wound near his spine. I carefully touch his back as I examine the wounds. All of them are closing, and if he feels any pain, he doesn't show it. Reznor slowly turns, exposing a chest littered with bruises and more slash marks. And that is definitely a matching exit wound from the gunshot. If this is what Emanuel calls a 'hit or two,' I never want to see what Reznor looks like to classify it as an actual injury.

"I'm taking longer to heal than usual; it's because of the full moon." Reznor watches my hands move to each of his wounds.

"I was going to be a nurse; you should have come up here so I could have helped you." Looking at his injured chest, I'm hit with a wave of anger. He stayed away even though he knew I could help him.

"I'll be fine, I don't need your help." He snatches my hand that had been resting on his arm. "Go to bed."

"Rez—"

"Liara, it's not a big deal. I got hurt, it happens." He's quickly retreating away from me and steering toward the bathroom.

"Why won't you let me help you? I care about you Reznor. I just want to help."

Reznor stops on a dime and turns around with utter disbelief and rage on his face. "Don't go there, Liara, I didn't come up here to have a fight with you."

"I'm not trying to fight. You scared me, Reznor!" I try to reason with him, but that just seems to set him off even more.

"You'll have to get used to it. This is nothing, I'll let you know when you should worry," He snarls.

"No, you don't get to act like that now, not when we finally start to get along." I point my finger at him, and he laughs at me. "You're an arrogant prick! I'm here offering to help you because I care about you, and you're shutting me out."

"I didn't *ask* for your help, and I don't *want* your help." Reznor stalks forward, getting closer until he's looming over me. "You know the last person who called me that ended up with a broken arm and a busted lip."

"Are you going to hit me, Reznor?" I pronounce each word with as much venom as I can muster, but even then, it can't convey how angry I am.

Without warning, Reznor grabs me, pulling me toward him, causing me to collide with his chest. His eyes flare red as his anger takes over. His grip locks around my waist, not giving an inch of space. He inches his face closer to mine. "I don't hit women, not unless they ask me to."

"Then you'll be waiting a long-time jackass."

If I hadn't already been pushed against him, I might have fallen. The bond is overwhelming my senses, and I can't think straight, but even my anger can't completely dissipate. All I know at this moment is that I want to prove a point. He wants to use his body to distract me, well, I can use mine to distract him too. Not allowing myself a moment to think, I push up on my toes and close the gap between us, pressing my lips against his.

Check mate, Reznor.

The moment my mouth brushes his, a wave of pleasure crashes into me. The bond flutters, enjoying every moment of this. Reznor immediately relaxes against me as he reacts to the kiss, then I use that moment to shove him back with a smirk on my face. Free from his grasp I turn, walking back toward the bed. I don't get a single step further before he picks me up and tosses me onto the bed.

Reznor is quick to get on top of me, pinning me in place with his body. "Oh, so you think you can tease me, huh?" He mocks with a devilish grin.

"It worked, didn't it?" I start to struggle against him, but it only works to his advantage as it pushes us closer.

"No, because I always win."

He claims my mouth, moving his hands to my hair, titling my head back further. My plan was to not kiss him back, but my body betrays me when my lips begin moving against his. Reznor's grip on my hair tightens as his tongue brushes against my lip. At first, I'm determined not to give in, but as he bites my lower lip, I whimper and open my mouth for him. Needing to touch him, I sink my fingers into his hair. Reznor wraps my legs around his hip, then presses in closer. We continue kissing like this, only breaking when I need air. He takes the opportunity to press open mouth kisses along my cheek, jaw, then down my throat, but as he reaches the point where my neck meets my shoulder, I feel something sharp graze my skin. Reznor abruptly pulls away from me. In the next moment, the door is slamming shut with a hollowing thud. He's gone, and I'm lying here on the bed, flustered and confused.

Chapter Thirteen: Red Like Fire

A knock on the door startles me out of bed. I flip right over and land on the floor.

Reznor remains gone for the rest of the night. I tried to wait up, but my efforts were useless. I know whoever's at the door isn't him because he wouldn't have knocked.

"What?" I groan from the ground.

Charles peeks his head out from around the door. "What are you doing on the floor?"

"Just hanging out."

"Mhm, hate to break up your party, but you need to get dressed." Charles sits down in the nearest chair and closes his eyes.

I take my time getting ready, wasting as much time as possible. Even after I get dressed, I remain in the bathroom, sitting on the floor until I can't linger any longer. Just as I'm ready to leave the bathroom, I hear hushed voices coming from the other side of the door… Reznor has finally returned, but I'm not going out to meet him. Even though I shouldn't be, part of me is embarrassed. The other part of me is ready to yell at him for playing me. My plan backfired, and Reznor got the last word, then ran out on me.

Reznor's muffled voice seeps through the door, followed by another slam. Charles is still in his spot, but this time with his head is in his hands. "What happened last night?"

"Nothing, what happened out here?"

"Nothing." Charles sits up and grabs my bag from the floor. "Want to skip breakfast?"

"Yes please."

Charles looks around the room. "Let's go for a walk. We stay here and Reznor is going to come knocking."

I practically skip to the door. "Lead the way."

Charles and I wander the grounds aimlessly. The entire walk, Charles carries my bag slung over his shoulder, refusing to let me carry it. He doesn't try to force me into talking, he just accompanies me and laughs when I get a little too distracted by some flowers. They look like regular daisies, but when I lean down and touch it, the flower turns from white to baby blue, the next one turning orange, and so on until the entire patch is full of color. Charles' eyes go glossy a few times, but he ignores it, until he starts to wince and flinch.

I try to ask him about it, but he only ushers me further and points out more magical flowers to distract me from it. Still, each time we get further from the manor; the more Charles reacts. One is so bad that he stops walking and clutches at his head.

"Let's go back, it's not worth it."

Charles groans. "We're going to be heading back anyway."

Reznor comes storming around the corner with Emanuel on his heels. He doesn't yell, scream, nor even look in my direction as he ever so politely asks me to follow Emanuel to the car. Giving Charles a sparing glance, he jerks his head, telling me to go.

Emanuel speaks the second we're far enough from Reznor. "He's pissed."

"Because I went for a walk?"

"Just wait in the car, I can't explain for him."

The car ride from hell comes to an end and Reznor gets out of the car the moment it's parked. It's as if he can't get away from me fast enough. It had been like that for the whole ride. Him silently glaring at me, me looking out the window and not saying a word for the five-hour drive. It was absolutely friggin blissful.

"So much for progress," I mumble, grabbing my bag from Emanuel's hand.

I receive multiple questioning looks as I storm through the manor. I'm not entirely surprised when they start avoiding my path for the rest of the march to my room. Except when I enter my room, I half wonder if I'm in the wrong place. What once was the living room is now filled with carts of gowns, and Anisa's head pops out from one of them the second I open the door.

"You're back early," Anisa hurries over and pulls me into a tight embrace. "How was it?"

"Considering I just spent the last five hours getting glared at, it went swimmingly." I slam the bag onto the floor. Gods what I wouldn't do to punch something right now…yes, I know the anger management skills need improving.

"I'm going to need you to explain."

"Last night, there was an attack in Greensboro. Reznor and Arnold were ambushed. Rez got injured and naturally, I got pissed off because he was avoiding me. I offered to help, and he just snapped… then one thing led to another…" Even thinking about the kiss sends shivers down my arm. "We kissed, and it escalated slightly, and then he bolted out of the room, and stayed gone all night."

Anisa gapes like a fish. "Well how was it?"

My cheeks heat instantly. "It was nice, very nice until he walked out. The whole thing was just to prove a point, he said so himself that he wanted to win. I fell for it."

"What exactly happened before he left?"

"He was kissing down my neck, and then he was just gone." I really have no further explanation. Anisa's face flashes with realization. "Anisa, what is—" I'm cut off by a gut-wrenching pain that cuts through my body. Gripping at my stomach, my knees give out, buckling beneath the pain.

"Liara!" Anisa reaches out, stabilizing me. "Is it happening again?"

All I can do is nod. I grit down on my teeth. I swear, I'm going to kill him. This is wrong on an *entirely* different level.

Anisa carefully maneuvers us to the bed. There, she's able to help me in. "What do you want me to do?" she coos, pushing some fallen hair back behind my ear.

"It's worse this time," I cry out in pain, clutching at anything and everything. "Keep everyone out until it's over," I groan loudly, even though I'm trying to stay quiet.

Anisa hurries to the door, locking it, then rushing back over to my side. She can't help as I writhe in pain. I don't know how long it is, but eventually, it stops. By then, I'm covered in sweat and am a panting mess on the bed. The relief doesn't last long because it starts back up again a few moments later.

That bastard.

I nearly scream as the pain becomes the strongest it has ever been. It's like someone is peeling my skin away piece by piece, then dousing alcohol on the exposed flesh, like my bones are snapping, ligaments tearing. It's all overwhelming, as it becomes too much to bear.

"Anisa," I gasp out, gripping her hand. "I'm going to pass out. Don't tell anyone please," I beg her as tears run down my face.

"Liara, I don't think—"

I cut her off, gripping her hand tighter. "Please, Anisa, just don't tell anyone…please," I beg, gripping her hand with both of mine. "For the love of God, Anisa please don't get him." I'm fragile, and vulnerable at this moment, and I don't want anyone else seeing it. Let alone have Reznor come in right now because if he did, I'm sure I would beat him with my shoe.

"Okay, just try and relax," she coos, speaking calming things to me as the black blotches overtake my vision, and I'm taken under by the blackness. The last thing I think before I black out is that I'm indebted to Anisa for the rest of my life.

Something wet is pressing against my forehead, then it moves to my cheek, then repeats. I force my eyes open. Anisa's blue-grey eyes stare back down at me with a look of relief.

"Thank Gods you're up!" She tosses the rag into the bowl.

"How long was I out?" My voice comes out raspy as I move up on my elbows, wincing at the pain that aches across my body.

"You've been out for hours. If you weren't going to wake up soon, I was going to get Reznor."

I glance at the window, and sure enough, the sun is about to set. "Thank you, Anisa. I mean it, thank you."

She smiles softly, but I can see the guilt she feels hiding behind her eyes. "You looked absolutely dreadful, you kept thrashing out." Her face pales as she stands, taking the bowl with her to the kitchenette.

"When did it stop?" When I blacked out, I couldn't feel the pain, but my body seems to think otherwise. Every muscle in my body aches.

"Maybe thirty minutes ago..."

That meant Reznor and Serena have been going at it for hours. I suddenly become enraged. Once again, he spent last night with me, but is sleeping with her today. That won't be happening ever again, or he can kiss his precious powers goodbye. The urge to beat him with my shoe rises again. The ring on my left hand suddenly feels heavy.

"Wow, they sure like to fuck, don't they?" I hatefully snide, dragging my body from the bed.

"Liara—"

"I'm going to take a bath, then we can do whatever is needed for the ball."

Anisa frowns as she follows me into the bathroom, running hot water, then pouring in soaps. I did the timely task of undressing, and that's when I see the blackness has spread; it's all the way down my stomach, back, and it runs down my thighs, stopping at my knees. Maybe he is killing me. Anisa sucks in a startled breath when she sees my blackened skin, but instead of pointing out the progression, she helps me step into the tub.

A sigh of relief escapes my lips as the hot water soothes my aching muscles. I plan on enjoying the bliss of this bath for as long as possible.

"We are a little behind schedule. What kind of dress do you have in mind?" Anisa asks as she offers me the baskets of soap. I take one aimlessly.

"Is there a theme to the ball, or anything?"

"No, you have free range; it's your ball, but you are supposed to make an entrance with Reznor."

At the sound of his name, the anger ignites inside of me again. "I won't be making an entrance with Reznor. He can have his grand entrance with Serena." I stop as a brilliant idea blossoms in my head. "Red. I want something red, tight, and sexy. Still, it needs to be able to cover whatever this is." Luckily from the shoulder blades up, my skin remains untainted, and most of my breasts are left unmarked.

Anisa grins, walking towards the door. "I have the perfect dress in mind." She hurries out of the bathroom, leaving me alone.

With Anisa gone, it gives me time to reflect on what happened today and what I'm going to do about it. He was making out with me last night but sleeping with her this morning…and the rest of the day. I'm ready to even the score; he wants to play games, and this time, I plan on winning.

I stay in the bath until the water turns cold, taking as long as possible for everything. I'm going to make sure I'm late, and so is Anisa. She takes her time brushing my hair then curling every strand to perfection before pinning it into an intricate updo, leaving two tendrils near my face. She wants to show off the crest that rests on my neck, and this just helps the plan by showing more skin.

The makeup is a dark smokey eye with black being the primary color. She then uses a red color on my lips that matches the dress perfectly. We agree a necklace won't be necessary, instead, we place onyx studs in each ear. That is all the jewelry I will be wearing.

There's a bang on the door as I strip off my robe.

"She needed to be downstairs five minutes ago!" Emanuel shouts from outside the room.

"I'm naked!" I holler back.

Anisa and I both cackle as she helps me into the red dress. She takes her time lacing the corset all the way up, making it hug my figure. We dismiss another bang on the door.

Wasting a little more time, I gaze at the beautiful outfit in the mirror. The fabric is a fiery red with sparkles glistening all the way down the mermaid shaped gown. The layered material at the bottom drags the floor with a small trail following behind me. The cut of the dress reveals plenty of cleavage, yet another thing to piss him off. My favorite part of the garment would have to be the flame cut material that rests atop my breasts. They rest on each side, leaving the valley between exposed. The blackness is just hidden underneath the material. Thankfully, Anisa carefully places, and tightens, every piece of the dress to ensure it stays hidden.

As Anisa slides on my black heels that will remain hidden by the length of the skirt, the boy's barge into the room.

"Look, she has to get down there—" Emanuel starts to speak then stops.

Charles and Emanuel stop in their tracks, taking in my appearance. Their reactions alone are enough to cause my wicked grin.

"Reznor is not going to like this at all." Emanuel sighs deeply, running his hands over his short hair.

I wiggle my brows. "That's the point."

Anisa's fawning at her work, her approval obvious. Earlier, I had even forced her to get ready before me. She wears a black servant dress but has taken the time to add a little makeup.

"Look, you have to get down there now. He already had to go in by himself," Charles stresses. I motion for him to go first, so he leads, but Emanuel doesn't move until I do.

We brisk through the manor until we stop behind a black curtain outside the ballroom. Music can be heard from inside the room, along with lots of chatter and laughter coming from the guests.

"Go down, and go straight to Reznor," Emanuel begs.

Anisa shoos him slightly as she adjusts my dress and hair one final time. "You look beautiful, remind him who and *what* you are," she whispers beneath her breath.

I smile, thanking her for everything, then I take one final breath before she pulls back the curtain, and I began descending the grand staircase.

Chapter Fourteen: All Eyes On Me

It becomes quiet in the room as I ease down each step carefully. The ballroom has tables filled with guests along with a large open dance floor. Crystal chandeliers hang from the ceiling, and extravagant light fixtures line the walls along with the colors of Reznor's flag. The room is something straight out of fairy tale along with the guests filling it. People stop to stare at me, but the person who catches my eye is Reznor. He moves swiftly, but elegantly, as he makes his way to the base of the stairs and waits for me. He's dressed in an all-black suit with a black crown on his head, holding amethyst stones that match my engagement ring. The crown has pointed ends that look so sharp I'm sure it could slice something open. He looks every part of a king in this moment, a menacing one at that.

The second I touch the floor, he has me in his arms, pushing me flush against his chest. I'm still mad, but the aches from earlier soothe the moment he touches me. "You embarrassed me!" he hisses in my ear, his voice sending chills down my spine. I try to step away from him, but he holds me firmly against him. "No, you're staying with me. You've caused enough red flags to fly."

I smile up at him, dauntingly. "Well, I'm about to give them one more." I lean up, whispering in his ear, before I pull from his grasp then gracefully stroll to Tatiana.

"You look gorgeous!" she praises as she hugs me tightly.

"Keep me away from Reznor for a while; he spent a little too much time with Serena." I quietly say into her ear as she hugs me.

When she pulls back from the hug, she has the biggest smile on her face as she drags me around the ballroom meeting her closest friends. It isn't much fun for me, especially with the soreness building again, but it keeps me away from Reznor. It's worth it.

Reznor's getting mad. I can feel it in my bones. I manage to avoid him for a while, but my luck comes to an end. I'd been so lost in conversation with a faerie that I didn't notice Reznor until he slid his arm around my waist. That is the end of my fun. He keeps his composure until the faerie walks away, leaving me alone with the furious king.

Conjuring up my sweetest smile, I turn in his arm. "Is something wrong, Rez?"

His eyes flash red, lingering a moment before turning back to dark blue. He places his other hand on the other side of my waist, trapping me in his grip. "What the hell are you doing? This is not the time, or place to be acting like this."

"I don't know what you're talking about." I glance over my shoulder, looking for anyone who could save me, but that won't be happening. "I am shocked you were able to be here at all; I would have thought you'd be worn out." I drop my stupidly sweet act as the anger boils over.

He eyes me with confusion that quickly turns to realization. "We'll talk about this later." And based on the flare of his eyes, I knew it wouldn't be a pleasant conversation.

Reznor doesn't release his grip on me or leave my side from that moment on as we talk amongst his people who congratulate us. Some of the guests are dressed like someone out of the renaissance, whereas others dress more modernly. The fashion is all over the place, but I keep looking at their eyes.

"Their eye color is strongly linked to their magical heritage. Notice how not many have light blue eyes? That's because they have to be crossed with a warlock and a demon. Their powers are dormant, or they have one half of the power. I'm the only hybrid in these lands," Reznor whispers into my ear after he notices my focus on their eyes.

I continue to monitor the eye colors. It's sometimes difficult because some won't meet my eye because of who stands beside me. I can't say I blame them; I want to avoid the man next to me also.

Reznor radiates power, and even I feel intimidated by it at some points. I catch glances of admiration, disgust, and hatred from different people we meet, but I'm not sure who it's directed at. Me, or Reznor. If they're brave enough to be rude, Reznor is quick to put them in their place. He even makes a man bow to me even though I haven't been crowned yet. I was enjoying myself until the red-haired demon makes her way toward Reznor and me. The moment she reaches us, she runs her hand down his arm flirtatiously. That isn't even the worst part—she dares to wear white, and I'm willing to bet my life that it's a wedding gown. The tight dress has pearls and other jewels lining her shoulders, while white lace clings to her form.

"My King," she practically moans, smirking at me as she grips his arm.

"Serena," he says blankly, though his grip on my waist tightens. "You're not supposed to be here, you need to go."

She steps closer to him, but with one swift move, I block her from getting any closer to Reznor. As I lock eyes with her, lightning strikes outside, followed by a loud roll of thunder. "Touch him in front of me again, and I will have you on your knees, begging for my mercy," I grit, as a wave of rage roll through my veins.

Her eyes flare with anger. "We'll see about that. You won't be able to stop me when he's in my bed tonight."

Lighting strikes three more times outside. People gasp as the thunder shakes the large glass windows, stepping back as they rattle.

"Remember what you are, and who I am. I'm going to be queen while you're a disposable plaything." I hiss, stepping forward, causing her to take one back.

"Now get your skanky ass out of my ball before I *make you*."

I don't wait to see if she listens or what Reznor does. I hold my head high, and keep my shoulders straight, as I waltz over to Tatiana again. The people who heard the little altercation seem to approve as I breeze past them.

"Do you realize how long I have been waiting for someone to put that bitch in her place?" Tatiana is beyond thrilled with my outburst.

"Too long," I mutter as I make a point to keep Reznor out of my line of sight. If he were smart, he would give me space. I don't appreciate being humiliated, but I'm more embarrassed about my reaction. I'm not sure why I acted that way, but I do know I'm going to blame it on the bond.

"Let's go get a drink," Tatiana suggests, sensing my anger.

A servant takes a straw full of my drink, tasting it before handing it to me. I look at Tatianna, questioning the action. "She tastes it to make sure it's not poisoned. They know what the poisons taste like." Tatiana acts as if people risking their life for me is normal.

"Oh," I mumble, horrified, before drinking from the glass. A crisp, sweet red wine meets my tongue. I linger against the wall as I drain another glass while Tatiana complains about Arnold wanting to dye his hair.

Charles walks over, bowing his head to Tatiana. He remains silent as I finish yet another glass before taking it from my hand. "Let's dance," he suggests.

I laugh, and protest at first, but allow him to lead me to the dance floor. He twirls me one time before releasing me into a warm broad chest. Shit. The tingles against my skin tell me that the muscular chest belongs to Reznor.

"Sorry," Charles whispers as he hurries off the dance floor. He's smart not to meet my eye as he retreats because he would see the hateful glare, I'm sending his way.

I'm suddenly thankful for the hours of dance lessons Anisa forced upon me a few weeks ago as Reznor moves his hand to my waist, enclosing his other hand around mine. I place my free hand on his shoulder as I follow him across the dance floor quickly.

I planned to try and break Reznor's grip and head back to the crowd, but he is quick to guide me into each dance. We move to the melody in silence, dancing in a slow rhythm as we glide across the floor. People stop what they're doing to watch Reznor saunter me across the dance floor. He twirls me with ease, and I enjoy it, but when he dips me toward the floor, and gazes into my eyes…it makes me feel things I shouldn't along with nearly stopping my heart in the process.

We dance for a few songs. I had lost count of the number of dances by the time Reznor takes me off the dance floor. Due to the amount of touching during the dances, he probably assumes I'd calm down from his touch, but he is wrong. I am still royally pissed.

"She wasn't supposed to be here," he says quietly. It's obvious he feels bad. His shoulders sag further when I roll my eyes. I step out of his grip, disappearing further into the crowd of people. I know he feels bad, but I'm too mad to care; he made his bed, now he can lie in it.

"Liara…"

I stop moving, and suddenly I turn to face him. "I don't want to talk about this now…and certainly not here." I scan the room of smiling people laughing amongst themselves. This is not the place to unleash the feelings I have going on deep in my chest.

Reznor grips my chin, turning my eyes back to him. "I do want to talk about it."

"Then, I want to talk about what happened yesterday, and what you did all day today." I spitefully pull my chin from his grasp.

Reznor drops his hand immediately. "It's not what you think, Liara, I didn't—" I ignore him as I catch Anisa come in through a side door looking frantic.

"I have to go."

Reznor startles, clearly worried. "What? why?"

"Rez, please I'll explain later." He sets his jaw but steps back. I rush to Anisa, who is pacing and fidgeting against the wall. She can't stay still.

"Anisa, what's going on?"

"I saw something I shouldn't have." She fumbles with her hands nervously as she searches the room and those around us.

"What did you see?"

"I saw Serena sleeping with one of those men with a tattoo on their necks," Anisa says in a rush.

I stare at her, puzzled. "Are you sure?" She nods her head eagerly. "Where?" I press further, but Anisa goes rigid. I track her eyesight and see Reznor walking our way quickly.

"In one of the closets upstairs. I don't want to tell him; he won't believe me." She hurries away, practically running toward Emanuel.

Great, that means I get to tell him that his lovely girlfriend is sleeping with another man. I mentally start counting a million ways this could go wrong.

"What's going on?" Reznor asks as his eyes follow Anisa's retreating figure.

"How long till the ball is over?" I ask, trying to block Anisa's exit from his eye with my body.

"People are leaving now. Everyone should be gone in thirty minutes. Why?"

"We'll talk when everyone's gone." Reznor watches me skeptically as we make our way to the exit, thanking our guests for coming.

The ballroom clears out quickly, leaving only the servants and the guards remaining in the room. The second our last guest leaves, Reznor turns to me. "What is going on?"

I look around the room, my eyes landing on Charles, Emanuel, and Anisa standing in the corner. "Serena is sleeping with one of the men with tree tattoos; a servant caught her in a closet upstairs during the ball."

"No, she isn't," he says in disbelief.

"Reznor—"

He cut me off, dismissing my words with his hand as he takes a few steps back from me. "You're really that jealous, aren't you? You're really going to lie about this? You want me to stop seeing her that bad?" His voice echoes in the room around us, servants flinching at the sound.

"Don't turn this around on me! God forbid your whore sleeps with someone besides you!" I shout back. This is one of the many things I predicted to go wrong.

"At least I was upfront about her!"

"Don't go there!" I turn away from him, starting toward the stairs. If I don't walk away now, things will only get worse. I did my part, I told him. What he does with the information is on him.

"At least I'm telling the truth!" he practically spits. "She wouldn't lie to me."

I freeze in place. "I'm trying to protect your dumbass! If she is so truthful and righteous then maybe you should marry her!" I take the ring off my finger and throw it at his face. "Make her your queen! God knows you treat her better!"

I storm up the stairs, not wanting to hear another word from his mouth. He pushed my one trigger which is trust; he thinks I'm deceiving him, when I'm actually looking out for him. I've had enough. I don't want to be married to a man who doesn't trust me. I'm not even sure if I want to try to be with him anymore.

Reznor shouts after me, but I brush him off. I hear footsteps following after me, but I know it's not him. He's too busy growling in the ballroom. He roars so loud it shakes the walls, causing pictures to tumble to the floor. Temperamental Tribrid, he should come with a warning label.

Throwing the door open, I kick off my shoes the second I stomp into the room.

"Liara?"

I whirl my head around. Anisa has tears running down her face as she hesitantly steps inside. My plan of breaking something goes out the window. "Please just help me out of this dress."

She rushes over, unlacing the dress. "I'm sorry," she cries as she quickly works her fingers against the back of the dress.

"It's not your fault," I say in an attempt to ease her guilt.

She sobs quietly as the dress finally comes unlaced. I step out of the fabric and wrap a robe around myself quickly. Another roar shakes the manor; my balcony doors shake at the force.

"You should tell him. He'll believe you if he sees…he needs to see." She gestures to the lines across my legs.

I shake my head, crossing my arms over my chest. The marks won't change anything. But what happened tonight changed everything. I won't be his arm candy any longer.

"Can you sleep in here tonight? He won't come in here if you're here." I ask her, hoping she would agree. I don't know what I will do if he barges in tonight.

"Let me go change into my nightclothes and tell Emanuel where I'll be staying." She leaves me alone, standing in the dimly lit room.

I creep to the balcony and look up at the moon. All the events of the day are running over and over in my head. How it turned this bad, along with every moment since he went out the door last night. It's all escalated since then, but this explosion was bound to happen at some point; I just hadn't expected it to happen tonight.

Chapter Fifteen: Alliances In The Woods

The next morning, Anisa wakes me up for training like last night had never happened. She cooks me breakfast, dresses me, then sends me on my way down to the field. She doesn't even react when we find that the black in my veins had spread after the fight with Reznor. It crawls completely up my back and chest, ending at the tops of my shoulders.

Walking alone across the field, I see two familiar figures conversing back and forth. Charles and Emanuel stop talking as I approach, the silence instantly becoming uncomfortable.

"I'm going to go run the trail..." Charles nods but doesn't respond to me.

I run through the trails, trying not to think about what happened at the ball last night, or the blackness in my veins. All I want is to clear my head, but my mind is working at a rate I can't keep up with. The trail ends too quickly, and I'm forced to go over to the boys. They remain silent as I walk up yet again.

I'm on the ground stretching when Charles finally speaks up. "So, are we going to talk about last night?"

I wait a moment to think about my response. "No, there's nothing to talk about. I'm not going to be disrespected like that."

Emanuel clears his throat, though he appears saddened. "Let's get to work then."

Charles puts me to work immediately. This might be the hardest he has ever pushed me in training. That, or he is mad and punishing me again. Either way, it's a brutal practice filled with fighting, boxing, and running, then more fighting. Charles and I are fighting each other under the hot sun; the chilly morning had turned to a hateful afternoon. He swings hard for my stomach, but I throw out an arm to dodge the punch. Swing. Dodge. Punch. It repeats over, and over as we move across the grass.

I land a punch, hitting him square in the jaw. "Oh, my god, I'm sorry."

Charles takes a step back, laughing deeply even as he holds his jaw. "She got you good," Emanuel cackles, holding onto his stomach as he looks at the pink mark that's already blossoming on his skin. Charles stops, then, lunges at Emanuel.

The two start to fight one another as I slide to the ground beneath a nearby tree. Closing my eyes, I listen to the two fight while I enjoy the shade of the leaves. Twisting my fingers into the grass, I twirl it around my fingers. I'm calm here, and now underneath the tree, and for the first time that day, my brain actually stops thinking. I'm just here sitting under a tree, playing with the grass.

It's pleasant until it's ruined.

I smell him before I see him. The moment his scent hits my nose, it feels like my body is covered in fire. I refuse to open my eyes as I hear him approach. The boys cease their fighting as Reznor calls out. I can't focus on what he's saying. I'm too busy trying to control the invisible flames that dance along my skin. My body is calling to him, begging for him.

There is some shuffling followed by a whining voice. It's like nails screeching on a chalkboard.

My eyes snap open instantly. Standing across the field is Serena. The rush of anger is immediate, my grip on the grass tightening as she calls for Reznor, yet her eyes are locked on me. Her fear is palpable as her gaze focuses on my eyes, then tracks to my hand.

"Liara…" Reznor calls hesitantly.

My gaze shifts to him, both he and the boys are focused on my hands also. What had once been grass is now ash.

"Liara," he calls again. When his eyes meet mine, lightning strikes in the distance as the wind picks up speed.

"You don't learn, do you? Or maybe you just can't take a hint," I snap as I drop the ash from my hands, watching it blow away in the wind.

"We need to talk." Reznor glances over his shoulder toward the redhead then back at me.

I shake my head. "We don't have anything to talk about."

Reznor sets his jaw. "Really? Because your eyes just turned dark grey; you don't think we should talk about that, huh?"

"Then why is she here?" I throw my arm toward the sparingly dressed redhead, who twinkles her fingers back in response. The action has me rising from the ground; I'm ready to cross the field and pummel her.

Reznor notices, appearing before me in what seems like a second, he takes me by the arm. I wasn't prepared for the touch; I fumble slightly as he steers me toward the tree line. Even Reznor seems surprised by the force of the bond because the second we are deep enough inside, he practically throws my arm from his grip.

"What is going on with the bond?" he hisses, shaking his hand.

"I don't know. I could smell you from halfway across the field." I didn't mean for it to sound disgusted, but it comes out that way.

"It shouldn't be this strong." Reznor stuffs his hands in his pockets. "Does it hurt?"

"Does what hurt?" I'm suddenly panicked that Anisa told him about the marks. She had been rather adamant about it last night.

He sets his jaw. "When I'm not touching you, but near you, it physically hurts me. I take it that doesn't happen to you."

I shake my head, averting my eyes. "But when I'm around you, I have the overwhelming need to be touching you, or be closer to you." I cross my arms over my chest, trying to close myself off from him even more. I focus on a rock near my boot. Yep, this bond is more trouble than it's worth.

"The bond's getting stronger for some reason. I don't know why, but it is. I almost marked you the other night. My fangs came out, and I couldn't stop them, so I left."

"That's why you left?" I'm puzzled by his sudden confession. Last night, I called off our engagement, so he decides now's the time to let me in?

"Yeah, trust me, I didn't want to leave, but I had to, or I would have marked you, and everything would have been ruined."

I chuckle to myself; everything was ruined last night. "They take this marking stuff seriously, don't they?"

"When it's between a king and queen, yes. It's the final part of fusing the bond, and marriage." Reznor takes a slow step toward me but doesn't take another when I speak.

"Well, I gave you your freedom, might as well go enjoy yourself," I say bitterly as I turn away from him, but he reaches out and stops me.

"I didn't want freedom from you, Liara." He's starting to struggle with his words, "If I didn't want you, or want this bond, I would have never brought you from the human world." He draws in a deep breath, his eyes flashing between red and blue.

"You have a funny way of showing it, Reznor." I pause, contemplating my next words. "You didn't want to come to get me remember? Ever since I've been here, things just keep getting worse. We *keep* getting worse."

"I don't care for people in that way. It clouds my head, and as you pointed out, brings them danger. I haven't cared for someone like that in hundreds of years. Having someone in that way makes them a target in my world. People are trying to kill you already, and we aren't even married yet!"

"Not to mention your girlfriend is sleeping with one of them."

Reznor stiffens, taking another deep breath. "We aren't going to solve anything if you don't let me apologize. If you want space, then say the word, and you won't see me until the ceremony, but I don't think that will solve anything."

"What I want is for you to actually look into what I told you. I never said I didn't want to see you. I enjoy being around you when you aren't being a prick. Plus, last I checked, I ended our engagement if you can even call it that."

"If I do this, we'll get married, you'll go through with everything?" he asks, stepping closer to me. He's so close I feel like I should take a step back…but I don't.

"I should say no, Reznor, last night…it shouldn't be like this."

"I know Liara, I'm sorry, I never intended for any of this to happen. I never meant to stay with her this long or for things to be this difficult for us." He reaches for me but drops his hands as his shoulders sag.

I'm not sure what to make of his admission, but I know I left my world for him. I left literally *everything* for him. He can have his one last shot. "If you look into what I said, then yes I'll go along with everything." I hurriedly add a witty comment to try and release some of the tension. "Up until this point, I've been rather compliant if I do say so myself."

He laughs, scoffing slightly. "That is simply not true. Last night was anything but compliant."

My lips turn up into a smirk quickly. "I was, too. I wore a dress, I went, I mingled."

"Ah, yes, that dress." Red flashes behind his eyes, the simple action exciting me.

"Did you like it?"

"I did, you looked beautiful. But I would have rather if everyone hadn't seen that much of your breasts. You also avoided me for most of the night."

I take a step forward, poking his chest. "Ah, ah, ah, you deserved that. You came home and fraternized with Serena all day then expected me to hang off your arm all evening. Plus, I could have acted a lot worse, I could have tackled her to the floor, or drug her out by her hair, but I didn't." I wait a moment before adding my final demand. "I did change my mind on one thing. You keep sleeping with her, and I'm done with all of this: no wedding, no ceremony, no marking, no me, I'd rather decay in the mortal world than watch you be with her. I don't trust her, Reznor, and I don't want her around you, or hurting you."

He pulls me flush against him. "She means nothing to me; you need to know that. I'd choose you over her a million times a day." He brushes some of my stray hairs back. "But how do you know about that?"

I'm so focused on the sensation from his touch, and his declaration of choosing me, that I nearly forget he asked me a question. "The bond," I mumble while I trace the pocket over his chest with my finger lazily. "So do we have a deal, Your Majesty?"

"You don't get to call me that, I'm your king, and you will be my queen. But yes, we have a deal." Digging through his pocket, he pulls out the engagement ring, sliding it on my finger slowly. "I am already investigating what you told me. Her being out here is only part of the plan." He smirks at my gaping mouth.

"Was last night part of the plan?"

"No, last night was real, unfortunately…" His thumb brushes against my cheek bone. "The more I thought about it, the more I realized it's a possibility. I'm sorry about last night, Liara, I shouldn't have said any of that. I never meant to hurt you; my rage just took over."

I smile meekly up at him, reaching up, brushing back a lock of his black hair. "We can work on that big guy. Starting with proving I'm right about Serena, then we can do anger management together. I wouldn't lie to you, especially about this. Not when these people have attacked you, too."

He completely brushes off my anger management dig. "If you're right, I will definitely make it up to you. *Only* if you're right."

"So, what is this plan?"

"It's something that only Emanuel and I know, and I'm not telling it to you for your safety. It has nothing to do with trust; it's about protecting you."

"Alright, but if you need my help, I'll do whatever I can."

"What I need is for you to storm out of here like I pissed you off. Yell at me and make it good."

Now, this is something I can do easily.

Smiling brightly, I step out of his grasp, only to be pulled back immediately. Reznor ducks his head down, kissing me softly. It's quick. One second, his lips are there, then the next, they aren't.

"I'm sorry Liara, truly."

I turn away as a blush creeps to my cheeks, but I shove it down. Setting my jaw instantly, I take on the persona of an angry person, which isn't hard for me.

"You're a fucking asshole!" I bellow, stomping back onto the field.

"And you're overdramatic!" he yells back. "Make her train the rest of the day!" he screams so loud birds fly from the trees. Serena is overjoyed at the outburst of anger from Reznor. She's even more pleased when the second he's close enough, he pulls her against him possessively.

The pain is immediate, but I'm prepared for it. Keeping a composed face, I politely give them the finger.

Both boys look at me with gaping mouths. "What?"

They glance at each other before taking a step back in unison.

"Calm down, guys." I try to give them a smile, but they step back again.

"You're not going to try and strike us with lightning again?"

"No promises." I give a wink for a little razzle dazzle.

"Oh, this is going to be bad," Emanuel groans.

The brutal assault that's called training, continues through the rest of the evening. By the time it's over, I'm limping back to the manor in the pitch blackness of the night. We had trained long past dinner, and this action has its consequences. I have blisters on the back of my feet, on my hands, and even have bruises cascading my body. Charles and Emanuel look beaten, but not as beaten as me.

I wince with every step as I climb up the stairs. The brief moment of relief when I step off the top step fades when I see my bedroom door has been torn off. The thought of calling for help is immediately dismissed when I creep closer to the room; it has been utterly demolished. The door is snapped off the hinges, the table is broken, the fridge on its side, the bed torn with deep slashes through the mattress. The room is in ruins. Carefully I step around the broken glass when there is a shuffling from the closet.

I freeze when a smash of glass rings out.

"My Gods what happened here?" Anisa sputters from outside my room.

I try to hush her, but it's no use. She's already alerted the intruder. The man in all black comes rushing from the closet, attempting to strike me. I block it, but with my weakened body, it isn't successful. Flipping me onto my back, I use my powers to send him flying across the room.

Reznor! I shout through the bond as I scramble off the floor, but the man recovers just as quickly. He advances on me again. I'm quick to stop his advances, taking him to his knees. I had used abilities so much today that again, I'm not as strong as I should be. Even with the force of my magic, he's climbing to his feet again. Glancing around the room, I look for anything I can use as a weapon. I find a large piece of wood from the table and whack the man upside the head with the board. Once. Twice. Swinging for a third, he snatchers it, breaking it across his knees.

Shit.

Reznor, I know you're busy with your plan, but I need help! I shout down the bond as I resort to scrambling away from him toward the kitchen where I spot a knife on the floor. I dive for it while praying help will get here in time. The second I grasp the knife, he snags my foot, dragging me back. I roll onto my back, hurling my other foot into his face. He falters as my foot cracks his nose but doesn't release my foot. I thrash out, trying to dig my knife into him, but he quickly gets on top of me, pinning me to the floor. He reaches for my knife that's trapped in my pinned hand. Before he can pry it from my hand, he's ripped from atop of me. Reznor has the man by the neck in a hold with an arm wrapped beneath his head. Reznor eyes the knife in my hand, then nods.

I rise from the ground then drive the knife into the man without thinking twice. I stab him in the heart, twisting to ensure it's a killing blow.

Once I pull the knife from his chest, Reznor throws his body to the floor. He reaches out for me as he assesses me from head to toe for injuries, but my eyes remain glued to the bloody knife in my hand. I carelessly drop my hand, allowing the blade to fall to the floor as Reznor tilts my face to look up at him.

"Are you alright?" he asks.

"Holy shit, I just killed someone." I wipe my bloodied hands on my pants. I intentionally avoid the question as I'm not sure how I feel. I'm not really upset, and that seems like it should be an issue.

"What happened?"

I hadn't even noticed until now that he's slowly leading me out of the room. "I came back from training, and I saw the mess. I had only crept inside when I heard the crash from the closet. Anisa had just gotten there when he came out of the closet. I tried to take him down, but it wasn't working, and well, you know the rest."

Reznor swears angrily. "You're staying with me from now on. Anisa have the other servants pack up her clothes, move them by tomorrow. Grab her something to sleep in tonight and bring it to my room. I'm done taking chances."

I stare at him, startled by his decision. "What?" I croak out, but he's too busy ordering the staff and the guards to answer my question. If I stay with him, he will see the blackness that runs along my body. But there is no changing his mind. This wasn't part of his plan, and with our enemies within the walls, he isn't risking it. Reznor also must think he is slick as he whisks me away from the room as they prepare to move the body.

He takes me across the manor, and I mean *across* the manor. My room is the farthest point in the house from him. The doors leading into his room tower over both of us with large symbols engraved into the doors, six different ones on each side.

Reznor pushes them open, allowing me to enter the dimly lit space. His room isn't as modernized as mine had been. A colossal bed sits in the center of the wall with black bedding. The walls are a dark grey with a large fireplace opposite of the bed. A grey couch sits in front of the fireplace along with a drink cart. The one thing that immediately catches my eye is the large windows near the bed, but they look fake. The last interesting feature is a doorway that leads to his closet, yet there is no door to the closet, which leads to a large open bathroom…with no door. He's going to see the marks sooner or later. This is not going to end well for me.

"I'm going to go see Emanuel. Anisa will bring you some clothes to sleep in." Reznor tugs on his hair anxiously.

"Was this the plan?" I rub up my arms and they ache back in response.

"No, this was not the plan…but this changes things. They got inside, they knew where your room *was*," he hisses angrily, his eyes flaring red.

"What do we do?"

Reznor looks at me, smiling suggestively, "We get creative." He takes careful steps toward me. "If it is her, I know exactly how to bring it out of her, and I'm going to need your help to do so."

I return his look as I also take a step toward him. "What exactly does that require?"

He slowly drags his hands down my side, smiling as he does so. "It's going to take a lot of touching," he whispers in my ear, his lips slightly brushing it as he speaks.

I shiver, and shake my head disapprovingly, taking a step back from his grasp. I need the space to think clearly. "I like the way you think; she can have a taste of her own medicine."

Reznor smiles brightly, but he doesn't get to respond thanks to a small knock on the door. He lingers a moment before stepping away to open it. Anisa stands with her head bowed, her gaze focused on the floor.

"Anisa, you'll be allowed to enter freely now since I have invited you in. Do so wisely," Reznor warns before stepping out of the room, shooting me a wink before closing the door.

"What does he mean you can enter freely?" I ask Anisa as she walks in, carrying a small bag.

"His room is warded. You can't enter unless he opens the door and invites you in. Only four people have been invited into this room." My face is asking the question for me because she continues, "Kora, his servant, Morana, me, and now, you." Anisa scans the room for a moment, quickly finding the bathroom.

She stays in the room as I shower quickly, then she dresses me in one of the few long nightgowns I have. She even brought a sweater to help cover the marks on my shoulders. I'm beyond thankful, and again, she came through for me without question. We don't speak as she walks me back out into the bedroom. She bids me goodnight then leaves me alone with my thoughts. Questions are a better way to put it. How did it come to this? How would Reznor and I do living in the same room? What happens now? Will this help things or make things worse?

I climb into the bed, not wanting to think or drill myself with questions any further. The sheets are cool against my skin, but it's the smell of Reznor lingering on the sheets that calms me down. I'm sore, exhausted, and mentally and physically drained, but none of those things matter as I allow myself to soak in his scent and drift to sleep before Reznor even returns to the room.

Chapter Sixteen: The Moon Is Rising

I wake up wrapped in Reznor's arms, securely pressed against his bare chest. The moment my eyes open, I feel the goosebumps that rise wherever he touches me. I glance around and realize my shoulder is exposed, revealing the black. Slowly, I reach back and tug the sweater into place, sighing in relief that the black marks are now hidden.

Reznor has a single arm behind my back, the other thrown behind his head. Laying my head back against his chest, he rustles and pulls me closer to him, but he remains asleep. It's still early in the morning; it's almost too easy to fall back asleep.

The next time I wake up, I'm alone, but not for long due to my guardian angel Anisa coming through the door. She gets me dressed then eats breakfast with me in the garden. After that, Charles and Emanuel accompany me to the forest, where we walk deeper than I've ever been into the beautiful woods. They want me to leave my scent in the forest for Reznor to chase because tonight, the full moon is rising.

The boys keep the conversation light, but they both seem anxious. "What is going on?" I ask as I stop to lean against a tree

"Nothing." Charles not so casually scans the tree line.

"Okay, now you have to tell me. What is going on?"

This time, Emanuel glances at Charles then at me before sighing deeply. "Reznor has no idea we're out here, and when he finds out, it's not going to end well."

It takes me a moment to realize why. What he really means is Reznor doesn't know where *I* am. Rubbing my eyes in annoyance, I ask, "Where exactly does he think we are?"

Charles chuckles loudly as Emanuel continues. "He thinks we have you in the study while he is at his meeting."

"And when does this meeting get out?" I push off the tree, walking toward the two men.

Charles opens his mouth to speak but is cut off when a roar echoes through the trees. I shiver at the sound as it pierces my ears. He's angry.

"Now." Charles scratches the back of his head, flinching at the mighty roar.

"You better tell him where we are." I cross my arms as I continue strolling through the trees.

"No, you just need to pick up the pace. This will keep him distracted tonight, so you don't accidentally end up marked and mated before the ceremony." Emanuel motions for me to move faster. I'm too sore to run, but we all briskly walk deeper into the forest, the boys flinching every so often.

It isn't until we're nearly out of the woods when Reznor appears, halting in front of us. He has been running, and by the looks of it, he has been running a long time. He grabs Charles and Emanuel by the collars of their shirts, slamming them into a nearby tree. The boys don't even try to defend themselves as Reznor yells at them for disobeying his commands. I step in when it looks like he's going to kill Charles for his snide comment about Reznor's 'separation anxiety.'

I hurry over, placing a hand on his arm. "Rez," I say his name in such a low and calm voice it sounds like a whisper. He shivers at my touch on his bare forearm. Snapping his head in my direction, his eyes are completely red. Even his canines protrude from his gums.

He lets go of the boys, dropping them to the ground with a thud, then he pulls me to his chest where he wraps his arms around me as if he is trying to protect me from anything and everything. Without saying another word, he leads me out of the woods and back to the manor with Charles and Emanuel sulking behind us like lost puppies.

Reznor is still livid, even now as he paces in his study. He is pacing so much it's starting to make me anxious. I quickly stand up, blocking him from moving any further. "Sit." I point to the armchair closest to him.

He rolls his eyes but complies. He sits for a moment and tries to get up. I quickly move, placing myself in his lap. "I'm not moving till you calm down." I say, while I try to move as little as possible.

Reznor goes stiff the moment I sit down but recovers quickly, snaking an arm around my waist, dragging me closer to him. Charles chuckles distantly from across the room causing Reznor's eyes to flash red.

"Will you cut it out? Now is not the time to be doing this." I try to reason with Charles, who only holds his hands up in surrender. Reznor's hand grips my waist, but I ignore it. "What's the plan for tonight?" I ask anyone that will answer.

"You're going to stay in my room, hoping that my scent will mask yours. Emanuel and Charles will stand guard outside. Everyone else thinks you're staying in a cabin at the edge of my territory. I'm hoping I stay outside long enough to not start things."

Charles breaks into a fit of laughter at Reznor's fumble in words.

"I will keep him in check, Sir." Emanuel swats Charles behind the head. "We will take the decoy to the cabin." Emanuel practically shoves Charles out of the room.

Reznor hitches both of my legs across his lap, cradling me against him. He begins tracing the seam of my pants that run along the outside of my leg. Slowly, his thumb takes its place as he strokes my thigh. "You wore a lot of layers to bed last night."

I raise an eyebrow at him. "And?"

"I recall, the last time we shared a room, that wasn't the case." He smirks wickedly, his dimples peeking from his cheeks.

"Well, last time we shared a room, you almost marked me. I figured it was better safe than sorry." A strand of his hair had fallen loose, and I can't resist the urge to tuck it back. It quickly turns to me just playing with his hair. He leans his head into my touch, which encourages me further. "Do I get to see this mighty wolf that you turn into?" I ask, but the moment the words leave my mouth, he freezes again.

"I don't think you will want to see that. It's more of a beast than a wolf." He stills his thumb on my thigh.

"But can I see it if I want to?"

He shakes his head slowly. "I would rather you not see me that way. It might scare you…"

I grip the back of his head, turning him to look at me. "If you don't want me to see it, you can just say no, but you haven't scared me yet."

He appears deep in thought for a moment before glancing back up at me. "I don't want you to see me like that, so it's a no…for now."

I smile at him softly. This is such a change of pace for us, but it's welcoming. We can spend more than five minutes together without wanting to annoy the other.

"I have to get ready for the moon, want to come?" he asks as he carefully lifts me from his lap.

"Sure, but first, pick me out a book to read tonight while you're out."

Reznor combs through the shelves before he grins, pulling a deep purple colored book from the shelf. "I don't know if you'll be able to understand it all, but read this one tonight. It's one of my mother's favorites."

I take the smooth book into my hand, then he takes my other hand in his before we walk back to his bedroom. I lounge on the bed as Reznor goes to the closest, and that's when I notice the ceiling. It's painted like a starry night with a crescent moon amongst the clouds and stars. The moon has a constellation right below, matching the one that sits on my neck.

"I was wondering when you would notice that," he comments, striding back into the room wearing black sweatpants. He has another pair along with a hoodie in his hand.

"What is it?" I ask, admiring the artwork.

"It's the Nightlighter constellation. Morana painted it when I was younger to focus on my future as I slept. I never had the heart to cover it up because she is so damn proud of it."

"It's beautiful, I don't blame her."

Reznor nods in agreement, waltzing over to the bed while pulling a white shirt over his head along the way. "Wear this tonight. It might help mask your scent with mine." Reznor hands me the black hoodie.

When I break into a burst of laughter, he looks at me quizzically. I slide the large hoodie over my head before elaborating, "In the mortal world, giving a girl your hoodie is a big deal."

"Humans." He rolls his eyes, but I catch the small grin that lights up his face for a second.

He moves around the room, stretching and preparing for the moon. The closer it gets to dark, the more anxious he becomes. Abruptly he jumps up and walks over to the bed, grabbing the pants from the mattress. "All right, I have to go now." He pauses, turning to me slowly. "Liara, please stay in the room tonight. You won't have to put up with this much longer, but I need you to do this for me."

"I will, I promise. Be careful tonight."

Reznor turns to face me, welcoming me into his arms. "You're worrying about me now?" he asks cockily, with his lips tugging upward.

Raising my shoulders dismissively, "I mean, it's possible, but not in a trash manor kind of way."

Reznor chuckles deeply. "That's playing dirty."

"Hey, I just needed to even the score, baby." I can't hold back the devilish look on my face, which he quickly mirrors. The gods knew what they were doing when they paired us together.

Reznor leans down, quickly kissing me, beckoning me closer, tugging on my hips till we're flush. Our lips move against each other's, but I feel the shiver ripple through his body, moments before he pulls back, loosening his grip.

"I have to go now, it's time. I'll see you in a bit." He leans down, pecking a kiss on my lips one more time, then he's gone.

I'm halfway through the novel when a bang sounds from the door. I creep forward slowly, but then I hear Charles' voice call out.

"Liara, open the door, we need you!" Charles whispers loudly.

"What's going on?" I ask, pushing the door open further to talk to them.

"Reznor is in trouble, the Tree People are in the forest; they're hunting him. We need to lure him out of the woods. It's a lot easier to injure him in this form, and he is too far away from the manor for us to get guards to him in time," Emanuel says frantically.

"They already took out a set of our guards," Charles adds as he glances down the hallway.

"Okay, what's the plan?" I ask, shutting the door behind me.

"It's late enough that he can turn into his human form now, but you still will have to be careful with him. The urges of his beast will still be there since he wasn't able to run long." Emanuel leads the way with his sword drawn as he stalks ahead, leaving Charles lingering at my side. "First, you're going to need to call out to him, then you're going to have to take his hoodie off and stand outside with us. He is going to need to smell your scent. Shake your hair out and move, do whatever you can."

"Emanuel and I will watch guard, but we need to get him back here quickly. You may have to cut yourself; your blood will draw him near, but that is a last resort," Charles adds quietly as we creep through the manor. We come out the back of the manor at the large courtyard that leads directly to the woods. At the bottom of the steps sit the stack of clothes Reznor had earlier.

"Okay, take the hoodie off and call out to him," Emanuel says as he surveys the area.

Without the hoodie, the cold air bites at my skin, but I push my focus on calling out to Reznor.

Reznor, come back.

Reznor, come back to the manor.

Reznor, they're following you, be careful. Rez come back to the manor.

I call out to him over and over in my head, but nothing comes back through the bond. "He isn't responding, now what?" My concern starts to grow as the seconds pass, my skin starts crawling, my heart beating louder in my ears.

"Shake your hair out, jump around, do something to get your scent out there," Emanuel suggests. I reach behind my head, pulling down my hair from its braid, raking my hair out with my hands. I shake my clothes and jump, but still nothing.

Gunshots come from the forest, and my stomach drops. I yank a knife from Charles's belt and slice the palm of my hand open. It isn't big, but it's deep enough that blood starts to pool down my fingers. "Reznor!" I shout.

Silence.

Then, off in the distance, a howl is heard, and a few minutes later, the sound of something large heading our way.

Emanuel quickly wraps my hand with a cloth he pulls from his pocket. The thrashing in the woods comes closer and closer until a large black wolf appears from the tree line. With fur black as night and eyes a fiery red, a growl erupts from its throat as its eyes watch me intently.

I admire the large wolf as he stalks toward the house. He's massive, easily the size of a large SUV, with long, muscular legs and razor-sharp teeth. Then, in a clash of fur and skin, he's suddenly Reznor again. Well, Reznor with red eyes. Emanuel and Charles both jump in front of me simultaneously as he tugs on the black pants.

"Move," he growls.

Emanuel and Charles bow their heads, stepping away from me immediately. He picks me up, wrapping my legs around his waist. "I thought I told you to stay in the room?" he snarls, carrying me toward the house. I don't dare say anything; instead, I just hold onto him, allowing him to take me right to his bedroom.

"Rez..." I say hesitantly as he slams the door shut behind us, still effortlessly carrying me in his arms.

"I thought I told you to stay in the room," he growls again as he crawls onto the bed with me still wrapped around his waist.

"They were hunting you, what else—" I'm cut off by his lips on mine as he pushes my back into the mattress, hovering over me. The kiss is needy, and hungry, as his mouth claims every inch of mine. Our tongues clash against each other as Reznor's hands roam my body. I tug him closer by the back of his neck. One of Reznor's hands move to my butt while the other continues to roam my chest.

He breaks the kiss, only to begin kissing down my neck. I try not to moan when I feel his calloused hand touch the bare skin of my back. It sets small fires across my skin, causing my back to arch into his touch. He growls into my neck before abruptly flipping us over, placing me on his lap. He crashes his lips against mine once again, taking a fistful of my hair in the process. He tugs my head back by my hair, baring the column of my throat.

His canines graze the soft flesh. "Rez," I try to warn, but it ends up sounding more like a moan.

A growl escapes him before he reconnects our lips. He tugs me closer, dragging me until our hips press together. A muffled moan escapes my lips from the sudden pressure between us. Reznor breaks the kiss, tugging my shirt off my head, and I don't have time to stop him. He's too fast. His eyes go wide as they take in the sight of my black filled veins.

Chapter Seventeen: Illness

"What is this?" Reznor asks, his voice too calm.

I fumble, trying to get off him and cover myself up, but he holds me in place. "It's nothing," I try to reason, reaching for my shirt, but he refuses to let me do so.

"This isn't nothing, Liara! It looks like tar in your veins!" Reznor argues as he gently touches one of the black lines running through my skin. We both shudder at the feeling, goosebumps erupting across my flesh. The bond is calling for more, especially now with us pressed so close together.

Averting my eyes, I focus on anything but Reznor; his scrutinizing gaze is enough to make me want to crawl within myself. Reznor groans as he hands me my shirt. I scramble off his lap, hurrying to cover myself.

He strides to the door and shouts for someone to get Anisa.

"Reznor no, she isn't a part of this." I jump up, moving to block the doorway. "Please leave her out of this."

Reznor's eyes flash red. "No, if you're not going to give me answers, she will."

"Rez…"

Anisa arrives at the doorway before I can try to persuade him to leave her out of it. She had been asleep. it's still evident by the look in her eye and her disheveled hair. She quickly bows her head. "You called for me, sir?"

Reznor's hands flexed before placing them on his hips. He's still furious. "Do you want to tell me anything, Anisa?" Reznor asks, raising his voice slightly.

She doesn't speak. She only looks at me, sheepishly.

"Something along the lines of something on her body?" he yells, losing his temper again.

I stand in front of Anisa protectively. "I told her not to tell you. This isn't her fault." Already Anisa looks as if she's going to cry at any moment.

"You're admitting she knew?"

"Yes, but I told her not to tell anyone. This is not her fault. If you want to blame someone, blame me."

Reznor digs his hand into his hair, tugging on it. "What is it?"

I'm not sure who he's asking, but I answer, so Anisa doesn't have to. "I don't know… it just showed up one night." It's true I don't know what it is, but I know Reznor will not accept this answer.

"Liara, this is a big deal!" he snaps with his back to me. He really is trying to compose himself. "When did it show up?" he asks, turning back around quickly. My eyes drop to the floor, feeling guilty and sick to my stomach just thinking back to the memory.

"The last full moon is when it showed up, but it got worse the night she had the incident in the closet." Anisa answers for me, breaking under the pressure of the powerful gaze of her king.

"This has been going on for a month!"

"Yes," Anisa answers again.

Reznor's chest starts heaving with anger as he storms toward the closet. Anisa and I both stare at each other with confusion as he sulks away.

"How did he find out?" Anisa asks me quietly.

"One thing led to another is how it happened. He and I have got to stop kissing; every time we do something happens!"

Anisa puckers her lips, looking at me in surprise. Then a chuckle falls from her mouth. She slaps a hand to her face, attempting to smother the laugh. I open my mouth to say something but stop when my name is called.

"Liara, come here," Reznor hollers from the closet.

Anisa, and I glance at each other before I slowly walk into the closet. "Get dressed in fresh clothes, we're going to see Morana." He's gripping the edge of the dresser so hard his knuckles are turning white. "Why didn't you tell me?" he asks, keeping his back to me as I take off the shirt, replacing it with a long-sleeved purple blouse that ties in a bow behind my back.

"Because I didn't know what it was, and I didn't want to cause any more problems."

"Liara, if you don't tell me things, I can't fix them or help you." Reznor's voice softens as he turns to face me.

"I know, I'm sorry. Honestly, I was hoping it would just go away, but it only got worse here recently." I focus on the ground, hearing him shuffle towards me.

Reznor kisses the top of my head, taking my hand in his. "Well, let's go get some answers."

We arrive at Morana's just as the sun rises, and even though it's early, Morana sits on her porch in her favorite rocking chair. She seems to be the only one awake in the town of Nightsend.

"Reznor!" Morana is positively beaming as she pulls him into an embrace the moment he's out of the car. "I'm so happy to see you."

Reznor chuckles as he holds her. "Morana, you just saw me a few days ago."

I can't stop my smile as I watch the pair—Reznor's tall figure looming over the short woman in a tight embrace. She's like a mother to him, and he like her son.

"As much as I love seeing you, I assume you have a reason for this early trip?" she asks, removing her arms from him only to wrap them around me. "It's good to see you again, love." I laugh and hug her. Reznor watches us, or better words would be, he gawks at us.

"There is something you need to see. You're the only person I could think of who would know anything."

Morana looks between us suspiciously. "Alright, let's get inside then."

I trail after Morana, but Reznor lingers outside to speak to Charles and Emanuel. Leaving Morana and I alone in the foyer, she tsks before pulling me by the hand further into the house.

"How have you been, dear?" she asks, pouring me a cup of tea in the kitchen.

"Good, mostly, how about you?" I ask as I survey the kitchen, seeing it has been repaired completely.

"I'm wonderful, especially now that you two are here. I see you two have improved since I last saw you."

Nervous laughter erupts from my throat. If only she knew, I wouldn't call what happened back in his bedroom improvement. Luckily Reznor chooses that moment to bless us with his presence and prevents me from explaining.

"Alright, let's see this thing you speak of," Morana says, leaning against the counter.

Reznor peers at me, clearly, he's not going to explain.

He's useless. I lift up my shirt, showing Morana my abdomen, letting my body do the explaining for me.

She gasps, touching my skin. "My Gods, I haven't seen this in years! How bad is it?" she asks me, but Reznor looks as if he wants to know the same thing.

"Well, I can't strip in front of him to show you."

"That means it's advanced," Morana mutters, practically dragging me to her study where I show her all of it. She continues to gasp and curse as she examines me, only to storm to the door to shout for Reznor. I scramble to put my clothes back on, barely getting my pants buttoned before he comes barging in.

"You and that stupid whore!" Morana shouts while slapping Reznor with her cane.

Reznor swats away her next hit. "Morana, what are you talking about?"

"She has the mating illness," she hisses, slapping him upside the head in disapproval.

"Morana, I don't even know what that is," he argues, looking at me, but I have no answers for him.

"It's an illness that can force the body to reject the mate bond!" she shouts angrily, digging through her cabinet. "It's bad too. The marks are all the way up her back and almost all the way down her legs. Poor girl, I'm surprised she didn't tell you sooner. The pain is unbearable."

Reznor's head whirls in my direction, and I quickly turn my head to the wall. It works for a moment until he stands directly in front of me.

"The illness is stimulated from when the mate is with another. It allows the mate to know of infidelity. By the looks of it, you and Serena are still sleeping together," Morana snarls, still digging through the cabinet.

"Liara, why didn't you tell me?" he asks once again, trying to keep the anger out of his voice, but there is a hint of hurt that lingers.

"You wanted time. I was trying to give you time," I babble trying to defend myself.

"That's how you knew at Greensboro," He pauses, then adds, "and at the ball!" His head drops. Now he's the one avoiding my eye.

"You're a strong girl, Liara, because that is probably the worst case I have ever seen. How did you manage the pain?" Morana asks as she mixes some herbs at her desk.

"I didn't. I just went through it, but this last time, I passed out for most of it."

Reznor remains silent in the corner of the room.

"You two are lucky. She was one more time away from you either being forced to mark her through the intensity of the bond or her body rejecting you completely," Morana says the words so casually it hurts. "Did you two not feel the bond intensifying?" She acts like it's the most common explanation.

"We didn't know why it got stronger. Hell, I was practically forcing myself to sleep with Serena so I wouldn't mark Liara early," Reznor speaks up from the corner of the room, looking disgusted.

I'm not sure how I feel about that comment. Good, or bad? I don't know.

"Well, that can't happen anymore. She needs to drink this once every day at bedtime, but you two have got to spend as much time together as possible. Touching each other frequently will help the bond rebuild on its own. Now I'm not saying have sex or mark her, but just be near each other as much as possible. Skin to skin contact helps."

My face reddens at the thought of her reminding me of my grams—the last person I'd want knowing about my sex life.

"The herbal solution should help speed things up. It will cause the illness to recede from her skin. Keep an eye on it, and I do mean both of you. If it suddenly starts spreading, come back immediately."

Morana hands me a large glass bottle with a black liquid that shimmers. "Just a cap full each night. This is strong from the olden days and be wary of the side effects." Morana smiles at me, "Will you give me a moment alone with Reznor?"

A sweet smile I don't believe in the slightest, but I walk out of the room, shutting the door behind me. As I'm retreating, I catch Morana say, "Reznor, what is going on? She is finally here, and you let her develop the mate illness. What's the matter with you? You both could have died!"

With that, I retire quickly to the front porch, waiting with Emanuel and Charles. I try to give them a reassuring smile but neither seem to buy it.

"Are you going to tell us, or do we need to wait for Reznor?" Emanuel asks, crossing his arms.

"I have the mating illness." They return confused facial expressions. I flash them a small portion of my stomach, just enough for the black marks to be seen.

"Gods!" Emanuel exclaims, but Charles's face washes with realization.

"That day on the field, it wasn't cramps, was it?"

I shake my head as I fiddle with the bottom of my flowing shirt. I'm starting to realize I should have told someone a while ago. But I can't change the past.

"What does it mean?" Emanuel takes a seat next to me in a matching rocking chair.

"It means Reznor, and I are going to be spending a lot more time together." I don't mean for it to sound so somber, but my voice holds sadness. I'm taking away the time he asked for, and I feel guilty for it. Once again, I've shaken his world.

"Well, that's good at least. You guys can get to know each other better, maybe you can cool out the hothead," Charles teases.

"And who is the hothead?" Reznor appears suddenly.

Charles' face transforms into a boyish smile. Reznor rolls his eyes in annoyance, "Let's go." He takes my hand, walking me to the SUV. He's fuming; I can feel it. I don't say a word. I'm not about to fight with him in front of the boys. Not over this, and certainly not here.

Reznor opens the door for me with his jaw set, still avoiding my eyes. I know what this means, so I'm not entirely surprised when he gets in the driver's seat while Emanuel sits with me once again. I have to hold in my laugh as he mouths me an apology. I've grown used to pissing off Reznor, although I know this time is different due to the severity of the situation. If my body had rejected him, a lot of things could, and would have gone wrong. Not just for me but for us.

When we get back to the manor, I practically leap from the car, hoping to get inside before Reznor. Or rather, to someone who can keep me away from him. I know a fight is coming, but I'm going to put it off, if possible.

Luckily, Anisa is waiting at the front of the manor for our arrival. I briskly trot up the stairs to her, gripping her outreached hand. "Do you know what it is?" she asks in a low voice, not wanting others to hear.

"It's called the mating illness." I try to guide her somewhere else before Reznor catches up, but she isn't taking a hint. I didn't get to elaborate further as I watch Anisa's face pale and her eyes dart to the ground. Seconds later, an arm slides around my waist. Tingles work their way across my back.

Shit.

"Anisa, why don't you go work on things for the wedding? I need a word with Liara." Reznor's face remains impassive. He doesn't allow her time to respond or for me to object.

He takes me straight to his bedroom. The moment he shuts the door, he leans against it with his finger splayed against the dark wood. I wait for him to say anything, but he's silent until I feel like I'm going to explode with anticipation.

He slowly turns to face me. "I need to see it, all of it."

I go to speak, only opening my mouth, but he stops me.

"You didn't tell me about it, or how bad it was. Now, I need to see it so I can monitor it since I can't trust you to tell me yourself."

A pang of guilt strikes me in the stomach, and I frown slightly. Still, I nod, undressing until I'm down to my undergarments.

He stalks toward me, walking around, looking at the black marks all over my skin. "Do you realize how serious this is, Liara?"

"I do now." I cross my arms, attempting to cover myself, feeling ashamed.

Reznor abruptly takes a step forward, his eyes flashing red. "I doubt that because if you did, you would have told me a month ago!"

"Look you're not the easiest person to talk to. I'm sorry, but there isn't anything we can do about that now."

Reznor stares down at the marks again, his face a pool of emotions. "You could have died, Liara. I could have died from this. Mates don't live long without the other. We both could have died because you won't tell me things."

"I didn't want to burden you any further. The first time I met you, I was almost ready to leave based on our encounter in the dining room. You wanted time, so I was giving it to you. I will not take all the blame when it comes to this mess."

"Liara, I brought you here. You haven't been a burden to me. I want you here, I just didn't want to have to give in to everything else. I have spent my entire life doing what I'm supposed to because of this fucking curse!"

I process his words, thinking of what to say as he walks away from me. "Then what do you want to do? If you want to break the bond, we—"

He storms over to me, putting his fingers over my mouth. "I never said that's what I wanted, Liara."

"Reznor, then what do you want to do? I came here because I wanted to. You choose what we are doing here. I'm never going to force you into doing something. That's why I didn't tell you. I didn't know how you felt for Serena. I didn't know anything about any of this. I'm still learning every day. It's all new to me: magic, this side of the world…you. So again, I ask what do you want to do?"

He soaks up every word I say, but then says the last thing I expect. "I want to go to sleep."

I open my mouth slightly, then shut it. I reach down for my shirt. "Then go to sleep. I'm going to go help Anisa. We can deal with the rest later."

He takes the shirt from me before scooping me into his arms and crossing to the bed. "No, I want to go to sleep with you." Reznor sets me on the mattress, then hastily undresses before slipping underneath the covers with me. He drags my body toward him, holding me against his chest. Without a word, all the lights in the room disappear, turning it black. One of Reznor's hands move to my back, strumming his thumb along my spine.

Chapter Eighteen: More Plans

Reznor's standing in the doorway to the closet when I woke up the next morning. He's adjusting the cufflinks on his shirt while watching me. Yesterday, we spent the day in bed doing absolutely nothing. We woke up only to lounge around then sleep again, yet even after all of that, I'm still exhausted.

I roll onto my side, facing away from him as I yawn. I do not want to get up yet, and his bed is so damn comfortable it should be illegal.

"You need to get up. Charles and Emanuel are waiting for you to train. I have a meeting today so I can't join you. Tonight however, we need to go over some things for the ceremony and the wedding." I hear him walking toward the bed as I make no effort to get up. "As much as I love seeing you half naked in my bed, you need to get up and put clothes on, or neither of us will be leaving this room. That black drink has side effects, and it's working."

My eyes shoot open at the sound of lust in his voice. I lean up on my elbows, trying not to laugh at his serious expression. Slowly he stalks closer to the bed, and that serious look turns lustful. Nope, not happening today; if we start, we won't be stopping.

I quickly jump off the bed, scurrying toward the closet. "You made your point."

He spanks my ass as I pass him, a smirk on his face. "I see that."

Reznor watches me get dressed into my training clothes. His playful mood turns sad as he tugs on the thin straps of my top. The black marks are on full display, but I don't care. Reznor knows now, we're working on it, and that's all that matters. He doesn't comment on the marks, instead he takes my hand in his. We leave his room and meet the boys in the foyer. Reznor shoots the boys a warning look, daring them to say anything, but for once, they don't as they see the marks on my skin.

"I'll see you later. Be careful." He kisses the top of my head then strolls away with his hands stuffed deep in his pockets.

"Be careful." Charles dramatically throws himself into Emanuel's arms, acting like a damsel in distress. He even goes as far as to cradle a hand against his temple, while puckering his lips.

"I will, my dear." Emanuel flutters his eyelashes.

"You two are awful." I try my best to act disgusted, but it ends up turning into laughter.

"What are you three laughing about?" A nasally voice calls from behind me. Low and behold Serena has come to ruin my good mood. She wears a skimpy yellow dress that leaves nothing to the imagination. When she realizes none of us were going to answer, she narrows her gaze on me. "Have you seen Reznor?"

Emanuel, immediately at attention, steps closer to me as I step toward Serena. "He's in a meeting, better run along and let the adults do their work."

"Hmm, well, I'll be sure to see him after. Give him a little reward for all that *hard* work." She smirks, then playfully licks her lips.

I go to step forward again, but Emanuel holds me back, shaking his head. "Let it go," Emanuel warns.

I bit the inside of my cheek, desperately trying to keep the words I want to say to myself. Charles and Emanuel must have sensed my control weakening because they take me from the house, ordering me to run the trails before I have the chance to give Serena a piece of my mind.

When I'm done with trails, I'm still hyped up on my anger, but Charles has a solution to that. They run me ragged all day. We train hard like we had the other day, but this time my powers don't deplete like they had before. But my body is another story.

Emanuel launches me to the ground for the last time. I wave my hands in surrender, mocking a white flag as I try to catch my breath. I swear I can feel my pulse behind my closed eyelids.

The sound of footsteps get closer to my head. Great, one of the boys must be coming to drag me back to practice. Digging deep, I try to find the motivation to get off the ground before they get here, but that doesn't seem to be happening.

"Tough day?" It isn't either of the boys that stand above me, but Reznor.

"You could say that," I breathe out tiredly.

He moves to stand in front of me, reaching a hand down and helping me to my feet. "How are the powers coming?" he asks as we watch Emanuel and Charles fight with swords.

"Good, I'm able to do more now. Some of them I still can't get a hold on yet." I know a lot of my powers are fueled by emotions, and this is a problem because I can't use those powers without unleashing my anger. "I accidentally caught a tree on fire last week because I was pissed off. Lightning struck the tree and caught it on fire. I turned grass to ash, but other than that, my main powers are the shields, healing, and telekinesis."

Reznor smiles softly. "You'll get the hang of it."

I scoff but thank him for the vote of confidence. Then, because I absolutely cannot control myself, I ask about Serena. "So, your lover was looking for you this morning."

Reznor casts me a glare. "I know, Emanuel told me."

I eye him suspiciously but don't press it any further. He hadn't been with her. I would have known. Reznor however, is not leaving the topic alone, "Feeling jealous today, are we?" He asks with a cockiness in his tone that matches the grin on his face.

"No, just thought you would want to know," I say coolly before turning and heading back to the boys.

I had expected Reznor to leave, but he doesn't. Instead, he flags over Charles with this finger.

Emanuel tosses me a sword as I approach. I swiftly catch it, twirling it in my hand once. Swords are still my biggest weakness in fighting, but I have improved…somewhat. I square off my shoulders as I get into a fighting stance. Emanuel swings his sword with little effort at me. I deflect the blow before swinging at his legs. Again, he deflects it.

"Can I ask you something?" Emanuel asks as he dodges my next strike.

"Shoot." I duck, sliding to one knee before coming back up in one fluid sweep, avoiding the pointed end of his sword.

"Do you think Anisa has been acting strange lately?" Emanuel asks as he strikes me harder this time, I have to use both hands to deflect his sword.

"I haven't seen her lately, so honestly, I don't know. Why do you ask?"

Emanuel takes a step back, holding his sword at his side. "She isn't sleeping, and she just keeps doing odd things. Every night this week she has had the door locked before I even get to the room." Emanuel scratches the back of his head with the hand he holds his sword in. "Can you talk to her and see if she tells you anything? I tried, but I didn't get anywhere."

"Sure, I'll talk to her tonight."

Emanuel nods his head, looking down at the sword before snapping back into fighting mode and swinging at me.

I jump back, missing the sharp blade. "That was a dirty move." I strike back, putting my entire weight behind the blow, and for the first time since fighting Emanuel without using my powers, he stumbles backward.

After Emanuel's stumble, he does not let me win the round as he sends me flying to the ground again. Reznor and Charles just watch as I climb from the grass slowly. "You know what? I'm done," I pant, arching my back in pain, "You win." I toss the sword to the ground. Emanuel calls for me to come back, but I've already turned toward the manor. He didn't do anything wrong; I'm just too tired to be tossed around anymore.

I make quick time as I shower. I want to be dressed before Reznor comes back to the room. Luckily, Anisa is there waiting for me with a nightgown in hand. I take the dress from her hand and hurry into it as I hear the bedroom door open and close. Anisa tries to leave as she hears Reznor, but I stop her.

"Hey, Anisa, are you doing alright?"

Anisa walks further into the bathroom, leaning against the counter as she fumbles with her fingers. "I've just felt a little off lately. It's nothing to worry about."

She's lying, and she's terrible at it.

"Are you sure? If you need anything, you know you can tell me, right?"

"I know, thank you. I'm fine." Anisa can't even look at me as she lies, and she doesn't allow me to ask any more questions either as she leaves me alone in the bathroom.

I understand what Emanuel meant now. Anisa is acting strange. She always talks to me and has spent a great deal of time with me over the last two months. Now, she always seems in a rush to leave, and is talking less and less. I don't understand it, but maybe Emanuel and I can figure it out together.

In the bedroom, Reznor sits on the couch with a stack of papers in his hand, looking diligently at the page before him. He only tears his eyes from them when I settle down next to him, nudging my knee against his. He glances at my crossed legs, his eyes catching where the black silk ends a couple inches above my knee.

"We need to go over some things for the wedding and ceremony." He averts his eyes back to the papers in his hand. "We have to decide whom you want your guest to be for the marking, along with who you want at the ceremony."

"For the guest at the marking, I would like for Anisa to be there. As far as the ceremony goes, I don't really have a preference. Whoever you think needs to be there can be there, I don't have any family here. Plus, I'm just being deemed a queen."

Reznor set the papers down, turning to me. "Well, technically, you do have family here. They just haven't met you because they hate me."

"Ah, you mean the part of my family that asked the gods to steal your magic then tried to prevent me from being born. I'll pass."

Reznor laughs at how easy it is for me to dismiss them. "Fair enough. We'll keep it small then. There will be plenty of people at the party leading up to the ceremony and twice that many at the wedding." He almost groans the word wedding.

"Are you being hassled as much as I am when it comes to the wedding?"

"Yes, that's what today's meeting was about. Actually, I had to meet with my advisors on who to invite and who to place where. I would rather have no guests at all, honestly, but that doesn't work seeing as I'm the king."

Laughing at his snide remark, even though I agree with it, I never thought I would have a big wedding, yet here I am, engaged to a king. "I guess I'm lucky Anisa is planning everything for me."

"If our wedding is ugly, I'm blaming it on you," he teases as a grin appearing on his face.

"It's Anisa. The wedding will be perfect."

Reznor nods again, proving my point even further.

The other planning is minimal, a preference on the menu and cake. I am, however, disappointed to learn we don't get a honeymoon. No honeymoon is another downfall of being royals, apparently. Personally, I think it's bullshit; I want hot sex on the beach in the middle of paradise somewhere hot.

All this talk of planning things reminds me of Reznor's plan for Serena. "Care to enlighten me anymore on this plan with Serena?" I cross my arm, eyeing him.

He groans, "In two weeks, there will be a tithe, but I do it differently than the other kingdoms. I only collect fifteen percent from the wealthy lords and upper members of society. Ten percent I fuel back into the lands and some of the less fortunate members of the land. The remaining five percent of all the upper members goes into the kingdom's funds. Then, the next tithe I collect eight percent from the town members, that way the people have more time to prepare the money. This one is for the upper members, which means Serena has to come to give her portion." Reznor stands from the couch, unbuttoning his shirt while standing in front of me.

I'll admit it's rather distracting.

"The beginning of the tithe I'll do alone, but toward the end, you will come to assist me. Serena gets jealous easily, and she doesn't like you therefore, we're going to do just that and make her jealous. We want her to slip up and send an attack on you the next day when I tell her you're going to be spending the night in your old room." He walks toward the closet with his back turned to me. He stops, then calls over his shoulder, "You're going to have to put on a hell of a show." For some reason, those words feel like a challenge…and I like to win.

Chapter Nineteen: Fighting Back

For the first time since switching rooms, I go to bed and woke up alone. Reznor left late last night heading to Greensboro for an emergency with Tatiana. Reznor was hesitant to leave, but in the end, he went, taking Emanuel with him. He didn't tell me what it was about, only that he was leaving and would be back tomorrow. I hardly slept that night. I had grown used to sleeping with him, and now sleeping without him has become a struggle.

I'm awake staring at the ceiling when Anisa comes to gather me for the day. I startle her as I shoot up in bed, hoping it's Reznor returning. Although disappointed, I'm happy to see Anisa. I don't get to spend as much time with her now. Anisa, doesn't even speak as she gets me ready for the day. I try multiple times to start a conversation, but she says nothing. Then the second I'm dressed, she's out the door, leaving me to eat my breakfast alone.

Charles collects me for training, even running the trails with me that morning. He has no idea why Reznor and Emanuel left last night.

"It was weird, right?" I ask him.

He nods in agreement as he stretches after our run. "Yes, it's strange. I found out this morning from one of the security guards."

"I guess we'll find out when they come back." Charles doesn't let the conversation continue as he motions for me to sit on the ground with him.

"I want to see if we can get you to turn something to ash again." Charles pulls a piece of paper from a journal, crumpling it in his hand before giving it to me. "Now you were angry last time, but let's see if you can do this on command. Think about turning it to ash, changing its form into something new."

Taking the crumpled ball into my hand, I stare down at it doing as Charles said, I focus on changing its form. The process of becoming something new, taking what was once whole and turning it into something deconstructed. It doesn't work at first, the ball staring back at me, its form never changing… but then suddenly, the paper turns to ash, floating away in the light breeze.

Charles smiles brightly at me. "You did it!" he cheers, putting a fist into the air. "Your eyes changed color again, but they went back instantly."

"Why does it keep happening?" I ask while taking another ball of paper into my hand.

"I've never heard of it in any book before. So, I'm not really sure," Charles says, as he watches the dust fly away.

I turned the ball into ash again. Charles watches me do it over repeatedly. I turn paper to ash, then stone, then grass. When Charles has his fun with the ash, he has me float him around the sky. I trapeze him through the air, twirling my finger around in circles causing Charles to do the same slowly.

"This might be my favorite power," I say. Some of my other powers were destructive, but this one was fun.

"If I had this power, I would use them all the time."

It suddenly dawns on me. "Charles, what are you?" I ask, spinning him back around to face me.

"I'm a warlock... well I was. I lost my powers to my brother when he siphoned them from me. He wanted the powers I had because I'm stronger. A spell was used to tranquilize me, and then he took them for himself." Charles looks down to the ground with sadness on his face. "Once you lose your powers, you can't get them back, so I trained to be a warrior, and eventually, I was turned into a demon by an ex-girlfriend."

"You what?" I ask, bewildered. "How does that even happen?"

"Trust me, you don't want to know how. She turned me as payback for breaking up with her through carrier pigeon."

I can't stop the laughter that erupts from my mouth. I hold my stomach, and in my fit of laughter, I forget to keep Charles afloat. He drops suddenly with me stopping him an inch above the ground.

"You can put me down now." He nervously laughs.

"Sorry, my bad. So do you have any powers?"

He nods, conjuring a fog creature that takes a step forward before he demolishes it with a snap of his fingers. "Not all demons can form fog monsters, some are incubus succubus others can shift their form, and the strong ones can possess others. Tope level demons can do pretty much everything. Yet we all have enhanced abilities like strength and speed."

"That's kind of creepy, no offense."

"None taken. I hate what I am now and if I ever get the chance to get my powers back, I'll gladly return to warlock life."

With Charles's feet firmly planted on the ground, he decides it's time to fight, and today, it's with our fists. He takes the time to wrap my hands, glancing off to the tree line every so often, but he never elaborates on what he's looking at or what he's looking for.

Squaring our bodies against each other, we start fighting. I throw the first punch, but Charles blocks it swiftly.

"Playing dirty, are we now?" He challenges, swiftly kicking at my leg. I block him with my arm then spin to strike him with my leg. Block. Punch. Dodge. I miss his hit by an inch, scraping past my shoulder. I use that distraction to take him to the floor.

Charles does not let that go unpunished. He rises off the ground quickly, standing back on his feet. We fight each other hard till we end up on the ground with neither of us willing to fight any longer.

"You've gotten stronger." Charles compliments me as he pours some water on his head.

"Well, you and Emanuel have beat me for two months. I had to get better at some point."

He snorts, jumping from the ground. "You're going to get stronger again. Go run the trail," he cackles in a burst of fake evil laughter.

Much to my disappointment, He refuses to run with me. He said that finishing before sundown is a privilege and that I should be grateful when in reality, he doesn't want to run.

I start jogging when the all too familiar path comes into view. I run this every day, twice a day. I like to run, so tackling the trails isn't a punishment but rather more my alone time. The perk of running the trail every day, you learn when something is out of place, and today, something's out of place.

A tree that had fallen, but leaning against its sister tree, is now lying a different direction than usual. I study the log, looking for a reason why it's been moved but see nothing. I continue jogging when there's a snap of a twig coming from a dense patch of greenery on the right. Then a rustle of branches from the left. I slow, staring into the shrubbery, then seeing black move behind the brush, I take off, sprinting down the trail.

My sudden movement is enough to send the men flying out of the woods. I'm in the middle of the course but know of a shortcut about a thousand yards ahead that I can use to get back to the manor quickly. Dashing down the path, I don't get far before one of the men jumps in front of me, coming out of another part of the woods. He reaches for me. I dodge his grasp, taking my elbow and sending a blow to his face before turning quickly and taking his feet out from underneath him with a swipe of my leg.

The other men are now aiming to fire, one of them firing the gun before I send him flying through the air. I can hardly think, acting on instinct alone as all hell breaks loose. The bullet landed in a tree on my right. The gunshot echoes in the trees, sending birds flying. The two remaining men start coming toward me at the same time, one shooting an arrow at me. I stop the arrow with my shield before launching it back at him. The arrow sinks into his chest, taking him to the ground. The first man that attacks me is now on his feet again. He picks me up, grabbing me around the waist. I kick and fight, beating him with my arms. I manage to wiggle in his arms enough that I'm able to take my elbow and hit him in the eye. He curses, throwing me to the ground, but I'm quick to jump back up to my feet. I take no chances and crash his head against a nearby tree.

 I stammer back a step only to feel a gun touch the back of my head. "Walk, or I shoot." I still, thinking of what to do, then it hit me. I freeze him in place with my powers. He fights against it, trying to wiggle free, to no avail.

 "Why do you keep trying to kill me?" I ask the man, but he spits in my face rather than give me a response. I punch him in the face before sending him flying through the air without a second thought, hearing him smack into a tree in the distance.

 All the men are down on the ground, some dead, others not, but either way, I'm not waiting around to see if they're going to get up. Racing down the path and taking the shortcut to the manor, I get stopped by Charles and six guards running toward the tree line.

 "Liara! Are you okay?" he shouts the second I dart out of the tree line.

 "They were following me. I took them out, but they tried to take me this time," I say breathlessly.

"You take her back to the manor and guard her door. The rest of you, you're with me." Charles points to a random guard who accompanies me back to Reznor's room.

Inside the room, I sit down on the bed, trying to calm my nerves when I hear shuffling coming from the closet. I slowly creep in and find Anisa rocking herself back and forth in the corner of the room.

"Anisa, what are you doing?" I step toward her as her head shoots up, tears running down her face.

"I'm sorry, I just needed someplace quiet where no one would bother me," she cries, scrambling to her feet.

"It's okay. What's wrong?" I try to stop her from leaving the closet, but she scrambles around me.

"It's fine, I'm just tired." She walks for the door.

"Anisa, talk to me." She pauses with her hand on the door handle.

She turns with a sweet smile on her face. "I'll be okay, I promise." Swinging open the door, she practically runs from the room.

What is going on with her? She has never acted like this before, even Emanuel is nervous about it. By the time I decide I want go after her, it's too late because now Charles is camped outside my room, forbidding me from leaving until Reznor gets back. I pace inside the room waiting and waiting. The sun is setting now, and Reznor still isn't back.

Anisa returns but only to start bathwater without saying a word to me. She comes into the closet quickly, grabbing my nightclothes and placing them on the counter. She fills the tub with water and purple soap.

"Get in the tub," she tells me, pointing to the full bath.

"Will you stay and talk to me?" I ask, hoping to get more details about what has been bothering her.

"Fine, but only till Reznor returns." She folds her hands in front of her, looking at the ground. She remains this way until I sink into the soft purple water with bubbles that cover all my body except my shoulders, arms, and tops of my knees that poke through the sea of bubbles.

"How's the training going?" she questions, taking a seat on the counter, finally looking at me.

"It's going good, just hard. I'm getting better."

"That's good."

I contemplate scaring her off again but ask the question anyway, "What's going on, Anisa?"

She doesn't speak for a while, and I honestly didn't think she was going to answer the question. "I've been on edge lately... I found a note saying that if I told anyone what I saw that they would hurt me. Then I felt like someone was following me today and I freaked out and hid in here," Anisa admits as a tear trails down her face.

"Why didn't you tell Emanuel?" I ask, gripping the side of the tub.

"I didn't want to scare him." She wipes the tear away as another one falls.

"Anisa, you should tell him—"

"No, not until I know if it's real, or not. Liara, promise me you won't—" she's cut off as the bedroom slams shut.

"Liara!" Reznor calls out.

Great he has impeccable timing. "In here," I holler back as Anisa jumps off the counter, moving toward me, although she relaxes when Reznor darts into the room.

"Anisa, can you give us a moment?" he asks her as he crosses to the bathtub.

Anisa nods, scurrying out of the room. He sits on the edge of the tub near my feet. "I heard you had an interesting day." He won't meet my eyes as he runs his finger through the bubbles.

"I did, but I handled it. What about you?" I carefully tuck my arms into the water.

"I think they set a trap, knowing I wouldn't drag you with me because of how emergent that errand was. The only reason I didn't make it back sooner is because the drives so fucking long." He splashes me with water suddenly. I quickly attempt to cover my face, but I'm too late. The water hits me right in the cheek.

"Playful today?" I tease, flicking some bubbles at him.

He chuckles as he sits down on the floor next to the tub, moving closer to me before leaning his head against the edge of it. He closes his eyes tiredly. It's evident by the dark rings around his eyes.

Reaching out with my wet hand, I run my fingers through his hair, interlacing bubbles into his black locks. He hums in appreciation as I continue. "Why don't you go to bed? You're tired," I tell him, as I place my hand on the porcelain.

He shakes his head and reaches behind him, placing my hand back in his hair. I can't help but continue to swirl my fingers around his silky strands.

Even after his hair became damp, he let me sit there and play till the water turned cold.

"As much as I enjoy this, we need to sleep. Finish up." He strolls into the closet, sending Anisa back into the bathroom.

She smirks. "That seems to be going well."

I try to hide the grin by sliding myself under the water, soaking my hair. Of course, that doesn't stop Anisa.

She taps my knee, signaling for me to come up. She hands me a bottle of soap. "Well?" she prods.

Lathering the soap into my hair, "Yes, it's going well," I replied.

Anisa smiles brightly for the first time today. "That's what I like to hear." She beams as I rinse my hair out, hurrying me through the rest of my bath.

Sending me to bed in a nightgown that is definitely shorter than last night's, she chuckles at Reznor's reaction when I enter into the room.

Reznor's gaze follows every step, his eyes growing dark with lust. I try not to let it affect me, or rather act as if I hadn't noticed it at all.

"I turned the shower on for you, Your Majesty." Anisa ducks her head then scurries out of the room.

Reznor strides past me, making sure to kiss my head and run his hand across my stomach to my waist before he goes to the shower. Goosebumps rise across my skin the second he touches me, and even linger as I get into the bed, grabbing my book.

Reznor returns after his shower, carrying the bottle of black liquid in his hands wearing nothing but a towel around his waist. I keep my eyes on him as he hands me a capful that I down quickly. He smiles triumphantly before going back to the closet, returning in pajama pants. He crawls into the bed, snatching the book from my hand.

"Hey!" I protest.

"We're going to bed." He turns off the lights once again as he hauls me toward him, resting his head on mine and wrapping his arms around me tightly. In the darkness, I don't see the kiss coming as he leans down, pressing his lips to mine.

Chapter Twenty: When A Plan Comes Together

Anisa wakes me before dawn, dressing me in a light grey, floor-length silk dress that has matching silk quarter sleeves. After the attack yesterday, Reznor decided I'm to be with him from now on, and that means attending all his ridiculous meetings today.

Three meetings in, and I'm ready to kill him. I'm perched on a chair next to him and he keeps a hand on my thigh throughout each one. Rez is purposely toying with me today for some reason. I almost spill my coffee when he hikes my dress up, dragging his hand along my bare leg through the small slit at my calf. He maneuvers the fabric up to my knees. Doing so in a room filled with other valuable members of his society. The best part, they never notice a thing as he completes the task with stealth.

He glides his hand back and forth or strums his thumb along my inner thigh. I have done a great job of composing myself until a younger nobleman questions Rez's judgment. Reznor squeezes my thigh so tight I gasp. Eyes shoot my way, but they must have thought it was due to the threatening words that leave Reznor's lips. Then, that same man has the bright idea to check out what little cleavage is showing from my dress.

"Fifteen-minute break now," Reznor growls.

The young man scurries from the room along with the rest of the noblemen. Reznor rises gracefully, removing his hand from my leg as he follows them, then slams the door behind them. He locks it before placing his head against the tall frame. Breathing in deeply, he turns back toward me.

"That child," he hisses, prowling rather slowly back over to where I sit, "is testing my limits today." When I didn't comment, he pushes back my chair, standing in front of me with a devilish smirk. "Not talkative today, love?" he asks as he glances at my dress that's still hiked up to my knee.

"No, not really. I don't like meetings." I reach down, readjusting my dress, smoothing it out.

"Well, I don't like them either, but you have made today's rather fun." He drags his bottom lip between his teeth.

Shaking my head in disbelief, I rise from the chair, attempting to walk past him, only to be stopped by his large hands. He grips either side of my hips, pulling me closer to him.

"What's exactly in that black drink?" I ask, leaning into his touch. I feel practically drugged when I touch him. Whenever our skin touches, endorphins shoot through my body, begging me to touch him further.

Nestling his head into my hair near my neck, he breathes deeply against my throat, "I'm not sure, but I think it's working."

I grasp his shoulder to prevent myself from falling as his gravelly voice weakened my knees. I lean further into his body. "What side effects did Morana say it could cause?" I ask, feeling him pull me closer though there hadn't been much room left between us.

He starts placing soft kisses on my neck, humming, "Something about heightened senses, and more attraction."

Running my fingers through his styled hair, I murmur, "That means this probably isn't a good idea."

He draws back, looking at me with darkened eyes. "You're probably right."

But even he doesn't listen to his own words as he kisses me deeply, with a hand gripping the back of my neck, securing me in place. Our lips move against each other as he picks me up off the ground using one arm. He turns, sitting me down on the table, spreading my legs as he moves to stand between them.

I gasp as he hoists my legs around him, exposing the length of my leg as he pushes the fabric up my thigh. He takes the chance, delving his tongue into my mouth. His hands caress my body as I pull him closer, my hands gripping his lower back. Reznor pulls back as a knock comes from the door. He groans, releasing me from his grasp. "Don't move love," he raps before striding to the door and jerking it open. Serena saunters into the room the second the door is wide enough for her to slip through.

"Hi, Rezzie," she coos, dragging her hands down his chest.

I feel the pain in the places she touches. Reznor quickly moves out of her grasp. As he stalks back over to me, the look on her face is priceless. She takes in the sight of me on the table with my dress hiked up along with Reznor's disheveled hair. Her anger is obvious, and a smirk is plastered across my face. Checkmate bitch.

"What do you want, Serena?" he asks in a flat voice, standing between her and me.

I'm not sure if it is to keep me from her, or to keep her away from him. Either way, I still want to slap that shocked look off her face.

"You let her sit in on the meetings?" she crows in disbelief.

"She's going to be queen in less than a month, so yes, she is sitting in on meetings." I eye him suspiciously. So, that's why I'm being forced to sit in on meetings.

"Look, we're busy, can you leave?" Reznor points to the door. She pouts, but in the end, she leaves the room without a word.

"Am I really sitting in on these because I'm about to be queen?" I ask as Reznor stands between my legs again.

"No, I want to spend time with you." He scoops me off the table, sitting in his chair, placing me on his lap.

"Why didn't you just tell her that?" I watch as Reznor begins toying with my fingers loosely.

"Because she always wants to sit in on these meetings, and I never let her do so," he sighs before kissing the palm of my hand.

"Now, you're using me to make her jealous," I tease.

He opens his mouth to respond, but the nobles enter the room again. I try to get up from his lap, but Reznor holds me tightly against him. He seems to enjoy the glances we get from the surprised nobles, but either way, he keeps me perched on his lap for the remainder of the meetings that day.

I'm graced with Anisa's presence, saving me from the last three meetings of the day, but I'm being forced to do fittings for dresses. Today, is selection day for my wedding dress, along with a dress for the reception.

Anisa is quick to shoo the seamstress out of the room the second she measures me for the dress for the ceremony. I'm being fitted for the dress in the grand hall, but I can hardly focus as I take in the cluttered room. The hall has been filled with eight racks of dresses along with boxes, upon boxes of decorations for the wedding. Boards are set up all over the place with ideas and fabric swatches. Along with at least a hundred different pairs of shoes and tables of accessories, tiaras, veils, and garters! There is a wall of mirrors attached to the far wall. She truly has the room set up for the utmost efficiency.

"I know it's a lot, but we don't have much time left until the wedding, and seeing as Reznor stole you today, we are behind schedule," Anisa says with her back to me as she poured a glass of bubbling liquid, handing it to me.

I take the glass willingly. Sipping the drink, alcohol hits my tongue. I'm delighted. She knew this fiasco would overwhelm me. She waits until I finish the glass, then she tears the first dress from the rack.

"We'll start with the dress for the reception. There are less of those to pick from." Anisa quickly helps me into the first of many.

Halfway through the first rack, I find the reception dress without having to look any further. I love it, and trying it on, Anisa agrees it's the one. However, finding the wedding dress is not as easy because Anisa has a style that is very different from mine. Half of the dresses were immediate no's, but the final dress on the last rack is my yes, and it fit perfectly.

Anisa nearly dies of shock when Reznor tries to come into the room with the two dresses hanging in the open. She practically slams the door shut in his face before hurrying to stuff the dresses into two black garment bags. I stand in the middle of the room, giggling as it unfolds before me.

Reznor enters the room, eyeing Anisa. "I'm sorry, sir, but you can't see the dress yet," she chastises him. Again, I giggle at the challenging look Reznor casts her, causing both to look in my direction.

Reznor saunters over to me, eyeing me suspiciously. "Are you drunk, Liara?" he asks, taking the glass out of my hand.

I pucker my lips. "I might be a little tipsy."

Reznor sighs, turning to Anisa with his hand pinching the bridge of his nose. "Are you done with her? It's almost midnight." Reznor does not look pleased, and I'm not sure if it's because I've been gone for hours, or because Anisa kept feeding me champagne.

"Yes, I'll plan the accessories, and everything else without her. Don't forget we have the wedding rehearsal in the morning."

"What?" Reznor and I ask in unison.

"I'll wake you up for it," she cheers.

Reznor sighs before he grabs my hand, starting to lead me from the room when he stops, eyeing the garters. "Don't worry about dressing her tonight." I whirl at him confused, but he just tugs my hand, leading me from the room.

The second he opens the door, he points to the bed. "Get in, I'll grab your tonic."

I don't feel like changing. Instead, I untie the silk robe and crawl into bed in my undergarments. Reznor comes back into the room a little startled when he finds my robe on the floor with me beneath the sheets taking my hair down. He hands me the capful; after drinking it quickly, he sets the bottle on the nightstand.

"I can't believe Anisa got you drunk," Reznor teases, sitting on the bed next to me.

"I'm tipsy, not drunk. I've never been drunk actually."

He chuckles. "You've never been drunk?" he utters in disbelief, eyeing me carefully as I sink beneath the covers further.

"Nope, I get a buzz then stop. I take it you've had many drunken nights?"

His face goes from a smile to a grimace. "Yeah, I have. I drank a lot in my early teens," he scratches the back of his head, "well, actually, my teens in general." His stare lingers a moment longer; I had asked him why, but his face tells me he's contemplating telling me, or not.

"Like I said, I'm called a ruthless king for a reason, and back then, I couldn't live with it, but now I can. How are you doing with what happened in the forest yesterday?" Reznor slides into the bed, lying beside me as we stare at the ceiling together.

I try not to think about what I did to the men, but it was them or me, and I want to live. Although it's a morbid thought, it's the truth. "I'm good. I feel bad about what happened, but both times they were trying to kill me. I'm just used to healing rather than hurting."

He snickers, "I always found it ironic that the only power they didn't take from me was my healing power...you're the only person I've ever healed."

Turning my head, I watch him. "Just because you can heal people doesn't mean you have to, but I appreciate you healing me."

Reznor smirks. "I'm always there for a damsel in distress."

I lean up on my elbows, "Are you saying you saved me?"

Mocking my position, he shakes his head. "No, but sometimes I like to tell myself I did," He teases, which earns him a swat to the shoulder.

Being awoken in the middle of the night to practice a wedding is not at all what I wanted, yet here I stand, half asleep, leaning against a wall in my night attire. Reznor seems just as displeased as I am, and I know for a fact it's not about my clothes. He, however, is able to look somewhat awake while I shamelessly could care less. I should be in bed right now, not standing in the throne room. Reznor and I had only slept a few hours before being dragged out of bed.

Anisa bursts through the door with a smile on her face. In one hand she holds a bouquet and heels, while the other held a cup of coffee. I hope the coffee is for me, but Anisa bypasses me before handing the cup to Reznor. I glare at Anisa with a pointed expression. This day is off to a bad start. No coffee and now heels? I don't think so.

Reznor, seeming to read the look on my face moves to stand next to me by the wall. He passes the cup out to me, and I gladly accepted it. I take a sip of the warm liquid, lavishing in the pleasant heat that travels down my throat.

"Thank you," I murmur as I lean my head against his shoulder.

"You're welcome." He slides a hand to rest on my lower back, his head tilting to lean against mine.

I'm aware of Anisa speaking, something about the wedding, but I'm more focused on how tired I am, and how comfortable Reznor is. Although as the time passes, I realize I should have been listening, but it's too late for that.

Another blissful moment is ruined by Anisa coming over and dragging me away from Reznor by the hand. I barely have time to give him back the mug before she forces me out of the throne room.

"Why are we leaving the throne room if you just brought me to it?" I ask, well, groan.

"Had you been listening, we are starting from the top. That means you are walking down the aisle." Anisa smiles, with a light in her eyes that I find repulsive this early in the morning. I don't get to object because she forces the heels onto my feet and shoves the bouquet into my hands. She smiles, squeezes me on the shoulder before she opens the door, and shoves me down the aisle.

Chapter Twenty-One: The Tithe

The two weeks leading up to the tithe fly by. Reznor and I spend all our time together. He trains with me, and I go to meetings with him. I have quickly grown feelings for him as I spend more time with him, and learn more about his past, and his life. The discovery of the mating illness actually brought our relationship closer together. Although we never speak of it, I think we both can agree we have come closer together.

He and I fell into a pattern of how we are together, and sure enough, that once cold man is starting to warm up every single day. I don't fear what he can do, and I don't hide things from him anymore. I swear I have never seen him so relieved when he realized the illness is almost cleared up entirely.

One moment we're in bed talking, and the next, he's ripping off the covers to look at the black lines only to find them remaining on the upper part of my abdomen. He was ecstatic. I couldn't be happier with how much progress we've made, but with sky highs come crashing lows.

The morning of the tithe is pure chaos. Servants running around, setting everything up in the manor. I haven't talked to a single soul this morning. They all were too busy rushing around. I saw Reznor long enough this morning to say hello while he passed me in the hallway. He smiled, but it hadn't reach his eyes.

Reznor has been on edge for the last three days. He would rise from bed early and come to bed late. It seems like all we have done the last three days is share a bed. I blamed the lack of communication and appearances on the tithe rather than something else because I couldn't have done anything to upset him.

Anisa however, has been cooped up in the grand hall preparing everything for the wedding. I only see her in the mornings and at night when she helps me dress. Each time she brags about how beautiful the wedding is going to be. She has calmed down about the threat. She thinks it had just been a way to scare her. She had returned to her smiling, bubbly self, and it pleases Emanuel tremendously.

While everyone is rushing about the manor, I wander back to my old room. I find it restored to its pristine condition. Going to my favorite spot, I sit on the balcony facing the mountains. Not a single soul is out in the large field behind the manor. It gives me a moment to appreciate the beauty of the land as fall rolls into Nightsend. The trees' leaves have started turning into orange, red, and yellows. It's breathtaking to watch as the light breeze sends them whisking across the land.

I observe the landscape for hours, just watching and enjoying the sun, but it comes to an end when Reznor's voice rings in my head.

Where are you?

I'm startled at the sudden noise looking around for him when I remembered the bond. *I'm in my room.*

No, you're not. Anisa is there now looking for you.

The realization hits me. He thought I meant his room. *Correction, I'm in my room, not your room.*

Reznor scoffs through the bond. *My room is your room. Now go back to our room and get ready. It's almost time.* I don't respond. Instead, I head back across the manor.

Anisa is pacing the room when I step inside, her head shooting up in my direction. "There you are! I was worried." Anisa places a hand over her heart, releasing a deep breath.

"I know; you told Reznor on me. I'm sorry I was in my old room. I wanted to sit on the balcony since his windows don't open, or I would have stayed here."

"Sorry about that." Anisa motions to the closet. "This is the only room in the whole house without real windows. His mom made them build this room special with no windows, so no one could come in other than through that door. She did it that way to protect him. They cast a spell on the magic windows to mimic what's happening outside," Anisa tells as she rummages through my drawers, picking out undergarments to fit under the dress. Turns out a bra isn't an option today.

Taking a seat on a chair in the bathroom, she curls the strands of my hair.

"Not that I don't appreciate the history lesson, how is Reznor today?" I ask, making eye contact with Anisa through the mirror.

"He's distracted and annoyed. He hates having the tithe; he always feels guilty about it. It's the law of the council, and he can't change it. That's why he's been so irritable these past few days," Anisa explains, curling another strand. I mumble an 'oh' in response.

Anisa is quick to fill the silence, talking of the wedding and the ceremony as she gets me ready for the tithe. She pins half of my hair up, leaving the rest in loose curls down my back. She paints my lids with a dark smokey eye and a red lip. She takes her time adding wings to the liner.

The makeup pairs perfectly with the black dress. It's a clinging, silky material with a slit halfway up my thigh. The dress ties at my lower back with strips of black ribbon crisscrossing over my bare skin. Between the back, slit, and the plunging neckline, a lot of my skin is on display.

Anisa kneels before me, sliding black strappy heels to my feet. The final touch is a small tiara with black stones that she places upon my head.

"Should I even be wearing this?" I question as I gently touch the tip of the tiara.

Anisa smiles, standing up. "Reznor actually picked this one specifically for you to wear tonight. Come on, you have five minutes to get to the throne room. When you get there, Emanuel will be waiting outside. He will tell you what to do." Anisa grabs my hand, helping me up from the chair.

I walk alone to the throne room. I've passed it many times, but I have only been inside of it once for the wedding rehearsal, and I barely remember that. The doors leading to the throne room from this side of the manor are closed with Emanuel standing guard in black leather pants, and a black shirt with a leather breast strap bearing the symbol of the crescent moon and wolf from the flag.

Emanuel chuckles when I stroll up to him. "Reznor will either love this, or absolutely hate it."

I nervously laugh, "I absolutely agree with you this time." Reaching down, I fumble with the hem at the slit of my thigh.

Emanuel checks his watch. "Alright, let's go." He reaches for the door, but I stop him.

"Wait, Reznor never told me the rest of the plan."

Emanuel shakes his head, opening the door further. "Follow his lead."

One wrong move in this dress, and a lot will be on display. "This is a terrible idea," I mumble, walking through the dimly lit hall to find the massive throne room that is twice the size of both ballrooms.

It's filled with guards lining the walls, all dressed in the same apparel as Emanuel. I walk along the wooden floor close to the wall making my way toward Reznor, who sits on a massive black throne with symbols of a moon, wolf, and fire engraved into the top of it.

Reznor's wearing all black with the top button popped open, revealing his tanned chest, and the same black crown on his head. The moment I enter from the hall, his eyes land on me, watching every move I take toward him. Taking careful steps as I walk up the stairs, Reznor locks eyes with me, and I try to keep a placid face to hide my nervousness.

When I got a few steps away from him, he reaches a hand out to me. Gripping mine, he tugs me toward him, carefully placing me on his lap. He secures me against him, while I cross my legs across his lap, the slit droops to show even more skin.

His hand darts out, strumming his thumb lazily across my exposed thigh, sending goosebumps down my leg instantly. "I don't know how I feel about this dress," he says quietly into my ear, causing a small smirk to cross my face.

"I could have worn nothing, but the tiara." His thumb stops moving on my leg as he grips my thigh.

"Save that for the bedroom, love." He kisses me right below the ear. "You look beautiful. The tiara suits you," a slow smirk tugs at his lips, "but a crown would be better."

"Thank you. So, how does this work?" I ask Reznor, glancing around the elegant empty room that sits before me.

The tall ceiling has large, silver chandeliers that hang all the way down the long hall. The room's painted light grey with silver crested walls that seem to give the room a dark, but elegant appearance.

"Right now, we are waiting for the next person. Serena is after him. We just need to make her mad enough to slip on an attack." Reznor stiffens at his words, shaking his head in disgust.

"Okay, but how far are we taking this?" I turn my head to look at him.

"As far as it takes to get her mad. She won't leave this room until she's furious...or felt like she's won." Reznor eyes me at the last part of his sentence.

"I'll let you in on a little secret, Rez. I'm very competitive, and I like to win. She can try, but she won't succeed." I smile wickedly, settling myself into him further.

A man wearing gold saunters into the room, two men behind him carrying a large trunk, a dazzling smile on his face as he approaches us. He strides through the hall, bowing before the king. The man's eyes linger on me, but as Reznor clears his throat, the man averts his attention.

"I present gold for my tithe, sir." The man flicks his wrist toward the two men who open the trunk, revealing glittering gold.

"Thank you for your tithe." Reznor waves a finger, and two guards take the trunk to a side exit. His grasp tightens on my thigh, as the man stares at my exposed leg again. The man visibly shivers before dashing out the door, eager to get away from the king's watchful eye.

"That's it?" I whispered to Rez, who nods his head.

"Trust me, doing this all day is brutal. You'll understand by the next one when you get to sit through the whole thing with me," Reznor sighs. He looks tired today, although his fatigue can be seen only in his eyes.

Reznor stiffens as the door opens to reveal Serena dressed in little clothing, strutting into the room without a care in the world. She wears orange crystals over her breasts then a light, orange skirt leaving little to the imagination. She makes my dress seem conservative.

The anger boils beneath my skin but simmers away as Reznor starts running his hand up and down my thigh, sending tingles across my flesh. Spreading my legs slightly, allowing him more room, I watch his eyes flare red as I move my ass against him in a slow sensual motion. He places a kiss on my shoulder, then my neck as Serena prowls toward us.

I tug his left hand, moving it closer to my breasts while I angle my head to the side, giving him more access to my skin. Reznor props his leg between my now spread legs, taking his free arm around my waist, dragging me further into his front. He did all of this without once lifting his mouth from my skin. I know this is an act, but I was enjoying it.

Serena gives us hateful glares as she clears her throat, waiting for Reznor to give her attention. But Reznor is too focused on moving his hands down my body to even realize she's spoken. He drags a single finger down the bare skin between my breasts as he asks for Serena's tithe. He doesn't spare her a glance, not as he watches his finger move slowly down the valley of each curve. He's captivated by my breasts, and how my body responds to his touch. My breath picks up some; I can't help it, but I'm not ashamed. Okay, maybe I'm a little embarrassed. It shouldn't be this easy. For him or me.

Serena snaps her fingers, and a man opens a small tote filled with jewels. Reznor glances at the jewels, stopping his hand, his palm now resting against my breast. I continue gyrating my hips softly. Serena only looks annoyed rather than angry.

"That's not enough to cover your tithe," he calmly addresses her as his hands move across my chest, to cup my breast.

I hold in a gasp at the sensation. I wasn't able to wear a bra with this dress, and with the thin material, his hands against me, and the bond magnifying his touch, it's almost too much to handle. Shifting in my seat, I feel his erection pushing into my ass. That's when I realize the plan might be working a little too well.

"I offer my body, too, as part of my tithe," she purrs. I freeze in my seat as lightning flashes through the bright windows, thunder shaking them slightly.

Easy, he murmurs down the bond as he gives a reassuring squeeze to my thigh.

"I don't need your body Serena, and I'm sure as hell not accepting it as part of your tithe," Reznor hisses, grabbing at my thigh harder.

Maybe he is the one who needed to calm down. I start kissing up his neck then to his jawline. He stares down at me, his eyes flashing red before kissing me hungrily.

"Are you sure about that, Rezzie?" she calls.

Reznor pulls back, sighing in annoyance. "Yes, Serena, I'm sure. Pay the rest of your tithe now or pay double next time." He focuses on the shift of my hips as I grind myself against him.

Serena looks as if she's about to explode as Reznor grips my hips, pushing them even further into his. "You didn't need her once, and those days weren't that long ago. Don't you remember how you were complaining to me about having to get married? How she ruined your life? How I was the one you wanted to marry?" Serena takes a step closer, but Reznor growls, causing the glass on the wall to shake.

"Serena, if you're going to lie to hurt Liara, you should realize I only tell her the truth. The truth is I never loved you and never cared for you in that way. But you knew that already, so you just said that to plant a seed. You wanted to be queen and I told you repeatedly that it would never happen because I was waiting for her. I've waited over a thousand years for her, and I sure as hell wouldn't leave her for you," Reznor practically spits at her as he cradles me tightly.

Easy. I murmur down the bond, repeating his words from earlier. He's angry, no, outraged. He's almost crawling out of his skin. Taking one of his hands into mine, I try to calm him down before he ruins the plan.

Serena mumbles something before storming out of the room, angrily slamming the doors behind her. I flinch at the loud noise that radiates through the room. Reznor's breathing deeply, his eyes staring off in the distance.

He keeps me secured in his lap for the remainder of the tithe, still seething with anger up until the last person is finished. He doesn't speak as he motions for the guards to leave the room, keeping his hands resting against my sides.

He's furious as he labors in deep long breaths. "What she said wasn't true. I never said any of those things, Liara," Reznor states quietly, with our faces inches apart.

"I never thought you did." I had never believed it, not once.

He leans forward, slowly meshing his lips to mine. Kissing me deeply, he moves his hand up to my throat, drawing me to him. The kiss quickly turns from something slow and sweet to something fast and hungry as he moves a hand down my chest, only stopping to scoop one of my breasts into his hand. I moan into the kiss as he grips and kneads my breasts before toying with my nipple. Breaking the kiss, he starts down my neck, sucking lightly where my collar bone meets my neck.

"Rez," I warn, feeling his teeth graze my skin.

He growls as he continues kissing back up my neck slowly. His teeth skim along my jawline as I tug on his hair, arching my back which pushes my breasts further into his hand. He moans against my neck again, gripping me harder at the waist to keep me from moving.

Prying my eyes open, I find Reznor eyes flashing red. We need to slow down, or he's going to mark me.

"Rez," I gasp out as he sucks along my collar bone. If he leaves a bruise, I'll kill him. "You'll mark me if you don't stop," I warn.

Reznor groans but tears his lips from my skin. "You're right," he mutters, his eyes remaining a vibrant red.

I use this moment of clarity to scramble off his lap. "You should take a cold shower, love," I tease as I saunter toward the door.

"And you should fix your dress," he calls in a tight voice.

I glance down at my dress to see one of my breasts practically falling out of the thin material. I turn away from Reznor mortified as I head for the bedroom.

I had just changed when sure enough Reznor comes sulking in. As I comb through my hair in the bathroom mirror, I catch him turning on the shower. I can't stop the grin as I see the temperature's set to the coldest setting. It seems I got the tribrid king hot and bothered.

Chapter Twenty-Two: Screams Ringing

"Emanuel, if you punch me in the face one more time, I'm going to kill you." Charles spits a glob of blood to the ground.

Emanuel only holds his hands up in defense with a challenging grin plastered across his face. The boys are fighting for sport in the rose garden while I watch lazily. There was no training today, and Reznor is god knows where busying himself. After last night's *activities,* I can't help but feel like he's avoiding me today. Perhaps it broke his pride a little that I flustered him so easily. If so, I'm going to take pride in that, still he shouldn't avoid me. But it's a nice surprise when Charles bangs on my door to wake me up. Our collective boredom led to us hunting down Emanuel and dragging him with us to wander the grounds.

I made the mistake of asking who fought better, which led them to fighting for sport in the clearing between the dying rose bushes. The boys dance on their feet, careful not to fall into the unforgiving thorns of the dead flowers. They weren't meant to live in the fall, not even in the magic realm.

At a sudden thud, I look up to see the men planting themselves down onto the bench next to me on either side. "Emanuel tells me you put on quite a show yesterday in the throne room. How was that?" Charles teases as a slow blush creeps to my cheeks.

Trying to play off the embarrassment of yesterday's very public display, I smile. "I don't know what you're talking about. I played the role I was asked to play." It was revealed to me this morning that Charles knew of the plan the entire time. He just acted as if he hadn't to keep it under wraps and to prevent me from asking questions.

"I don't buy that for a second," Emanuel chimes in, squinting his face slightly.

"Has anything come from the plan?" I would ask Reznor but seeing as he slipped out of bed before I woke, I decided I won't be doing that. The men beside me look between each other before Emanuel nods his head to Charles.

"Reznor hasn't told us of anything yet, and she hasn't tried anything. He made it known to her this morning that he was taking you to the lake this afternoon. Now we wait to see if anything comes from this," Charles replies for both of them.

"Thank you for telling me." I don't like being kept in the dark about things, especially not with the attacks becoming more frequent. "If this doesn't coax her into an attack, what next?"

"Then we go back to the drawing board. We don't know who else it could be at this point," Emanuel is quick to respond.

"Does she want me dead that bad?"

"The attack at Greensboro was on Reznor, not you, and now with them trying to take you, something has changed." I can see the gears working behind Charles's eyes as he remains deep in thought.

"If it is her, how are we going to get the truth out of her?" I ask.

Charles, and Emanuel share a knowing glance. "We will get our answers one way, or another…" Emanuel's voice drops off at the end, leaving me to decide for myself what that meant.

Charles watches me a minute longer. "Don't think about it too much; some things, Liara, you don't want to know." He's right, but I'm still curious. However, they also don't leave room for questions. Instead, they beckon me to follow them toward the manor.

The boys take me straight to the grand hall that Anisa has turned into wedding central. She sits in the center of the room, surrounded by black twigs and small glass cylinders.

"What are you doing?" I question, as I sit down on the floor near Anisa and watch as Emanuel stops behind her, placing a soft kiss on her head.

After smiling sweetly at Emanuel, she turns at me. "I'm making centerpieces for your wedding." She carefully intertwines the sticks around the cylinder, securing them with little ties. Once she assembles the elegant but simple centerpiece, she grins brightly. "I only have one more, then I'm going up to the top garden to finish off the altar I've been growing."

"You grew an altar?" I utter in complete surprise.

Anisa nods shyly, "It's for the ceremony. The wedding is elegant, whereas the ceremony will be more…rustic and natural." She has done so much planning for this wedding.

With it a mere two weeks away, she's in overdrive with last minute details. She has everything planned out from the second I'm to start getting ready, to the moment Reznor is to declare me his queen and wife. She has a real knack for this kind of thing, and it will come in handy over the years.

"Did you hear about the steamy show they put on in the throne room yesterday?" Charles teases me, which only leads me to give him the finger.

"I think it's good they are…" Anisa pauses, looking for the words, "furthering their relationship." She sends all of us into a fit of laughter, which turns to her criticizing us for laughing at her choice of words.

We had been laughing so hard we didn't notice the doors open with Reznor waiting in the doorway, his hands deep in his pockets. "What are you laughing at?" Reznor calls out, startling me slightly.

Charles is the first to try and explain, but Emanuel stops him, "At utter nonsense." Charles looks disappointed as he lost the chance to strike a killer joke. I am thanking God he didn't get the chance to do so.

"Liara, I need you to come with me, you too Emanuel." Reznor lingers in the doorway, not walking in any further.

Emanuel strides through the door first. I, however, take my time getting up; I thank Anisa for doing such a lovely job with the decorations and to keep up the good work before tracking after the men. Walking a step or two behind, I follow them to the study. Reznor keeps a watchful eye on me as we cross the manor, ensuring I don't lag too far behind.

Inside the study, Reznor sits behind his desk, Emanuel and I taking our places before him. He reaches into his desk, pulling out a file. Opening it, he tosses pictures onto his desk. "It seems Maura has crossed back into our world." The photos on his desk reveal my mother creeping along the forest through various images.

"What the hell is she doing here?" I gasp, bewildered, picking up one of the pictures with my mother's silhouette standing outside of a cave, a long sword in her hand.

Reznor trails a hand down his face. "I don't know, but I'm assuming it's to get you back."

"I highly doubt that. The last time Liara was with her mother, Maura tried to kill her. If anything, she is coming here to stop the marking or wedding," Emanuel practically snarls my mother's name. Images of Emanuel tied up in our basement splay into my mind. It had been Emanuel who saved me, and unfortunately, he knows all about my crazy mother. "How long ago did she come through?" Emanuel asks while shuffling through the pictures. It's the second time I have seen Emanuel look angry.

"She came through early this morning. Border control is hunting her down as we speak," Reznor speaks of my mother as if she is some feral animal. "If she hates Liara as much as you claim, then perhaps she is the one conducting the attacks while she was in the mortal world."

"What?" I narrow my eyes in on Reznor.

I can't believe those words fell from his mouth. How could she? She couldn't even get contacts over here to give her the herbs she needed to prevent Rez from finding me. How in the hell would she be able to find people who have been off the maps for years?

"She could have done this, Liara. Don't act surprised. You and I know two very different versions of your mother." the annoyance in his voice sets my blood boiling.

"It is something to consider," Emanuel adds, which only fueled my anger.

I open my mouth to protest but I'm stopped when a blood curdling scream echoes through the manor. Within seconds Reznor and Emanuel are on their feet and out of the study. I dismiss Reznor's order to stay as I follow them down the halls toward the scream that rings again.

We sprint down the grand staircase and out the front door of the manor. At the main entrance, servants and guards are gathering in a small circle around something. Some of the servants are crying. One young woman is practically being held up by another.

Reznor cuts through the small crowd and freezes. Emanuel shoves past Reznor and it allows enough space for me to see the foot of someone lying on the concrete. Reznor moves quickly, blocking me as I try to see who it is. He places a hand on either side of my waist, trying to take me backward away from the scene. I shove out of his arms, and the moment I do, I regret it instantly.

Anisa lays dead on the ground, blood seeping out of her mouth, nose, ears, head… her neck bent a way it was never meant to. But worst of all, a dagger is embedded in her stomach. It's a gruesome scene, and I couldn't tear my eyes away.

Emanuel has tears running down his face. He drops to his knees, taking Anisa's lifeless body into his arms, cradling her head against his chest. Her blue grey eyes open but no longer filled with life. It's watching this scene that causes the sob to release from my mouth. Anisa has been murdered, an unjust and painful death. She was alive minutes ago, and now she lay cold, and broken in her love's arms.

This time I allow Reznor to drag me from the scene as tears stream down my face, my heart breaking for my friend. Anisa had been my first friend here, someone I confided in, and now she's gone. I wouldn't be able to heal her or bring her back; magic can't even fix that…she's gone.

Reznor guides me back inside the manor, shutting the doors softly behind us. He's trying to prevent me from seeing Anisa's damaged body again. "Liara," he approaches me hesitantly with open arms, but I'm filled with sorrow and rage.

"You still think my mother is behind this?" I snap, taking a step back from him.

His face falls as he watches me back away from him. Reznor reaches out for me, but I dodge his arms, turning and sprinting out of the room. He calls after me and even attempts to chase after me, but I put up a shield to prevent him from following me out of the foyer. He yells after me again, but I take off running to the one place in this manor that makes me feel safe: my old bedroom.

Heading straight to the balcony, I sink into the couch, pulling my knees to my chest as I unleash the horrid sobs, I've been holding deep inside me. I cry for the friend I lost, for one of the purest souls I had ever met. Weeping for the person who taught me so much about this world, the one who quickly became family to me. Crying for the woman who wasn't afraid to call me out, and who has never let me down in the short months I'd known her.

Anisa had been alive half an hour ago, and now she lays dead out front. Her death is a message, and I won't forget it. Something dark stirs in my chest as the wind picks up, the once beautiful day turning into a brooding storm. Black and grey clouds start gathering in the distance near the mountains but are quickly gaining speed.

I sit there as the storm rages on, hitting the manor with forceful winds. I stay outside as lightning strikes and thunder rolls. Letting the rain mix in with the tears that will not stop falling. It's like the skies are grieving with me. I stay as I'm battered by the weather, the wind chapping my skin, the rain soaking my entire body. Still, I remain rooted to the damn couch.

The storm continues to rampage, but eventually, I stop crying. I can't muster up any more tears to shed. It's as if my body stops producing them altogether, but I don't dare move from my spot.

Reznor has been shouting in my head for at least an hour, but at some point, either he stopped, or I stopped hearing him. Either way, I don't care. I know who killed Anisa, and once this is over, she will die for her crimes. Serena may be able to fool Reznor, but she won't fool me. They all will see who she is soon enough.

I linger outside until the rain stops, only coming inside once the storm has simmered to angry black and grey clouds that float through the sky. Wandering into the closet, I find some spare clothes that had been left. It's as if Anisa knew I would end up back here. Taking the clothes with me, I go into the familiar bathroom and turn on the shower to its highest temperature, then sink to the floor inside.

I wash away the remainder of the day's memories when I feel pain erupt through my body. Knowing exactly what this means, I shout into Reznor's head.

You better stop whatever you're doing right now! I hiss at him through the bond, feeling the pain stop instantly.

His voice booms back in my head, making me flinch, *Where the hell are you? I've been looking for you for hours!*

I stand from the shower angrily. *You seem to be getting along just fine on your own.* I jump out quickly, dressing as I hear a growl shake the manor windows.

Liara, I won't ask again. Where are you? He should have been able to find me based on my scent, but maybe the rain, along with the shield, blocks my scent from him.

Enjoy your time with your whore Reznor. I send the line silent, going back to the bedroom, crawling into the bed. That's when the tears start up again. I cry until my body shakes, until my eyes burn, my lids grow so heavy I gladly allow them to close. Only to be awoken by nightmares of her blue grey eyes and from a thud echoing outside the door.

"Liara, open this damn door right now!" Reznor growls outside of the room.

I guess my magic doesn't stay up when I'm sleeping. Contemplating whether to open the door or not, I wait until I hear a crack coming from the wood. I scurry from the bed, throwing the door open to find a furious Reznor with red eyes staring back at me.

"Don't be a brute!" I yell before taking in his appearance.

Reznor is completely disheveled. His hair is a mess upon his head, his shirt wrinkled and untucked from his pants. Not to mention the dried mud all over his pants and shoes. He doesn't let me move as he hauls me into his arms, pressing me against his body. He doesn't say a word as he tries to take me toward the steps. It's only when I start fighting him that he throws me over his shoulder, carrying me back to his room.

He tosses me onto the bed. "You're not leaving this room, Liara. Anisa was murdered, and you're not joining her on the other side!" He points an angry finger at me before he drags his fingers through his hair. Sighing, he casts me one last glance before he turns for the closet.

I do what he says, staying in the room, knowing he will only drag me back again, and again. I, however, am not sleeping in the same bed as him while knowing he had his hands on Serena today. Trudging out of bed, I snatch a pillow and a blanket, then move myself to the couch.

When Rez comes back into the bedroom, he frowns, noticing I'm on the couch, but he doesn't force me to get in bed with him. Instead, he turns off the lights and crawls into his bed alone. I try to sleep, but I'm boiling with anger and sorrow. Then, suddenly, I become drowsy. It feels like I had been drugged. I turn sluggish and find myself struggling to stay awake. I try fighting, not wanting to give in and wake up to a nightmare. I will not sleep this night…I can't.

Chapter Twenty-Three: Words From The Dead

At some point in the night, Reznor brought me to bed. I lay in bed with him now, my head against his chest, his hands at my waist. This only annoys me. Not only had I fallen asleep, but the ass brought me to him. I carefully remove myself from him and shuffle to my side of the bed. Adjusting the pillow, I hear a small crunch from beneath it. I freeze, then move the pillow again.

Beneath the pillow is a grey envelope with my name written across the front. I recognize the handwriting instantly. It's Anisa's. I carefully open the envelope but stop as Reznor shifts in the bed, groaning slightly. He sends out a wandering hand feeling for me in the bed, his hand freezing when he doesn't find me. I quickly tuck the envelope underneath the book on the nightstand just before Reznor's eyes flash open. He lifts his head up, looking for me, then rolls his eyes as he finds me on the far side of the bed, glaring back at him.

"If I wanted to sleep in the bed, I would have," I bite as I cross my arms over my chest.

Reznor groans, shutting his eyes again. "You were thrashing around; I was worried you were going to fall off, so I put you in the bed. I'm sorry if it's not what you wanted." He counters, adjusting himself in the bed to lay facing me, his eyes still closed. "Nothing happened yesterday with Serena," he adds, which only leads me to get out of the bed.

"Did you forget I can *feel* when you touch her?" I add, as I go to the closet, pulling on a robe before snatching the book off the nightstand, heading for the door.

"Don't go out that door, Liara," Reznor calls with his eyes still closed, obviously ignoring my question.

"Why?" I challenge, standing with my hand on the handle of the door.

"Because Anisa was murdered, and you're not being alone right now. You can be mad at me all you want, but you're not being alone today. It's not safe. I don't want anything happening to you." I watch Reznor say the words, his eyes landing on me, then glancing down to my hand on the doorknob.

Taking my hand off the door only to go back to my spot on the couch, then open the book up to continue reading. It's enough to please Reznor because he falls back asleep quickly. I read a few pages of the book waiting to ensure he's actually sleeping, but once he's breathing slow, shallow breaths, I open the envelope.

Inside the grey envelope is a letter written by Anisa, and it's dated with yesterday's date. She wrote this the day she died.

Dear Liara,

October 12th

I write this to you with a heavy heart, and if you're finding this, it means that I'm dead. The last few weeks leading up to this letter, I have noticed someone following me, and that's why I locked myself in the grand hall the past couple of weeks. I knew I would be safer this way, but after the ball, it all changed. I found a dagger stabbed into the back of my door with a note. The note bore a red 'X,' and it was at that moment I knew I was going to die soon. I didn't ask for help because I knew it was the only way for you all to see the truth. I didn't want to die, but none of us could have stopped it.

I know who killed me, but so do you. Don't take my death in vain, for I did it to protect you and for the good of your people. I know, without a doubt, that Serena is behind my murder, whether it be at her hand, or one of her followers. She knew I saw the one thing that could take Reznor from her and ruin her plans. She wants to be queen and has had plans to get rid of you all along. I did some digging. In her room, I found letters between her and another talking of your locations and where you would be staying in the manor. I dug up everything that I could on her, but the night I found the letter, all the evidence that I had gathered was gone. I had no proof. I tried to prove her guilt and treason, but she took all of my proof except one thing. Now, I need you to find it, and give it to Reznor for me.

  Deep into the forest, near the old maple tree in the northeast quadrant, there will be a box buried beneath a silver stone near a patch of wildflowers. Take Charles with you, but do not tell Reznor until you have the proof. You may not understand what is in the box, but Reznor will. Do not go out alone because, as the wedding approaches, she has grown anxious to see you gone. I watched her bury this box the day after you arrived, and I only recently realized what she is hiding inside. I have two last things I need to ask of you.

  One, watch over Emanuel for me. Let him know that he is not alone in the wake of losing me and that I will be waiting for him in whatever lies beyond this life. Tell him that I loved him deeply and always will. Let him know that it's alright to grieve and miss me, but he should move on and find another one whom he can live out the rest of his days with. I won't be mad, and I hope someone will love him the same as I loved him. Lastly, tell him I'm sorry that I had to go so soon and without a goodbye. Watch him for me, Liara, let him be sad but not for too long.

    The last and final thing is for you, my friend, I cannot thank you enough for being such a good friend to me over our short time together. You were a blessing in my life and will continue to be a blessing to Reznor, Emanuel, and Charles's life's along with the people you will lead. I know being queen will be scary, and challenging, but I believe that no one else was meant to rule these lands alongside Reznor. Rule with your head held high and with a strong heart, but do not let them walk all over you. You are the queen we have been waiting for, and now it is time for you to rule.

    Take care of my boys and live a long, happy life. I can only ask that you don't forget me, but don't let my death ruin you. None of this was your fault, and I never want you to feel that way. I loved taking care of you and wish I could have done it longer. I wish I could see you walk down the aisle and be crowned as Queen Nighterious, but because I can't, I'll cheer you on from the skies. The wedding, ceremony, and ritual are completely planned, I even have arranged for a special friend of mine to come dress you on your big day. Victoria will care for you and dress you as the strong queen you shall be Plus, I taught her everything she knows.

  This is my goodbye to you Liara, I wish you and Reznor the best along with many years together. You two were made for each other, although you may not see it, I see the love that has started to blossom between you two. It's been a joy to watch it grow, and now I can only wish that love will continue to grow over the years. You didn't give up on him and are actually trying. That's when I knew without a doubt, that you would be the one to repair the damage of years past. I'm giving my boys to you, love them and care for them as I would. I'll miss you, my dear friend.

The Magic Stolen

Love,

Anisa Woods

I have tears streaming down my face by the time I'm done with the letter. I'm in shock of her sweet words to me. I read and re-read the letter repeatedly, trying to make sure I don't miss a single detail. I want to show this letter to Emanuel, but I need to wait until I find this box and its unknown remains. The first thing I need to do is formulate a plan on how to get away from Reznor long enough to get it.

I'm going to need a majority of the day to be able to get there. The northeast quadrant is far away from the manor, past the town, I think. This will be a trip Charles and I will have to make alone, and one we have to do with stealth. The first task of the day would be Charles getting me away from Reznor without him knowing what I'm doing. I could risk telling him, but Anisa asked me to do this, and I'm following her wishes.

I creep to the door, opening it enough just to be able to speak to the guard outside, "Can you get Charles for me?" I ask the young guard who is stationed at the door. The man nods, stepping away without another word. While he is getting Charles, I change quickly and quietly into some training clothes before he arrives. I sit next to Reznor, who is sleeping. I carefully wake him, his eyes flashing open and immediately taking in my appearance.

He rises onto his elbows. "Where are you going?"

"I'm going to go for a run. I asked Charles to come with me," I say.

"No, I'll come with you."

"No, you're going to have to help Emanuel; he has to be a mess right now." Reznor doesn't argue that.

He takes my hand, "Be careful Liara." He leans forward, kissing my cheek, lingering a moment to rest his head against mine. In the moment it makes me want to stay and seek out the simple comfort he gives, but I know I can't.

Charles appears saddened as he walks with his hands stuffed in his pockets. He follows my lead as I take us toward the running trail. Stopping once we're out of view from the manor and hidden just inside the tree line, I pull the letter from its hiding place in my jacket. "I need you to take me to the northeastern quadrant tomorrow, and no one can know." Before Charles can object, I shove the letter into his hand, telling him to read it.

Charles groans deeply once he finishes reading the letter, "Gods," he mumbles, dragging his hand down his face.

"Charles, I need you to take me there tomorrow. We have to get the box before Serena goes looking for it."

"I'm assuming you have a plan?" Charles asks, looking through the pages again.

"I do…but it's going to make Reznor really mad once he realizes we're gone."

"I know this place. We can drive to the northeastern quadrant, but it will be a hike to get to that tree. It's going to take at least an hour to get there and then another to get back to the car, not to mention it's about a three-hour drive. We would need to leave before dawn to make sure we have enough time to be back before sunset." Charles glowers, as he scratches the back of his neck.

"That means Reznor will know I'm gone the moment he wakes up, and it won't take him long to realize I'm not on the property." I huff. This will not be easy.

"Well, it's that, or try to find this in the dark and risk being out there even longer. It's hard to see at night. It would take twice as long." Charles has a point; we would just have to be quick enough to get out of the manor before Reznor wakes up.

"I'll leave a note saying we went for a morning hike behind the manor so he can check that first, buy us some more time," I suggest.

"You better hope that box is still there, or Reznor is going to be furious."

I scoff, "He is going to be furious either way, but Reznor is already questioning Serena's involvement, and I need to prove I'm right."

"Then we leave before dawn. Take the servant stairs near Reznor's room all the way down. It will take you to the garage. I'll meet you down there."

"One more thing. We need to get rid of the guard outside of Reznor's room."

Charles smiles. "Oh, don't worry, I can take care of that." Charles and I put the last few details of our plan in place before returning to the manor to begin preparing for tomorrow.

I find a black backpack in the closet, which I stuff with the letter, a flashlight, a knife, and some water before shoving it beneath the bed on my side. Taking the hoodie Reznor lent me a while ago, I tuck it on top of the bag beneath the bed. My part of the plan is in place, and now I just have to wait.

I go to bed with a wet head that night, trying to leave as much of my scent on the bed as possible. Taking an extra measure of wearing a sweater that I can take off and leave in bed with Reznor, allowing my scent to linger.

I wait for Reznor, but as the night goes on, he still doesn't come back to the room. When I go to sleep, he still hasn't returned, and when I wake up at four in the morning (thanks to the shocking bracelet Charles had given me), he still isn't there. This is alarming to me, but I don't have the time to worry about it.

Jumping from the bed, I dress quickly into black clothes and Reznor's hoodie. Grabbing the bag from beneath the bed, I sneak out of the bedroom door. The guard is gone from outside the door, allowing me to make a leisurely getaway. I creep along the hall heading in the direction of the stairwell when I hear Reznor's voice. Shit. I speed up the pace, reaching the steps before he can get any closer.

Reznor's talking to someone, but I don't know who. I freeze on the steps, just out of his sight as he passes by the stairwell. His steps falter before he hurries down the hall toward his room. I take off sprinting down the stairs, pausing at the roar that erupts through the manor. It's all I need to hear to run faster down the stairs towards the garage.

Where are you? Reznor shouts in my head. I wince hard this time as his voice booms against my skull. I dismiss it, going down another flight of stairs. *Liara!* he shouts again. I flinch as goosebumps rake down my body. The garage staircase comes into view as I dash down toward the running SUV.

"I thought you were going to stall him!" Charles shouts, jumping into the car.

I do the same, scrambling into the passenger seat. He doesn't wait as he steps on the gas, shooting out of the underground garage and heading toward the town. We don't miss the growl that erupts across the lands, shaking the windows on the car.

"He wasn't back by the time I left the room. I had just ducked down the stairs when he got back to our room," I gasp out of breath.

Charles winces next to me, "Well, he knows you're gone. No turning back now."

Chapter Twenty-Four: Deep In The Ground

Charles winces frequently over the hours as Reznor shouts to him. It didn't take Rez long to realize that Charles and I are together. Reznor yelled through the bond numerous times, but eventually, he went silent, though I can still feel his anger and rage lurking, but beneath it all is the stench of fear. By the time we get to the quadrant, I have a pounding headache, thanks to Reznor's emotions shooting down the bond.

Charles pulls off the road, parking the car inside an old barn. "This is an old storage barn; no one will know the car is here."

Groaning, I climb out of the car. "Let's make this quick. Reznor is sending something awful down the bond."

Charles shuts the barn door. "Enjoying that mating bond, aren't you?" he teases, smirking as we head for the densely wooded area.

"No, this part sucks."

Charles only snickers as we start our hike through the woods. The hike to the tree is long and hard. Uphill, downhill, through a stream, but as we come up a final hill, across the open field is a tall maple tree.

Trotting through the tall grass, the sun casts a glow down onto the field. The tree looks as if it's on fire, the orange leaves creating a glowing appearance against the bark. It's a sight that takes my breath away. For a moment, it makes me forget about the aching pain in my skull.

The wildflowers are easily spotted from either side of the tree in large patches. "Look over there, and I'll look over here."

I find the large silver stone hidden within a patch of flowers, "Charles, over here." Charles hurries over, pulling a shovel out of his backpack, unfolding it and digging down into the soil.

He digs down, scoop after scoop, and yet there is no box. "Liara, I'm starting to think there isn't a—" The shovel strikes something hard.

"Never mind." Charles kneels, reaching deep into the hole, pulling a metal box from the ground then hands it to me. Anisa was right. It's exactly where she said it would be.

Inside are a few papers tied with string, along with a silver knife that has swirls engraved into the handle of the blade. The thing that catches my eye is the ring that sits inside the box. When I pull it out, Charles gasps as he catches sight of me holding the band in my palm.

"We need to get that and you back to Reznor." He emphasizes the word 'you' as he drags me to my feet then practically shoves me down the hill.

"Charles, slow down, what is going on?" I jog the remainder of the hill to try and catch up with him.

"Nothing. Reznor will explain, but we need to hurry…" Charles stops, turning his head to the woods. He glances around the forest before drawing a gun. "Liara, run now." Charles and I take off running through the woods until we get to the stream. I'm yanked back by Charles, he hides us behind a tree, putting a finger over his mouth. He slowly peeks around the tree, then motions me with his finger to follow him again.

We creep along the stream, going further down than we had before. This time the entrance isn't dry. We jump from a steep ledge into the stream. Mud and water splash up my pants, across my arms, and I even take some to the face as Charles splats down beside me. He doesn't laugh. He only ushers me forward.

We work quickly through the stream. The water here is deep and moving swiftly. I almost lose my footing a few times as we wade our way through the murky water. On the other side of the stream, we climb up a steep, muddy slope. Gripping onto the top of the ledge, I haul myself onto the embankment, Charles is next to me moments later. Then we were both are on our feet running again. I have to follow Charles's lead because I have no idea where the barn is from this direction.

We run until the old barn comes into view. I watch guard as Charles opens the door. Then hurries to get into the car, he wastes no time starting the car and speeding back toward town. We both are breathing deeply, trying recover from the last half hour of running and climbing.

"Why did we just run all of that?" I ask breathlessly.

"The Tree People were following us… I think… I didn't want to take a chance!"

I pin him with a death glare. "You just made us run all of that without knowing if we were being followed?" I yell.

"What? I was worried! If you die, Reznor kills me! I have felt that man's wrath before, and I'm not getting his mate killed!" Charles admits, looking a bit embarrassed.

"You're lucky I don't kill you."

"Consider this your training for the day." He smiles brightly at me, raising his hand for a high five, which I oblige, only to end up laughing along with him. We did it; we got the box and didn't die in the process.

After almost two hours of driving, my thoughts escape through my mouth, "How mad do you think Reznor is?"

"Probably fuming, but he won't do anything stupid." Charles rounds a corner, taking us closer to town. He presses harder on the gas pedal on the way back. Something in the box is making him want to get home quickly, or maybe he really is that scared of Reznor.

When we get back to the manor, guards are stationed outside, some even wandering through the grounds. The car has just come to a stop when Charles is pulled from the driver's seat along with my door being flung open, a male guard pulling me out of the car.

"Get off of me!" I shout, yanking my arm from his grasp. Charles is being dragged from the other side by Emanuel.

"What the hell were you two thinking?" Emanuel shouts at us as he shoves us up the stairs, well he guides me, but he almost takes Charles to the ground.

"Emanuel, let us explain," Charles tries to reason, but Emanuel stops both of us in the hall.

"It's not me you need to explain yourselves to. Reznor is in the throne room, and I suggest you not keep him waiting." Emanuel stares down at Charles and me. "You two are a mess!" he hisses as he shoves Charles down the hall again. Emanuel takes us to the guest entrance of the throne room, meaning we both have to walk across the long hall to reach Reznor.

The room is dimly lit by the sun. Not a single light is on in the place. It casts a dark shadow onto Reznor's throne, where he sits with glowing red eyes. He watches every step I take. His eyes remain locked on me, scanning me from head to toe. It's so dark where he sits, I could barely see anything, but his red eyes blazing like a fire.

Charles and I stop just before the steps leading up to his throne. Charles bows his head in submission while I can't look anywhere but his eyes.

"Where have you two been?" Reznor asks, with his voice cold as ice, sending chills down my back.

"I asked Charles to take me today. It wasn't his idea." I quickly defend Charles, which only angers Reznor further.

He stands from his throne, prowling toward us with slow steps. "I didn't ask for an excuse. Where have you two been?"

"I took her to the old maple tree, sir," Charles answers, keeping his head down.

Reznor pauses, standing on the last step, his red eyes glaring Charles down. "And why did you take her there without *telling me!*" He breaks his cool demeanor by yelling.

"Because Anisa wrote me a letter. She knew you wouldn't believe her till I had proof. I went to get proof!" I take off the backpack, pulling the metal box and letter out and handing both of them to Reznor. "She said you would know what this meant. That all I needed to do was bring it to you."

Reznor takes the box and letter before climbing back up to his throne. Sitting, he reads the careful words that Anisa had written to me. First, his eyes turn back to blue as he goes over the letter. He's calming down…thankfully. Folding the paper, he moves onto the box. He picks up the blade first, then the letters, his jaw set as he flips through them. He stills as he reaches inside the box, grabbing the ring, his eyes turn back to red.

"Bring me, Serena," He snarls her name, sending a servant fleeing from the room to complete his demand. "Charles, I'll deal with you later, you're dismissed." His voice is clipped and short. Charles bows at the waist, thanking him before retreating through a side door, leaving me standing before Reznor alone.

"Rez…" I start quietly.

"No, Liara, don't pull a stunt like that again." He's trying to calm himself, his eyes flashing between blue and red. "Especially, if you plan on running around with another man."

"I could have gone alone, but I chose Charles because we both trust him. He wouldn't allow me to get in serious danger, you know that."

Reznor's eyes turn that vibrant red again. "That doesn't change the fact of what happened. I don't care that you took someone I trust, I care that you left without telling me." The doors fling open behind us, ending our conversation. I will not be letting this topic go. He needs to understand why I went.

Serena saunters her way across the throne room in a sheer white dress, a smirk written on her face as she approaches. "You wear that to greet your king?" she mocks as she eyes my dirtied clothes, "Rather pathetic, you look worse than usual."

"Don't speak to my mate that way," he snaps.

Her eyes quickly fell on the box in his hands, her mouth dropping open slightly. Reznor pulls the ring from the box before coming down the stairs. "Do you recognize this?" he asks Serena.

"I can't say I do."

"That's funny because the last time I saw this ring was about three years ago when you found some of my mother's things. The next day it was gone along with some letters my father wrote to her, and his knife," he hisses, moving closer to Serena to the point that she's straining to look up at him. "You knew that ring was meant for her. Why did you take it?"

"I didn't take it; she's lying to you." Serena steps toward me, but Reznor is quick to grab her by the throat.

"She doesn't even know what this is." She stumbles back quickly as he releases his hold. "Why did you take it, Serena?" he yells again.

"Because she doesn't deserve it. I was supposed to be queen! It was supposed to be you and me, not you and this ugly bitch! It almost worked too. If she had been killed months ago, none of this would have happened!" Serena shouts as she flings her arms about in her fit of anger.

"You apologize to her now," Reznor hisses. Serena only laughs, turning to walk away from Reznor. He grabs her, forcing her to look our way again just before he plunges his claw tipped hand deep into her chest. "You shouldn't have tried to kill my mate," Reznor growls in a voice laced with venom and spite.

"He'll never let you get your powers," she gasps, blood coming out of her mouth, "one way, or another, he will win…he always wins."

With a sudden jerk, Reznor rips his hand from her chest, removing her heart along with it. Blood drips down his hand, falling to the floor in a steady stream.

"Send this to Lord Nostics. Let him know that his daughter committed treason; inform him it started when he hatched a plan to kill my queen." Reznor places the heart into a small wooden box that a guard holds. Watching him hold the heart in his hands oddly, doesn't make my stomach queasy. He takes a cloth from the guard, cleaning the blood off his hands, "Get rid of the body. Nico, bring Emanuel to my study."

Reznor walks past me, gathering the things from his throne, then leaves out the side door without a word to me. Everyone exits the room, leaving me standing there in utter confusion with Serena's dead body on the ground before me.

I turn away from the body and the bloody mess on the floor. Going straight to Reznor's bedroom to shower, I scrub away the mud and grime while the image of Reznor ripping out Serena's heart replays over and over in my head. My biggest problem with what happened is that he didn't scare me. Not even when he held her bloody heart.

I don't leave the room again. I don't want to annoy Reznor further, and I certainly don't need any more disgraceful looks. But the face he wears when he returns that evening has me wishing I had fled before he came. Reznor's features are stone cold as his eyes land on me. He sets his jaw, then shuts the door slowly before crossing the room and heading into the closet.

"Liara," he calls over the sound of the shower from the bathroom.

I say a silent prayer before slipping from the bed, focusing on the cold tile as I walk to the bathroom. Reznor's standing before the shower; he's in the process of undressing when I come in, his pants unfastened, and his shirt is laying on the floor.

"Tell me what happened today," he says with his back to me, discarding his pants and stepping into the shower.

"Where do you want me to start?" I ask, taking a seat on the bathroom counter, the steam from the shower blocking me from seeing his body.

"From when you snuck out of our bed this morning."

Alright, he's still mad.

"I woke up, and you weren't in bed, so I got dressed, then I went to the garage."

"After you snuck past me, with my hoodie on in an attempt to cover your scent," he adds.

I grimace and nod along, although he can't see it. "Once I got to the garage, we took an SUV and headed to the maple tree."

"While ignoring my questions and asking you to stop."

"Once we got close enough, we parked the car in a barn and hiked to the tree. We found the stone, dug up the box, then we ran back because Charles is paranoid and thought someone was following us."

"Someone was following you."

My gaze jerks from the floor to his hidden figure in the shower. "What?" I ask, surprised.

"A guard in that quadrant followed you two," Reznor states.

"Then why are you asking me what happened today?" I question angrily.

"I wanted to see if you were going to lie to me Why didn't you tell me what you were doing?" he counters.

"Because you wouldn't have believed me." Crossing my arms over my chest, I suddenly feel like a child and hate him for it. I remain on the counter as we sit in silence for the rest of his shower.

Reznor emerges, wrapping a towel around his waist, his sculpted chest dripping with water along with his hair. "You don't know that because you didn't tell me." He stalks toward me, "You assumed because of Anisa's letter that I wouldn't believe you. You assumed that I wouldn't let you go." He now stands between my legs. "You assumed that I was defending Serena," he rests one hand on the right side of my thigh, "You assumed that I wouldn't trust you." He moves the other to the left, hovering over me, causing me to strain to look up at him. "You assumed, yet again, that you can't come to me. I haven't lied to you, given you any reason not to trust me. Yet you Liara, you're giving me a ton of reasons not to trust you, seeing as you keep deceiving me."

His words struck me, leaving me feeling guilty, and looking up at him, I see the anger rolling off his form. He's right. I did everything the way I did because I didn't think he trusted me enough to allow me to do this. His deep blue eyes search mine, a storm raging on in those beautiful orbs.

"I'm not trying to deceive you, Reznor. I was trying to protect you and prove that I'm not going to be just another burden in your life." I lean forward, pointing a finger into his chest. "Yes, I didn't think you would let me go, and I went anyway because I knew Serena was behind this, and I just needed to prove it. I didn't want you to think I was just some jealous woman. I was just trying to care for you in my own way and—"

Reznor cuts me off, pressing his lips to mine. His slowly kisses me, his hands moving to my thighs, tugging me closer to him. My hands find their way to his hair, gripping the wet strands, opening my mouth wider for him as he slides his tongue into my mouth. Our tongues glide against each other in a heated kiss.

Reznor pulls back, taking his thumb and running it against my lower lip. "Tell me next time. I don't want anything happening to you." Leaning in, he kisses me softly one last time before pulling back and strolling out of the bathroom.

It's been four days since Anisa died, three days since Serena's heart was ripped from her chest, and since I told Reznor I cared for him…but today is the day we are laying Anisa to rest. How is it that so much happened in four days?

In this world, funerals are at night, and they aren't called funerals, but a passage ceremony. From what I have been told, a passage ceremony is similar to a funeral, but it takes place after sunset, and at the end, they burn the body. Reznor told me a little about this but didn't give me further details than they burn the body at the end; he wanted me to be prepared.

Nothing, however, could have prepared me for seeing Anisa dressed in a baby blue dress, resting on a flowered wooden platform ready to be set ablaze. Reznor's at my side, with my arm looped through his, we cross the open field. It's been decorated in bright flowers and glowing jars on the ground leading to where Anisa lay.

Guests are walking around the platform, taking flowers off nearby tables, and placing them on Anisa's body, surrounding her as they bid their goodbyes. Everyone's dressed in black, causing the bright flowers to glow in the soft light of the candles. Many are crying, but as I search the faces, I can't find Emanuel amongst any of them.

Pulling Reznor off to the side of one of the tables, I ask quietly, "Where is Emanuel?"

Reznor looks puzzled as he searches the service. "I'm not sure, I'll go ask around." He removes his arm from mine, but I stop him, re-looping mine in his.

"I'll come with you; funerals creep me out." I step closer to him. Death has been something I never handled well. When I had my first run-in with death, I sobbed for weeks, and even now, I hate the thought and hate funerals even more.

Reznor smiles sadly, "Okay, let's go find him."

We stroll, looking for Emanuel, and finally find him. He's sitting against a tree, watching everyone walk up to Anisa. His face is blank of emotion, but his eyes show the pain he feels as he sees the woman he loves being prepared for her passage into the next life.

"Anisa would have hated all of these people crying over her," Reznor says, causing Emanuel's eyes to drift up from Anisa's platform to meet his eyes.

"You're right, she would have hated this many people being here. She never liked being the center of attention," Emanuel's voice is practically a whisper.

"Have you been up to see her?" Reznor asks as he takes a seat next to his friend. Emanuel shakes his head no, his eyes darting back to the crowd gathering by the platform. Reznor motions for me to come to him, so I do. He has me sit between his legs, leaning my back against his chest, crossing my legs at my ankles as I rest against him. "We'll stay with you till you're ready to go up there." Rez grips Emanuel's shoulder, giving it a gentle squeeze before moving his arms around my waist.

"Anisa wrote me a letter the day she died." I try to keep my voice even while pulling the letter out of the pocket in my dress. I take the page where she addresses a section for Emanuel, then hand it to him. "I think you should read it."

Emanuel holds the paper like it's a newborn, cradling it gently in his hands. His eyes light up as he scans the paper, taking in her words. He smiles for the first time in four days. "Only Anisa can make a death threat sound like an adventure," he chuckles, swiping his thumb over the edge of the paper. "She wouldn't want me to be sad, but I just don't know how to live without her. I grew so used to having her around, and now I have to sort through this world alone." Emanuel has tears running down his face now.

"We all will have to learn how to live in a world without Anisa, but we will do it together." Reznor's words take me by surprise, but they warm my heart at the same time. "We are all going to sit here till you feel ready, and then we will go say goodbye to Anisa and grant her passage into the next life." If I hadn't known I cared for Reznor before, I would have known now. His words remind me why I care for him in the first place.

While we sit in silence supporting Emanuel, Charles arrives to join us. Taking a seat next to Emanuel, he takes a different approach, pulling out a flask and handing it to him. Emanuel drinks from the flask before giving it to Reznor, who does the same, and we keep going till all of us take a turn. When it returns to Charles, he pours some out into the grass before raising the flask, pointing it toward the sky.

Watching person after person walk up to Anisa, Reznor keeps me against him. It isn't my first funeral, but it is the first one where I didn't feel like I'm suffocating, and I know it's because of him. We sit with his arms around me while my thumb traces slow circles into his hand. Every so often, he will rest his head against mine or strum his thumb against my sides, little gestures to comfort me. I appreciate every small gesture, stroke, and touch that he gives as it soothes me and makes tonight much more bearable.

Emanuel rises from the ground after most people have dispersed, leaving only a few stragglers. "Alright, it's time." We all get up, heading to the entrance of the lit trail leading toward the platform, each of us grabbing a flower to place on Anisa.

Charles is first, placing a flower next to her head. He kisses his fingers and presses them to her forehead, whispering his goodbyes, then steps aside. Next, is Reznor and me, one hand holds his flower, and the other has my hand as we stand before Anisa.

"Thank you for all you've done and given. May you find peace on the other side," Reznor speaks his words quietly as he places the flower next to her side.

It's now, standing before Anisa, that it all sinks in. Tears well in my eyes as I take in her appearance. She looks every aspect of an angel— her blonde hair curled perfectly, her makeup giving her a soft glow, the blue dress making her appear lively. Breaking the stem in my hand, I step forward as I place the flower in her hair and whisper, "Thank you for being my friend in this new world. I'll never forget you. I'm sorry this happened to you, Anisa, but I'll try to make you proud…" I pause, brushing her hair from her face, "I'll watch over *our boys*." Stepping back, I let the tears fall as I allow Reznor to wrap me into his arms, pressing my head to his chest.

Emanuel walks to Anisa hesitantly, grabbing onto the edge of the platform, sobbing. "I'll love you forever. I'm going to be sad for a while, but I promise Nisa, I'll live the way you would have wanted me to." He takes the flower and places it in her hand before placing one final kiss to her lips. "Goodbye, my love." Emanuel grabs a lantern from the ground, then takes a step back after he lights the podium.

The podium starts to light slowly at first, but then it spreads across the platform, quickly flooding the dark sky with a burst of light. The flames light up our faces as we watch the podium burn, taking Anisa's body with it. Tears fall down my face as the floodgates open, watching Emanuel sob for the woman he loved—watching a woman we all had grown to love—be put to rest.

Reznor grips me tightly to his chest as I cry silently against him, his head leaning on mine. Holding each other tight, I watch as the fire casts a glow across the boys, the heat of the fire warming my skin. I understand in this moment why they burn the bodies. Standing here before the flames, the heat, it feels like a final hug from the person you love—their warmth wrapping around you one last time.

We stay until the fire goes out: we stay as her ashes float through the air, we stay as the lingering candles burnt out, we *stay* together on the ground until the darkness of night gives way to a gorgeous morning. The sun rises, lighting the sky in shades of purple, blue, and pink. The colors paint the sky, and, in those colors, I'm reminded of Anisa. It's at this moment that we all agree, we would avenge the death of Anisa, and the wrongdoing that has been done to our *family*... my family.

Chapter Twenty-Five: Let The Festivities Begin

The final two weeks leading up to the ceremony have been filled with long hours of training along with Reznor leaving every day to go work with his soldiers. He's preparing for a war that has yet to start, but Reznor must know something I don't because troops start training harder, and more guards linger amongst the manor.

I have hardly seen Reznor over the last fourteen days. It's mainly in passing, mealtime or when he returns for bed. He and Emanuel are often gone before the sun rises, then return late after it's set. They are working hard and preparing for something much larger than I know. Charles fills me in on what he can, but it turns out he knows as little as I do.

Charles has taken up the role of being my form of personal entertainment. When we aren't training, he's telling me about his past loves or flings rather. He jokes of his impeccable taste in women who are crazier than they seem. His stories never get old, but if we weren't talking about that, we were finding things to do to keep us laughing. We are trying to find a new normal after Anisa, but it's just not the same…nothing is.

The passage ceremony had been a night of bonding, especially for Rez and I. However, we have somehow split into pairs after that night. Reznor and

Emanuel are preparing for something while Charles and I laugh and train. We've become an odd duo that the staff find amusing. I've never had a sibling, but this is what I presume having a big brother would be like. Some days I enjoy it better than others, but today it's a welcome distraction from the events that will be occurring over the next forty-eight hours.

Charles and I are training by the lake with long wooden sparring sticks. Crashing our beams against each other, we remain silent. Still, he keeps throwing me a glance of confusion every so often. With a swivel of my stick, I send his pole flying to the ground, landing with a thud near the lake.

"Spill it," I say, annoyed with the glances.

Charles bends down, picking up the stick before he turns around to stare at me. "Aren't you supposed to be getting ready or something?" he asks, pointing his stick to yet again another cluster of people who are moving decorations far across the yard.

"The ceremony isn't until later, I have plenty of time to get ready."

Charles snickers.

"What?"

"Nothing, you're just not like any other queens I know," he chuckles.

"That's because I'm not a queen."

A wide grin crosses his face. "Not yet, but you will be soon," he teases, making kissy faces into the air.

"You're a child." I smother my smile, trying not to laugh.

"Perhaps, but I'm still your favorite person, and you cannot tell me otherwise." He beams, placing an invisible crown onto his head. Charles is probably the one person I enjoy being around all the time. Reznor probably won't be fond of that answer, but what he doesn't know won't hurt him. "Have you and Reznor even talked lately?"

"I don't see him much, but when we do…" I pause thinking of what to say, "we exchange words. He is anxious about something. I can feel it through the bond. If he wants to talk about it, we will, and if not, we won't."

Charles scrunches up his face. "That sounds like an awful idea. You guys are getting married tomorrow. I feel like there should have been more talking by now." Again, Charles had a point, but the truth is Reznor and I have just found a comfortable routine; we don't need to talk. I can lay there and read a book while he works on his papers, and it's enough to just be in each other's presence.

"Well, it's a good thing this isn't your relationship then."

Charles places a hand over his heart as if I wounded him. The playful charades come to an end as his eyes glaze over then return silver. "We can't catch a break, can we?" he groans. Looking around the area, he cocks his head toward the manor. "Let's go, something happened. Reznor called for a shelter call."

"What's a shelter call?" I ask as we jog back toward the manor.

"It's when something's happened, and Reznor wants everyone inside. Everyone has to go into their homes. It's the safest way to get everyone out of the woods and out of the open." Charles picks up the pace after his eyes glaze over again, leading me to do the same. "Reznor wants you to go to your room, and I'll stand guard outside."

The closer to the manor we get, the more people I see scurrying inside. Servants and guards are flocking out of the woods. Climbing the concrete steps, a growl echoes through the trees, and I know exactly who the growl came from…Reznor is furious.

The sound of his growl alone is enough to send me taking two steps at a time, getting inside the door quickly. The second I'm in the house, Charles turns, and locks the door behind us.

"Lockdown protocol," he explains before motioning me further.

Three guards join us as we climb the stairs leading to my bedroom. The guards remain outside while Charles accompanies me inside my room. He crosses over, locking the balcony door. "I don't think this is the room he meant."

I instantly groan, he's probably right, but this is just where I went naturally. "Reznor can yell at me for it later." I throw myself onto the bed, sighing.

"Is this it?" Charles asks, touching a garment bag that's hanging on the door of the closet.

"Yeah, all of my dresses are being delivered one at a time. Something about the safety of the fabric." They are very particular about the events for the next two days.

"It makes sense. We don't need someone hexing you." The thought is funny to me, but according to Charles's face, this is serious.

"They do that?" I utter in disbelief, sitting up on the bed.

"Magic is a powerful thing…" Charles says something else, but I miss it as another growl shakes the windows, sending shivers down my back.

"How often does a shelter call happen?"

Charles' face blanches, "Not often, that's why people were running." His words are fearful enough to make a call out to Reznor down the bond.

Be careful.

Rez is quick to respond, *Are you inside?*

Yes, I'm in my room, as you requested.

Good, stay put; this isn't good.

Two hours later, Reznor lifts the shelter call, allowing the servants to start the decorating again.

You're not in our room, where are you? Reznor calls down the bond, sounding annoyed.

I'm in my room.

I can practically hear him sighing before he summons me to his bedroom. The guards and Charles follow me to the room, the bunch lurking outside while I go inside.

In the sink, Reznor is washing blood from his hands, his grey shirt is covered in it along with slashes scattered across the front and back.

"What happened?" I check him for injuries. He winces when I touch his shoulder, seeing blood pooling through the shirt.

He allows me to unbutton his shirt, staring down, watching me undo each notch. "There was an attack on a family in town; they killed them all." He pauses as I pull the shirt from his body. "It was a massacre. We arrived as they started in on another family. It was only Emanuel and I against twelve of them. We got them all, but it's a message. They know the ceremony is tonight, and we can't reschedule it. I thought things might get worse before they got better." I listen as I clean the slice across his shoulder, one of many. There is no way these are going to heal in time for the ceremony. "Security is going to be doubled for tonight and tomorrow, but we are moving forward with the plan."

I chuckle, moving onto the next slice, this one looking like a stab wound. "You make our wedding sound like a business arrangement."

He grabs my hand, stopping me from treating him further. "I didn't mean it that way."

I smile up at him. "I know. Can you let me finish now?"

He releases my hand, allowing me to continue to clean his wounds. "They will heal, it's just taking longer than usual." He doesn't even flinch as I clean the deep wound crossing his abdomen. The idea springs into my head to heal him, solving the problem altogether.

Splaying my hand over his heart, I pull at my magic, allowing it to flow from the tips of my fingers. The light has changed this time… it's grey instead of the blinding white it had been before. It moves from wound, to wound, closing them as it goes. Once every injury is closed, I lift my hand from his chest.

"If we get attacked tonight, you'll need to be in your best health," I say, smiling now that he's healed.

Reznor's eyes are wide with shock as he looks down at me. "That's impossible… you shouldn't have been able to do that."

"Why?"

"Because last time someone tried to heal me, it didn't work. I almost died when I was sixteen because my injuries were too extensive. They found a healer, but it didn't work…" I shrug, having no answers. Everything about our relationship has always been a patch of grey.

"You keep surprising me." His hand grazes the side of my face, pushing away a strand of hair that's fallen loose. An unwanted blush creeps to my face as he leans forward, placing a light kiss onto my forehead.

My arms snake around his waist, hugging him, while his hands slide to my neck, titling my head back to look up at him. Leaning down slowly, his eyes search mine before he kisses me. His lips barely touch mine. He pulls back only for me to reach up on my toes and connect our lips. Reznor smiles into the kiss.

Pulling back, I detangle my arms from him. "It's not nice to tease," I pat his chest, smiling. "I have to start getting ready for part of our business deal," I mock, walking out of the bathroom, but he catches me quickly in the closet.

"But you're a tease," he whispers throatily into my ear, snatching me up by the waist.

"I am not," I argue, but he laughs in response, setting me back on the ground.

He slaps my ass as I start toward the door. "Don't call our wedding a business deal," he hollers after me.

I cast him a smile over my shoulder. "Then, don't make it sound like one." I swiftly shut the door behind me and walk away with that smile still on my face.

Kora, Reznor's servant, has my bathroom set up when I return to the room. She wears the same outfit as all the servants, keeping her greying hair tied back in a bun. She speaks with a thick accent I don't recognize, but she is a kind lady. She chatters while she tackles the mighty job of getting me ready.

She zips up the dark blue dress that hangs to my body. The full gown has lace straps along with lace patchwork over the breast panel, and patches of lace flowers throughout the soft tulle at the bottom. My hair is in a fashioned updo atop my head, showing off the crest at the back of my neck. The makeup is silver and grey, causing my eyes to seem brighter. Before we leave the room, Kora straps on the tall, silver heels.

She trails behind me, following me down the stairs as we head for Reznor at the back of the manor. He stands talking to Emanuel and three other guards, his eyes skimming over my face the moment I come into view. He wears a black suit with a blue tie matching my dress, his crown sitting on his head. Reznor sends them all away with a wave of his wrist.

"You know how to clear a room." A smirk grows on his face as the words leave my mouth.

"It's a perk of being king." He crosses over to me, slowly running a finger down my exposed back.

"Let's go make our grand entrance since you're actually on time for this one."

"Still mad about that?" I tease, taking his extended arm, looping my own through it.

"Oh, tonight's going to be fun." The tone in his voice has me worried as we walk to the back doors leading to the party outside. After Reznor gives a lingering servant a nod, the doors open to the courtyard that has been decorated with lights and flowers. People are scattered throughout the lush space, talking and smiling, but all eyes focus on us as we descend the concrete stairs.

Reznor's face is made of stone, radiating power, and in front of all these people, you can tell who the king is. The only question is if I can live up to being his queen? I shove the thought aside as he leads us down the stairs then over to the priests that stand apart from the guests.

"Welcome to the Ceremony for our future queen. Let the festivities begin," a priest in black robes with a drapery that matches the colors of Reznor's flag calls out, raising his hands so that everyone claps. Music erupts as people began to mingle again. Reznor takes me with him as we head toward Tatiana.

She rips me from Reznor's grasp, hugging me tightly. "You look beautiful!" she compliments me as she pulls back to admire the dress. When she releases me, I step back into Reznor's grasp, which causes a bright twinkling smile to rise on her face.

"Thank you."

"Better soak up this small gathering because tomorrow's going to be a madhouse." Reznor chuckles as Tatiana warns me.

"She's right, you're going to meet a lot of people over the next two days," Reznor speaks up from beside me.

Unfortunately, we don't get to stay with Tatiana long. We have to work through the guests. Reznor takes us through the party, greeting more and more people. Some I recognize from the ball, but most of them are strangers. I smile and greet them all, using all the queening lessons Anisa had given me, but I still can't help but feel guilty for not being able to name any of them.

I wander away from Reznor as I catch sight of a blonde-haired little girl crying on the ground by the fountain. Kneeling next to the girl, "What's wrong?" I ask, as I wipe a tear from her cheek.

She sniffs and points to a cluster of kids across the way. "They called my dress ugly, and stole my doll!" she cries again, a purple flare in her eyes.

"Oh darling, your dress is beautiful." I offer my hand, helping her onto her feet. She throws her arms around my neck, hugging me tightly. Rubbing my hand across her back, I soothe the child until the tears stop flowing. She removes her head from my neck as I swipe the last tear away from her cheek, smiling sweetly at her. "Let's see what we can do about getting that doll back."

The small child clings to my hand as we approach a cluster of girls holding a doll that looks exactly like the little girl whose hand I'm holding. "Is that your doll?" I ask the little girl with brown hair, pointed ears and bright green eyes. She glances from the blonde girl to me. Shaking her head, before staring at the ground.

"Then why did you take it?"

"Because I wanted to play with it."

"It's not kind to take things that aren't yours. Can you give the doll back, please?"

The little girl hands back the doll, looking somberly at the toy. "I have an idea. Why don't all of you play together nicely?" The brunette's eyes meet the blonde's. They both smile, nodding eagerly, the other girls joining in.

"You should do well to take your own advice," a voice calls, coming from the woods just behind the courtyard. The girls flee behind me in fear as a man with white horns protruding from his forehead steps into the clearing. Menacing grey eyes, silver hair running down his back, with sharp angular facial features, his fierce scowls promises violence. I keep the girls hidden behind me, the little blonde refusing to let go of my hand as she stands at my side. "It would be a shame if something happened to these little ones because of someone else's foolishness."

My power surges in my veins with the anger of his threat. "You will not threaten these children nor anyone else here." My voice comes out firm while I shout for Reznor through the bond, *Reznor come over here now.*

"I will do much worse than threaten them." His fingers grow into talons.

I throw a shield up, creating a barrier between us. Lightning strikes far in the distance as he tries to advance toward me, but I freeze him in place, preventing him from moving any further, but he fights it hard. If I didn't have children with me, I would have done so much worse. Thankfully, Reznor comes over quickly, along with Emanuel and Charles. The sight of the man sends Reznor's eyes red, taking in the scene before him.

"Liara, take the kids back to the party," Reznor says calmly.

I keep the shield up until I have the blonde on my hip while ushering the other kids back to the party. The girl clings to me; she isn't going to let go of my neck anytime soon.

Tatiana rushes over. She smiles at the little girl in my arms who keeps tracing the lace straps on my shoulder. "Reznor will handle it," Tatiana says, trying to reassure me as I keep glancing in the direction I had just come from and where he still lingers.

"Is King Reznor, okay?" the little girl asks.

I push her soft curls over her shoulder. "Yes, sweet girl, King Reznor will be just fine."

She freezes in my arms and gawks up at me. "Wait, are you the new queen?" When Tatiana answers for me by nodding, the little girl squeals and hugs me tighter. "I'm Star!" She beams up at me.

"I'm Liara, it's a pleasure to meet you."

She smiles in my arms; it's contagious, causing a matching one to cross my face. A gust of wind comes from above the trees as a black figure shoots across the sky. It startles Star in my arms, who only clings to me tighter.

Reznor emerges from the woods, adjusting his jacket as he speaks to Emanuel and Charles while focusing on my direction. The moment they're done speaking, he crosses over to me. Reznor wraps an arm around my waist, causing the little girl to giggle out. "Why don't you go find your mommy? You can come see Liara later," Reznor says gently.

"Okay, King Reznor!" I place her on the ground. She waves, hugs his leg, then darts off into the crowd while shouting something about meeting the new queen.

"You have a way with kids." Tatiana nods her head in approval.

"Who was that, Rez?" I ignore her comment. I am not having a conversation about kids right now.

Reznor rolls his eyes at his cousin, then turns his head to me. "We'll talk about it later. Right now, we need to follow the priests, it's time for the ceremony." Reznor tries to take me toward the priests, but I stand my ground, not moving from my spot. Sighing deeply, he moves to stand in front of me. "I promise I will explain everything after the ceremony, but we have a limited time frame to do this. We need to go."

I eye him warily, but give in, following him over to the priests. They lead the way, heading to the tree line. Emanuel, Charles, and Tatiana, along with two others, walk behind us, remaining a few paces back. We stroll through the woods, passing by some flowers that float through the air, glowing in a beautiful, soft light. It's the light from the flowers and lanterns on the ground that pave the way to the cave.

Outside stands two guards on either side, bowing their head as we enter the dimly lit opening. The cave has a slow breeze flowing through the high tunnels as we zigzag through, coming to a stop in a room with a pool of water with white flower petals floating on top. The bank starts out shallow, but the further out it goes, the deeper it gets.

The priests stand before the water while the other guests move to stand behind them. Reznor escorts me to the edge of the water, stopping just before the swirling flowers.

Kora drifts from the wall, removing the heels from my feet. Taking them with her, she steps back to the line of guests. Reznor holds my hand, remaining on the edge of the rock while I step into the flat, shallow waterbed. Releasing my hand, he moves to stand next to the priests.

"Let's begin," the priest in the middle speaks with his eyes closed. Reaching out, he takes the hands of the other two. "We present the queen to be before her king, and the closest members of her circle. You are to hold her accountable for her duties to the kingdom, to the land, to her people, and to her king."

The next priest continues the piece, "She will watch, guard, love, and protect those of her land and of her home. She will stand with her king in unity to serve this land until their end comes."

The final priest speaks, "The queen shall serve with compassion, but guard with ferocity for her people and her land. If she accepts these tasks, then tomorrow she can be anointed queen. Liara, do you accept to guard, protect, love, and care for these lands, these people, and this king?" he asks, all of the priests opening their eyes at once.

I pause only for a moment. "I accept." I refuse to meet Reznor's eyes. Instead, I focus on the trio before me.

"Take to your knees," the priest instructs, each of them watching me as I gracefully and carefully kneel in the water. "Close your eyes and bow your head." The three of them surround me, the cold water lapping against my legs with each step they take. I close my eyes, listening as they revolve around me, talking in a foreign tongue.

They go around chanting five times, stopping as a light casts through the cave and shines brightly onto me. Even with my eyes closed, I can see the brightness through my lids.

"Liara has accepted the title of this land as King Reznor Nighterious' queen, blessed be." They say one more word in that foreign tongue before the room erupts into gasps.

I pry my eyes open to find the white flowers in the pool have turned black, and the dress that was once blue, is now black as the night.

While everyone else has shocked expressions, Reznor simply smiled, reaching out a hand for me to take. Rising off my knees and out of the water that has ceased to wet my dress, Reznor guides me from the cave without a word, but he still has that same radiant smile on his face. Barefoot, I walk beside him in the soft light of the forest.

"Why did my dress turn black?" I ask, running a hand along the black tulle.

"It should have turned white, but I'm guessing because you're a Nightlighter, it turned black." He stops, bracing me in his arms, he leans down, kissing me, "A woman who knows darkness enough to handle all of mine," he adds before we start walking again.

The party has been cleared, not a single person remains except for the servants cleaning. I expected us to stay, but Rez is guiding me elsewhere. I must admit it's a relief to be alone with him. With all the people I greeted, and the mass number of bodies, I couldn't be happier for us to be alone now.

Reznor takes me up to my bedroom, us both sitting on the balcony. "Better enjoy tonight because, after tonight, you're stuck in *our* room." His face takes a promising smirk. He is always teasing me.

"I just like this view. A room is a room, but this view is beautiful." I gaze off at the mountains, the moon casting a soft glow against the peaks.

"Whitehorn is a creature my father fought back in the first war. He wanted to rule everything. He was jealous of my father's relationship with the God who blessed me. He felt he deserved to have them, and he's part of the reason my magic was stolen from me. Tonight, he came to show that he still wants to rule all the lands, and he knows he cannot be the ruler of all without my powers."

"He said something to me about people taking what doesn't belong to him, so that was him referring to your powers?"

"Yes, the equivalence of my abilities with my tribrid status are…god like. Everyone fears that amount of power, except for Whitehorn; he's hungry for it."

I reach forward, taking his hand in mine. "Are you nervous about getting your powers?"

"No, I'm more worried about what comes after I get them… people hate those who have more power."

"Well, we will handle whatever comes with it." I squeeze his hand lightly.

Reznor stays with me for a while, eventually departing so I can get ready for bed. He doesn't breathe another word of what tomorrow holds as he places a soft kiss to my brow then leaves.

My mind reels as I enter to the bathroom and continues as I soak in the tub. Even after the day has been washed away, and I've changed, nestling myself into bed my brain won't shut off. I toss and turn in the bed, unable to sleep. I'm not sure if it's the fact that today, I will be getting married and becoming a queen, or if it's the problem that I've grown so used to sleeping with Reznor that my body won't allow me to sleep without him. I do know one thing: I don't want one last night of freedom. No, for tonight I just want it to be normal and casual one more time. One last time as Reznor and Liara, not as King and Queen Nighterious.

Rez, are you awake?

A moment of silence then, *Yes even though I shouldn't be.* Another beat of silence. *Did you want something?*

I don't need to question my next words because I have been wanting to ask them since he left my room earlier. *Will you come sleep with me?*

Reznor chuckles down the bond, *I thought you'd never ask. I'm on my way.*

I snicker because it seems we both were thinking the same thing. Reznor comes and crawls into the bed without saying a word. I shift into his arms, laying my head on his bare chest.

The tingles seep into my cheek, sending shivers along my skin. "Will the tingles stop? Once you mark me." I ask as I run a lazy finger across his chest.

"I hope not," he murmurs, drawing circles against my skin before giving up and pulling me closer to him. Our bodies mold against each other, fitting perfectly together like a puzzle and its last piece.

"You're distracting me. I'm supposed to be sleeping. Beauty rest and all that."

Reznor laughs. "I'm not tired."

Me either…this does not bode well for us.

Chapter Twenty-Six: Wedding Bells Ringing

When I wake in the soft light of day, I'm alone in bed. I'm not sure when Reznor had left, but these last few weeks, I've grown used to waking up alone. It still sucks no matter how often it happens; I hate it.

I take my breakfast out to the balcony, sitting in the soft breeze. It's already the start of a beautiful day. Today is my wedding day, and I can't tell if I'm nervous, but the one thing I do know is that I'm excited. Every little girl dreams of growing up and marrying a prince, and today I'm going to do just that. Well, I'm going to be marrying a king.

Hearing the bedroom door open and close, I wait for Victoria to appear, the woman Anisa had arranged to ready me for the big day. Instead, a familiar face steps through the doors of the balcony. I leap to my feet, taking her into my arms. My grandmother hugs me tightly as I cling to her with tears spilling from my eyes. "Grandma," I cry out.

She combs her fingers through my hair, soothing me. "I missed you dearly," she coos, wiping away a tear as I pull away from the embrace.

"What are you doing here?" I'm afraid to let her go, worried she'll disappear, and it all will have been a dream.

"Reznor invited me. He wanted you to have some family here. He knows this is hard on you. He told me about the attacks…"

Anisa's blue eyes flash into my mind, causing another tear to slide down my face.

"He planned on inviting me since you came here. He was willing to invite your mom, but with everything going on, we both decided it was best if only I came."

"He's been planning this the entire time?" I utter in shock.

She beams brightly. "Yes." She moves to sit on the couch, and I take the seat next to her as she continues. "He seems to have grown very fond of you."

I cackle as she wiggles her eyebrows at me with suggestive eyes. "Grams!"

"What? When I was younger, I thought he was the most handsome young man there ever was, and now, look, he gets to marry my granddaughter."

"I could have gone through today without knowing you think my fiancé is hot," I tease, and nudge her arm.

"It's true, but it makes sense why he waited for you." She stares down at her hands. "I'm sorry I helped keep you from him, but I did do it to protect you, Liara. I disagreed with what your mom did, but I knew I wanted to protect you at all costs."

"Grams, I don't blame you. You have nothing to apologize for; Reznor and I turned out just fine."

"Do you love him?" she asks, stunning me into silence as I think about her question.

"I care about him, but I don't think either of us love each other right now," I admit, looking out at the mountains. I always thought I would be in love when I finally got married but caring about him and wanting to be with him is better than marrying someone out of obligation.

Grams appears saddened, but she's still smiling. "Maybe if you had come back sooner, you two would have fallen in love before the marriage."

"It'll happen someday, just not right now. You know me, Grams, my life motto is I don't do feelings."

She gets a twinkling in her eyes. "Or maybe you never developed feelings because your heart knew it would belong to Reznor eventually."

"Maybe you're right." I had a number of boyfriends over the years, but I never loved any of them. It never felt right, plus, my taste in men always led me to getting hurt.

She beams before standing abruptly and sticking a hand out to me. "Let's start getting you ready!"

I furrow my eyebrows at her. "Grams, it's not time yet."

Growing impatient, she takes my hand, wrenching me to my feet. "Honey, we've got to prep you from head to toe. Victoria has been setting up the bathroom this entire time."

The prep for the wedding is extensive. I have been waxed and plucked of any hair on my body that isn't essential. I soaked in a face mask while my nails were painted, then my feet were scrubbed and painted with a matching grey lacquer. By the time they're done scrubbing me, I swear whatever scent I had before is now gone.

My hair is meticulous, every piece in place, loose curls hanging down my back with half secured in a braid across the back of my head with baby's breath interwound in the locks. She spent the longest on the makeup, painting my face like a mural on display for everyone. A grey smokey eye, with winged eyeliner and a dark purple on my lips. Yet no matter how simple the look, she took her time ensuring everything's perfect.

Now, I sit in a white, silk robe before Grams and Victoria, each of them holding a box. "What's this?" I ask as Grams hands me a small crème box.

"We have a few gifts for you to open. This one is from me." Grams smiles, ushering me to open the box. Pulling loose the dark blue ribbon, I carefully removed the lid. Nestled inside is a hair clip with blue stones and amethysts nestled in a swirling pattern atop the silver clip. "Now you have something old, and something blue. I bought that the day your mom told me she was pregnant with you, I've been saving it for this day."

Placing the pin back into the box, I hug her tightly. "Thank you, I love it."

"This next one is from Anisa." Her name sends a pang of sorrow to my heart. She planned this day but wouldn't be here to see me walk down the aisle. Opening the box, a snort escapes me when I see a black garter for my thigh. The black lace is soft to the touch with swirling flowers in the fabric. What catches my eye is the initials "RSN" stitched in red thread in beautiful cursive at the front of the garter. Reznor is going to love this, I just know it.

Victoria hands me a final box, and inside is a pin of the crescent moon, "Something borrowed, we're going to pin it inside the dress." Victoria says, smiling again. "The only thing left to do is get you down to the grand hall and into the dress."

I hardly register the walk to the grand hall. We don't pass a single soul on the way there, and once we step into the room, it's empty of all the wedding décor that had once been there. The only thing in the room is my dress hanging off the mirror, my shoes sitting on the floor next to the elegant gown. I fight back the urge to cry as I touch the material and think of Anisa again and how much time she had spent in this room. But I don't have any more time to think because it's time to get me into the dress.

Grams and Victoria are unbuttoning the dress while I slide the black garter up my thigh before removing the robe then carefully stepping into it. Victoria stands behind me, clasping each button, ending just above the middle of my back. The lace straps hang off my shoulders. Crochets of lace litter the bodice offering glimpses of my skin before diving off into a full skirt with matching crochets through the tulle, ripples of the skirt and the train that flows behind me. The dress is gorgeous and elegant, and it's everything I could have ever hoped for. More and more, this day is becoming like a dream I had as a child.

My grandmother is standing before me, clasping her hands against her face, tears of joy in her eyes. "You look beautiful, Liara," she cries out, taking in my glowing appearance in the gown.

"Take a look at yourself," Victoria gushes as she steps back, allowing me to turn to face the wall of mirrors. I can't help the small gasp that falls from my mouth. Yes, this was exactly like my childhood dream. I look like a princess...no, a queen.

I'm taken aback by my reflection. My eyes feel like they're being deceived as I gaze at the woman before me. She's beautifully bathed in white lace, her face glowing, her light blue eyes piercing back in the mirror as I study myself. I rarely give myself compliments, but right now, in this gown, I have never felt, nor looked more beautiful in my entire life.

At the same moment I'm admiring my reflection, I feel Reznor down the bond. He doesn't speak at first, but I can feel his presence like a feather touching my skin, it's an affirmation that he's there, waiting for me.

I will make a timely entrance this time, I taunt him, a small smile rising to my face.

I hope so, I've only been waiting for twenty-five hundred years for you. I can hear the grin in his voice, his words sending chills through my body. *But I suppose I can wait a little longer.*

I anxiously wipe my hands against each other, waiting outside the doors to the throne room. What in the hell did I get myself into? No one is here to talk me down as the nerves grow in my stomach. Grams has gone inside to get a seat, while I remain outside of the throne room with Victoria and the lurking guard who watches the hallways tentatively. She's pinning the veil into my hair along with the clip from Grams. The veil is the only thing that I had done with *Reznor* in mind. The veil is white, except the lace trimming is black. It's a little message for him that I have the same darkness, and I'm willing to display it as he does, but only for him.

My attention is brought back to Victoria as she does all the final touches: fixing the veil, straightening the train, touching up the curls, ensuring to reveal my bare shoulders except for the sliver of straps hanging off them. She even instructs a guard to hold the bouquet, so she can finish up her work, and he had taken it without an ill word.

When she's satisfied with her work, she stands in front of me, handing me the bouquet of flowers. The nervousness hit me all at once as I hear the music start from inside the throne room, "When they open the doors, keep your head up and walk to Reznor. He will be standing at the front of the steps. He will crown you before you two kiss, then announce you as king and queen afterward." Victoria reminds me of the plan before she steps to the side. She will follow me down the aisle and will oversee managing the dress, while Kora will be upfront to deal with the bouquet.

I take a deep breath in an attempt to calm myself, 'just walk,' I repeat in my head, 'just walk.' The doors open, and I go rigid. Dear God don't let me fall!

Just focus on me, Liara. Reznor calls in my head, coaxing me as I walk into the room slowly. I gaze at the people around me, trying not to wretch all over my dress. *Look at me, Liara, focus on me.* Reznor's gentle voice is precisely what I needed as I gaze down the aisle, zoning everyone else out, only focusing on the man waiting for me down the line.

Reznor's eyes captivate mine. They follow me as I get closer to him. With each step nearer to him, I feel more confident, the stress rolling off my shoulders as I find comfort in him there waiting for me. A small smile rose to my face as I appreciate him. A swirl of warmth starts in my chest while I take in that smile and the man that beholds it.

Yes, I still have questions, and yes, I have doubts, but with Reznor looking at me the way he is…I don't think I could have pictured anyone else waiting for me at the end of the aisle. I don't think I could have pictured myself with anyone other than the brooding tribrid king.

The dress flows down the aisle along with the train of the veil behind me. I feel like a princess while Reznor looks menacing to everyone else in his black tuxedo and signature pointed crown. But to me, he only looks devilishly handsome, but then again, he always does.

He's a sea of black and I a sea of white, except for my black trimmed veil that seemingly ties me to him. It's then I realize I'm the brightest thing in the room. The rest of the room has been draped in the colors of his kingdom. From the curtains to the flowers, even the candles are all in the three colors of his flag: purple, blue, and black. It's beautiful. The room is darkly decorated, but I love it. Anisa has done a fantastic job.

I reach Reznor, stopping beside him before the priests that stand on the first step. Reznor's throne sits empty without him to occupy it. Each priest holds a different object: one holds a black box, the middle a book, and the farthest one has a staff. The priest holding the book motions for the people to sit before starting the ceremony. I see Kora to the left of the stairs waiting to take my bouquet when it's time.

"On this day, we are gathered to wed King Reznor Nighterious to Liara Norrison. These two have been the stories of many books, a tale that has been waiting to be finished. Now that she has come, it is time to join them in matrimony before their people, friends, and family." The priest pauses only to pray over us in a tongue I have yet to understand before asking us to join hands. Kora walks over, taking the bouquet from my hands, then steps back without a word.

"On this day, October 31st, we ask you King Reznor Nighterious, do you accept this woman to be your wife, your queen, your equal to the throne and in all aspects of your life? Do you accept to cherish her, love her, and protect her as she walks alongside you for as long as you both shall live?" The priest asks.

"I do," Reznor says, swiping his thumb across my hand.

"On this day, October 31st, we ask you, Liara Norrison, do you accept this man to be your husband, your equal, and your other half? Do you promise to obey and serve alongside him for as long as you both shall live? Do you agree to rule these lands and guide him should he stray? Do you accept to cherish him no matter what is to come?"

I feel the weight of Reznor's watchful eyes on me before I meet his gaze, "I do." The fluttering sensation of his presence comes again through the bond as we share another form of affection, one that is only for us to see.

"We present these rings to thee, we bless them with prayers of protection, prosperity, and holiness." Reznor slides the wedding band along my finger. I recognize it instantly from the box Serena had buried. The ring that has been meant for me this entire time. I slide a solid black band onto Reznor's ring finger, shivers igniting across my skin as my hand glides against his.

"Liara, please bow before your king one final time, and let this not be in submission but of gratitude, for he will crown you." The priest holding the box speaks, moving to stand before Reznor as I bow before him. Then a weight is placed upon my head. When I rise, it's to see that same smile on his face. The smile that had been there last night in bed and so many times before. He retakes my hands. "You may kiss your bride and queen." Reznor wastes no time, leaning down and kissing me sweetly, his mouth moving against mine, the tingles erupting across my skin as he holds me.

The kiss doesn't last long. Reznor breaks it, stepping back and holding my hand once again. We turn to face the people, *our* people. "I present to you King Reznor and Queen Liara Nighterious."

All at once, the people bow their heads. The hundreds in the room bowing in unison before us all rise at Reznor's command and watch as he and I walk back down the aisle, this time together.

"You look gorgeous," he says when we're alone, waiting outside the throne room doors. We have to thank and say goodbye to our people while the other guests will be heading to the reception area in the ballroom.

"Thank you," I rise on my tiptoes, attempting to press my lips to his cheek, but he turns his head, causing our lips to collide. It's sweet and slow as our mouths say things we can't. We only break apart when we hear the sound of shuffling bodies.

Our people start filing out of the throne room. Although we don't talk to everyone, we wave and thank as many as we can. Some are crying, others are beaming with smiles. Only a few look as if they could care less. Reznor doesn't smile much as the people clear the manor, keeping his reputation intact. But nothing could have stopped the grin on his face as Emanuel and Charles come prancing out of the throne room. Charles throwing flower petals like confetti, Emanuel allowing himself to be drug along. Even Emanuel cracks a smile for the first time in what feels like forever.

Anisa planned the perfect wedding. The throne room looks gorgeous, and the ceremony was just the same. Everything would have been perfect if she were here, but even with her gone, we all can tell how much work she poured into planning this day. I just wish I had been able to thank her for it.

A tug on my hand pulls me from my thoughts as Reznor dismisses the calls from Charles, who stays behind us as we head toward Reznor's chambers. It had taken a while to thank everyone, and now it's time to change and go to the reception.

Kora's waiting outside the room when Reznor and I arrive at his door. She's the other servant that has access to his room and has been his servant since he was a baby. She follows me into the bathroom, but while Reznor attempts to linger in the doorway, she sends him away before helping me change into the next dress.

This one is my favorite of the two. Mainly because it's more my style rather than the dress from before. This gown is silk, except for the lace long sleeves with trim that runs up from the small cut at the breast, and over my shoulders going all the way down to my lower back where it buttons with the lace resuming at the small train. This fabric's form fitting, hugging my figure at my hips, sides, and breasts. With the crown sat on the counter, I'm able to take in its beauty and its resemblance to Reznor's.

This crown has large, pear shaped, black stones surrounded with a small metal piece each holding a black diamond with smaller purple stones on either side of the large pears. Black stones line the rim, and it even has matching spikes like Reznor's between the gems. It also matches the style of the rings on my finger. I wear his mother's band, and the simple thought saddens me as I realize none of his immediate family was able see him wed.

Kora slips the black strappy heels on my feet before securing the crown to my head once again. She then gathers my dress from earlier and takes it with her as she leaves the room. Rez is drinking from a glass as he stares into the fireplace, the flames lighting his features.

He notices my presence immediately. Looking over to me in the new gown, his eyes rake across my body. "Yet again, you look beautiful." He downs the rest of his glass, placing it on the cart that holds the liquor for his room.

"Thank you, you look dashing yourself."

He slips his jacket back onto his shoulders. "As much as I would love nothing more than to rip off that dress and ravish you right now," he buttons his jacket, keeping his eyes locked on me, "we have a party to attend." I don't get a moment to be shocked by his words because we exit the room the second they leave his mouth. But his words did *make* an impression on me.

Our names are announced again as we come down the stairs into the ballroom, the remaining guests cheering loudly. Reznor raises a hand in thanks, the party immediately resumes as they sit down at their tables. We stroll around the room, talking to the guests and thanking them.

Just as Reznor is about to lead us to another table, Star comes out of nowhere, hugging my legs tightly. "I like your dress." She smiles, pulling on the silky material at my thighs, and I release Reznor's hand as I kneel to her level.

"I like your dress too; you know purple is my favorite color," I say sweetly, touching the tulle on her shoulders.

Her dimples poke through her cheeks. "Will you play with me, Queen Liara?" She struggles to pronounce my name.

"I would love to, but I can't right now." Reznor chuckles behind me as Star pouts her lips. She then hugs me tightly before running off in the direction of a group of little kids darting through the room toward the dessert table. Rising from the ground, I step back into Reznor's arms, who is trying to keep a smile from his face. "What?" I probe as he starts chuckling.

"Nothing." He smirks, brushing his thumb against my back.

As the party starts to wind down, the guests leave after hours of mingling and dancing. They began exiting one by one, and eventually, the room is empty except for the servants. The guests for the ritual are upstairs waiting for us, but instead of Reznor rushing me, he takes my hand and leads me to the dance floor, pulling me into dance, though there is no music. He holds me against him as we rock back and forth, just enjoying each other's presence.

"Thank you for inviting my grandmother. I really appreciated it." Reznor nods, but then shrugs as if it were nothing. I reach up, caressing my hand across his jaw then moving to rest it on the side of his face. "I mean it, Rez, it meant a lot having her here with me…with us." He studies my face but is silent as he does so.

Taking my hand from his face, he twirls me away from him, allowing me to pause a moment before spinning me back into his arms. "My mom always said the woman I would end up with needed to be like me," he pauses, dipping me, before slowly bringing me back up. "She said she would have to understand the darkness in my heart and not fear it." He places his hand on top of mine. "She was right, and I didn't understand that until I met you. You understand it without having experienced what I went through. You were worth waiting for."

His words stir something in my chest that I have yet to name. Reznor is someone who drives me absolutely mad—his teasing, his possessiveness, his willingness to protect me. He's rather bizarre, yet I don't think I would change a single thing about him.

    We continue to dance, holding each other until Emanuel appears at the edge of the dance floor. "They're ready for you two; the moons almost all the way up."

    Reznor stops swaying us, his eyes focusing on mine. "Let's go."

Chapter Twenty-Seven: Teeth Sinking In

We had barely left the ballroom when Reznor's eyes glaze over. The moment they correct, he growls in anger. Stopping, he turns to Emanuel. "How long do we have until the moon is too high?"

"Forty minutes maximum, and I mean she has to be marked by that fortieth minute, or you have to wait till the next full moon. You'll shift after that if you don't mark her."

"We have a situation to deal with," Reznor says, removing his hand from mine. He unbuttons his jacket, tossing it onto a nearby chair. "Liara, your mother is here. It seems she's just broken into the bottom of the manor. Would you like to join us or wait in our room?" he asks, rolling up his sleeves.

"I'll come; she would absolutely hate seeing me in a crown." Reznor winks, taking my hand in his.

At the bottom of the manor near the dungeon, we find six guards surrounding my mother, who is on her knees with her arms bound behind her back. Reznor and I step out of the darkness into the light before her. Reznor clenches his jaw while looking down at her; she shoots daggers at him through her eyes. "What are you doing breaking into our home on our wedding night, Maura?" Reznor's voice is laced with hatred, holding a bite that I don't hear often.

She doesn't look at Reznor. Instead, her eyes drift to me and then directly up to the crown sitting on my head. "You're pathetic." She spits at my feet, causing Reznor's eyes to flare red. "You two will never be happy. You were never meant to have her! You don't deserve to be happy; you're a monster, and so is she!" Reznor's hand that was in the middle of my back moves to squeeze my side, gripping it firmly. I don't know if it's to calm him down or to soothe me.

"You don't get to talk about her that way. The only monster in this room, Maura, is you." Reznor strolls around her with his hands deep in his pockets. "Liara, it's your call. What do you want to do?" he stills, standing behind my mother.

"Why did you come?" I ask, crossing my arms over my chest, which only causes her to snarl.

A guard steps forward, handing a bag to Reznor. "You came here to kill me, didn't you?" he pulls a dagger out of her bag, "It'll take a lot more than this to kill me." The expression on my mother's face gives away who the blade was actually meant for.

"No, Rez, she came here to kill me." My mouth goes dry at the thought—she'd try to kill me for a second time. She doesn't deny it, and she doesn't need to; we all know it's true. That dagger wouldn't have killed Reznor because he would have healed... but it would have killed me.

Reznor's eyes flare red as he recognizes the truth in my words. He drags my mother to her feet by the collar of her shirt. "You broke into my home, to kill my wife, and you expected not to get caught?"

She barres her teeth to him. "If I can't have you, then you don't get to have her. They'll kill her eventually." Her word choice is what makes everything fall into place; she's aggravating him on purpose. It makes all her actions become clear. She knew that if she came, we would have to stop whatever we were doing to deal with her. She wants to stop the marking ritual, and that's why she came now when the wedding is over. The ritual has yet to be completed, giving her time to still kill me, and that was her plan all along.

"Rez, take me upstairs now. She wants you to wait and torture her instead of marking me." I step further into the light, my white dress almost glowing in the dark room. His eyes land on me, then shift back to her, his face seething in anger.

With Reznor's eyes still flaring red, he drops Maura to the ground. "Take her to the dungeons and lock her up. We'll deal with her in the morning." Reznor steps over her, taking my outstretched hand.

Maura screams out behind us, cursing and yelling profanities. Reznor and I ignore it as we ascend the stairs. His eyes keep shifting back and forth from red to blue. I know he wants to go back down there and find out all the information she has. But he also knows I'm right—Maura is just playing another game to manipulate our lives.

We enter an empty bedroom across the hall from his. Inside the room wait three priests, four noblemen, along with Emanuel and Grams. The bed has been made, flowers and candles decorate the room. I found this cliché, but I didn't say anything about it. Judging by the look on Reznor's face, he thinks the same.

The cluster of people stand around us as we come to a stop at the end of the bed. Grams hands me a shot glass filled with a dark blue liquid. "It's a contraceptive," she whisper in my ear. I blanche, but down the shot quickly. Why did my grandma have to be the one to tell me that? I mentally groan. She hands the bottle off to Kora. She lingers at the edge of the room, talking with Grams in a hushed voice before taking the bottle with her as she exits. Reznor seems amused by my embarrassment as he laughs down the bond.

Don't even, I warn, which only makes him laugh harder.

"Let us pray, then you two shall begin," the priest calls.

Reznor and I join hands while bowing our heads. The priests start chanting in the foreign tongue again, but their words sends shivers across my skin. The moment the prayer ends, all eyes fall on us. Reznor removes the crown from his head, handing it to Emanuel before doing the same with mine and giving it to Grams.

He takes another step toward me, pushing the curls back over my shoulder, exposing my neck to him. His eyes focus on a spot on my neck as his hand trails to my throat where he brushes a single finger over the area that caught his attention. My anxiety spikes as the weight of guests stares falls heavy on my shoulders. Reznor's face swirls with emotion; the observers don't seem to bother him at all. His gaze darts from my eyes to my lips, down to my neck again, then trail back up to my eyes.

Ignore them, act like they aren't here. Reznor advises while he presses closer.

That's harder than you think buddy, I counter.

He proves me wrong. Leaning down, he brings mouth to mine. His lips slide from mine, trailing down my jaw while moving one of his hands to my throat, his hold claiming. He draws my head back, baring myself to him.

He skims down my jawline to my throat, leaving open mouthed kisses until he reaches the base of my neck where it meets my collarbone. His canines graze my skin, the sensation making me weak in the knees, thankfully, he's cradling my body against his, or I would have fallen. After the first graze, he sinks his fangs into my flesh, marking my skin with the imprint of his teeth. It's a sharp pain initially, but it quickly disappears, being replaced with an overwhelming sense of Reznor. It's as if I'm now hyper-aware of everything he's doing, and how everything *feels.*

His tongue brushes against the wound as he licks away blood that runs from my neck. The sensation is enough to tear a small moan from my mouth. Reznor was right all those months ago, telling me why he would be marking me in the bedroom. I want him right here, right now. The sensation of his mark on my skin is enough to make me melt into his arms.

The moment he withdraws his teeth from my neck, there's a shudder that shakes the manor as Reznor's powers enter his body with a force. Reznor pays it no attention to what is happening around him. Instead, he picks me up, hoisting me into his arms. I quickly wrap my legs around his waist, wanting him as close as possible. He's focused on one thing and that one thing is me.

"Take me to *our* room," I whisper against his lips, before meshing our mouths together. He brushes past the small crowd in the room that seem too stunned to leave. Reznor opens our door with ease before slamming it shut, pushing me against the wood. He claims my mouth with his tongue, invading every inch. He tugs on my bottom lip with his teeth as he pulls away, lowering me to the ground, dragging me down his body so every inch of me is pressed against him. Claiming my mouth again, he turns us back to the room.

With my feet on the ground, I walk backward while unbuttoning his shirt. The back of my knees hit the bed, but before I can crawl onto it, Reznor quickly tosses his shirt, then drops to his knees in front of me. He lifts the dress and starts unfastening my heels, taking his time to brush his warm calloused hands against my skin.

Rising back to his feet, he picks me up again, taking me onto the bed, our mouths still moving slowly together. Even as he lays me down in the middle of the bed, his lips never leave mine. One of his hands goes to my leg, wrapping it around his waist before sliding it beneath the fabric, skimming across my flesh. The sensation I had been afraid to lose before the marking has only magnified, causing me to push myself further into his touch.

He freezes as his hand skims the lace resting on my right thigh beneath my dress. He tears his mouth from mine, pulling back then quickly hiking my skirt up to see the black garter, a hungry look crossing his face as he peers at the initials on my thigh. With a renewed vigor, he smashes his mouth to mine while my hands graze down his bare back. His hands skim the buttons at the back of my dress, undoing them deftly. Taking his time to gather the material, he brushes his hands along my sides while moving the dress up and off my body. I lay before him, naked from the waist up, only wearing the black lace undergarments that match my garter.

His eyes go red with lust as he kisses me, our tongues gliding against each other, his hands moving across my exposed skin. My nails tug through his hair, twisting it between my fingers. The second my back arches against the soft bed again, his hand dips between my legs, causing a moan to escape my mouth and into the kiss.

"You're so wet for me. I bet you taste like candy," he says against my throat before pushing a finger inside me. He adds another, pumping and curling them slowly. "I've been thinking about having you like this all day."

Reznor moves down my body, attaching his lips to my breast, toying with my nipples while his hand still works below. Arching my back further, I push my breast further into his mouth and grip his hair tighter. A throaty moan flees my mouth as his teeth graze my nipple. "Rez, please." The mark, the bond, it's too much; I need him now.

Reznor disentangles himself from me completely, standing at the edge of the bed, his eyes watching me as he unfastens his belt then his pants. Sliding his pants down along with his underwear in one fluid motion, his erection springs free, standing at an impressive, girthy length. Climbing onto the bed, he uses his knee to spread my legs, grasping my underwear in his hands. I lift my hips, helping him as he drags them down my legs. Open mouth kisses are placed up my thigh, then one just before the garter.

"You're keeping this on," he breathes against my skin before continuing upward.

Skimming up my chest, he leaves chaste kisses along my stomach. then each of my breasts, up my shoulder, and over my mark before crashing his lips against mine again in a feverish kiss. He reaches down, positioning himself at my entrance, his lips never leaving mine as he slowly sinks inside me. Reznor moans into my mouth, a primal sound that turns me on. He fills me up tightly, his size stretching me to the brink of pain, but a delicious burn that makes it enjoyable.

Reznor grips me at the thighs, dragging me further down the bed and closer to him before he slams himself into me again. Holding me steady as he continues to thrust, our hips crash against each other. His mouth moving to my breasts again while I angle my hips upward, meeting his, "Rez," I moan, pulling his mouth back to mine.

His hand grabs mine, pinning them above my head. "Say it again," he purrs.

"Rez," I moan again as he hits my core deeper with a powerful thrust. With his head pulled back, his eyes flash between red and blue as he gazes at me beneath him. Releasing my hands, he moves a hand to my throat, holding firmly.

"Yes," I gasp as I relinquish control to him.

"Hmm, thought you'd like that." He uses his free hand to stroke my hood, tracing it quickly. I shudder as I come dangerously close to finishing.

"Hold on, baby," he murmurs in my ear as his thrusts start to become sloppy, my hands clawing at his back as I draw him closer.

With another hard thrust, I lose it, coming undone around him, my hands gripping his back as I moan out his name, "Reznor!"

He finishes in me shortly after, calling out my name just before he releases my throat then slumps against my body, attaching his lips to mine in the bliss of our passion. We're a sweaty mess pressed against each other above the sheets. Through it all, the garter has stayed on my leg with his initials facing outward, displaying who my body belongs to. He belongs to me, and I belong to him.

Reznor moves to lay beside me, pulling me close to his chest. An intense sensation rakes across my naked skin as we lay against each other. Whatever tingles we had felt before now seem like little volts of humming electricity wherever our skin touches. Reznor traces shapes onto my thigh without rhyme or reason. That's when I notice the tattoos on his arm. I still his arm, bringing it to me, examining the marked skin.

"Rez look." I trace the swirls of black that tattoos his arm. It starts at his hands, then continues all the way up his arm in the pattern of smoke that swirls in different directions as it wafts up his arm and across his shoulders.

"Must have come with the powers. I thought the sensation was just because I was touching you," he murmurs against my head as he tilts his arm in the soft light that comes from the fireplace. He doesn't say anything else as he tilts my chin up to face him.

Leaning down, he presses his lips to mine. "I'm not done with you yet. I've been waiting a long time to have you like this, naked, and on display in my bed, and I plan on taking advantage of that all night," he huskily says, pulling me onto him before shoving his tongue into my mouth.

Chapter Twenty-Eight: Can't Catch A Break

A large weight is bearing down on my chest when I wake up the next morning. Reznor's head rests atop my chest with his arms beneath my waist. I admire the sleeping man before me, the black locks that are usually styled back now hanging loose. His firm jaw is relaxed in his blissful state of sleep. He looks peaceful as he sleeps against my chest.

Tracing my fingers along the tattoo on his shoulder, I follow along the black and grey smoke until it ends in between his shoulder blades. Reznor stirs beneath my touch, my fingers freeze, as he nuzzles his head lazily against my chest. Groaning, he opens his eyes before leaning up on his elbows and looking around the room before laying back down.

Tracing the tattoo again, Reznor trembles beneath my touch. "You better stop that, or we won't be leaving this bedroom at all today," he warns while keeping his eyes shut. His shoulders start to ease as my hand stops at the base of his neck.

"My bad," I tease, then start to run my fingers through his hair instead. Reznor hums in appreciation as I twirl it around my fingers. He groans as my fingers grip close to his scalp. This simple action is enough to pull Reznor out of his groggy state. He lifts his head from my chest, his eyes red as they bear down at me.

He studies me for a moment before unwrapping his arms from around my waist.

He presses a hand into the mattress next to my head as he hovers over me. His lips are a mere centimeter from mine, peering down at me with lust, hunger, and something new… admiration. Reznor lowers his lips to mine, only allowing them to brush against them for a short moment before he pulls back with a teasing grin.

He climbs up from the bed, "We need to shower," he hollers over his shoulder before striding off in his naked glory. Leaning up on my elbows, I appreciate his finely toned ass walk through our closet. "Are you coming?" he shouts over the now running water.

Taking my time to roll from the bed before walking into the bathroom, Reznor's silhouette can be seen through the steamy glass door. He's washing soap from his hair, running his long talented fingers through it.

Steam rolls out of the shower as I open the door and step in behind him. The heat rolls off his shoulders as he drops his hands down to his sides. Just as I'm about to reach out for him, he turns slowly, his eyes raking over my body. Opening his arms up to me, a small grin rises as I willingly go into his arms, then reach up and drape my arms behind his neck.

Water falls from his shoulders, splashing down onto my chest as he tugs me under the stream of hot water. He leans down to kiss me, our lips slanting against each other. Pulling away, he reaches out, brushing away the hair that's resting against my chest, exposing my neck.

He places a light kiss against my cheek, then my throat, then one on my mark, which turns my insides molten. "I like this," he murmurs against my mark, sucking on it lightly. "And this," he adds brushing his lips against my wedding ring.

"Now you have a wife," I chime in, grabbing his hand, tapping the black band on his finger.

One of his hands go to the back of my neck, the other going to my waist. "No, I have a queen who happens to be my wife." He kisses me fiercely, his tongue tangling with mine as he invades every inch of my mouth. Unlike our kiss moments ago, this one is heated, filled with hunger and desire.

His large hands move to my ass, squeezing as he seizes me into his arms. Snaking my naked legs around his waist while gripping the back of his neck, he walks us until my back hits the cool tile wall.

The coolness of the damp wall against my back makes a gasp escape from my lips. I instinctively arch away from the cold; it only pushes me further into him. I tug on his hair harder, trying to pull his body closer to mine, although I doubt that's possible.

"King Reznor?" Kora calls from inside the bathroom somewhere.

Reznor groans and curses under his breath. "Yes, Kora?" he asks with a hint of annoyance in his voice.

"We have a situation; we need you immediately."

Reznor places me on the ground in front of him. "Layout some clothes for Liara and I, we'll be out shortly." He hands me a soapy washcloth. "We'll finish this later." He winks, squirting soap onto his hands then combing it through my hair with his fingers.

"This is why we needed a honeymoon," I point out.

Reznor doesn't wait for me to get dressed. I send him away, much to his dismay, but he finally gives in before practically running out the door. Kora makes speedy time braiding half my hair into a bun, leaving the rest to flow straight down my back. Apparently, because I'm queen now, I need to look presentable at all times. She dresses me in a red blouse and slim black jeans before setting black heels onto the ground.

The moment I step into the heels, I hurry out the door. She wasted enough time, and I'm not going to allow any more to be wasted with makeup. Reznor told me before he left that they would be in the dungeon, but entering it still feels eerie.

Reznor yelling is the first thing I hear as I go down the narrow steps leading to the dungeon. "You mean to tell me she has been gone for hours and you didn't realize until now?" His voice echoes across the four walls of the dungeon.

"Yes sir," a guard says while keeping his eyes on the floor. I step into the soft light, Reznor's eyes darting to me. Yet I can only look at the gore. The room has blood thrown across the floor, the walls, and even the ceiling is painted crimson. Eight guards have been brutally murdered. They are thrown across the room, each of them lying in a pool of their own blood. The dungeon itself is frightening on its own with steel cells, not a single window to be seen on either side of the long hall. But the room is much more menacing with all the blood.

"What happened?" I step over a pool of blood, moving further into the horror scene before me.

"The Tree People broke in and kidnapped your mother," Charles says coolly while placing his hands on his hips. Everyone looks to Charles, who holds his hands up in defense. "What?" he asks.

Reznor runs a hand down his face in annoyance. "You could have explained with a bit more detail." He squats staring into the face of one of his fallen men.

Emanuel stands silently against the wall, the gears behind his eyes working as he analyzes the room. Looking from person to person, weapon to weapon, he looks at everything. It isn't until Reznor stands that Emanuel's eyes stop roaming.

"Get the names of their next of kin, and I'll reach out to let them know what happened." Reznor grimaces, walking around a dead body, reaching a hand out for me.

I take it, following him out of the room; he's tense. His emotions are coming in a lot clearer through the bond. Reznor's in my head now more than ever. The marking ceremony has increased everything through the bond. He's flooded with emotion, but it's mainly fear and rage. Those two emotions together are not a good combination.

The moment we get into the study he drops my hand as he shuts the door, lingering a moment with his head against the wood. The window catches my attention; outside is a beautiful fall scene, the trees shining in the late morning light. It's peaceful, unlike the incident that had unfolded downstairs.

"They broke in and took your mom last night, killing the guards on their way out. They have been dead for hours. This means your mom has been gone for a while. They were in and out of our home without us knowing."

Noting his annoyance at their ease of entry, I try to change his direction of thinking. "Why would they want to take my mom?" I ask, turning from my place at the window.

Reznor sits at his desk chair with his head poised on his fist. "They both don't want you with me, but I've marked you. I have the powers now, so what good is she to them?" He gnaws on the inside of his cheek in deep thought.

"I don't know, but we need to figure it out." Crossing the room, I recline on the couch, facing him.

"I don't like this. We need to up all of our security and figure out how they keep getting in," he says more to himself rather than to me.

Four hours later, Reznor is still interviewing the members of the guard from the night before. I wander the halls aimlessly before Charles finds me lying on the floor, staring at a chandelier in the throne room. "What are you doing?" He's clearly puzzled.

"I like this chandelier." The beaded crystals that glisten in the light. It casts out little crescent moons against the ceiling.

"But what are you doing on the floor?" Charles asks again, sticking a hand out to help me up. I grasp his hand, tugging him down onto the floor with me. He lands with a thud and a groan.

"Look," I point my finger to the crescent moons that litter the ceiling from this angle.

"I've lived here over eight hundred years, and I've never seen that before," Charles comments as he assesses the ceiling.

"What can I say? I'm a sucker for the little things." Charles snorts as Emanuel and Reznor walk into the room.

Reznor stops behind my head, staring down at me. "What are you two doing?" He too has confusion, and amusement lacing his voice. I curl a finger at him, summoning him to the floor with me. He narrows his eyes but moves to lie beside me. He follows my finger to the crescent moons shining through the crystals. "Only you would find something like this."

The three of us linger there for a moment with Emanuel watching the room, surveying those around us. He stands guard until we all get up from the floor. Reznor tells the boys to check in with the guards before we exit the throne room and head back to his study. I plop myself down onto the couch, briefly shutting my eyes.

"You seem chipper today." He sits down next to me, draping his arm against the back of the sofa. I shrug, ignoring his suggestive smirk as he probes further. "You're sure it doesn't have to do with last night's festivities?"

I cackle, "Don't give yourself that much credit; you might need to have sex to function, but it's just a bonus to me." I mock, but that might have been the wrong move based on the look that intensifies as he moves closer to me. I try to scoot away from him, but he tugs me onto his lap quickly.

"Are you saying I'm bad in bed?" he asks while dragging my hips closer to him, causing me to straddle him. "Because the way you were screaming my name last night should be proof enough, but I will gladly show you again." He takes my earlobe between his teeth, a shudder coursing through my body, not only by his actions, but at the intent in his words.

"Did you find out any information about the attack?" I ask while he continues to kiss down my neck, keeping his hands planted on my ass, pushing me further against his groin.

"No, nothing useful," he mumbles against my throat.

I tug at the back of his head, pulling his face away from my neck. "So, what are we going to do about it?"

He sighs, "I'm going to increase the guards, and we are going to start circulating shifts of checking in on each other to ensure we don't have any more time gaps. As far as your mother goes, we have been trying to track the Tree People, and now we'll look for her too."

I search his eyes before a dark thought crosses my mind. "If you find her, send her ass back to the mortal world." I lean forward, pecking his lips, then pulling back again. "She doesn't get to try and hurt *us* again."

"Such a dirty mouth," he smirks, guiding my mouth back to his.

For a second time today, Reznor and I are interrupted during an intimate session, this time however, we're interrupted by Tatiana. She fumbles into the room looking distraught, her short hair thrown in all different directions. Black mascara runs down her face over her tinted cheeks, her yellow eyes looking dull as a tear rolls down her cheek.

She startles at our positions on the couch, her lip trembling. "Arnold is dead…" she cries, "They killed him." Reznor and I gape at each other, shocked expressions on both of our faces. I scramble off his lap, Reznor rising to his feet the moment I'm off him.

"What?" He hurries to Tatiana, catching her falling body as soon as he's close enough. He cradles her against him, not allowing her to fall to the floor.

She grips onto the collar of his shirt. "They killed him then hung him from the flagpole," she sobs against his chest. Reznor's eyes dart to me, his eyes wild as we exchange horrified looks. After taking in her expression oner more time, his eyes glaze over.

Emanuel and Charles burst into the room with four other guards in tow. All their eyes going to Tatiana sobbing in Reznor's arms. Seeing that Reznor needs to talk to the guards, I take Tatiana by her hand, gently tugging on it, guiding her into my arms. Reznor observes as I take his brittle cousin to the couch. He's stunned for a moment until he starts speaking to Emanuel, Charles, and the guards in hushed voices while taking their conversation outside of the room, giving us space.

Tatiana breaks in my arms while I comb the back of her head, attempting to soothe her pain. Eventually, her tears stop, the heavy sobs cease, along with the shaking of her shoulders. It all stops as if she has turned off her sadness.

After a few moments, she lifts her head from my chest, her yellow eyes looking at me with a blank expression. "Do you need anything?" I ask softly as she shifts into a sitting position beside me.

"Will you call Reznor? I need to tell him what happened so I can go home." She hastily wipes away at the black smudges beneath her eyes.

"Are you sure you want to do this now?" I pause, grasping her hand in mine, "You can wait to talk to him."

She shakes her head. "No, I can't. I need to do this so I can go home and plan a passage ceremony for my husband."

Respecting her wishes, I call out to Reznor, *she wants to talk now.*

He doesn't respond, instead, he comes into the room minutes later, his sleeves rolled up to his elbows, revealing his marked arms. Tatiana's eyes go directly to his tattoo, then to my neck, where no evidence of his mark can be seen; Only mates can see their mark for protection.

"You don't have to do this now, Tatiana." Reznor leans against his desk as he looks down at her.

"I know, but I want to. I need to get this over with so we can put him to rest." She sniffles, and for a moment, I think she's going to cry again, but she hastily shakes her fallen hair from her face.

Can you give us a moment? Reznor asks, giving me a pleading look.

I squeeze her hand a final time before standing up. She tries to give me a smile but can't seem to bring herself to do it. Outside the door, Emanuel stands with his hand on his blade, his stare going to the significant wet spot on my shoulder.

"Come on, I'll take you upstairs to change while they talk," Emanuel says quietly, offering up his arm for me to take. Once I loop my arm through his, he pats it softly. "I've been taking five minutes each day to talk to Anisa." Emanuel's words surprise me as he continues. "Five minutes each day I talk to her, I tell her I miss her, that I love her, and what my day has been. For those five minutes, I forget that she's gone, and everything feels like she is alive." He pauses as we turn a corner, climbing the stairs toward my bedroom, "But then the five minutes are up, and I allow myself to be sad for two minutes after that. I grieve her for two minutes just to help myself heal."

As we reach the top of the stairs, I stop him. "Why have you been so quiet?"

"I've always been quiet, but it was Anisa who got me to talk more, and now that she's gone, I don't find myself having much reason to talk," Emanuel admits.

I look to the ground as we get closer to the bedroom door. "I'll talk to you, or I'll get you to talk. Emanuel, I know Reznor asks you to watch me and protect me, but I like to think we're friends, and I like to talk to you. If you ever want to talk about Anisa, I will gladly listen."

Emanuel smiles down at me. "Reznor doesn't ask me to watch you or protect you. He doesn't have to because you are my friend, and I want to protect you not only as my queen, but as my friend," he pats my arm again. "As far as Anisa goes, I'm not ready to talk about her now, but I will be eventually if you don't mind waiting around for me to be ready."

"That's something I can do."

We both turn and cross to my bedroom door, but a small brown box halts us in our tracks. I warily bend down and gather up the box, taking it into my hands. The moment I remove the lid, I gasp in horror as my eyes land on a bloodied heart sitting inside a box with a note on top that reads,

Although he wasn't my target, he served a purpose. You'll lose this war, Reznor, and when I'm done destroying your kingdom, I'll rip her heart out while you beg for her life. Liara will die, and your kingdom will fall.

"We need to get Reznor," I say eerily calm as I hand Emanuel my death threat, "It looks like things are about to get more complicated."

Chapter Twenty-Nine: Felt Across The Lands

I pace back and forth in the bedroom across the hall from our room with Emanuel as we wait for Reznor. I called out to him immediately, but he hasn't responded yet, and that was nearly an hour ago. I had been so focused on my steps that I didn't hear the door open until I feel Reznor's eyes on me.

"Sorry I came as soon as I could, what's going on?" he studies me intently. Emanuel stares at me, and I realize that I will be the one to tell Reznor.

I point to the box with a finger. It sits closed on the bed, the lid hiding its contents. "That box was left at our bedroom door. I'm guessing it's from Serena's father." I finally stop my pacing as Reznor reaches for the box.

The moment he opens the box, his anger flares down the bond. "You two found this?" he asks, holding the note in his hand.

"I came upstairs to change, and it was just sitting outside our door." Reznor tosses the note back into the box and shuts the lid before turning back to face me.

"We can't tell her, not yet." He set his jaw, striding for the door. "We'll tell her after the passage ceremony, until then we up all the guards. They came to our bedroom door, they invaded our home again, and this will be the last time. Emanuel, do not leave her side for any reason." He seethes before opening the door, leaving Emanuel and I gaping at each other.

"He's really mad," I state, causing Emanuel to chuckle.

"Someone just threatened to kill his wife, yes, he is mad."

It's been three days since Arnold was murdered, and ever since then, Reznor's been tense and irritated with everyone. Hell, even I've started to avoid him because he's in such a foul mood. But I won't get to avoid him much longer because soon we will have to go down and pay our respects to Arnold for his passage ceremony.

My reflection in the mirror staring back is dark with my long black dress. Lace sleeves hang down to my waist, a matching lace belt around the center of my abdomen just above my navel. My eyelids are shaded black while my hair's styled in a braided updo with my crown upon my head.

It's weird…wearing a crown. I said a few words, and suddenly I'm a ruler of lands unknown to me. I'm a queen, a wife, and one day into my reign, I received a death threat. Within four days of my marriage, I've started avoiding my husband because his mood is too unbearable to be around.

A movement behind me startles my thoughts as Reznor approaches me in the reflection of the mirror. He regards me through the mirror, reaching out and wrapping his arms around me from behind. He kisses the side of my neck. "You look beautiful."

I lean into his touch, "Thank you." Reznor and I look like a matching pair with our crowns and black outfits. We're the King and Queen of Darkness... or so the people like to call us. I turn in his arms to face him. "How are you doing?" His jaw instantly sets as the words leave my mouth.

"I'll be a lot better when this day is over, and we're home." His voice is almost spiteful. His tone makes me pop an eyebrow up at him in suspicion. He yanks his hands from my body then storms for the door.

"Reznor," I call after him, making him halt in his tracks. He doesn't move as I come up behind him. Sliding my hand along his shoulder, "If you don't want to talk about it, then we won't talk about it, but I'm asking you what you need right now so we don't go down there, and you bite someone else's head off for trying to comfort you."

Reznor lifts his head up. "I appreciate the thought, but please Liara, I don't want to talk about it. I just want some space." He shuts the door softly on his way out.

That is not what I wanted to happen. I'm usually very good at consoling people, but Reznor is still foreign ground that I'm learning to navigate. I want to help him, but if he wants to be left alone, then that's what I'll do. I knew it's risky to even ask if I could help, but I can sense how he is hurting through the bond. Reznor feels guilty, like this is his fault, but treason was declared when the attacks started on me four months ago. It isn't his fault, yet he continues to believe that Arnold's death is blood on his hands. But as sad as it may be, Arnold is a causality of war just as Anisa had been one. It's not fair that we lived, and they didn't, but now we have to find a way to live with this guilt.

I linger a moment longer before walking out the door, or instead, I tried to, but Emanuel's back blocks me from doing so. He quickly steps aside once he notices the now open door. I raise an eyebrow quizzically, but he keeps a placid face as he stares ahead. It seems the quiet giant is on guard duty. I note Emanuel stays three steps behind me. He has been my shadow since the box arrived. I don't know if it's Reznor's asking, or Emanuel's volunteering. Still, either way, everywhere I go, he tags along.

A small group of servants, along with a few guards, stand outside of a bedroom. All of them talking amongst themselves in confusion and concern. "What's going on?" I ask no one in particular, but they all turn in union, bowing their heads to me.

"The queen is refusing to leave her room, Your Majesty," A little servant girl answers quietly.

"I'll speak to her." The sea of servants part immediately, allowing me to walk through them. Some of them whisper as I pass, 'That's the new queen,' 'I heard she is stronger than King Reznor.' I chuckle at the naive comments; none of us know what Reznor can do yet. I grasp the silver handle, knocking before pushing the door open, entering the large bedroom. The only light comes from the fireplace where Tatiana's form can be seen sitting on her knees before the fire, a black dress and robe covering her skin along with an orange gold crown upon her head.

I kneel down, staring into the fire alongside the broken-hearted queen. We sit in silence for a few moments before I repeat the same advice that Emanuel had given me a couple days before. "We're going to sit here for five minutes, and you're going to grieve the loss of your husband, and then you and I will get off the floor. I'll straighten your crown and touch up your make up, we'll walk out of this room and go down to pay our respects to your husband. You can be sad the entire time, but we cannot let them win. You will get revenge for what they have done to you, I will ensure that."

She grips her hand in mine. "But until then, you have the next five minutes to let it out. Then you have to be the queen all of your people are looking up to and needing right now." She sniffles, then the sobs wrack her body. Gripping my hand and one of Arnold's shirts in the other, she trembles and cries for the full five minutes. But the moment I say time is up, she rises to her feet while still holding my hand. She sits at the vanity, waiting for me to fix her crown. I touch up her makeup quickly, knowing she will cry it all away again later, but for now, she appears like a put together woman. The only signs she's been crying are in her yellow eyes. They aren't as bright as usual.

With Tatiana now ready to face the crowd outside, I loop my arm through hers as we exit the large double doors of her bedroom. The staff outside seem shocked, but quickly bow at her presence. Tatiana paves the way but refuses to move unless I'm with her. I squeeze her arm as we pass more servants bowing their heads in respect as the two of us ease down the hallway along with several guards behind us. Emanuel stays closer than the rest, but the other guards make no move to stand any closer to us than they already are.

The moment we top the stairs of the courtyard, Tatiana freezes as she takes in Arnold's body on the podium. It's massive, fit for a king. Littered with thousands of flowers and little mementos belonging to the king, along with a large mural of Tatiana and Arnold created out of flowers that stands on the large podium with him.

It's my turn to lead. Her yellow tear-filled eyes meet mine, giving her a subtle nod, she grimaces. Before turning to the hundreds of people below, I put my shoulders back and tilt my head up. Tatiana copies my stance as we descend the stairs, but the entire way down, I'm tracked by a pair of eyes I've come to know so well. Reznor's feet are planted in the ground, not moving an inch as we descend into the ceremony.

Tatiana fists my sleeve as we move through the crowd but keeps her composure. "Take me to say goodbye," she whispers, her voice barely reaching my ears. Crossing up to the podium we climb the stairs. I only release her so she can have her moment to say goodbye. But she begs me not to leave the podium without her.

I linger a few steps behind her as she kneels next to her husband, a stray tear falling down her face. I hand her a yellow sunflower, which she graciously takes and places next to her fallen king. The sight shatters my heart as I witness the love and sorrow flow through her eyes as she holds her husband's hand.

I wait patiently for her to say goodbye, knowing she'll need me to descend the stairs. Our agreement not to cry lasted for a short while, but she rises up after placing a gentle kiss against his lips one last time. She retakes my arm before we both retreat down the stairs.

I need a drink, so I take initiative and go over to the refreshment table where our wines are tested and smelled before we're each handed a glass. I take a rather large swig, allowing the sweet liquid to run down my throat.

I don't get another one before Tatiana's wandering eyes find Reznor across the party observing us. "What is your husband doing all the way over there when we are over here?" she asks, annoyed.

I take another sip from my glass. "I asked him what he needed, and he said space, and that is why he is all the way over there." I clarify as Tatiana turns her head to me, bewildered.

"We are going over there right now because if I can't be alone, then he doesn't get to either."

I detach my arm from hers. "You can do that but, I will not." She casts me a glare before stalking off toward her cousin with anger in her eyes. At the same time, I turn to face Emanuel instead of watching the conversation that I know is about to occur. "Why are you lurking, Emanuel?" I ask, shifting closer to him, and more importantly further away from the passage ceremony. They still creep me out; death is not something I was fond of, or something I can grow used to.

He offers a small smile to me. "I'm protecting my friend and queen."

"Did Reznor ask you to be my personal guard?"

Emanuel shakes his head. "No, actually, I asked him if I could do it." My shock tears my attention from the floating lantern as he continues. "From here on out, I will be your personal guard except when I'm needed as the second in command. This means I will die for you, Liara, and if you run off, I will find you as will Charles and Reznor. We won't let anything happen to you."

"You don't have to do that. Just be my friend Emanuel, that's all I want." It saddens me to hear he would die in place of me, even more so, all three would be willing to do so.

"I would die for you as your friend."

"Well, if you die for me, I will never forgive you. Instead, live for me." Emanuel's eyes track something behind me. Reznor arrives next to me, Tatiana hanging off his arm.

"I've found a new chauffeur, Liara," Tatiana announces. However, she doesn't smile like she usually would have.

I wink at her then study Reznor, who, much to my surprise, doesn't look annoyed. "That's good. In fact, I think you should have him lead you around to speak with some of your guests."

Tatiana smile is small, but it's still there, "I think that's a grand idea." Reznor gives me a pointed expression.

You'll pay for this later, love.

I'm merely granting your wish to be left alone, you can be alone with your cousin. He doesn't respond to my smart mouthed comment, nor do I expect him too. I hadn't done it to be spiteful, I did it to distract him, but he doesn't need to know that.

As the ceremony's winding down, it's time to set the flame. Tatiana summons all the guests, presiding before the podium with a lit torch in her finely manicured hand. "May you find joy and prosperity in the afterlife, my love. Gods bless this king on his passage home," she calls to the crowd. Reznor lingers near the front, waiting for her while Emanuel and I hide at the back. Tatiana lights the podium, and slowly, it starts to go up in flames. Arnold's people, family, and friends all watching as he begins his journey to the next life.

As the flames rise higher and higher, Reznor and Tatiana make their way through the crowd until they find Emanuel and I leaning against a pillar in the courtyard. Tatiana releases Reznor, motioning in my direction with her now free hand. Reznor ignores it and takes her arm again before he starts for the house. He stops next to me, planting a kiss on my cheek. *I'm going to go tell her about the letter. Do you wish to come?* he asks through the mate bond.

No, me being there might only complicate things.

Reznor gives a jerk of his head, then strides for the castle with Tatiana looking confused as she follows him up the stairs. Emanuel and I linger until finally I deciding to retire to the castle. We'll leave in the early hours of the morning, and this day has caused me to grow weary.

As we pass the study, we hear yelling coming from Tatiana. I flinch and hurry past, steering down the hallway briskly. Two looming figures stop me from progressing further. Emanuel notices immediately and pulls out his sword, shifting into a fighting stance in front of me.

 The two figures turn to four as the hallway widens after they make it through the door frame. I reach for my powers in my mind, throwing a shield up around the two of us. Stepping closer to Emanuel as four more come from the other end of the hall. They all attack at once, and having no weapon on me, I use my powers and send two of them flying through a nearby window before they can advance another step. Emanuel's fighting the other four, keeping them away from me as I square up to spar with the other two. They were too close for me to launch them anywhere but the wall. I spin to avoid a strike from their long blades. Something's different about their swords. They have a large orangish-yellow stone that sits on the hilt.

 A glace over my shoulder tells me the other four all have the same stones in each of their weapons, the action being costly as one tries to grab me. I turn him to ash the moment his hand touches my body, causing his sword to fall to the ground with a clank. This only angers the other guard as he lashes out and swings at me. Quickly, I jump back, throwing a hand out, freezing him in place, before sending him flying through the air knocking over two of the guards Emanuel's fighting.

 The commotion brings Reznor out of the study just as another set of guards come down the hallway running at me. The guards don't falter as they both act to attack me. Just as I'm about to strike at the guards with my powers, the castle shakes as a dark purple light erupts from Reznor. It travels in a misty dance toward the two guards. The second the purple matter touches them they began clawing at their own skin before falling to the ground.

Reznor's eyes glow red as he unleashes his power. He takes all the remaining guards to their knees, their bones crunching and snapping as they fall. They scream in agony, but Reznor doesn't stop till they're dead. Only then does his eyes return to their dark blue. He sprints down the remaining length of the hallway toward me. He assesses for injury before sliding an arm around my waist, bringing me to his chest. I huff a breath of relief as he holds me in the now destroyed hallway. "Are you alright?" he asks, his voice tight, a clear sign of his anger.

"I'm fine," I say quickly as I hold onto him tighter. This will be the last time I travel without a weapon. There's no doubt in my mind that whatever power he just used was felt across the lands. He busted the windows out, knocked paintings from the walls, he literally wrecked the hall. Through the broken window, people below search for the source of power they felt.

I close my eyes, breathing in Reznor's scent deeply, which quickly calms my nerves, and my being close to him is doing the same. He isn't as tense now as he was few moments ago. I almost forgot we had an audience until I hear Tatiana's voice.

"My people will fight with you, no matter what the cause is, my people will fight for you," Tatiana calls, gawking at Reznor holding me against him.

"We'll leave tonight. I'll send back guards to you when we arrive back at the manor. They'll protect your lands while they're here waiting for word of the first fight," Reznor's hold tightens.

As more guards arrive at the scene, Tatiana barks orders to get our car and things ready. We will be leaving immediately.

Reznor doesn't leave my side until Emanuel and I both are sat in the car, while he converses to Tatiana outside. Emanuel's somber when I glance in the rearview mirror. "Thank you, Emanuel, for protecting me."

His eyes meet mine in the mirror. "My pleasure, although I wish it wouldn't have happened at all."

"Why did their swords have those stones?" I ask, inspecting the one sitting in the passenger seat next to Emanuel.

"I'm going to figure that out." Emanuel doesn't say anything else as Reznor climbs into the car. He sits next to me, snaking an arm around my waist, dragging me closer to him.

The second we arrive back to the manor, Reznor helps me out of the car. My heels dangle from one of his hands while his other is wrapped around my waist as we climb the steps. Charles meets us halfway up, listing off things that he's already done.

I don't wait around to listen. Instead, I stand on my toes, place a kiss on Reznor's cheek, then go upstairs with Emanuel and now two more of my guards in tow as they trail me to our bedroom. In the bathroom, I remove all the pins from my hair, setting them on the counter next to my crown that Reznor will put away when he returns. I quickly change into a nightgown before retreating from the closet, only to go still when I enter the bedroom. Reznor sits on the bed with his head hung.

I stand between his legs, gently pushing his head back. "You said you didn't want to talk about it, so this is all I'm going to say." I move my hands to either side of his face. "Today was not your fault, just like Arnold's death is not your fault. You're not alone in any of this, Reznor, not anymore. If you need me, just say the word and I'm there." He briefly closes his eyes the moment I let go of his face.

"I'm tired of this. I'm tired of people dying, but most of all, I'm tired of people trying to take you." He stops, his eyes opening only to glare at the ground before looking up at me. "I need you." Those words are enough to bring me right back to him, taking his face into my hands. "I just need you." He leans up and kisses me as his hands tug on my waist, pulling me onto his lap.

"Reznor, you've always had me," I say, before leaning in and placing my lips on his.

We kiss slowly, our tongues and mouths molding against each other. Reznor leans back, taking us to the mattress, his hands keeping me splayed against him.

I tear my mouth from his. "I don't think this will solve any of your feelings."

"I think it does, because you remind me that things aren't as bad as they were and have been in the past." With those wise words, I don't respond out of fear that my words will fail me, so I take my nightgown off then bring Reznor's lips back to mine and do my best to distract the man I care for from the thoughts that haunt him.

Chapter Thirty: A Surprise Guest

When I wake the next morning, Reznor's still holding me tightly in his sleep, his arms wrapped around me. I take my time waking him up, slowly, and sweetly. Reznor sure does enjoy it, I might add. Even as we sit in the study, he keeps shooting sultry glances over the book I'm reading. He caresses the back of my neck through the bond, making me shiver.

I cast him a warning look, but he only smiles tauntingly and does it again, this time lower. Snapping the book shut I hop up, sliding my feet into the flats that sit by the edge of the couch. As I walk past him, I give him a swift swat to the back of the head that sends Emanuel and Charles into a roar of laughter. Reznor slaps my ass before I get more than a step away from him, my wide eyes and gaping reaction has him joining in on the laughter. Leaving the papers at his desk, he follows me out of the study. "I'm almost done with these plans, then I need to go into town and meet with one of the commanders, do you want to come?" he asks while toying with the black clasp on his jacket.

"I'm going to stay here and read, but how about next time?" I take a step closer, causing him to lose interest in the clasps.

He grins down at me as he lowers his head closer to mine, "Okay, but next time I take you, I'll show you some interesting places in town." Judging by the look on his face, I'm guessing it won't be a sightseeing tour. Reznor presses his lips, still in a smile, against my mine, which makes me do the same. Pulling away, he tousles my hair before kissing me once more. Even as the door opens, he doesn't pull away till he's ready.

"Gross, I hate when Mom and Dad kiss in front of us," Charles teases as he shudders with disgust.

"The thought of you being my offspring is not pleasant," Reznor scrunches his nose up, shaking his head. "I know too much about your personal life." His choice of words send all of us into a burst of laughter again.

I stroll with the boys to the entrance where the cars are waiting to take them into town. Reznor lingers with me just inside the manor while the other two remain on the steps. I catch sight of Emanuel swatting the back of Charles' head as he cranes over his shoulder to get a glimpse at us.

Reznor pays them no attention as he pecks me on the cheek. "Call me if you need anything," he calls over his shoulder as he struts out the door.

Emanuel went with Rez into town while Charles seems rather excited to laze about the manor with me. He even picks out a room for us to lounge in, and that room is the sunroom. It's more of a greenhouse, but it allows us to enjoy the sun without the coolness of late fall. I've never been in this room until today, but grateful Charles has shown me to this hidden gem. The room's a decent size with a table set before the large window, while at the back of the long room rests two couches that face towards a towering windowpane, I know instantly the plush brown sofa is where I'm going to spend my time, and that's exactly where I sit while Charles sinks into the couch next to it. Folding his arms behind his head and crossing his legs, his eyes soak in the light and warmth of the bright sun. We're silent as I read for an hour, and I'm presuming Charles grows bored as he speaks, breaking the tranquil silence that we've created.

"We need to start your training again; you've had a long enough break."

I scoff, "Charles, it hasn't even been a week, but I agree; I do need to start training again. I have these powers, yet I still feel weak."

"That will change over time. You haven't used your powers on a mass scale," he pauses as he turns up to face me, "I promise Liara, *when* you use your powers at a mass scale, you will feel like the most powerful thing in this world." I note that he says *when* and not *if*.

"When do you think this war will happen?" I close my book completely, knowing I won't be able to finish it now.

"I'm not sure because right now, it's not one. I feel there will be one soon, and I don't think anything is going to stop it from coming."

"I can't die," I blurt out. "It's not that I'm afraid to die, but I am afraid of what Reznor will do if I die. He's lost enough in his life, and I don't want to add to that list. I can't die for him, and neither can you or Emanuel."

Charles smiles softly at me. "I see you're starting to care for the big brute," he teases. "No matter what, when we go to war, people on both sides will die, but I will try to ensure that you, Emanuel, and I do not." He slaps his thighs. "That being said, don't go getting pregnant because it will cause Reznor to go absolutely mad if you're in danger and pregnant with his child."

My face blanches at the thought. "I don't plan on getting pregnant any time soon; I've hardly had any time with Reznor, and I want that time before I am to bring a child into this world. I'm not even sure I want kids. Plus, Reznor is religious when it comes to time for my contraceptive potion, so if I get knocked up, it's on him." I admit, which seemed like a pure shock to Charles.

"I think you're the only woman I've ever met that has said she might not want kids!"

"I'm from a different world, or rather I grew up in a different world."

"I wish you had grown up here," he looks away from me. "I wish you and Reznor could have done all of this properly." He doesn't have to say the words, but I know what he means. Reznor and I have known each other for a short time, and now we're married and bonded when we should have had years to do all of these things rather than months. The time range doesn't matter because I knew from the day I looked into his eyes that I would fall for him eventually, and now I guess I'm just waiting for my heart, or brain to catch up.

"Well, he and I will just have to learn as we go," I add, focusing on the fluttering leaves that fall. The manor's so large it should really be called a castle, although Reznor hates when it's called that. The sunroom must be close to my old room because I can see the white caps of the mountains from here, just over the tops of the trees and open fields ahead.

"Queen Liara?" a servant calls as she stands in the doorway with her head bowed.

"Yes?" I ask after taking a moment to realize she called me queen.

"You have a guest waiting to see you and King Reznor; he's waiting in the throne room." Charles and I both glance at each other. It's surprising news to both of us.

"Who is it?" I abandon the couch, leaving my book behind.

"All he said is that he is a friend of the king. He knew the password at the door to get in."

Charles tramples ahead of me while three guards trail behind as we march into the throne room. A man with long blond hair tied behind him stands before us, his gaze darting up to me instantly. His eyes are a steely grey, dressed in black breeches tucked into his brown knee-high boots with a loose green blouse and leather vest. He must live in the lands that still live like the olden times. He beams brightly at the sight of me along with the many guards flanking me.

"You must be Rezzie's wife! My apologies that I couldn't attend the wedding," the man winks, and Charles starts laughing as he crushes the man into a hug. The guards stand down, but still remain in a spacious circle around me.

"Liara, this is Maximus. He's one of our friends we gained in the last war!" Charles explains as he places a firm hand on his shoulder. I walk through the guards who move right along with me.

"Nice to meet you," I greet, sticking my hand out for him to shake. He scrunches his eyebrows. Instead, he takes my hand in his and kisses the top before releasing it. The second his lips touch my hand, I hear Reznor's voice down the bond.

What are you doing? he asks suspiciously.

Your friend Maximus just arrived.

Reznor's response is immediate, *What? What is he doing there?*

"Not that I don't enjoy meeting a new face, but what is the reason for your visit?" I ask.

Maximus's smile fades. "I came to talk to you and Reznor, whispers of war near my land."

I convey the message to Reznor, moments before his anxiety simmers down the bond, but he covers quickly, *I'll be home soon, keep him company till I get there... but not alone.*

"Reznor is out at the moment. Would you like some tea while we wait for him?" I offer.

Maximus smiles brightly. "That sounds lovely!"

I turned to one of the guards. "Can you ask one of the servants to bring tea to the sitting room?" The guard bows his head before quickly exiting the room, another guard moving from the wall to take his place in the formation around me.

The guards linger along the walls of the sitting room, which doesn't seem to faze our guest, thankfully. Max and Charles are exchanging stories from the war. They have all but forgotten my presence until the tea arrives, and the servant woman asks me if I need anything else. I politely reject and thank her for her service.

Maximus eyes me suspiciously. "You're a very nice woman, considering you grew up in the mortal world with that awful mother of yours."

I sip the warm tea and shrug; he's correct. My mother's a difficult person, and the mortal world indeed is an awful place. "I'm not a product of my environment."

He smiles again. "And how do you like it here in Rezzie's castle?" He's probing for an answer that will never come from my mouth because it's untrue. He wonders if I'm using Reznor or not. I'm insulted, but I try my best to hide it.

"I have grown very fond of these lands. They're beautiful, and the people here are extremely kind."

His eyes roam across my body. "You wear no crown, or dress?" he critiques as he gestures to my black pants and my burgundy sweater. I must admit I don't look like a queen sitting here right now, but this is how I like to live.

"I do when I need to. Are you done analyzing me, Max?" I place my teacup back onto the saucer before leaning back into the chair.

He raises his hands in defense. "My apologies, Reznor doesn't have a good reputation with the women in his life."

I feel a twinge of jealousy but shove it down as I give him a soft smile. "It's alright. It's better you get over with it before Reznor gets here because if you look at me like that in front of him, friend or not, he will kick your ass down the hallway."

Maximus laughs at my words but turns to look at Charles, his straight face emphasizing that I'm not joking. "Thanks for the heads up." He adjusts his leather vest, clasping it up another notch. "So have you swum in that lake yet?"

"No, have you?" I counter, which leads him to tell me the elaborate story about the monster that lives beneath the lake. The beast is the reason whenever you throw something into the lake, Lily pads rise instead. Apparently, it uses the flowers as a warning of the creature's home below. By the time he's done with the story, I question if that kind of magic is possible here.

"Reznor pushed me in a couple hundred years ago, and I swear I saw something big and green move deep below. I jumped out of that water so fast," Charles admits between his laughter, holding a hand to his chest.

He's so focused on laughing he jumps when Reznor opens the door. He's startled, which only makes us cackle again. Emanuel motions for the other guards to leave, and they do so with a bow of their heads.

Maximums opens his arms up to Reznor. "Rezzie!" he cheers. Reznor chuckles as he hugs him back. The second Max releases him, he lets out a sigh of relief and sits down next to me. He gently places his hand on top of my crossed thighs while I sip my tea.

Tense love? I tease.

A little, he admits. Feeling bad, I stroke him down the bond.

"So, what brings you, Max?" Reznor probes, and Max smiles suggestively.

"Your lovely mate called me the same name."

Reznor's hand tenses on my thigh, his claw tips starting to appear. I quickly place my hand on top of his. I pray Maximus isn't stupid enough to look where Reznor's hand rests. I've done a lot of research on mates lately, and the temper of a mated male can be ruthless. They act off instinct rather than logic.

Maximus continues, either not noticing, or ignoring the shift of energy in the room. "Judging by the number of guards that surrounded Liara, I'm assuming the whispers of war are true."

"There have been multiple attacks made against Liara and I recently. I declared treason against Serena's dad because he ordered the attacks against Liara."

Maximus rubs his forehead. "Then you and I are speaking of two different wars. Whitehorn has been moving troops out of his territory a lot lately. They have been moving through Lord Nostics lands, along with pushing in through some of my father's. We've been trying to stop it, but we can't seem to catch them in the act."

Charles curses under his breath as Emanuel breaks his silence. "Are they working together?"

"I'm assuming so. I haven't seen them together in our territory, but the lands surrounding us are saying Whitehorn is preparing for war. You're supposed to be King of All and take leadership now that you have your powers: he isn't happy about that."

"I don't want to be King of All; the council knows this." Reznor sighs, his hand squeezing my thigh while I caress his palm with my thumb.

"Whitehorn doesn't listen to his own council reps, and he isn't going to listen to you either," Maximus clarifies.

"How long have the troops been moving around?" Charles asks as he pushes his tea away from him.

"About a week or two. They started moving heavily in the last few days, but that's not all. Whitehorn has been reaching out to the lands. He's looking for allies. He never tells them what for, he just sees whose territory will stake allegiance and who won't."

"If you find out what, contact me immediately, or if you hear anything new. Tatiana's lands have been attacked, and we can't afford any more surprises." Reznor's growing restless quickly with the new information we just learned.

"I will, but I must go. I've probably been gone too long as is." Charles embraces Maximus first, then Emanuel. Reznor goes last, then watches Maximus bow to me as he bids goodbye. He stills at the door. "Keep him in check, Liara, although I'm guessing he has to do the same with you. I must admit I like you already," he teases before he ducks out the door with Charles and Emanuel, leaving me with a displeased Reznor.

"Did he touch you?" he presses, which causes me to choke on my tea.

"What?" I set the cup down, knowing this is going to require my full attention.

"When I was in the village, right before I called out to you, it felt like my hand had been dipped in acid, and then suddenly it just vanished."

"He kissed my hand when he greeted me, but that was it. I had four guards with me, along with Charles."

Reznor growls, towering over me as he rises from his chair. "The bond tells me when someone touches you intimately."

"Rez, I would have punched him had he done anything else. Not to mention the guards and Charles all would have done the same. A kiss on my hand is nothing, I promise."

"Next time he does that, I want you to punch him regardless. I don't like anyone touching you." He means every word, no one gets to touch the tribrid's mate but him. Reznor hauls me into his arms as he nuzzles his face into my hair, breathing deeply against my throat. A laugh erupts from my mouth as I see the jealous side of Reznor once again, but I understand it completely. I had felt the same with Serena, although when it came to her, I won.

Chapter Thirty-One: A Golden Letter

Over the next few days, Charles has me up at dawn to start training yet again. However, being queen has its perks because now I get to leave training early to attend meetings with Reznor. The meetings are rather boring, and Reznor seems as uninterested as I am, but I still go to every one I'm supposed to and sit next to him, giving my opinion if needed.

Today, however, I have no meetings to attend, and Reznor is off to the village again, so that means I have to endure all of training today. Reznor spent last night in the town dealing with a situation. He gave me no further information other than he would return later today.

It's odd sleeping in our bed alone. It smells like him, but it still doesn't feel right without his body next to mine. When I had woken up, I was sprawled across the bed diagonally, indicating that I didn't mind his absence in the bed too much.

Kora only chuckles at me as she drags my sleepy self from the bed. All too quickly she has me dressed and fed before sending me on my way to Charles. He accompanies me on the run this morning, and I appreciate it greatly because if he hadn't, I probably wouldn't have finished it. I'm sluggish today, silently praying today will be an easy day.

I'm wrong. Oh, so very wrong. Emanuel and Charles are fighting with me brutally this morning.

We're hardly halfway through the morning session. My muscles are already aching and protesting at the swing of my fists against their bodies. It's a sparring drill, and they aren't holding back, but neither am I. I may be shorter in stance to them, but I sure as hell am not going to let them win.

Fighting them both at once, I use my legs to kick Charles away from me while Emanuel's attempting to haul me over his shoulder. I swiftly knock him in the ribs, freeing myself from his grip. I roll away on the ground, jumping back up into a fighting stance. Charles grins, an all too familiar taunting look. The next thing I know, I'm thrown to the ground by Emanuel.

"That isn't fair," I protest, as Charles and Emanuel both snicker lightly as I get to my feet, wincing at my aching back. I use my powers to pull Charles' legs out from underneath him, sending him falling to his back. He recovers quickly and jumps back up, shaking off some dirt from his clothes.

"That's all you got, princess?" he mocks, and for some reason, it causes a spark in me. I fight harder the next round and am able to take both boys to the ground rather quickly. Emanuel nods in approval while Charles soothes his broken pride.

"Maybe you should recognize her title as queen, and she wouldn't have kicked your ass." Emanuel comments.

"If getting her mad makes her fight like that, then we will need to do it more actually. Imagine if she uses her powers or yields a sword at the same time. she'll be lethal." Those words take us into our next part of training, using a weapon and my powers. This time

The Magic Stolen

I'm not just fighting with Charles and Emanuel; I'm fighting them along with four other guards.

It's hard fighting against that many people, and at first, I fail over and over. Especially as the Lycans all semi shift under Charles' orders. Turns out Charles and Emanuel are the strongest warriors Reznor has, physically, and in their abilities. Charles wants them to try and match their strength in order to train me fully. If this had been a real fight, I would have died nine times by now. The feeling of being weak creeps down my shoulders, stirring me into a fierce fight. I know when my eyes turn a smoky grey as I tap into my powers, the sky crackles with lightning as I take two of the guards down before striking two others. I disarm Emanuel before freezing Charles in place with a forcefield, his body unable to move. The other guards quickly recover, but I continue fighting until I have landed what would have been killing blows on each of them. The smokey grey retreats from my eyes, allowing me to see everything clearer now.

I learned that when my eyes change color, the world fades a little bit. It's like the world goes quiet while I'm using my powers. Everything turns glossy, but the moment they clear, my vision returns to normal. I shocked the youngest guard when he saw my eyes change color. His falter is what allowed me to strike my mock killing blow.

With the first half of training over, all of us retreat back to the manor, taking lunch together in the dining room. I eat my entire meal and then some while they tell me stories of training and what it's like to prepare for war. Some of them grew up in these lands while others migrated here and competed to join Reznor's army. They all willingly signed up for the brutal task, each earning great honor in doing so. These soldiers are killing machines, skilled in more ways than one to bring a person down.

These aren't ordinary soldiers and guards; they're the elite of Reznor's personal protection staff, and now mine. All the soldiers in Reznor's armies are extensively trained and if I thought what I endured today was hard, I'm wrong. These guards have faced far worse to ensure they can survive and protect in any situation. The most unique thing about his army is that it's made of all breeds, and that makes them twice as lethal. He has soldiers of all makes. They are taught to fight in the same brutal way, but with the advantage of knowing how to kill certain breeds. The army consists of Lycans, Warlocks, Demons, and Shapeshifters, and a Troll or two. All willing to lay down their life at any moment for Reznor, for me, for our home.

The guilt starts to seep in the longer I sit with them. They're all willing to die for me along with thousands of others, yet I don't even know their names. I will never be able to recognize all of them, and that only disheartens me further. I thank the guards with me today for their service and make a mental note to try and learn as many of their names as possible and thank them when I can.

I'm torn away from the conversation when Kora hurries into the room with worry on her face and politely asks me to step into the hallway with her. "Queen Liara, there is a royal representative from the council approaching. We must change you quickly before they reach the manor." We rush into the study, where a grey dress is waiting for me along with my crown. She fastens the flowing gown, the only exposure of skin coming from the plunging at the chest along with the tops of my shoulders exposed from long fitted sleeves. She twists my hair up, securing it at the back of my head before sliding the crown on and adding light makeup. It's a hurried job, and she knows it. She mutters under her breath as she slides my heels on before ushering me to the throne room. Emanuel and Charles are lingering in the hall to take me downstairs, already changed into their official uniforms.

"Did anyone tell Reznor?" I question as we hustle to the throne room.

"Yes, he won't be back in time. They're already approaching." Emanuel throws open the doors to the room. My heels clink against the floor as we cross toward the throne, actually thrones. An exact copy of Reznor's sits to the right of his, except this one has been engraved with my moon at the center.

"Your throne awaits you," Kora offers me her hand. She escorts me up to the chair and bows once I'm seated. Kora then hurries to the side of the room waiting in the shadows.

Charles and Emanuel flank either side of me, watching, but more importantly scrutinizing the man dressed in gold slacks with a red jacket strutting across the throne room, holding a gold envelope in his hands. He has yellow eyes like Tatiana, and I'm sure she'd love his bright appearance. It's a lot of gold to look at. Even his hair looks gold as it shines in the dim lights of the throne room. He stops a little ways off from the steps leading to the throne.

"It's a pleasure to meet you, Queen Liara. I'm Casper." He bows before me, rising as he continues, "I come bringing a letter from the council. Will you be receiving this, or shall we wait for King Reznor?"

"I'll accept it. King Reznor is occupied at the moment." Even I'm shocked at my own words as I mimic the formal speech Reznor uses when speaking to members of power, or council officials. Casper steps forward to bring me the letter, but Emanuel intercepts him, walking down the steps and taking the item from his hands. Emanuel inspects the outside of the envelope before handing it to me.

"Most kings don't allow their queen to have a throne the same size of theirs," he notes as he regards my throne, then Reznor's empty one. "It's a sign of weakness."

My eyes flicker grey, "I see it as a sign of strength and unity, but you can think what you please." His face twitches in surprise, but he only smiles and bows before leaving the throne room. Charles trails after Casper to ensure he's leaving while Emanuel steps closer to me.

"You were right to put him in his place. He was challenging you," he informs from my side.

"I almost said something else, but I don't need my first solo meeting going back to the council that I'm a hateful queen."

"No, you just proved that you're a strong one who is allowed to act without her king."

"Other queens can't?" I ask as I tear my eyes from the gold envelope in my hands.

"No, you're lucky, a lot of the kings don't even let their queens have thrones or speak at functions.

Reznor is not one of those obviously. If he had made that comment with him here…that would not have ended well."

"Should I open it or wait?" Twirling the envelope in my hand, looking at the wax seal that's imprinted with a crown above a cursive capital 'C.'

"That's up to you," Emanuel says like a wise owl, he knows the decision's up to me, but I'm hesitant to make it.

Charles crosses to the throne room at a slow jog. "You haven't opened the damned thing already?"

That's all I need for me to carefully break the seal and open the envelope to find a folded golden letter inside. "It's an invitation to a meeting with representatives from each court. It's set for next week." I give a breath of relief, thinking it could have been something worse.

Reznor's reaction, however, is not the same as mine. "Shit!" he curses, tossing the letter to his desk. He groans as he leans back into his chair, dragging a hand across his tired face. He looks exhausted. Thoroughly, and utterly exhausted.

Keeping his eyes averted, he says, "I will attend the meeting, and you will stay here with Emanuel and the guards. It's a three-day trip. I'll let you know what comes from the meeting when I return."

"Why can't I come?" I'm a little shocked that it wasn't even an option for me to go to the meeting. I thought we were moving past this stuff.

"Because you can't, you need to stay here." Reznor adds blankly.

"But why?"

"Because I will handle it. I've handled the meetings for years without you, I can certainly handle them without you now." His voice raises higher and higher as he speaks; it's loud but not a yell. I know if I push much further, it will lead to yelling.

I swallow the anger that's scorching my throat, "I see," is all I can bring myself to say as I fight down the urge to scream at him. I exit the room, dismissing the call of my name just before I shut the door. I know he's tired and anxious, but it's no reason to pick a fight. Since I'm still wearing the dress and the crown from the meeting, I head to our bedroom. I had waited in the throne room till Reznor returned, and now that we're done discussing the matter, I'm getting out of this dress.

Kora helps me out of the gown and returns the crown to its place. She lingers in the bathroom, waiting for me to finish washing. The sun has just started to set according to the magic windows. Now that I'm in more comfortable clothes, it's time to unwind. I retreat to the sunroom with a book in one hand and a glass of wine in the other.

I never understood the reason behind us having modern clothes here along with some older styled ones, but I'm thankful, nonetheless. It reminds me that this world is still somewhat familiar to what I had known. Before I can reflect on being saddened by missing the way things used to be, I dive into the book.

Reznor enters the room, remaining silent as he crosses to stand in front of the large window that faces the glorious view of the mountains. I peek at him, but don't speak. Focusing on the book again, I have to re-read the page because his presence is distracting me. He abandons the window, and instead of asking me to move my feet, or shift from my lounging position, he crawls onto the couch until he can hold me against him. My book is a lost thought as he combs his fingers through my hair, holding me tighter against his chest. We both lay on the couch intertwined in each other's limbs.

"I'm sorry for yelling at you. I shouldn't have done that," Reznor murmurs while still playing with my damp hair. "I want you to come, but I *need* you to stay here."

Refusing to give into the bond's attempts to soothe my anger, I keep my stare on the page as I say, "I can respect you not wanting me to go. I just wanted to know why. Me asking a question is no reason for you to yell at me to make yourself feel better."

"I'm sorry. Liara, I would love it if you came to this meeting with me, but I need you to stay here at home. I don't trust that this meeting isn't a setup. I'm worried there will be an attack of some sort there."

"Then why didn't you just tell me that?"

"Because it's hard for me to talk like this," he peers at me. "Liara, I need you to stay because I need you here, protected in our home. I care about you too much to take you into the lion's den, and that's what this meeting is going to be." He searches my eyes for something, an argument maybe. "I can't make you stay, but I'm asking you to."

"I'll stay, but next time you talk to me like that again, I'll go just to spite you. I'm not a toy you get to use when you see fit. We are meant to do things together, Reznor, don't forget that. Plus, based on the comment the court official made, I don't think I would be suited for a meeting of this type anyway. I was actually going to ask if I could sit this one out had you given me the opportunity to."

Reznor tenses under my head as I rest it against his chest. "What comment?"

"Something about our thrones, along the lines of us having the same size throne makes us seem weak." His rage down the bond is instant. "I told him that he was wrong, that it made us unified, stronger as equals."

"Maybe you should go to this meeting," he teases, his fingers continuing to work into my hair. "I'll kill Casper if he speaks ill about you or our kingdom again."

It's me who laughs this time. "Reznor, you can't kill everyone we have a problem with."

"I can try."

Chapter Thirty-Two: Protecting My Home

After Reznor's little outburst last week, he slept for hours. He'd been exhausted, the stress of everything having gotten the best of him. He felt guilty for how he had treated me. He apologized endlessly before slumbering away, and I decided it was good enough.

I'm thrilled when I found out that Reznor's frequent contact with Tatiana has resulted in them going to the council meeting together. She's had a rough time since losing Arnold, and I think it will do both her and Reznor good. There's nothing we can do for Tatiana but support her right now, and we're trying our best to do that. However, she is just one of my concerns, the other being the meeting that Reznor is leaving to attend in a few short minutes.

Reznor's fast asleep after our activities prior to lying down, but I can't sleep a wink. I know I won't be sleeping anytime soon because in a few minutes, Reznor will have to get up and leave. I'm just enjoying lying with him, waiting for the inevitable moment when Kora will come to wake him. I study the beautiful sleeping man, his dark long eyelashes, his sculpted face, not a blemish on it except for a small scar atop his brow. He's absolutely beautiful. Suddenly, I wonder why I wasted my time on light hair, light eyed men before. Although no one could ever compare to Reznor, I've known this since the first day I met him.

I don't care if I wake him up early as I gently tousle his hair while he rests upon my chest. He doesn't flinch or move as I caress his hair and face. I know this meeting most likely won't be an attack, yet I still worry about him. My feelings for him have only grown stronger and wilder. He rustles slightly causing me to cease my movements as he grips my waist tighter. Even deep in sleep, he holds tight to me. My thoughts suddenly disappear as Reznor clutches me. A small smile creeps onto my face but vanishes as the door to our bedroom opens, light casting onto the bed, illuminating his face.

"Your Majesty, it's time to wake up." Kora herself looks tired as she wakes Reznor.

His eyes open instantly. They search for me, then close after he sees I'm still secured beneath him. He grunts to let her know he's awake, but he makes no move to get out of the bed. In fact, he settles deeper into my chest as he lets out a sigh.

"I'll make sure he gets up. Will you set out his clothes?" Kora nods shuffling off to the closet while I continue teasing his locks. She turns on the lights in the closet and one lamp in our bedroom before she takes his bag and leaves the room.

I wait five more minutes, combing my fingers across his broad shoulders. "Rez, you have to get up now," I coo softly, trying not to smile at my tired man.

He groans but shifts so he's resting on his elbows. He observes me for a moment, then he rolls off me and starts toward the closet. "You didn't sleep last night, did you?"

"I slept a little bit," I retort while grabbing my nightgown off the floor, sliding it back over my head and down my body.

"Mhm," Reznor hums in response.

I roll my eyes, moving into the closet, slipping on a robe and some slippers, as I watch Reznor get ready. He's slicking his hair with precise motion, styling it into his signature look, although sometimes I wish he'd just leave it down.

"I'll keep that in mind," he chuckles.

I furrow my brows. "Keep what in mind?"

"That you like it when I leave it down and unstyled."

"How did you know I was thinking that?" I screech bewildered.

"You said it." He gives me a weary look through the mirror. "You feeling okay love?"

"No, Rez, I only thought that—wait! Did you read my mind?" Oh, this is getting weird.

"Yes, this is getting weird…"

I stab a finger at him. "Hey, stay out of my head. You're in it enough with the mating bond."

"I didn't mean to." He tosses his hands up in surrender. "Maybe that's how my dad always knew when I was lying; the God gave me many of his same abilities."

I'm shocked at the mention of his father. He rarely mentions his dad. I'm just about to ask him a question when he moves from the bathroom heading back to the closet, slipping on his jacket. I follow him and linger until he's ready, then head for our bedroom door. He stops suddenly, causing me to bump into his back. He wheels around and scans me from head to toe. I realize what he's looking at. This nightgown is rather revealing. With a roll of my eyes, I tie my robe shut.

"Territorial bullshit," I mutter, stepping past him and out into the hallway, but he only smiles in triumph and takes my hand, kissing the back of it as we stroll through the manor.

The guards, along with Emanuel and Charles, wait by the door. Emanuel is the only one who seems awake of the lively bunch. Charles tries to look somewhat conscious as he catches the sight of Reznor and I descending the grand staircase. "Emanuel is staying here with you. I'm taking Charles with me." I'm not surprised by Reznor's words; he has told me about it six different times this week.

At the bottom of the stairs outside, Reznor has everyone in the car. They just need to go pick up Tatiana. He pecks the top of my head. "If you need anything, just check in with me through the bond." Then he leans down and claims my lips, searing me with a hot kiss before forcing himself away. "If I don't get in that car right now, I'll throw you over my shoulder and take you with me."

"Then go, or I won't let you leave." With great hesitancy, Reznor climbs into the car, soaking up my appearance before the car pulls off.

"He's nervous about leaving you," Emanuel acknowledges as we both watch the car disappear down the drive.

"I'm nervous about him going to this meeting," I admit, suddenly feeling empty now that Reznor's out of view.

"It's alright, he'll be back before you know it. Plus, I'm sure he'll be talking to you the entire time anyways."

The first day goes quickly, mostly because with Reznor gone, I'm in charge of meeting with the noblemen and various other members of Reznor's...our court. I didn't need to make many decisions, they mainly filled me on the status of the town, and we set a date for the next tithe. I also learn there's to be a fall harvest celebration planned along with a winter solstice party. Luckily, I have time to prepare both things, and I will be seeking some help from Reznor.

I've fallen asleep in his study, the sound of his voice startling me awake, *Liara, are you seriously still asleep?*

My head shoots up from the pillow, looking around the room, then remember he's gone. *Well, I'm not now.*

Good, I regret asking you to stay. It's been dreadful, Charles and Tatiana won't shut up.

I snicker. *You should have seen one of the noblemen's face yesterday when they told me I needed to plan a fall harvest party! A warning would have been nice...*

A low chuckle from Reznor, and even without seeing his face, I know he's grinning. *Don't worry, we'll have the same person plan it who does it every year.*

And who is that?

Morana, she loves planning the parties. I'm sure she'll enjoy your help if you would be willing.

I snuggle deeper into the couch. *I'm not sure I'll be of much help.*

Another laugh from Reznor then a feather-like stroke against my temple, tingles seeping into my skin. *I miss you.*

I miss you too.

We don't say anything else, but we return affectionate strokes down the bond. He does it randomly throughout the day, and each time he does it, I always stop and give one back in return. He, however, has been silent since the late afternoon, and now, with the sun setting, he still hasn't given a word, a stroke, nothing. I worried about him at first, but as a guard comes bursting into the study, I'm met with bigger problems.

"Unknown guards are moving into our territory at a fast pace and coming from four different directions," the young guard spiels between pants.

"Where?" Emanuel asks, grabbing a map, laying it across Reznor's table, all of us moving to it. He gestures to one coming from the East, North, West, and the South, the most alarming is the latter. That's where the town is, where our people are.

"Announce a shelter call for all the areas with people near the entering troops," I order but feel more confident when Emanuel nods in agreement. "We need to send troops into the town to protect the people in case it's a target, and to stop their advancements should they try and attack."

"We also need to surround the manor, two of these flanks can only come to one place, and that's here. That's also assuming the third and fourth division doesn't arrive here also," Emanuel adds, which none of us object to.

"Lockdown the manor, lock down everything." My voice is authoritative as it comes out. Emanuel seems proud as the other guard rushes off to start my orders, alerting every one of the plan.

"You might want to change out of that dress. I don't plan on you needing to fight, but if you need to run, it can't be in that." Emanuel's right as usual. We rush up to my room, where I quickly change. When I emerge from the room, Emanuel has a black leather jacket and chest strap in his hands.

He helps secure the strap in the back and hands me four daggers that slid into place across the front and side of the belt. The leather jacket is made of worn leather with strong sleeves, with shoulder caps made of swirling symbols. "It was his moms. She wore it when she had to fight in the first wars. You will wear it until we can get one made for you." I zip up the jacket and slide two more daggers inside each sleeve.

In the armory, I'm dumbfounded at the lines of men and women grabbing weapons and arming themselves. The first batch of soldiers has already been sent out, and the ones remaining are preparing to guard the manor. I'm handed a sheath that holds a sword that I quickly secure around my waist. Emanuel and I leave the armory, going outside to the front of the manor. In the distance, the sound of marching boots approach. The biggest problem being that our soldiers were sent to the village in large trucks.

"They're almost here." My words are quiet, but inside my head, they echo.

That's when Reznor calls out to me. *What's happening?* Reznor's voice is a mix between worried and angry, but I don't have time to focus on that as Emanuel and me race back to the manor. *Liara!* I flinch at his booming voice in my head. As we sprint up the stairs, guards come out and start flanking the estate in all directions. We weave through the ones coming down the stairs.

We have a situation, I tell Reznor quickly.

Emanuel and I are directing the soldiers when ten guards dressed in significantly different outfits come to my side. They're dressed in silver, all of them wielding multiple weapons and helmets to match.

"These are your personal guards; they're the best trained we have." Emanuel motions to the heavily armed guards with his hand. "Where you go, they go from now on till this thing is over."

"Okay fine, but Reznor is literally screaming in my head right now, so I need a minute where I'm not being followed. Just stand outside the door." None of them argue, guess that's a perk of being queen. They all linger outside of the study where I respond to Reznor's booming voice that's yelling my name over, and over.

Okay, I don't have much time—

What is going on? Reznor cuts me off before I can even try to explain.

Let me talk! There's silence, and I take that as my cue to start talking. T*here are four unknown guard divisions moving in from all directions. We have the manor on lockdown along with the village. We have soldiers in the town and surrounding the estate and we have others on standby if we need them.*

Do you have your guards?

Yes, I have ten of them lurking outside of the door as we speak.

Keep me informed on everything. I can't respond because a knock on the door tells me my time is up. The guards take me to the throne room. It's in the center of the manor. It has all the fastest exits from the manor in case of emergency. From the window, I can see foreign guards moving into view, but these aren't small divisions.

No.

This is an army.

Reznor...there are a lot more than we thought. Can you leave?

I'm not leaving unless I have to. I have powers, I can use them.

You leave if they tell you to, don't act brave, be smart about it. Liara, be careful please. I don't know if it's the commotion before me, or if I heard correctly, but it sounds as if his voice cracks when he says my name.

As the army presses in, a decision has to be made—if we play defense, or offense. I don't want to attack first, but the second I see the weaponry they wield as they approach, I know we will need to play both well.

"Get whatever sort of firepower, or big guns you have and get them ready because by the looks of it, they aren't here to fight hand to hand." Emanuel acts on my order quickly, and once he's done, I turn to face him. "Emanuel, I'm out of my depth here. I'm trying, but you have the experience, not me. If you have any suggestions or feel you need to take the lead at any time, do so, please."

"You're doing a great job, Liara, but I will make adjustments if I need to." I try to smile at him, but it doesn't feel right as more soldiers come through the woods. My woods. With the sun setting quickly, this fight is going to be even more dangerous. In moments, the sun will be disappear completely, the moon already rising in the sky.

Standing at one of the windows in the throne room, a massive fiery blaze hurls toward the manor. I throw my hand out, stopping the blaze in midair. "They aren't here to fight; they are here to take the manor." I launch the fireball back into the enemy. "I need to be outside. I can't protect the manor from here."

Ignoring the protest from all ten of the guards assigned to me, I sprint out into the courtyard with the soldiers on my tail. Outside, multiple catapults are being set alit. I summon all the power I can, pulling a shield from the ground up. It shimmers slightly in the moonlight as it snakes toward the sky. My eyes turn grey as I use a mass force of my powers, sealing in the only protection that I can offer my home.

The fiery blazes start launching one by one into the shield. I only wince as they become more frequent. Tossing them back if I can, but most of my focus is on the shield. The soldiers gawk at me in the beginning, but now their roars of encouragement help fuel my anger at the invaders. We start returning fire through the forcefield with whatever they could muster up on short notice.

A single person emerges and approaches my shield, touching it with his hand. It starts eating away my protection like acid, disintegrating in tiny spurts. It hurts terribly, like I'm burning along with it; I drop that shield only to send him through the air into his lingering army. I slam up another shield, only this one isn't as large.

Whitehorn.

What? Reznor asks, confused.

I glare at the man who moves to stand again. *The man leading this army is Whitehorn.* I can't respond to him anymore as the army starts running at the manor, firing at the shield. They're launching everything they have at it. "Get them ready, I can't hold it much longer." I yell out over the sounds of the army running full force in all directions for the manor. Emanuel shouts the orders, all of them getting into fighting stances. With one motion, Emanuel sends them running toward the shield. I drop it enough to let some of the enemy in, then I yank it back up, sealing the rest out. The soldiers eliminate the enemy with ease, taking down the cluster.

We continue this over and over, but with another touch from Whitehorn, my shields goes tumbling down. This causes a brutal fight with both sides charging at each other. Whitehorn's soldiers are coming too fast.

Moving further away from the manor as I hurry down the courtyard steps, I call out to the moon while lifting hundreds of soldiers into the air, launching them forcefully away. I turn to grab more soldiers and force them away, repetitively throwing them in all directions. This gives my soldiers barely enough time to block the ones advancing further into our territory. Sounds of metal clashing against metal echo all around with various shootings on both sides. My soldiers are fighting hard, striking, and killing everyone they can. They're ferocious. My pride for them blossoms as they fight, following my lead meticulously. The warriors don't hesitate, launching into each assault. I keep doing whatever I can to protect them and our home at all costs. I've been so focused on yielding my powers and assessing my warriors, I almost miss Reznor yelling down the bond.

Liara, Reznor shouts, but I'm growing weak quickly, or at least it feels fast. I'm not even sure how long we've been fighting. I dismiss him as I shove them back again, my vision blurring slightly. *Liara!*

Rez, I mumble as the black spots start clouding my vision. Catching multiple balls of fire then sending them back with the wind. They explode and shoot out amongst the enemy lines. I muster everything I can, forcing them back again, but there's just too many. A bright flash followed by a swirling black oval appears a couple yards away from where I stand. But I can't focus on it. My vision's blurring again. I'm using too much too fast.

"Liara!" My head shoots in the direction of Reznor's voice. He steps out of the swirling oval and runs to me, his eyes taking in the battle around him.

"How?" I ask, unable to finish the sentence as I wince, conjuring up a shield and launching another fireball. Reznor doesn't reply. His eyes are flaring red as he witnesses me struggling to protect our home. Moving down the stairs, he heads for the battle, a dark purple mist shooting out of his hands, capturing soldiers, killing them instantly. Wanting to help, I freeze them in place, making it easier for him to capture them as he wades deeper into the gore. A soldier throws himself at Reznor, but he kills him with ease. His purple mist works along the soldiers, shooting through them as if he were piercing them each in the heart. The mass of his strength is astounding; his new powers are something I've never witnessed before. Reznor yields them effortlessly as he fights using a sword alongside his new power. He's annihilating the battlefield, fighting hard and turning into a bloody mess. It's the evidence of his many kills as he navigates his way further into the field of bodies. Soldiers of our own guard alongside him, watching his back and protecting their king. Reznor's in his element here fighting in his own land, but I can sense the rage of an attack here. There's no way he's leaving this field until they're dead, and we've won, eyes flaring red as he tears through the battlefield that is usually our backyard.

 I keep my eyes on Reznor at all times. I don't think he knows it, but I created a shield around him, protecting him. They just keep coming, even as Reznor dents the number of soldiers quickly, only some start to fall back in fear. The fireballs cease, and the longer Reznor and his soldiers battle, the more they withdraw. Whitehorn is nowhere to be seen, but I doubt he's left. When I launched him, it was like tossing a stone, not even that would have scared him away. It worries me, but as I survey the scene, I can't find him anywhere.

 That's when I see him just before a massive, fiery blaze the size of a large house comes flying toward us. More importantly, it's heading right for Reznor in the heart of the battle.

I scream loudly, my body trembles as it takes everything in my entire being to stop the massive blaze in the air. Whitehorn is astounded as I yield the colossal ball of fire, launching it into the heart of his fleeting army. I stumble backward as large black dots start filling my vision.

"Liara!"

Reznor calls my name again, but I can't keep my eyes open any longer. I crash to the ground as nausea sets in. My vision becomes obscured as black creeps in. Emanuel is trying to either coax me to get up, or is trying to help me up, either way I'm not sure because my only thought is Reznor. "Don't let anything happen to him," I mumble as my eyesight fades quickly. Just before I lose consciousness, Reznor sends out a massive wave of purple mist. It shoots out and kills every remaining soldier of Whitehorn's within his reach.

Chapter Thirty-Three: Playing With Magic

I start with a gasp, jerking upright in the bed. A scan around the room tells me I'm not alone. Charles and Tatiana sit at the dining table in my old bedroom, both straightening upon seeing me awake. I try to rise from the bed, but a wave of vertigo hits me so fiercely I fall back, landing on my ass.

"Hey, take it easy," Charles coos while he helps steady me as I attempt to rise for a second time.

"What happened? Did they retreat? Where's Reznor?" I rapidly spew off my questions as images from the fight flash through my head. The sun's just starting to break through the night, the sky lightens only by a few shades. It's before dawn, but the sun will rise soon enough.

"I'll take you to him, but we should wait till you're feeling better," Charles says, while trying to deposit me into the bed.

Tatiana snorts at Charles' comment, coming up on my other side. "She isn't going to wait, and you know that," she grips my other arm and smiles at me, "let's get her downstairs before she attempts to go herself." Tatiana's right. I need to know what the carnage from the battle is. I needed to see if *he*'s okay.

The courtyard is filled with bodies, but luckily most of them are Whitehorn's soldiers. Standing amongst all the dead bodies and carnage is Emanuel and Reznor, both covered in dried blood and soot. The field's trashed along with a decent amount of devastation to the lingering forest. The fire balls have done plenty of damage, not to mention, the large searing path and bodies that are remnants from the final blast. A lot has been destroyed, but it could have been so much worse. I'm mostly upset about the damage to the forest I've grown so fond of. Moving down the stairs, we veer from the path. Charles and Tatiana are both at a loss for words as we wade through the gore. I try not to linger on the dead bodies for long, instead I focus on Reznor. He either hasn't noticed our approach, or he's too busy to acknowledge it.

"Gods, this place looks awful," Charles mutters under his breath as he steps over another dead body.

"You should have seen it last night," I mumble as I maneuver the same body, clinging to Tatiana as black patches hit my vision.

"He is going to be mad you're out of bed," she whispers in my ear, which only earns a scoff from Reznor as his eyes dart over to the three of us.

"Yes, he is, but he can also hear you," Reznor calls in a tired voice, his eyes lingering on where Charles and Tatiana's hands are steading me.

Don't go there, I send down the bond, which only makes Reznor glower. Within standing distance of him now, he reaches out for me, taking me into his arms and out of the other's grasps. He holds me against his side, keeping me steady with his hand at the small of my back. With the Generals still talking to Emanuel, Reznor focuses down on me.

"How are you feeling?" He seems exhausted, and even though I have been out for some time, I'm still drained from the night before.

"I'm fine. How are you?" I don't want him to worry about me when we have so much to deal with.

"I'm okay, just trying to sort some of this out." He studies the damage as his sadness seeps into my own through the bond.

I lean my head against his shoulder. "What now?"

"Now, we recover and make a plan."

Reznor keeps me on the field with him until we've talked to the generals and created a list of orders of things to be done. It isn't until almost noon that Reznor and I head back into the manor. He goes to the bathroom immediately, the shower echoing in the silent room. We haven't spoken much, and I'm too tired at this point to have any sort of discussion. Sliding the leather jacket off my body, I hang it up in the closet along with the leather chest strap still holding its weapons. I might have need for it later.

Barely having the energy to change into pajamas, I crash face first into the bed. I'm nearly asleep when Reznor crushes me to his chest, pressing a few kisses along my temple before he tucking his head against my neck. He inhales a deep shuddering breath.

"Thank you," he breathes out quietly.

"For what?" I strain to see his face in the dark.

"For protecting our home when I wasn't here to do it."

I hug him tighter to me. "Like you said, it's our home, and I will do anything to protect it."

'I'll do anything to protect you,' I think to myself but don't have the heart to say it out loud.

I cling to him, the same way he does to me. I hate to admit it, but I'm terrified of what would happen if I lost him. It's something I never want to happen, and something I decide I'm never going to let happen. I have never cared for someone like this, and I don't think I could ever do it for anyone else.

The next few days are spent cleaning up after the battle. Every time I'm amongst the soldiers, they go quiet instantly. They whisper about my powers and what I've done to save them. They were surprised I fought with them at all. I can't say I blame them; I haven't built much of a reputation here except that I am Queen Nighterious. Now, I am Queen Nighterious, the fighter, someone that fought for their home without question. They admire me for my actions. It's strange to get random thanks for something that I did out of love. I love these lands, and I don't want anything to happen to them. I didn't protect them out of obligation.

The sudden love for these lands are not the only thing that has shocked me over those few days. It's the powers that Reznor holds that surprises me more. He can open portals to any part of this realm with a wave of his hand. His mist, the ability to read my mind (which I'm still not a fan of) his strength and speed has all increased. He seems unstoppable at this point, even being able to use his warlock abilities. The tribrid is now able to utilize all three of his gifts.

Maximus sends word that he will be paying us a visit next week while we repair the damage. Along with the repairs came the decision of what to do next. Reznor's furious at the attack on the manor. He wants to even the score, and he wants to do it soon. We set our next plan into motion, which will be gathering allies. We need to see who will fight in this war with us, and to do that, we're going to throw a party. We'll be asking our guests to stand with us at the fall harvest. Until then, we plan a party, and we plan a war at the same time.

    It's no longer the time for words of peace. Reznor expresses each passing day that Whitehorn won't stop till he gets what he wants, and he wants Reznor's powers and this manor. Both of which he won't get without a fight. These next few weeks are going to be crucial in the war that's now raging on. It only concerns me further that Reznor is becoming more and more territorial over me. He's scared. Scared because Whitehorn might have realized something else that night, another thing he might want.

    Me.

Chapter Thirty-Four: Practice Makes Perfect

It's been over two weeks, and Maximus is still here. He and Reznor are combing any possible allies we can use in the war. Reznor tried to include me in as much as possible, but my opinion is useless on this matter as I don't know any of these kingdoms or their lands. While they plan who to call on for the war, I've been training. Charles has been training me longer and harder than he ever has. I train all day and late into the night to work on pulling my powers from the moon. It's hard, but I'm doing what I can to prepare in my own way for this war.

I haven't seen Reznor lately, other than when we sleep, and it's starting to irritate me. I'm not sure if it's because the bond needs him or if it's me just missing his presence, but either way, my mood has been rather foul lately. Charles also seems to enjoy making the mood worse by teasing me or pushing me a just bit too far.

Charles mocks me as he uses his strength to launch a large branch at me. "Are you going to speak or are you going to ignore me?" he teases as I deflect the branch, sending it flying across the field, aiming for the mass pile of cleared dead trees. The manor is still a mess from the battle.

"I'm going to ignore you," I mumble as I dodge another tree being thrown my way.

"Ah, she speaks!" He raises his arms in triumph. I roll my eyes while deflecting a large boulder one of the Lycan guards throws my way. I'm deflecting all the objects with a mere flick of the wrist, or a simple thought from my mind. Usually, training distracts me. It allows me a break from my thoughts of Reznor. I'll be receiving no escape today; my anger is still rageful. For some reason, when I rose this morning to an empty bed, I was furious. Even now, as I dodge the large objects being thrown my way, I'm simmering with anger at the thought of that cold empty bed. I have no reason to be mad, not truly, yet I'm fuming at the lack of interaction between us. I get it, he's making strategies, but five minutes of conversation won't ruin the war. Hell, being in my presence for more than sleeping would be nice.

My anger is what causes the tree being thrown my way to obliterate as lightning pierces through its bark. The wood from the tree splinters out in all directions, a large piece grazing my thigh, cutting my skin through the thin fabric of my pants. I curse as I assess my bleeding leg.

Charles jogs toward me. "Are you okay?" he shouts.

I raise a hand to stop him from moving any further. "I'm fine, let's keep going." Ignoring the pain in my leg, I put all my weight onto my other foot as I clear the splintered wood with a twirl of my wrist. Charles examines me hesitantly, then takes a few steps back before he sends two branches flying my way. I deflect them both with ease once again. "Can we do something else?" I've grown bored of this training exercise.

"You can run. We've completed all the other exercises for the day." Charles grins. That's enough to clue me in on the fact this won't be a pleasant run.

I run hard, ignoring the protests from my thigh as I sprint through the woods. My previous running trail was set ablaze by one of the fireballs from the fight, and many other trails suffered the same fate. This trail is longer, which I enjoy. But the one thing I don't like is the steep hill in the middle of the course. By the time I reach the peak, I need to stop and catch my breath. My plan to do that shifts as I throw myself to the ground, dodging a large boulder that's thrown directly at me.

I groan, rolling onto my back as Charles laughs wildly. "You're supposed to deflect them, not drop to the floor and dodge them," he teases, reaching a hand down to me. My thigh throbs at the action as I get to my feet, a patch of blood painted on the ground from my leg. Charles' eyes move from the dried mud that is stained red in fresh blood to the slice at my thigh. "You're bleeding! Why didn't you tell me?" Charles takes his belt from his pants along with ripping cloth from his jacket.

"I didn't know," I lie smoothly as Charles kneels next to me, casting me a wary eye.

"Mhm, you would have noticed." He jabs the wound with his finger.

"Ouch!" I hiss, slapping him on the shoulder.

"Exactly, you knew you were hurt. You're just as bad as him," he chastises while his hands work, pressing the fabric of his jacket against the wound.

What are you doing? Reznor calls down the bond while Charles secures the fabric with his belt before removing his bloodied hands from my thigh. I ignore Reznor, clearly still annoyed with him from this morning.

"Alright, you wrapped it. Can we get back to training now?" I try to move past Charles, who catches my arm in his hand, stopping me in my tracks.

"What's with you lately?" he quizzes. He appears concerned and confused, two things I don't want him feeling. I have been off my game since the attack on the manor, and I'm not sure why.

Liara, what are you doing? Reznor calls again, and he's dismissed again. I bet it sucks being ignored, but karma's a bitch.

Charles releases my arm as I settle onto on a fallen tree nearby, resting my leg out in front of me. "I'm not sure."

"Is it because of the attack?" He plops down next to me, shaking the tree.

"I don't know honestly. Since the attack, everything's changed. Reznor's treating me differently, people keep staring, whispering. It has me on edge."

"He isn't avoiding you, or treating you differently; he's trying to plan a war and figure out what's happening in the other kingdoms," he pauses a moment, "the other lands are getting attacked if they don't join Whitehorn. Reznor just has a lot on his plate right now."

"I know that..." I groan, annoyed with myself. He rubs a soothing hand along the tops of my shoulders. Charles is like the big brother I never had, but always wanted. It's nice to feel like I have a family again.

"Just give him some time I'm sure things will—"

Liara! Reznor shouts into my head, causing me to miss whatever Charles is saying as it's drowned out by the booming. I wince as his voice echoes against my skull, painful his voice causes chills to erupt across my skin—this stupid bond.

What? I hiss as I grip onto my forehead. Charles stares at me, warily. "Reznor is yelling," I explain as Reznor's voice comes again.

What are you doing?

I'm training

A snarl comes down the bond. *It doesn't feel like you're training.* I can hear the accusation in his voice. It sends my blood boiling. I get to my feet, wincing at the pulsing in my leg. If he has time to shout at me down the bond, then he has time to do it in person.

Charles hurries after me as I storm through the manor, slamming open the door to the study, all eyes in the room fall on me. Emanuel, Maximus, and the two generals all give me shocked expressions. Reznor sits behind his desk with his jaw clenched tight as his eyes shift from me to Charles, who is lingering behind me. "Out now," I demand. At first, no one moves, then lightning strikes outside as I yell., "Get. The. Fuck. Out. Now!"

All of them scurry past. Emanuel grabs Charles by the collar of his shirt as he drags him from the room. I can hear Charles defending himself to Emanuel as he's hauled away. Slamming the door the moment they're out, I turn to him slowly. "You got something to say, Reznor?"

Reznor picks up his whisky glass, downing the rest of the brown liquor while his eyes bore into mine. He places his glass down on the desk as he drags his bottom lip between his teeth. "You were doing an awful lot of touching today," he bites as he pours another drink.

"And you think that the 'touching' wasn't for training purposes?" I accuse, my voice seething as I move closer to the desk. He just stares at the glass, ignoring my words, angering me further. I take the final step, slamming my hands against his desk. His eyes shoot up at me, red shining in his eyes.

"I think he had no reason to be touching you in the locations he did," Reznor says calmly as he leans forward in his chair.

"One, Charles and I are nothing but professional when we train, and two," I lean forward a little bit more as I feel my eyes turning grey, "at least someone is touching me." I know the 'touches' between Charles and I have been nothing but appropriate. But Reznor pissed me off, and I'm going to let him feel my rage for once. I know the words will trigger him, but I don't care. That dark part of me that has been awoken wants to explode.

Reznor jerks up, knocking the chair back behind him. Mimicking my stance, he leans against the desk, splaying his finger centimeters from mine.

"You *want* someone to touch you?" The words are menacing, laced with a bite as he leans further over the desk, his eyes still flaring that fiery red and his mouth inches from mine.

I pull back with a smirk on my face. "No, I don't want someone to touch me. I can do it better than any of you can." Reznor's eyes go wide as I back further away from him. I turn away with that same taunting grin on my face as I leave the room, ensuring to sway my hips as I go. I slam the door to emphasize my anger, a chuckle leaving my mouth as I see the shocked expression of the men waiting outside the room. They flinch when I continue to grin snidely as a roar erupts from the study along with a smash of his glass. I stroll down the hall, a massive smile on my face as I get further away from the angry man.

I allow my feet to take me where they please. That's how I end up on the balcony in my old room. I pace back and forth trying to calm my nerves, but that only seems to amp them up further. I'm not sure if it's my anger or Reznor's that's coming through the bond. Either way, we both are exchanging mass amounts of rage. I can sense his blood boiling, and I hope he feels the coolness of my snide mood.

I stay on the balcony for a while, but with the adrenaline of our fight wearing off, the pain in my leg becomes a burden. It quickly turns into something that I can't ignore as the pulsating wound throbs with each step. It takes a great deal of effort and time to climb down the stairs, then across the manor. I find Kora in the large washroom on the other side of the manor. I limp into the room, leaning myself against one of the large washing tubs. Her eyes instantly drift to the contraption on my leg. It's something that Reznor had failed to notice earlier.

"What happened?" she gasps as she takes in the soaked rag tied to my leg.

"Rough day at training. Can you get me something to clean it?" I had looked in my old room for supplies, but the room's bare of everything but the furniture. Kora hurries out the door as I hoist myself onto the counter, cursing as my leg starts bleeding again. She comes back quickly with an arm full of bandages and antiseptics. I was going to take them from her, but she pushes away my hands.

"I'm going to clean this," she insists. "I can cut your pants off, or you can take them off." She holds her hands out like a tipping scale as she gives me the options.

"I'll take them off." With help, I get down from the counter before Kora assists in guiding my pants down my legs. I grunt as I climb back onto the counter. The long gash between the tattered flesh is worse than I thought. I'll probably need stitches. Kora cleans the wound seamlessly, but it's not until she rubs the cream against my thigh that I'm hit with a surge of anger— anger that certainly doesn't belong to me. The door to the laundry room flies open minutes later, just as Kora is done dressing my thigh in the white wrap. Both of us jump at the sound. Reznor stands in the doorway, his eyes fuming red.

A smirk rises to my lips as the realization crosses his face when he looks at Kora and my position, his eyes dropping to my injured thigh. Kora bows her head as she exits the room without needing to be told to do so. Although, I wished she would have stayed. Reznor walks over slowly, his eyes going back to their natural blue state.

"Still think I'm seeking out other people's company?" I point to the ripped jacket sleeve and the belt in the nearby sink. "Charles was dressing my wound, not fondling me." I spit the words out as I jump off the counter, my bandages tinging pink the moment I'm on the ground.

I try to walk around him but get stopped by his arm darting in front of my path. "Let me heal you." He peers down at me with guilt-driven eyes.

"No, I'm fine." I shove past his arm, walking out of the room in only my t-shirt and underwear.

The hot water rolls off my shoulders as I stand directly beneath the stream coming from the showerhead. I've been standing here for the last half hour, enjoying the warmth coming from the hot water as it pelts my skin. With my eyes closed and my head tilted up toward the stream, I'm so focused on the water, I don't hear the shower door open behind me.

Two strong arms wrap around my waist as Reznor envelopes me into his arms, moving his head down next to mine. As much as I want to resist, I lean my head against his, the tingles spreading across my skin wherever we touch. Closing my eyes, savoring his touch, his head nuzzles against mine. I'm mad, but I'm starting to forget why.

"Liara," he murmurs against my throat while placing open mouth kisses up my neck. I strain my neck, giving him more access to my wet skin. "Liara."

I reach up, grabbing his head. "Shut up and kiss me." Reznor crashes his lips to mine. I welcome his eagerly as I swivel in his arms so that I'm facing him. I push my chest against his, while the need for all of him rises. His mouth slants against mine, our tongues tangling as every part of my mouth clanks against each of his. Hands rake down my naked back as he detaches his lips, moving his head to my neck once again. He goes straight to the mark, sucking on it harshly. The action has my heart beating between my thighs as his tongue traces his claim. He hoists me into his arms, pushing me against the wall of the shower. I arch my back away from the cold wall, which only pushes me further into Reznor's chest.

"Reznor," I warn as his canines graze the flesh of my neck in a new spot. He skims the area one more time before taking the skin between his teeth, biting me, but he doesn't break the skin. The hold is just enough pressure to keep me in place as he plunges inside of me with no warning. I cry out in surprise as he thrusts harshly. Twisting my hair around his hand, he tugs my head back. He sucks and bites across my throat as his hips collide with mine, his body keeping me secured to the wall. A wandering hand trails to my thigh where my cut *should* have been. I wrench open my eyes to see my healed leg. "You sneaky bastard," I moan as he strikes my core just right. The statement was meant to sound annoyed; instead, it comes out in a hearty moan. My sounds encourage Reznor as he palms my breast and reattaches his lips to mine.

He breaks the kiss, snagging my lower lip between his teeth, tugging on it as he pulls away. "I wouldn't be sneaky if you would've let me heal it earlier. But you stormed off." His snarky tone pisses me off once more.

"Watch it, Rez, or the only thing you'll be thrusting into is your hand," I hiss before biting down on his neck. My words seem to trigger him; his thrusts become more forceful as he pins me against the wall. He secures my hands above my head while the other supports me between him and the wall. I tighten my grip with my legs on his waist. This only seats him further, a whimper escaping my lips.

He's mad, but I don't care. Attempting to drag my teeth down him again, he swiftly moves to avoid my mouth as he pushes me harder into the wall. I want to reach out and touch him, but with my pinned hands, I can do little but cry out for him. "Reznor," I moan as he starts a brutal assault on my neck while rocking his hips forcibly against mine.

He suddenly drops my legs to the floor, spinning me so that my chest is pressed against the wall. I grunt at the coolness as my chest collides with the damp tile. Reznor spreads my legs, then locks them in place by intertwining our ankles, his in front of mine. He pins my hands above my head with one hand before he shoves himself back inside me from behind. He trails a hand down my front, dipping it between my legs. I throw my head back, resting it on his shoulder as he continues to work me. All thoughts of anger are gone as he rubs my button and thrusts deep at the same time.

"Rez," I cry out as my climax creeps on me suddenly. I try to tug my hands free, but they're trapped. Slumping against the cold wall, Reznor finishes shortly after, coating my insides in a fresh batch of warmth. My name falling off his lips multiple times as his orgasm wracks his body. He slumps against me, pressing me harder into the cold tile, his head dropping to my shoulder. He releases my hands only to wrap his arms around my frame, pulling me back underneath the water with him.

"I'm sorry," he says before kissing my shoulder.

"I wouldn't do that Reznor, I don't want anyone else."

"I know I just got…" He breaks off.

When he doesn't finish, I shut off the water. "You're healing all of these marks on my neck before I meet with Morana."

Reznor left after our shower fanatics. He has one last meeting before coming to bed. Unfortunately, I also have a meeting. Mine's with Morana, and I'm hoping she won't comment on my pinkened cheeks. Tomorrow will be the fall harvest; we had some last-minute preparations to go over, but other than a few details, the harvest is planned.

Walking into the hall with a damp head, Morana smiles at me brightly. She doesn't note the short black nightgown and robe, but sure enough, she points out my cheeks as she hugs me. "So, that's why you were late."

My face blanches. "I don't know what you're talking about."

She breaks into a fit of laughter. "Mhm, I bet Reznor is sitting somewhere with a damp head just as you are right now."

"Morana!" I exclaim.

"I knew it was going to happen sooner or later. You and Reznor can't be avoiding each other like you used to. The mate bond will make both of you unbearable. Plus, we're facing war, and a pissed off couple won't help our problems."

I sit next to her at the table, flipping through the harvest book. "You agree that he's avoiding me?" I ask while tracing a colored leaf on the page.

"I think it wasn't intentional, but he is awful at expressing anything. Therefore, it could have felt like he was avoiding you when he wasn't." She's right. Reznor doesn't express his feelings, much like I don't, something we both really need to work on. She uses my silence to speak again. "He cares about you, you know that, right?"

I drag my head from the book. "That, I do know; he has conveyed that much to me." I chuckle, but Morana's eyes light up at the words.

"It took him four hundred years to tell me he loved me. Him telling you that he cares about you is a big deal, especially with what little time you two have had together," she pauses, "just give him time, he will always come back to you. He just has a lot on his plate; he has a war to think about, and now he has *you* to think about." She casts me a suggestive grin. "I wouldn't be walking around here in that little of clothing again. Reznor would likely claim you in front of everyone."

"Morana!" I exclaim again, blushing deeply. She waves me off.

Morana doesn't speak any more about Reznor and me. Instead, she dives into the details for the harvest tomorrow. I hadn't realized how long we've been going over the particulars until Reznor marches in, seemingly annoyed.

"Morana, it's almost one in the morning," he states before he sees me leaning over the table, the robe discarded on the back of the chair, my black nightgown raised higher due to my position. I don't make any sudden moves to get the robe, but Morana gives me an 'I told you so,' look.

"She can go," Morana smiles sweetly to Reznor, which only causes me to shoot her a begging glance to keep me. Reznor comes closer, snatching the robe off the chair while sticking his other hand out to me. I slip my hand into his, throwing Morana a final glance before Reznor and I exit the room.

Reznor tosses my robe onto the back of the couch as he passes it on his way to the closet. I watch him suspiciously as I veer to the bed. I crawl beneath the cool sheets and face toward the wall rather than Reznor's side of the bed. The lights turn off, followed by the bed dipping as Reznor slides in behind me. He shifts to the middle of the bed, wrapping me in his arms from behind.

"What's wrong?" he asks as he strokes my bare arm.

I sigh and close my eyes, enjoying his touch. "I'm sorry about today."

"You don't need to be sorry for anything. I overreacted, not you."

"Yes, but I allowed you to feed into it because I was pissed." Reznor snickers, agreeing with me, which earns a slap from me.

He rests his head against mine in the darkness. "Why were you mad today?" I freeze, thinking of an answer. I don't know if I should tell him the truth or lie. "Liara," he calls my name, which leads me to my final decision.

I groan. "I felt like you were avoiding me." Reznor's hand that had been moving along my side stops. "I never got mad when you avoided me before, but for some reason, I was furious this morning when I woke up, and you were gone again."

"Liara—

"Rez, I know you're busy with the war and all, it's not that I don't understand. I don't mean to cause problems, but it overtook me today." I rush out in an attempt to not sound like such a needy girl wanting attention.

"I was avoiding you," he admits, which hurts me more than I would ever be willing to admit.

"Why?"

He turns my face to him, the soft light from the magic windows lighting his face. "Because it's hard to plan for war when all I can think about is my future with you…" he pauses, caressing my cheek gently, "and whether or not we will get to have one."

"I hope we get one, but if not, you shouldn't avoid me if we don't know how much time we'll have together."

Reznor studies me. "What are you doing to me, Liara?" he asks before kissing me. It's funny, I could ask him the same thing.

Chapter Thirty-Five: Harvest Party

I'm sleeping with my head on Reznor's lap in his study when Charles' voice wakes me from my peaceful slumber.

Charles barges into the room, slamming the door with a thud. "Are you ready—"

"Shh!" Reznor hisses. I don't dare open my eyes. Hoping he'll leave, so I can fall back asleep I don't let them know I'm awake, but Charles has other plans.

"Awe, look at sleeping beauty," he teases, which annoys Reznor further.

"What do you want?" Reznor asks while shuffling the papers in his hands.

"Are you ready to come to the last meeting?" Emanuel questions in a quiet voice.

"You go. I'm going to sit this one out. Liara isn't awake yet." With Reznor's words, I groan and tear open my eyelids.

"I'm up, thanks to loudmouth." I lift my head off his lap, allowing him to get up, but he makes no moves to stand.

"I can skip it."

"No, it's fine. I'm sure Kora will be collecting me soon to get ready." I think Reznor still feels guilty about avoiding me these past few weeks. I'm not mad anymore, but I appreciate him putting in the effort to spend more time with me. Reznor nods before gathering his papers and climbing off the couch. He plants a kiss on my temple before heading to the door, and with a final glance he watches me as I snuggle back into the sofa. I don't get to stay on the couch much longer because Kora comes to collect me. Tonight, is the fall harvest, and that means getting dolled up for our possible allies. It isn't the ideal time or place, but it can't wait any longer.

Kora's incredibly excited about tonight's dress. Her daughter made it. She won't allow me to see it early, keeping it hidden in the garment bag. She spends a great deal of time on my hair, curling the long strands. Using gold leaves, she clips back the curls from my face. To match the golden clips, she does a brown smokey eye and a nude lip. When it's finally time to put on the dress, Kora can't hide her excitement as she unzips the bag. The dress is a beautiful brick red with gold shimmers across the gown. It has a thin golden belt with a cluster of golden leaves at the waist. The sleeves hang off my shoulders with matching leaves that outline the cut of the dress. Koras correct. The dress is stunning and wearing it now, it's also rather heavy.

Reznor seems dazed as he watches me come down the grand staircase, the dress catching the light with each step I took. He's waiting for me at the bottom in his usual black attire except for a brick-colored jacket instead of a black one.

"I see Kora got you to wear something bright," I tease as I ease off the final step off the staircase.

"I understand why she was so persistent; she wanted us to match." He extends his arm to me, and I gladly accept it. We walk through the fall decorated manor heading for the grand hall. Gold, red, orange, and yellow decorates the manor along with pumpkins and other fall apparel.

"This harvest seems like Thanksgiving," I tell as I compare the similarities of the two holidays.

"What's Thanksgiving?"

"It's just some human holiday."

Reznor cracks a smile. "Well, the fall harvest is to celebrate the fall harvest; it's sweet and simple."

"You probably wouldn't like our other holidays either; they get a little bazaar. For example, on Christmas we tell kids that a man slides down a chimney to bring☐" I don't get to elaborate further because we enter the grand hall, but Reznor's face contours in confusion which sends me laughing as we stroll in.

The heavily decorated room is lined with tables of food and guests who are talking amongst themselves. I catch sight of a blonde-haired little girl in a yellow tulle dress spinning beneath a chandelier. It seems we see each other simultaneously because she screams my name before running toward me.

I crouch down, hugging Star as she throws herself into my open arms. "You look so pretty," she cheers as she pets the shimmering dress.

"She does look beautiful, doesn't she?" Reznor asks as he smiles down at the little girl. Star blushes before running off giggling. I rise back to my feet, retaking Reznor's arm. "We will wait to talk to the royals after dinner. A lot of them are already in our dining room." Reznor leads us to an adjoining room where five out of the six closest kingdoms are waiting. Reznor and I are the last kingdom to join.

Tatiana seems relieved the moment we enter into the room. She waves us over to her with an eager hand. "This is dreadful without Arnold," she sighs before drinking from her wine glass.

"I'll leave Liara with you. I need to talk to Max and his dad."

"Can you explain to me who everyone is?" I ask, gazing at the couples before me.

Tatiana sets down her glass and carefully eyes the first couple. "The one in that awful bright pink gown is Queen Cheri and her husband, King Typhore: he is Maximus' father; they rule the Faeries." Cheri has matching pink hair and piercing green eyes like the grass in the spring. Typhore looks to be an older version of Maximus with his blond hair turning white in places. He, however, doesn't have the grey eyes that Maximus has. Instead, they're green. Tatiana nods to the next couple. "Next, we have King Westen and Queen Warra, the ones in all grey. They rule the demons which aren't hateful creature's contrary to what the humans say." They both wear silver from head to toe, but what stands out is how similar they looked. I originally thought they were brother and sister, not husband and wife. They both have matching blonde hair and light grey eyes.

"The ones next to them are Queen Allegra and King Norcaiste; they rule the witches." Allegra and Norcaiste are both older, but they both have piercing purple eyes that stand out against their dark skin. Allegra has long black hair that's fastened into purple bands at the end of each plaited piece, along with a symbol painted in the center of her forehead in a bright silver powder. The symbol resembles a trident—two outer lines pointing toward the center of the third. Her husband also has a matching symbol painted on his head.

Tatiana snorts in annoyance. "Then, lastly across from them is King Bellamy and Queen Sucrasa, they rule the Warlocks. He's the dumbass who gave Nostics lands and appointed him titles as Lord, essentially making him a mini king." Bellamy is an older man with salt and pepper hair, blue eyes with flakes of violet in them. Sucrasa won't look anywhere but her lap. The only thing I can tell from her is that she's a blonde…and a lot younger than him.

"You'll have to explain the difference between Warlocks and Witches to me later," I say quietly to Tatiana. I don't get to ask any more questions because Reznor returns to my side and instructs the servants to serve everyone.

The dinner holds pleasant conversation between the royals, although I'm not involved in it much, and I don't mind. They're all old friends, and I'm an outsider. I mainly converse with Tatiana, which she appreciates greatly because it stops the 'pity party.' She hates the apologies. Tatiana gets interrupted in her rant as Bellamy boldly addresses me, cutting off my conversation with Tatiana completely.

"You don't look like a Nightlighter. You don't look like you could hurt a fly," Bellamy snips with an underlying anger.

Reznor tenses next to me, but before he can speak on my behalf, I address Bellamy. "Don't judge a book by its cover," I match his tone as lightning strikes outside.

Reznor's face twitches into a smile as he squeezes my hand underneath the table. *You should have struck him with lightning.*

If I could control the lightning, I would have. Reznor laughs at my words down the bond, but he can't hide his smile.

"She could kick your ass with a flick of her finger," Tatiana adds in a defensive voice.

"Then why were we asked here? Because if she's so strong, why would you need our help in the war?" Bellamy's words stun me into silence.

Reznor is quick to step in. "I asked you here to ask for your help. Whitehorn attacked my manor a few weeks ago. We don't have the numbers to fight against Whitehorn and King Nostics."

"Is Whitehorn after your powers?" Allegra asks, her purple eyes flaring.

"Yes."

It's a mixed reaction from the royals upon learning the news, but Cheri seems to be the most appalled. "How did the manor come out unscathed?"

Reznor regards me. "Liara was able to use her powers along with our soldiers to drive back the forces until I arrived." All the eyes in the room shift to me. I try not to squirm under their gazes, but it's growing harder as the moments pass.

"She is strong then," Warra states instead of questioning it. "Why is Nostics at war with you?"

"He ordered attacks on Liara and used Serena as a ploy to get information about Liara. When I found out, I executed her for treason. He wants Liara dead, but lately, he's been attempting to capture her." Reznor rubs slow circles into my palm while he addresses the crowd.

"Are they working together?" Allegra asks again. She's inspecting me openly; it's starting to make me very uncomfortable.

"We don't know for sure, but if I find out they are, I will let you know." Reznor pauses, glancing down at me again. "I know I have no right to ask when these issues are both personal to me, particularly, but I have to. You all have watched me grow into my role as king. All of us knew this would come at some point. We all knew war would come with it, but I'm asking you to stand with me to protect my lands, my home, my people, and Liara." I'm stunned at Reznor's words, but what shocks me more is that they start agreeing to it.

"We'll fight with you," Allegra speaks first, a determined grin on her face. "I've been waiting to meet a Nightlighter, and since she is the last of her kind, we must protect her."

"We'll fight," Cheri beams, clapping her hands. I'm not sure how someone can be so happy about war.

"We'll fight because you fought for us last time," Westen says to Reznor. The only person not to speak is Bellamy. All eyes drift to him.

"No, I won't fight for a girl," he scoffs, rising from the table.

Reznor's mouth transforms into vicious grin, "That's fine, but know that I won't forget this."

Bellamy snorts, "That's fine because you're on the losing side of a war." He reaches for the door handle, dragging his wife behind him. "You'll never win, and she'll die. You should just accept that."

The room is silent as we digest what just happened.

Rez, he is just trying to make you mad; I soothe down the bond, trying to calm him, but it makes matters worse.

No, he isn't because their goal is to kill you.

Well, they can try.

"Will she fight with us?" Allegra asks, interrupting my conversation with Reznor through the bond.

Tatiana snorts, sipping from her wine. "We'd be stupid not to use her."

Reznor won't meet my eye as he speaks to the royals. "She'll fight with us if she wants to. Plus, I don't think she'd listen if I told her no." This earns a round of laughs from the royals, a heat creeping to my cheeks. He's right because if he's laying his life on the line for me, then I'm willing to do the same for him, for us.

For the rest of the dinner, the royals include me in as much of the conversations as possible. I tell them of the mortal world, and they tell me of their lands. It's nice but odd at the same time, and by the end of the gathering, they all made it clear they have no problem fighting with Reznor for our future. Many of them believe the prophecy that comes with my and Reznor's relationship. Most of them want to see the lands united again someday, but to do that, we need to win this war.

With the harvest party over and alliances made, Reznor and I tour the manor grounds as the sun sets, our hands intertwined as we stroll. We've been silent so long; I'm spooked when he speaks up. "That has been the first fall harvest I have enjoyed since my parents died." I lean my head against his arm. "Hopefully, we'll have many more."

"If not, at least we had one." I squeeze his hand.

He stops suddenly, crossing in front of my path to face me. "That's not going to be enough." He focuses on to the tree line, his eyes looking anywhere but mine.

Taking his face into my hands, his torn expressions tugs at my heart. "Reznor, even if we had a thousand years together, it wouldn't be enough. You and I both know that."

"I wish you never went to the mortal world." He looks despondent; it's evident in his dull empty stare as he looks without focus. In those deep eyes are a sadness he never allowed to show except for a few moments.

"I never felt right in the mortal world; I never felt like I belonged. But here with you, it finally feels right."

"That's because you belong here with me. You should have been here this entire time. You and I were always meant to be together." His words warm my heart and break it at the same time. Standing on my toes, I kiss him with as much passion as I can muster. I know standing here with him, with his lips on mine, that I need him, just like he needs me. I want a future with him. I want him, now and forever.

Chapter Thirty-Six: Better Together

Liara...

Liara...

Liara, wake up. I groan at Reznor's words in my head, wrenching my eyes open and find our bed empty yet again.

It would be a lot easier to wake me up if you were actually in our bed.

Reznor gives feather-like stroke against my cheek, *I didn't want to wake you before dawn, but next time—*

I cut him off quickly. *Nope, too late. What do you want?*

He sighs down the bond. *I need you to come to my study.* I reluctantly climb from the bed. I throw on some clothes that aren't pajamas but keep my slippers on before heading to the study. I'm presentable, but I still plan on going back to bed as soon as possible.

Charles is the first to mock me. "You look ridiculous."

"At least I don't look ridiculous all the time, unlike you," I tease with a snide grin. My annoyance is still fresh, and he's an easy target.

Charles eyes me boldly. "At least I don't look like a rat fresh from the bed."

I try not to laugh as Reznor swats Charles harshly. "Joke or not, I will hurt you," Reznor warns.

"Can we get down to business?" Maximus asks. They're all standing near Reznor's desk while I settle into the couch, draping the blanket around me. It's cold...too cold. Judging by the sun's location, it's hardly past dawn. Annoyance sets in again as I cast daggers into the back of Reznor's head.

Sorry, love.

You don't get to keep me up all night with sex-capades, then wake me up this early. Reznor laughs out loud, causing all eyes in the room to go to him as he tries to cover it up with a cough. But then when they focus on me, I keep a blank face giving nothing away.

"Anyway," Maximus continues, but Reznor's voice distracts me again.

If I recall correctly, you rather enjoyed our 'sex-capades.'

Keep it up, and you won't be having any more, I hiss. But Reznor gleams with amusement as he takes in my annoyed features.

I don't believe that for a second; you like it when I—

"They aren't listening," Emanuel calls, claiming all our attention.

"Gods listen, this is about you two." Maximus mirrors me, displeased to be up this early. With all of our attention, he starts again, "I think you two need to look into the lore on your bond. See if there is anything that could help us have another advantage to this war. Whitehorn's soldiers are ones he's created, and they are hard to kill. What he used here at the manor is nothing compared to the monsters he'll bring with him."

"What kind of lore?" I question.

"Your bond is one of the only other things written in scriptures as much as the gods. There is lore on what your bond is. Some of it is true and could help us. My father mentioned it to me last night before he left. It's obvious you two share the bond where you can communicate with each other, and that's one of the things in the lore."

"I don't know what you're talking about." Reznor grins playfully.

"Yeah, okay. We all see it. It's a good thing to have since she doesn't have the pack link like everyone else." Charles taps his temple.

"Pack link?" I ask confused.

"It's how I communicate to my warriors. I can send a message to any of my soldiers, or people. That's how they distribute my orders," Reznor explains while moving from the cluster of men over to me on the couch. "They receive the blood bond when they join my forces, or when they join my lands; it links them all to me."

"It'll be helpful in the war, which brings me to my next point. Before we move into battle —whenever that will be— we need to know who we are going to flee with if things get too bad, and we can't collect both of you." Maximus adds, not looking either of us in the eye.

"Reznor," I answer before Reznor even has a chance to speak. "He knows how to rule, I don't." Reznor goes deathly still. If looks could kill...well then, I'd be dead.

"No, you get her out."

"No, Reznor, we both know you're more valuable to the people than I am."

"Liara, we are not going to have this discussion. They all already have the orders. They have had them since the moment you got here. If it's down to you and me, they will save you." Reznor glares at me with red eyes, but even in those fierce red eyes, I can see the underlying fear that might actually come down to one of us surviving and not the other.

I lean toward him. "I'm not leaving that fight unless you do Reznor, dead or alive."

"I hate it when Mom and Dad fight," Charles groans.

"Charles!" Reznor and I snap in unison. However, the tension relief is always appreciated.

"See, this is why they gang up on me, then dad pouts and mom gets angry. It's a whole mess really." Charles adds, smacking a hand against his face.

"Give us the room," Reznor snaps. The boys try to leave, but he stops them. "Liara, I meant you."

You wake me up then kick me out? I accuse. Of course, he doesn't respond.

I glare at him for a moment then wipe my face of emotion. Rising from the couch, I discard the blanket onto his lap. They boys gawk as I leave the study.

"See, she's mad. Just know I choose her in the divorce," Charles jokes moments before he yells, "Ow!"

I'm mad, but not as mad as Reznor; he's practically shoving it down the bond at me. Ignoring him, I seek out Tatiana who is sitting on her bed in the guest room. The cream couch that sits in front of the fireplace accentuates the light grey walls of the area, a cashmere bedspread to tie it all together. "Your cousin is a stubborn ass!" I grumble while crawling onto the bed next to her, leaning against the large headboard.

"Are you just now figuring that out?" she laughs lightly.

I ponder a moment. "No, but he's worse today. Maximus asked who he should flee with if things get too bad, and I told him to take Reznor."

"Ah," Tatiana sighs knowingly. "He already made me agree to have my soldiers get you out of there if things got too bad."

"Why? He's the king. He knows how to rule; he is more valuable to the people."

"Yes, but you are more valuable to him than his own life."

"Tatiana, he has to live."

"If you two would focus more on fighting the war together rather than who is going to live through it, then maybe things would be different." She's right yet again. It seems everyone is right besides Reznor and me.

"I don't think it's about who is surviving. I think he is more afraid they will take me from him." I pause, being hit with guilt. "If I'm dead, then it's over, but if I'm taken…then he has to hunt me down all over again." Reznor's face from the night of my almost abduction haunts me…the fear in his eyes.

She takes my hand in hers. "Then stick together; if you need to fall back, fall back together. Make him agree to it. That way, you both walk off that field together."

Tatiana jabbers about Cheri for a few minutes when Reznor calls me back to the study. I take Tatiana with me in case Reznor becomes problematic again.

She seats herself next to Reznor on the couch, where he remains with my blanket still in his lap. I take a spot up by the fireplace. It's still too cold, but I'll freeze to death before retrieving my blanket from his lap.

"We need to see Morana. If anyone knows about our bond, it's her. One of us needs to look in the library and archives here while the others go into town," Reznor rubs his face.

"Tatiana and I can check the library and archives," I suggest, but Tatiana quickly shoots it down.

"No, you need to go with Reznor to see Morana." So much for Tatiana being useful.

"Charles can help you," Reznor says in a deeper tone than usual, but he doesn't object to the plan of me accompanying him into town.

With the plans set in motion, Tatiana and a complaining Charles head to the library deep in the manor, while Maximus heads to the archives. While Reznor, Emanuel, and I get ready for Morana's, and I quickly realize I should have fought harder to stay at the manor. Although Reznor sits with me in the back, he makes no move to speak to me as we travel into town. I'm the first one out of the car and the first into Morana's arms. She's waiting in her rocking chair on the porch, like always, no matter the weather or time.

"How did I know you two would be here today?" she releases me only to envelope Reznor into a matching embrace. It's still amusing to see his tall frame compared to her short one. He has to practically hunch over to hug the small woman.

"Because your king is a stubborn ass."

Morana cackles at my words. Reznor however, doesn't look pleased. I smile innocently, following after Morana into the house, where she takes us to her office. I sit down in one of the chairs facing her desk while Emanuel and Reznor linger near the wall. How times have changed since the last time we've been here; our previous visit is when she diagnosed me with the mating illness, and now, we are at war.

"What brings you by?" Morana adds sugar to her tea, or rather heaping it into her tea.

"What can you tell us about our bond?" Reznor asks from his place on the wall.

"What about it? I studied your bond a lot over the years," she adds another lump of sugar, and suddenly I'm wondering how she has any teeth.

"Anything that can help us fight."

Morana stops mixing the tea, her eyes traveling from Reznor, then to me. She steps from her desk and studies the bookshelf, pulling down an old leather-bound book. She flips through the pages until she stops, tapping the page with her finger. "This is the most accurate book I could find. It's written by the eldest scholar; he is the one who helped revise the curse before it was bestowed on Reznor." She hands the book to him.

"When it talks about Liara being created for you, it also means her powers were created to counter yours. Just like your powers will be stronger when activated with hers." She eyes me. "Your powers are meant to magnify each other, although you're stronger than Liara. She's your weakness, which makes you weaker. Just like Liara can draw off you to fuel her own powers. You two are meant to work as two parts to one whole, rather than separate pieces," she says with wild fascination.

"Your powers are meant to work together; it says in there that Reznor can bring out the moon in the middle of the day by blacking out the sun. That means Liara can call on the moon easier and make her powers stronger." Of course, he can block out the sun. He has powers from a god, I think to myself. I quickly say a silent prayer, hoping Reznor isn't lingering in my thoughts at the moment.

"And what does it mean about sharing blood? I can read it, but the phrasing is what I don't understand." Reznor finally moves from his place on the wall taking a seat in the chair next to mine.

"It means if one of you dies, then the other one can bring you back, but it has to be done through each other's blood. Joining your bodies like that leads to a whole different kind of bond. In some of the other books it says if you do it, then your powers become joint. You can both access all of each other's abilities." she takes a moment, almost looking uncomfortable. "It also says if you two do that, then you two will be immortal and essentially Gods."

"My father knew all of this before he cast the curse?"

Morana smiles softly. "That's why he had his God cast the curse. He knew he was going to die and wanted you to be able to have someone with you forever. There is a lot about this curse that neither of you know about." Reznor slams the book shut and tosses it onto his chair before he storms out and leaves the office without another word.

"What was that about?" I question, staring at the door.

"Reznor has a lot of issues with his father and what his father did to him…and to you." She takes the book and places it back onto the shelf. "I'd give him some space for now." Morana turns wary as she sits back down, casting me a sympathetic glance. It takes everything in me not to follow him, but feeling the pain being shoved down the bond, I know if I went after him now, things would only get worse. We would fight, and I do not want to do that, and he certainly does not need that either.

Reznor left Morana's inn, telling Emanuel to take me back to the manor. I argue with Emanuel for a while, but eventually, I give in and return. I seek out Charles, Tatiana, and Maximus, hoping to distract myself. They tell me of their findings, but none of them are as promising as Morana's. We take the rest of the day going through books and old testimonies. I try to focus on the words I read, but all I can think about are Morana's words and Reznor. Where the hell is he?

It isn't until late that night that he returns, but he doesn't come to find me. Instead, I follow his scent through the manor. I end up outside a door in the manor, in a corridor I have never been to or seen before. The corridor has been closed off, evident by the dust and dirt leading up to it. The hall seems completely and utterly abandoned. I know I'm in the right place because there is a fresh set footprints in the dirt leading to a closed door at the end of the hall. The tall door has a large cursive 'N' engraved across both doors. After hesitating a moment, I push open the door and wander inside.

The room's pitch black except for the light coming from the open balcony doors and the large glass wall. The room, like the rest of the corridor, is covered in dust and cobwebs. What catches my eye is Reznor standing out on the balcony. It has old steel furniture, along with empty flowerpots littering the area. I walk out into the cool night air, standing off to the side of him. I'm waiting for him to speak, but he doesn't. He just stares out at the vast manor before him.

From this spot, the rest of the estate is visible, all the lands in every direction. The entirety of the manor: the lake, the mountains, the pathway to the cave from the ceremony, courtyards, gardens, the maze. It all can be seen. This is the best view I have seen by far; I'm starting to wonder why he has this corridor shut off. I shove down my questions as I study the confused and tormented man standing next to me. He's been shoving down his feelings about his father for so long, and now this new information tears open old wounds. He looks miserable, the pain so evident I start to wonder what's going on in his head, or what memories he's thinking of.

"Rez," I say hesitantly. He doesn't acknowledge me, but I continue, "If you want, I can go, but I just wanted to check on you. I don't know what any of this means for you, but I'm here if you need me." After waiting another few minutes in silence, I turn to leave, but he catches my hand, stopping me.

"Stay." The single word is barely a whisper, but it's all I need.

He snakes his arm around my waist and tugs me in front of him. Keeping one hand on my side while the other rests on the iron railing before us. "I haven't been in this part of the manor since my mom passed. I had them seal it off completely that night. My mom died in this room, on that bed, and this is the first time in sixteen years that I have been near the corridor, let alone back in their old room. I wouldn't let them do a thing to these halls. I ordered everyone out and sealed it off like a tomb. Never meant to be opened again." He grips my waist tighter. "Yet, somehow, I ended back here, thinking all the same questions I thought back then." My heart breaks for Reznor. He has known so much loss and pain in his life. He's been burdened with the task of leading since he was nine years old, and now, he has to fight to keep what was supposed to be his since the beginning.

"I've resented him for so many years for casting his powers to me instead of using them to fight. I resented him for not protecting my mother. I resented them for leaving me alone in this world. Then, I find out he put a loophole into the curse to ensure I wouldn't be alone." He shakes his head in disbelief. "I've hated them both for longer than they were alive and now—" He breaks off, unable to speak anymore.

"Rez, you didn't know. You were nine years old and lost your mother and father months apart, along with being cursed. You're allowed to be mad; you're allowed to be hurt."

"That's the thing, I can't be mad anymore because he gave me the one thing I needed." He slides his hand to cup the side of my face. "I needed a way to have you forever, and he ensured that I get it."

"Reznor, you would have had me forever either way. It's you and me, Rez. It's us until the end."

"We're going to win this war, Liara, and I need your help to do it." He searches my eyes, and as I say my next words, his light up with a flare of hope.

"We'll win this war, Rez, but we're going to win it for us," I caress my hand against his cheek, "But you have to stop trying to save me when I'm not in danger yet. We need to work together. Stop telling the warriors to save me because I will not walk off that field, or away from that battle without you."

A slow smile spreads to his cheeks. "You're stubborn."

"Yep, and now you're stuck with me."

Chapter Thirty-Seven: Working Together

It's me who leaves Reznor alone in bed this morning. I have training 'bright and early' as Charles cheers from outside my door. I slap a hand over his mouth when I exit the room, chastising him for being so loud. He only laughs loudly in response, then sends me to run the trails. When I emerge, I'm surprised to find Reznor waiting with Emanuel and Charles. All three boys stare in my direction as I approach them. Reznor's dressed in training clothes along with the other two boys. I guess we all are training today. It's rare that I see Reznor in such casual attire, and looking at him now, I wish I'd get to see it more often.

"Morning," Reznor greets as I near his side, but he quickly dives back into his conversation while I settle on the ground to stretch. With my eyes closed, I rest my head against my legs, stretching them out before me. "We're going to be trying out our powers together." Reznor stands at the ends of my feet.

"How are we going to do that?"

Reznor sticks his hand out to me, "Like we used to; they're going to try and provoke us enough to try and get our powers to come together."

Allowing him to pull me from the ground, I snicker, "This is going to be a long day then." Reznor joins in on the laughter as he pulls me against his chest.

"Try not to kill them," I whisper quietly, rising on my tiptoes so my lips brush against his ear.

"I'll try my best." His expression is anything but promising. He steps back with a smirk that gets wider with each step he takes. This is going to be a long day…and not just for me: Emanuel and Charles are going to be sore by the time we're done.

"Are we even sure this is a good idea?" I ask, but my answer is Charles running toward me with a sword in hand. Reznor steps in front of me and flips Charles into the air, making him slam into the ground.

Charles jumps up to his feet, picking up the fallen sword from the ground. "Nope, but it's the only thing we can do, unless you want to wait until we're in a battle to try and figure out how to use your powers together."

"Alright, but if one of you gets hurt, we stop." I step around Reznor so I can see both boys.

"We'll see about that," Charles grins, running at me again while Emanuel runs at Reznor. I send Charles flying through the air. He collides with Emanuel taking both of them to the ground.

"Alright, new rule," Charles groans as he sits up, "no powers unless you're both trying to use them together."

That's how the training starts. I fight Charles while Reznor battles with Emanuel. I only use my powers if I need to, but we just can't get the hang of it. Using my sword to push Charles back a step, I call out to Reznor. *Want to try and use them at the same time instead of provoking them?*

Reznor is slow to respond as he's too busy flipping Emanuel over his shoulder. *Yeah, we can try that. Use your shield, and I'll use the mist.*

Won't the mist kill them! I whip my head in his direction. It costs me a blow from Charles' elbow against my side.

Pay attention, he hisses, *and no, it only kills them if I want it to.*

Tell me when. I struggle to push against Charles as he bears his sword down hard against mine. I use all my force, giving a little only to shove up harder and send him stumbling back a step. Charles approaches me again, his arm going back to build up strength. He's preparing to strike me hard.

Now! Reznor says as we both use our powers against our separate parties. Both of our powers listen to their commands, yet they don't work in unison. Charles stills in place, along with Emanuel being brought to the ground by a purple mist twisting around his ankles.

"This isn't working," Reznor huffs as he rests his hands against his hips, none of the boys have broken a sweat while my skin is damp with it. Not fair.

We're all supernaturally inclined, that's why we aren't sweating.

Reznor, stay out of my head! I shout down the bond while giving him a nasty look.

"Let's pick it up a notch then," Emanuel suggests as he grabs another blade from our stash of training weapons. Oh god, someone's going to get hurt today, and it isn't about to be me. Reznor laughs down the bond. *Reznor, I swear if you don't get out of my head!* I slap his chest.

Charles crosses in front of me with a sword and spear in his hand. I drop to the ground to avoid being impaled by the sharp end of the spear as he launches it at my chest.

"Charles…" Reznor warns, his eyes turn red as he fights with Emanuel, his gaze searching between me on the ground and his opponent. I scramble off the ground quickly. Charles always says the easiest way to kill an opponent is to get them on the ground. Now on my feet, I barely miss Charles' sword as he aims for my stomach. Reznor growls from somewhere behind me, but I can't focus on him right now. I dodge his strike only to send an equally powerful one back. Charles doesn't flinch as he deflects the hilt of my sword. There's shuffling on my right as the other two move in my direction, but I can't see how close they are as Charles swings at my face.

I don't get to block him. Reznor jumps in front of me, putting a protective arm out in front, moving me behind him as he swings with the other. With his arm lightly touching mine, I call out to my powers. As my forcefield meets with a purple mist, both Emanuel and Charles go flying in opposite directions away from us. I do mean flying. They end up at least eighty feet from where they started.

Reznor looks over his shoulder at me. We just used our powers…together. I grin up at him. "We did it!"

He laughs as he moves to stand beside me rather than in front. "I guess we just have to be touching." The smirk on his face implies more than his words do. Luckily, the boys don't catch it. Charles and

Emanuel both groan but slowly rise up from the ground. They glance between each other before looking back at us.

"Do you think you could do that with the force of your mist and her ash?" Emanuel asks as he collects his weapons.

"We can't test that out on you guys, but I'm assuming so." Reznor shuts down the idea of using our more destructive powers. My ash cannot be undone, and the mist he uses can be lethal, especially the more force he puts into it.

"We need to be able to test that, and how far you can cast your powers," Charles argues.

Reznor and I glance at each other before collectively shaking our heads. "It's too risky. That is something we will have to wait and see about. We can't risk using those yet."

I quickly add, "We can see how far out we can cast our powers, but that's it."

"Alright, let's go again then," Emanuel suggests. Reznor and I join hands. They go flying backward farther than before.

We continue fighting, Reznor and I using our powers while Emanuel and Charles try to separate and attack us. We were planning to train late into the evening, but Reznor gets called away for a meeting, so we end practice early. Charles and Emanuel escort me back to the house while Reznor goes to his meeting. They linger, not wanting to leave my side, but eventually they get called away on business of their own.

The full moon is shining brightly overhead as I sit beneath it on the concrete steps, gazing at its beauty.

My powers hum in my skin as I bask in the light from the radiant moon, my body feeling more alive when I sit beneath it. Soaking in the powerful rays that rejuvenate me in a way that nothing else can, a soft breeze starts up. With the gush of the cool wind, my hair twists in the invisible current. Goosebumps spread across my body. Rubbing my arms in an attempt to warm myself, the wind stops suddenly.

The world goes quiet around me for a moment. Everything's silent, but as steps are heard behind me, the world quickly becomes alive again. Reznor climbs down the stairs toward me with a pair of black sweatpants in his hand. He tosses them down next to him as he sits down beside me.

He sighs as he begins untying his shoes. "I had hoped when I got my powers, the need to shift into my beast would stop, but here I am wanting to shift just to subdue that side of me."

"What's it like?" I ask, tearing my eyes from the beautiful man next to me only to gaze at the moon overhead.

"Turning into a beast?" he asks as he removes his socks and his shoes.

"I don't think you turn into a beast," I peer at him, "I think you turn into a beautiful *wolf*."

He doesn't comment on my word choice. Instead, he starts unbuttoning his shirt. "It's painful, but I've grown used to it. It doesn't hurt like it used to, and it's nice not to have to turn every full moon, although the urge is there."

"When are you going to shift?" I return my gaze to the moon as he removes his shirt and places it on the growing pile of clothes.

"Any minute now, at least then the anxiousness will stop, luckily I get to choose when I shift now." He rises to his feet, heading for the woods. "Don't wait up, it'll be a while before I'm back on two legs," he teases, shooting me a wink. I watch him as he lingers near the tree line. He shifts so quickly, it's hard to process what just happened. My eyes thought they were deceiving me as the man turns into an animal in seconds. Reznor's wolf regards me with red eyes before he takes off, darting into the forest.

Be careful, I call only to get a chuckle from him. I don't reach out anymore as he goes on his run. Instead, I gaze at the sky. I appreciate its beauty, thinking back to the story of the man in the moon. I had read that story many times as a child. Even in the human world, I felt a strong connection to the moon. Whenever I read the story about the man in the moon longing for his love, the sun, it always saddened me. It would fill me with such despair, I would often cry at night, gazing at the sky, hoping, and longing for love like that. I wanted someone to love me the way the moon loved the sun, but as I grew older, I realized a love like that would never happen for me. Now I'm not so sure that's true.

I would die for Reznor without a second thought, which is terrifying because I hardly know this man, yet I feel like I've known him my entire life. He reads me like a book, and although his alpha male ego gets in the way sometimes, he does care for me in a way no one ever has. I, however, haven't decided how I feel about that. I've never been good at feelings, and I've relayed as much as I can on how I feel to Reznor. It seems we are similar there because we have expressed, we care about each other, but nothing further than that.

    I don't want to ruin whatever we have, but now it feels like whatever we do have is intensifying. I realize it more and more with each passing day that my feelings for Reznor might be more than I care to admit. Reznor and I are similar, yet so opposite of each other. He's hesitant to share his feelings but is willing to express he doesn't want anything happening to me or us. I have told him I care for him, yet I express myself mainly through actions rather than words. I would rather *show* him how I feel rather than *tell* him. That way, it doesn't hurt as bad if things fall apart. I'm afraid of what would happen if things did.

    I know I would do anything for Reznor, and I don't know if it's because of my feelings for him or the bond. It's been changing these past few weeks The bond is always changing like some living, breathing thing that pulses through both of us. It was when he was distant that I realized I was missing his words, his presence, his touch. It's something I've never experienced before, and it's why I'm so confused now. I care for him deeply, but I don't know in what way. Even now, I'm sitting here staring at the receding moon thinking all these thoughts that somehow always end up being about him. Even when he is not physically with me, he is always in my thoughts.

    It gets colder and colder as the night goes on. I return to the manor only to grab a blanket before retreating to my spot on the courtyard stairs. I'm not tired. The moon and my raging thoughts have me captivated. I'm so focused on the moon I hadn't realized the large wolf emerging from the forest. Glancing in that direction, I hear a low growl coming from the tree line. Reznor's red eyes meet mine as he walks out of the forest in his wolf form. His eyes pierce mine. I'm not sure what he's thinking as he lingers there, scrutinizing me. Feeling uncomfortable under his gaze, I focus on the moon again. A deep groan is followed by soft footsteps coming my way.

Reznor offers me his hand now in his human form. "I told you not to wait up." His voice is accusing, yet he isn't annoyed.

"I was looking at the moon. I wasn't waiting for you," I tease, taking his hand, allowing him to pull me to my feet.

He wraps his arm around my waist. "I don't believe that for a second."

Laughing, I pull out of his grasp, turning and heading for the manor. "Think what you want, but the moon has just as much a hold on me, as your wolf has on you." He lingers behind me a few seconds before reluctantly following me into the manor. He falls into step with me as we ascend the staircase heading for our bedroom. "Do you feel better now?"

"Yes, running in that form always helps me clear my head."

"What was bothering you this time?" I ask as we approach the top of the stairs.

"This war, and my stubborn wife; she is always defying me."

I glare at him. "Well, neither of those things you can control, best to get that idea out of your head."

Reznor's laugh is music to my ears as he smiles at me brightly. The kind of look that can make a woman feel a number of things, but it always warms my soul to see him so happy and carefree. I turn away from him, heading for the room again. The flutters I usually feel when he touches me are now dancing across my chest. I'm not a fan of this feeling, because he isn't *touching* me. Without the action, it makes me feel incredibly naïve because that means he's pleasing me for an entirely different reason.

"The only place I can control you is in the bedroom." He's swift in his advancement towards me, His teeth grazing my ear. "Although I think you would enjoy that too much; it wouldn't be a punishment."

I move my hand to the doorknob. "Well, wouldn't that be something to try." I force the door open, moving away from him quickly. "Too bad you won't get the chance."

Reznor prowls into the room, shutting the door behind him. "Are you sure about that?" he asks, stalking towards me.

I drop the blanket from my shoulders, tossing it onto the couch, "Yep, we can let that happen when I do something worth punishing."

Reznor takes on a heated expression as he stands in front of me. He tosses me onto the bed, suddenly causing a squeal to escape from my lips. Gone are the naïve thoughts of a girl. Instead, they're replaced with lustful thoughts for the man before me. I'm not going to be doing any more thinking tonight.

Chapter Thirty-Eight: Snow is Falling

It's been a month and a half since I got married, and within this short time, we have learned so much. With the daunting truth that war is coming, everyone has been training harder than before. Reznor and I train together for the first half of every day, then he, or I are whisked away on meetings within the manor. Our powers have blossomed, as we find new ways to use our magic together.

We learned that when we combined my telekinesis with his mist, we can launch the boys while smothering them. It keeps them subdued while we fight the other warriors. We started fighting our best guards, only allowing a few to know the secret of our joint powers. It helps to have these new opponents. Reznor and I have to learn how to physically fight with our backs to each other. His ability to read my mind has indeed come in handy because he knows my plan of attack before I make my first move. I, however, do lecture him every single time he invades my mind. 'It's for the greater good,' he'll argue. Although I think he just enjoys being in my head. However, things with the war aren't advancing in our favor like our powers are.

Whitehorn has moved his armies throughout the lands, a majority of them stationed in the Warlocks kingdom while the others are scattered through Lord

Nostics land. After many attempts to invade the other lands, the Faeries had to give in and allow Whitehorn's forces to march through their territory. They destroyed a lot of the town and killed many people in the process. Maximus showed up the next day. He told us not to send reinforcements, seeing as there isn't much of a town left to protect.

Instead, Maximus came and asked if he could move some of his soldiers to help guard the other lands. Typhore is willing to sacrifice his land at the beginning of the war, only to promise that it will be reclaimed later. They scatter their soldiers, dividing them up between the remaining kingdoms. Each kingdom got a portion of the warriors. Some of the witches created a warning sigil to warn of invaders on their lands as an extra precaution.

The kingdoms are working together, and it's something that will be talked about for years to come. Everyone's admiring Reznor for his skills in leading. He's able to instruct and negotiate with all the kingdoms. He has expressed many times he doesn't want to be the King of All, but I understand why he would be a great ruler for everyone. Reznor handles every situation with a level head. Well, he deals with every situation with a level head when it doesn't involve *me*.

Today, he's meeting with the other kingdoms at our manor. A representative from each kingdom has arrived this morning, and they have been locked in his study ever since. I opted out of going; he can't think clearly when I'm there. He'll need to get over this issue someday, but for today, I allow it. I'm not much help in these things anyway. I don't know enough about war or moving armies to be of any use. The queening lessons I got help with my daily duties, but there wasn't a class on how to plan a war. Instead of being hunkered down with the representatives, I keep Star entertained in the empty ballroom. Star is the daughter of one of Reznor's noblemen. He brought her with him today because his wife couldn't watch her. He was going to leave her with one of the servants, but I insisted I would watch her.

Seeing her twirl in circles in the ballroom is exactly what I needed. She's so full of joy that it makes me forget they're talking about war upstairs. She stops spinning, gripping onto her blonde hair, erupting into giggles before running to me. She dives onto me where I sit on the ballroom floor. Catching her in my arms, I join in on her infectious laughter.

She huffs once she pulls back, one of her gold locks moving away from the gush of wind. "My hair is in my face," she whines, dragging her hands through her hair, pushing it back and away from her face.

"I can braid it if you want," I suggest as I touch one of her soft curls.

"Yes!" she squeals, clapping her hands as she cheers.

With a finger, I motion for one of the lingering guards to come toward me. "Can you ask Kora to bring me a brush and stuff to braid a little girl's hair?" The guard grins down at the eager child in my lap before leaving to gather the items from Kora.

Star fiddles with the tulle on the grey dress I'm wearing. With the weather turning cold, my dresses are gradually becoming longer and thicker. Even sitting on the ground now, my tulle splays out around us. We could hide beneath it, that's how abundant the material is.

"I like your dress," she pulls at the fabric again, "it's soft!" She rubs her face against the fabric.

"I like your dress better." Her dress is light pink with roses lining the skirt that stops just above her feet.

Before we can discuss either of our dresses further, the guard returns with a basket full of flowers, a brush, hair fasteners, and clips. Star claps her hands and giggles as she sits down between my legs with her back to me.

Grabbing the brush, I start combing through her soft hair. "One braid or two?" I ask as the silky hair combs with ease.

"Two!" she cheers.

This little girl is easy to please. How blissful it must be to be a toddler. I had a hard childhood, although I don't speak of it often. My mom had always been hard on me and often acted crazily. She yelled at me repeatedly and always told me I wasn't good enough. She would never allow me to have friends over, and even when I excelled in things, she always told me I was a failure, and this is just the mental conflicts. I hope this little girl never experiences any of those things.

Maura has also been able to evade all of our attempts to locate her. She's like a snake in the grass, hard to see and dangerous.

I part her hair down the middle before braiding each side carefully. Once the hair is bound, I pin white and light pink flowers into her hair, tying matching ribbons at the end of the braids. Her golden hair is beautiful with the flowers lining it. Once I'm finished, she screams happily as she grips onto the mirror tighter, looking at herself admiringly.

"I love it! Thank you, Queen Liara." Throwing her arms around my neck, she hugs me tightly. Star jerks away, glancing down in the basket, finding a matching white flower like the ones in her hair. "You need a flower too." She pushes my curled hair over my shoulder before securing the flower next to my ear.

She smiles brightly, grabbing the mirror eagerly to show me my reflection. "Thank you, Star, I love it!" Her face twinkles with her giddiness.

Both of our heads turn in the direction of a low chuckle coming from the ballroom stairs. Reznor, Tatiana, and Star's father are all coming down the stairs. She crawls out of the tulle of my dress before sprinting in the direction of her father.

She throws her arms out for him. "Daddy, look, Queen Liara did my hair!" She shows off her braids to her father.

"I'm next!" Tatiana teases, raising her hand in the air.

"Thank you for watching her, Your Majesty," her father bows to me.

"You're welcome. We had a great time, didn't we, Star?"

She nods and points to the flower in my hair. "She let me do her hair also!" she gushes. Her father lingers to talk to Reznor a moment more before retreating with Star back up the ballroom stairs. I'm packing up the contents of the basket when Tatiana and Reznor approach.

"She's good with kids," Tatiana points out as she eyes Reznor suggestively.

"How was the meeting?" I ask as I hoist the tulle, attempting to stand without tripping.

"It was good, although I think you had more fun." Reznor smirks as he takes the basket from my hand.

"I think you're right," I admit while fixing my dress. I only wore this because I knew I would be watching Star, and she always loves to admire my dresses.

Tatiana's eyes dart back and forth between Reznor and me. "Reznor, don't you have a meeting with Maximus?"

He huffs, but nods his head. "Yes, I do. Excuse me if I want to greet my mate for the first time in twelve hours." Reznor hands the basket to Tatiana before he envelopes me into his arms, pecking my lips.

You alright? I ask down the bond as I hug him.

We'll talk about it later. Reznor kisses the top of my head before pulling away and leaving the ballroom. I'm already missing his presence, and I can't blame it on the bond this time.

"What did you do?" I ask as I veer toward the steps.

"I did nothing!" she argues, attempting to defend herself, but her smile is not convincing.

"You practically shooed him away."

Tatiana snickers, "Well, I wanted to talk with you, and he can't be present for this conversation." She loops her arm in mine as we reach the top of the stairs. She drags me in the opposite direction I had planned on going. Guess I'm not getting out of this dress anytime soon.

"Why can't he be present for it?" I ask skeptically as she takes me further into the manor.

"Because it's about him." I stop moving. She rolls her eyes, tugging me along. "It's nothing bad…just something I've noticed."

"And?"

"Reznor has changed since you've come, and for the first time in years, I find him to be slightly happy."

"How can someone be slightly happy?" I cock an eyebrow at her as she opens a door down the hallway. The door leads to another sitting room; this one is charcoal grey themed along with a wine-colored couch.

"I've seen Reznor at his worst, and I've never seen him be fully happy. But, with you here, I think it's the happiest he has ever been." Her words stop me. I knew Reznor had a hard life, but I assumed he's been happy before.

"I'm not following. Is this good, or bad?" I ask, removing my arm from her and sitting down on the red couch.

"Good, actually, it's terrific. With this war developing, I don't want him to lose this happiness to the war. I need your help. I want to fight on the front lines along with you and Reznor."

"Tatiana, I don't think I could get him to agree to that. Hell, he doesn't want me there."

She turns somber, twisting her wedding band around her finger. "I need you to try. Arnold died and I need to do something about it; this is my opportunity."

She sits down next to me, taking my hands into her own. "Imagine someone killed Reznor, and then the war came to—"

I cut her off immediately as an overwhelming feeling of sadness strikes my body like a physical blow. "I'll talk to him, just please don't speak like that. Not with the possibility of one of us dying sooner rather than later."

"Good, so—" I can't focus on what Tatiana's reply is because Reznor's voice fills my head.

Are you okay? His voice is full of worry. If I don't respond to him now, he will hunt me down.

Yes, why do you ask?

I just... his voice falters, *never mind.*

"Are you listening to me?" Tatiana snaps her fingers in front of my face.

"No, I wasn't. Reznor was asking me a question."

"You two and that mate bond." She rolls her eyes before starting again, "Let me know what Reznor says and if he says no, I'll go anyway and not tell either of you where I am."

I scrunch my face. "No, that's an awful idea."

"Well, I've got nothing to lose. I didn't even get to have a baby with Arnold. I have nothing left of him."

"I'm sorry about what happened to Arnold. I am truly sorry."

She smiles sadly. "Just promise me when you and Reznor have a baby, you'll name her after me."

I cackle but stop when I catch her straight face. "You're joking, right?"

"About the name, yes, about you two having kids, no." She grins. "I've seen you with Star. You'll be a great mother."

"Tatiana, I'm not even sure I want kids. Reznor and I just got married. I can promise you there will be no babies anytime soon. I can't even promise there will be babies."

Her face morphs into disappointment. "That's a shame. You and Reznor would make a beautiful baby. I can't say I blame you either. I mean, who wants to be pregnant fifteen months."

My mouth drops open in shock. "What!"

"Yes, it's awful! Magical babies take longer to develop."

"You never should have told me that because now there definitely won't be any babies."

Tatiana snickers again. "Yeah, maybe I should have let him tell you that, you know, after you were pregnant." Tatiana blabs on about babies for hours. It gets to the point I'm begging Reznor to come to save me.

Reznor, please come save me from your cousin, I plead, and at first, he's silent, but then a laugh is heard.

I'll be there in a few minutes. I count down the minutes until Reznor arrives. Precisely seven minutes later, he strolls into the room.

"Ah, Reznor!" Tatiana cheers.

I jump from the couch and hurry for the door. "I need Liara for a meeting. You'll have to finish this talk another time."

"Such a shame. I'm going to head home." Tatiana hugs me and pecks Reznor on the cheek before disappearing out the door.

"Thank you," I groan, resting my head against the closed door.

"What was she talking to you about?" Reznor eyes me before taking me into his arms, wrapping his arms around my waist.

I don't want to talk about babies, or us. "A lot of things, but she did make a request."

He raises a brow in suspension. "Oh, what was that?"

"She wants you to let her fight with us in the war. She also said if we don't allow it, she will just go off and do it on her own."

Reznor rapidly drops his hands from my waist. "No, if she gets killed, she has no one left to rule her kingdom. I'm going to catch her and tell her that." Reznor leaves the room, slamming the door behind him. I follow after with the intention of finding Reznor and Tatiana, but instead, I change out of the dress and into my nightclothes. I have had my fair share of people today, and for now, I want a break.

I retreat to the sunroom, where I cover myself up with a blanket. I'm too caught up in my own thoughts to read my book. Tatiana wants to fight, yet Reznor doesn't want to let her because if she dies, she has no one to rule her kingdom. Yet if one of us dies, there is no one to rule his kingdom either. This man needs to stop trying to tell the women in his life what they can and cannot do.

"I'm not trying to protect you from everything, or Tatiana, for that matter." Reznor stands in the doorway, his hands stuffed deep in his pockets.

"Stay out of my head, Reznor."

He strolls into the room. "It's hard when you're practically shouting your thoughts." I pretend to read the book in my lap as he continues. "She will take over our kingdom if we die, but if she dies, we have to take over her kingdom as next of kin." He takes the book off my lap, shutting it. "I'm not trying to control you two. I'm trying to prevent complete and utter chaos if all three of us die in battle. With you, yes, it's personal. I don't want you out there because selfishly, I want you to live. With her, yes, I love my cousin, and I wish her a long life, but I know she would hate to rule our kingdom and hers."

Scoffing, I snatch the book out of his hands. "Well, I'm selfish too then because I want you to live."

Reznor picks my legs up long enough to slide beneath them, moving them onto his lap. "I don't want either of you out there," he sighs, "but I agreed to Tatiana fighting with us."

A smile plasters onto my face at his words. "Good, stop trying to control us."

He frowns. "I wasn't trying to control you."

"Reznor, it's how you care for us, but you need to realize the people who care about you would willingly sacrifice themselves for you."

"I don't want anyone to sacrifice themselves for me. My parents already did that!"

This conversation isn't going anywhere. "Come here." Reznor doesn't move at first, but slowly he shifts next to me on the couch. He holds me while I rest my head against his chest. Closing my eyes, I breathe in his scent. "I'm sorry, I didn't mean to bring up your parents."

He kisses my head. "It's fine. I'm just trying to protect you both, so you don't end up dead." He rakes his fingers through my hair. "Look," he murmurs, pointing in the direction of the large window. Snowflakes start falling from the sky in a slow dance as they twirl toward the ground.

A smile tugs at my lips, gazing out at the falling snow. "Even in this world, snow is magical." When my eyes finally shift from the falling flakes, to find Reznor wistfully looking me, "What?" I ask, a slow blush creeping to my cheeks.

"Nothing." He turns sheepish before focusing on the snowfall. It starts slowly at first, but the longer we watch, the harder it falls.

Chapter Thirty-Nine: Winter Winds

The first day of snowfall was beautiful, along with the second. By the third day, it's pretty, but falling harder. The fourth day, it was a burden as the weather became unbearable to train for me and the troops. On the fifth day, the snow was thundering down, but by the sixth, it's as if the world will be covered entirely by the heavily falling powder.

Reznor is unsure if the snow is an act of the Goddess of nature or an act of magic. Either way, we won't be able to handle much more. The town is already under duress from the surge of the winter storm. The townspeople had no time to prepare because by the third day, the snow had already caused all the roads to shut down.

The cold is almost as bad as the growing inches of snow. However, the freezing temperatures are our biggest concern. All the doors on the manor have frozen shut, and that can only leave me to imagine how cold it is in the small-town houses in the square. Reznor's in a growing panic; he told me stories of past winters, but they have faced nothing as cold or as fast falling as this.

Reznor, Emanuel, and Charles are throwing out ideas. We're looking for any possible solution to help with this monstrous storm. I follow along with the conversation attempting to help where I can, but I still don't know much about the magic world. If only I had gotten more studies with Anisa.

"We could ask one of our witches for help," Charles suggests as he perches over the desk that holds a list of ideas we have already gathered.

Emanuel shoots down the idea quickly. "Our witches don't practice that kind of magic, plus, warlocks are the ones who work in elemental magic."

Reznor pinches the bridge of his nose. "We could see what kind of spells they could do to attempt to keep the villagers warm or lessen the snowfall."

Emanuel rises from his chair. "I'll put out a call." He leaves the study in a hurry, practically running out of the room.

"We'll have to see what else we can do." Reznor starts to chew on his lower lip as he inspects the frost-covered window.

"Don't we need to figure out if this is magic or just a terrible blizzard?" I ask.

"Yes, we need to go outside to find either a break in the storm or a symbol that will tell us if it's a blizzard or spell. Charles, get a vehicle ready. We'll leave within the hour."

Charles leaves the office with a nod of his head. When he opens the door, a cold gust of wind from the chilled hallway tumbles into the study.

"What do you want me to do?" I move from the couch and toward Reznor, standing by the blazing fire.

"You can come, or you can stay and sort through information on the witches with Emanuel."

"I'll come with."

Reznor and I dress quickly into our winter clothes. I wear fleece-lined pants along with a thermal beneath my grey sweater. I'm lacing up my tall winter boots when Reznor emerges from the closet in black jeans and a matching sweater, which makes sense considering I'm wearing one of his old ones. He has two winter coats in his hands. Kora's in tow with a box filled with gloves, scarves, and other winter apparel. She sorts through the box, picking out a grey set of gloves and a knitted hat. I slip the hat on before the coat, stuffing the gloves into the pockets.

Reznor and I sit in the back of the truck, and even with our many layers and the heat blasting, our breath is still visible. The roaring winds, along with the freezing temperatures, make unforgiving weather conditions. Too long out here and we'll certainly get frostbite, along with getting lost in the dauting snow.

"Keep an eye out for a break in the storm or a symbol in the snow, trees, anything that looks out of place." Reznor tells as he focuses out the window. The truck starts heading towards the village. We find a break in the storm after an hour of driving. The snow in the forest off to the side of the road looks undisturbed. The wind hasn't touched this part of the woods. Even the snowfall is light as we pull into the clearing and off the main road.

Reznor keeps a close distance to me as we wade through the snow. The snowfall here is uneven. We walk through an inch, or through half a foot of snow. It's hard to look for anything in the blinding white reflection from the fresh powder.

"Reznor, come look at this," Charles hollers from the left of Reznor and me.

"Stay close," Reznor warns before he steers to Charles.

I continue to the right. Scanning the ground, the skies, the bushes…nothing. I'm just about to head for Reznor when I see a symbol engraved at the bottom of a tree, barely poking out over the snow. I kneel, swiping away the snow from the emblem. When I touch it, I can feel the power surging through the tree—it's humming.

The symbol is a snowflake surrounded by a thick circle, then there is a curled letter that looks between a 'q' and a 'p.' One of the letters is at the four points of the snowflake, looking like points off a compass.

"Rez, I found something," I call out. It's as if I'm in a trance as I study the snowflake, feeling the hum from the tree enchanting me.

Reznor snatches my hand off the tree and curses under his breath. "This is an old blizzard spell. It's what the Gods used to cause the ice age in the human world."

Charles groans, "How are we supposed to break a spell that's as old as the Gods?"

Reznor examines my hand, peeling my glove off. "We can't. We can only find a way to lessen its destruction."

"What are you doing?" I ask as the cold nips at my fingers.

"That spell can freeze people to death if they touch the bare symbol, I'm looking to see if it pricked you or not." Reznor slides the glove back onto my hand. "Let's head back and see what we can find in the library."

We trudge back to the truck only to find it buried in snow and frozen sleet. The weather has gotten worse while we were in the clearing. The men struggle to get the doors open, and once they do, they fight even more to get the truck started under the freezing conditions. With a final groan from the truck, it comes to life, but as we approach the manor, it dies on the side of the road when we're still about three miles away.

"Gods!" Charles exclaims, slapping the steering wheel.

"What do we do now?" I ask as I peek out the snow-crusted windows. I can't see a thing.

"We have to get back to the manor," Reznor swears quietly as we all agree getting back to the manor is safer than freezing in a truck.

"Stay close. We won't be able to see you if you wander too far," Reznor orders as we start wading in the deep powder toward the manor. Reznor keeps a firm hand on mine as we trudge through the snow and ice. After multiple failed attempts to open a portal, we realize the storm is interfering with our escape plan. Reznor sent out a mind link for someone to come get us, but even the other magical vehicles won't start under the freezing temperatures. My legs are numb after the first mile. The cold has seeped into my pants. The snow I can handle, the wind I can take, but it's the sleet and the freezing temperature that are the problem. My teeth chatter even with my mouth clamped shut. I cling to Reznor for warmth as we walk closely together.

We're almost there, he calls down the bond as he pulls me tighter against his side.

I used to love the snow, but now...not so much.

Reznor's laughter warms my spirits, *what is it, too cold?* he teases, making me laugh down the bond.

No, not at all, in fact, it could be a little colder. It's the teasing and joking down our bond that makes the second mile bearable, but the third is the hardest. The storm has picked up again, battering us with heavy snow and ice pelting us in all directions as the wind whips around. The snow's up to midcalf and rising higher with each passing minute. I can't feel my arms or legs... I can't feel any of my extremities. Even Reznor's warmth has turned to coldness against my side. He keeps talking to me down the bond, but it's to keep us distracted from the cold, not for entertainment.

We need to go to the beach, even my voice sounds strained.

I promise I'll take you to the beach at some point, after this. I can't agree more, and the thought of Reznor relaxing on the beach will be a sight to see. I forget to respond to his comment as the large manor comes into view. We're close. Maybe fifty feet, with the storm, we hadn't even been able to view the silhouette of the building until now. Reznor squeezes my side, encouraging me to move faster, and I gladly do. We claw our way to the manor doors and shove them open. The moment we're inside, the servants are tending to the four of us, removing our frozen coats and replacing them with warm blankets.

Reznor and I clamber up the stairs as the heat starts returning to our frozen limbs. I could cry from joy when I see the steaming bathtub waiting in the bathroom. We both strip immediately before climbing into the hot water. Reznor holds me between his legs as we soak in the warmth. He takes my frozen hair down from its braid, working his fingers through it. We don't speak. Instead, we enjoy the heat from the tub while Reznor continues to work through my thawing hair. We stay in the tub until the water is too cool for our liking. Kora has clothes waiting for us when we emerge. Dressing quickly, the chill already attempts to creep back in. The best part is when I enter the bedroom, she has pulled the couch closer to the fireplace. She goes above and beyond by leaving a hot, minty chocolate drink waiting on the end table along with a tray of cookies.

Reznor cuddles with me on the couch. Although I'm still cold and trembling, Reznor's body temperature has returned already. "How are you so warm?" I ask as I pull the blankets higher, tugging them close to my neck.

Reznor's chest rumbles with laughter, "It's my beast—"

"Wolf." I correct.

He huffs, "My *wolf* is the reason I heal, and the reason I'm always so warm."

"Hmm," I shuffle closer into his arms, settling my head in the crook of his neck, the warmth from his body seeping into my chilled skin.

"I'm worried about our people," Reznor rubs slow circles across my back.

"Me too." The only reason the manor is this warm is because it's enchanted, and even with that, part of the manor is still freezing. "When I was doing some research for our bond, it said something about Nightlighters being able to control the weather." Reznor's hands still against my back. "I don't know how to use that part of my power, but I can try. Any time I've done something with the weather, it was based on my emotions."

"Maybe we just need to get you hot enough."

I glare at him. "Reznor, I'm serious."

"So am I. If we get you hot, then maybe you can thaw the outside." He sits up, taking me with him. I press my cold body against his warm one, sighing in relief as my icy hands grip his warm chest. He flinches at my cold hands but doesn't stop me.

"How about I try my way, and then if it doesn't work, we'll do it your way."

"Deal."

Chapter Forty: Thaw

Sitting before the windows in the sunroom, I close my eyes and focus on my powers. I chose this room because it's the closest I can get to being outside without actually venturing into the blizzard. It's the dead of night, and I'm the only one awake. I slip out of bed, wanting to try and use my powers against the hazardous weather without the pressure of disappointing the others.

Resting my hands palm up against my thighs, I start to think of warm thoughts—the summer, the ocean, the sun, hot concrete, a stove, the list goes on and on. I summon these thoughts, hoping it will call to the powers within. For hours I try to stop the harsh storm, but nothing helps. The vicious wind blows, snow pelting the window.

My abilities with the weather have only ever been triggered by emotions: when Anisa died, when I'm mad. I don't understand how to stop a storm with a feeling.

Venturing up to my old bedroom, I struggle against the balcony door, but eventually I get it. With the door finally open, snow tumbles into the room, and I regret this idea already. The snow seeps into my wool slippers. Still in my nightclothes, I won't be able to be outside long, but it's worth a shot. Stepping into the deep snow and crossing to the railing, my skin burns from the cold against my bare flesh. I've been outside seconds, and I'm already starting to grow a chill. I grip the railing, closing my eyes to focus on warming thoughts again. Sun, beach, concrete, boiling, I chant in my head. Peeking one eye open, the storm is still raging on.

Maybe I'm taking the wrong approach. Perhaps, I need to focus on calming down the storm rather than stopping it. Taking slow, deep breaths, my eyes close again, and I allow my powers to take control.

Calm, slow, warm, thaw.

I repeat each word slowly in my head over and over, and after the fifth time, the wind stops. I don't dare open my eyes. Instead, I continue to chant in my head while focusing on calming the storm. The sleet stops pelting me in the face. It's quiet. The storm finally calms.

Hesitantly, I open my eyes and find the clouds still lingering overhead, but the snow is no longer falling. Calling out to my powers again, this time I call for the heat, thinking of things that warm my soul. I think of my family that I've developed here, the people, and *Reznor*. Drops of water start to fall from the windowsills as the temperature rises. It's still cold, but no longer freezing. The ice begins to melt along with the snow.

Having a small grasp on the powers, I conjure up a wind and clean the snow off the balcony, sending it through the air with a flick of my wrist. It falls from the balcony and lands in the courtyard below. A smile tugs at my lips as my powers allow me to form a clump of snow. Pile after pile, I shift all the snow on the grounds below until a significant mass had formed. I leave the room only to walk outside through the front of the manor, standing on the top steps. I repeat the action until the front of the manor is also cleared. I do this, walking around until most of the snow is removed. The temperature is gradually warming the more I practice with the power.

With most of the paths clear now, I turn my attention to the clouds overhead that are still a nasty color. Conjuring up a massive wind that rattles the trees, leaves, and loose snow as the blast goes up to the sky, I send the gust upward. It breaks through the atmosphere and punctures the dark clouds. Through the hole, the stars twinkle back at me. With the small opening, I continue to shovel the winds to the sky, breaking the clouds till they're few and far between.

By the time I'm done, exhaustion and a coldness burdens my body. I trudge up to the bedroom, but as I try to go inside, Reznor opens the door the precise moment I reach for the handle.

"Where were you?" His face is still ridden with sleep. He must have just woken up and noticed I was gone.

"I went for a walk." I don't want to tell him about the powers now. I'm too drained.

"It's the middle of the night."

"Rez, we'll talk about it in the morning." I brush past him, kicking off my wet slippers and robe before climbing into the bed.

Reznor stares at me puzzled but moves into the bed with me. "You're freezing!" he hisses as he touches my chilled skin, tugging me to face him. "Did you go outside?"

"Yes, Rez, I stopped the storm. Can I sleep now?" I beg, trying to drop myself to the bed, but his arms keep me in place.

"How?"

"Rez," I groan.

He tucks me against his chest, wrapping his body around mine, blessing me with his warmth. "When you wake up, I want you to tell me what happened."

The storm has stopped in the town and across Reznor's land. After I sleep for a few hours, Rez takes me into town and across the part of our lands that has been plagued with the blizzard. I use my powers to clear the villages of its snow and help repair what I can. The townspeople marvel and cheer as I work. I'm not sure who is more in awe: the townspeople, or Reznor. He keeps glancing and smiling at me as I unthaw the world around me. He beams and watches me with admiration, something I've never experienced before. No one has ever looked at me and been proud or admired my work. He holds something else in those eyes that's more than admiration, but I can't…won't name it.

Chapter Forty-One: Winter Solstice

The winter solstice didn't come a moment too soon as the war is advancing in other parts of Dwimmér. People are scared and need something to look forward to, and this holiday is just that. The solstice is tomorrow. Today, we're decorating, and by we, I mean most of the staff. I'm merely following along, trying to learn about the holiday. Yet again, it reminds me of Christmas. They decorate pine trees and exchange gifts while celebrating the longest night of the year. On the day of the solstice, we will have a special tree lighting to celebrate.

A tree is in our bedroom waiting to be decorated, but Reznor has been so busy we haven't had the time. I help with the war in ways I can, but mostly I'm useless until it comes time to fight. I am learning to help; I've been watching the way Reznor leads and how he's moving the armies. Mostly, we're just rearranging our troops while Whitehorn is doing the same. We're making moves and countermoves, but more and more battles are happening across the lands. Reznor's ability to use portals has helped us immensely; he goes and speaks to the other royals, and then he revises. He even has been helping move in extra soldiers if he learns of a battle in time.

Today, however, Reznor is in the manor talking with Maximus over plans while I help decorate. It's fun. I always loved the holidays in the mortal world. I would go all out every year. My mom, however, disagreed, she often frowned upon it. Shaking the thoughts from my head, I help string the silver garland across the mantle. Morana and I have been decorating since dawn, and I've loved every moment of it.

"You're good at this." She smiles brightly as we place blue and grey ornaments against the garland. These orbs are glass, each of them holding hand-painted winter scenes on every globe. One is tree scene, another a snowflake, but my personal favorite is the moon painted globe. The crescent moon is painted on both sides with twinkling stars. They're beautiful.

"I've always loved the holidays."

She seems saddened for a moment. "This year will be kind of somber considering, but it will still be memorable." She steps down from the step stool. "How are things going with the war?"

"Reznor would be the one to ask."

"Ah, is he keeping you out of the loop?"

"No, I just don't know much about moving armies. They are moving their soldiers toward us but not directly. We are waiting to find a definite place to intercept."

We seek out the other staff decorating the towering trees in the grand ballroom. "You'll learn eventually, and Reznor will teach you."

"There is no time to learn or teach. We're at war, and I'm decorating a tree."

"You're doing more than that. You're probably about the only thing keeping Reznor sane." We both snicker, but eventually, it snuffs out. "You're willing to fight for us, and you're trying your best."

"I know, but I wish I could do more, but since I can't, I'm going to help plan this holiday and keep the spirits going."

"All you can do is your best." She touches my shoulder, giving me a warm smile.

We continue to decorate the ballroom. By the time we're done, it's a winter wonderland. We've done the ballroom, the foyer, and the halls. Even though my fingers were sore, there is one last room that needs to be done—our bedroom. Morana accompanies me, both of us carrying a box of decorations.

We start stringing the lights around the tall tree. It's gorgeous, a perfect shade of green full of long branches. The lights are single glowing orbs that we place throughout the full skirt and body of the tree.

"You know, the newlyweds are supposed to decorate their first tree *together*." Morana cocks an eyebrow at me.

"He's busy. Plus, I enjoy decorating with you."

Morana hugs me to her side. "I enjoy decorating with you! All my daughters hate the holidays. I'm glad someone enjoys it in this family!" she gushes before moving to grab a small white box. "I got this for you and Reznor."

"You didn't have to."

"Nonsense, open it." She places the box in my hand. Inside is a grey glass ornament with me and Reznor on our wedding day. My long white dress and his black tux. It's us standing at the altar, sharing our first kiss as husband and wife, king and queen.

"Morana, I love it, thank you." I place the ornament at the front of the tree, the light behind the globe illuminating our shadows. I hug her tightly as we admire the decoration.

"Now, if only the workaholic had been here," she teases. We continue to decorate the room and barely finished when Kora forces me to bed. I oblige and quickly wrap myself into the blanket, but I don't sleep, instead I think of past Christmas memories.

Standing before the mirror in the bathroom, I admire the blue gown that clings to my body. The dress has a fitted bodice with long sleeves and a thick skirt that goes to the floor. Small jewels line the cuffs, sleeves, and the very top of the dress where it rests on my shoulders. Kora curls my hair in an intricate braid with silver pins that resemble snowflakes. The makeup accents my eyes with silver and highlights my cheekbones. I'm shimmering like one of the many glittering ornaments that line the halls.

I stroll down the hall with my heels clicking against the floor, Charles and Emanuel in tow behind me, yet Reznor is nowhere to be found. I stop suddenly, turning around to face the boys. "Where is Reznor?"

"He's with Maximus in the study," Emanuel politely says as he tucks his hands behind his back.

"Hmm, Morana is not going to like that." Starting down the hall again, we reach the foyer where Morana stands in the center, directing guests.

"Where is your husband?" Morana asks after she moves the guests forward.

"He is busy. Want to be my escort?" I try and fail to keep the grin from my face.

"No, Reznor should be doing that," she hisses while she motions the boys forward with a finger. "Boys, escort her into the party." Emanuel and Charles offer me their hands.

"Oh look, my boys coming to the rescue." I link my arms through theirs as they escort me inside. The ballroom is lit by glowing lights, casting a soft glow that makes the ornaments and the grand tree twinkle. brighter. The room is marvelously decorated. It's a winter wonderland, and the perfect touch is the light snow that is falling outside the large windows.

We ease down the stairs, our arms still linked. Tatiana waits at the bottom, laughing as she catches sight of our trio. "Aren't you three just a matching set?" she snickers into her wine glass as she takes another sip.

"I think we look pretty good." Charles adjusts his blue blazer that happens to match my dress. The snazzy outfit shouldn't fool anyone because underneath Emanuel's and Charles' matching blue jackets, they're heavily armed.

"You three do look rather magnificent, but I am wondering why your husband, the king, isn't your escort to this party?" Tatiana places her empty glass onto a passing tray before picking up another.

"He is busy but take note of this; I showed up for the grand entrance this time, not him."

A quiet chuckle escapes from Emanuel. I have no doubt in my mind that we all think back to my first ball. Oh, how the times have changed. Tatiana lingers with us as I start the rounds at the ball. I remember more names this time. I wade through the guests, thanking them for coming and wishing them a happy solstice along with some small talk. I stop only when Star comes running across the dance floor and straight at me.

"Queen Liara," she cheers as she flings her arms around my legs, her face becoming obscured in the skirt of my dress. I'm thankful for Emanuel and Charles being near because she hits me with such a force both men have to help stable me, or I would have toppled over.

I kneel before hoisting her into my arms. "Well, hello, little one," I coo, "are you enjoying my party?"

"I love it. We match!" she gushes as she stabs at her dark blue tulle dress that has long sleeves just like mine.

I push back her soft curls. "We should match more often," I tease. Oh, how I've come to love this little girl. Carrying her as we work our way over to the large tree, I grab the silver box wrapped beneath it. I set her down on the ground, kneeling next to her. "I got this for you."

"Really?"

I nod. She waits only a minute before tearing into the box. She squeals with joy when she pulls out the light purple dress with matching shoes, but she is most surprised at the tiara. "Thank you!" she screams, throwing her arms around my shoulders.

"You're welcome." Star scurries off with the box to go show her parents. I rise only to find three sets of eyes staring at me.

"You're good with kids," Tatiana eyes me as she sips her champagne. When had she gotten that? Last I saw, she had wine.

"I know, but we aren't getting into that topic again." I willingly enter the sea of lingering guests to avoid this conversation. I'm so focused on the couple before me I don't even realize Reznor has come up behind me.

"Can you excuse her for a moment?" he grips onto my waist, drawing me away from the couple without waiting for their response.

"You're late. I've been greeting these people—" Reznor cut me off by placing his lips against mine, his hands gripping onto my waist firmly. His kiss is desperate, as his hand slips up my back, reaching beneath my hair to cradle my neck, while I open my mouth up for him.

"Sorry I'm late," he says quietly as he presses his brow against mine.

"Is something wrong?" I cup his cheek with my hand.

"No, I just missed you." he takes me into in his embrace again. We linger there, entwined together, the large tree shielding us from the crowd of people. Reluctantly, he takes us back to the party again. Reznor acts unusual as we make our rounds. He's tense and keeps whispering to Emanuel, while Charles is lurking at an even closer distance than usual. Reznor's tension only eases a little when it's time for the walk to the ceremonial tree lighting. He stands next to me as I change into silver winter boots that somehow still bear an elegant heel. "Are you going to tell me what's wrong?" I ask, while Kora laces up the boots as I hold up the heavy material of the dress.

He gazes out the window at the light snowfall. "Nothing's wrong."

"Mm-hmm, you're an awful liar," I snark, adjusting the skirt of my dress while Kora grabs a large grey cloak with fur lining at the rim of the hood. She fastens it beneath my neck, adjusting my hair so the curls can still be seen.

Sensing the tension, Kora surprises me when she speaks up. "Have you ever thought about cutting your hair?"

This question summons Reznor from wherever his thoughts have been lurking. "No, no, no." He practically rushes her away as he moves in front of me, pulling up the rim on the cloak. "Never cut your hair," he says with his mouth an inch away from mine before kissing me.

When he pulls away, I want to lighten the mood a little. "If you ever piss me off bad enough, I'm going to chop it off."

He genuinely seems mortified. "Please, never do that." Enjoying his shock, I take him by the arm.

We lead the party through the light snow heading to the large snow-covered tree that's been decorated for the solstice. We stroll through the woods that are lit with glowing lanterns. People sing local holiday songs and children cheer as they pass the different colored lanterns.

"I'm sorry I didn't get to decorate the tree with you," Reznor glowers, shifting me closer to him. "Or spend much time with you over the last three days."

"I understand, but you should thank Morana for the ornament she got us."

He stares down, confused. "She got us an ornament?"

"Yes, it's beautiful actually."

"I'll have to look at it. I hadn't seen it earlier. Hell, I've only been in our room long enough to sleep, change, then be out the door again."

"It'll slow down eventually…" I pause, "hopefully."

"You are something else."

I return his smile. "You're lucky to have me," I tease, nudging his side.

"That is true, but so are our people." He stops us just at the end of the twinkling trail. The large tree waits before us, the guests surrounding it on all sides. Reznor keeps his arm draped around me as he starts his speech. "I know these past few months have been filled with a lot of heartache and fear, but it's also blessed us with a lot of good things. We care for all our people and all creatures that live here with us. I know it's been hard, but things will get better. Instead of focusing on the troubles we're facing, let's focus on the holiday. Happy Solstice!" The moment he says the words, the tree lights up, casting a glow out to the surrounding crowd.

The tree's lit with red, green, blue, purple, and white. It is a magnificent sight. I tear my eyes from the smiling faces and the glowing tree to look up at Reznor, only to find him already staring down at me. A soft smile on his face, as he studies me, he nods for me to look back at the tree. When I do, I'm not disappointed. The guests have joined hands around the tree as they start to sing.

"Winter has come, and now the fun has begun,

May this year be filled with blessings sent from the gods above,

Blessed is the king, blessed is the queen, for who we sing,

It's come time to cheer, to celebrate the winters here,

Our hearts are filled with the gleam of a fruitful year,

Blessed be the king, blessed be the queen in the lands where we sing."

They repeat the verse three times while they sway and smile at the tree, the words falling blissfully from their lips. They're singing for us. I'm overwhelmed with the love that's rising from the crowd as they sing to the tree. The emotions are palpable in the air around us.

Do they sing this every year? I ask Reznor, not daring to ask the question aloud.

Yes, but this is the first year they have addressed the queen. They never sang that part until now. Tears sting my eyes. I'm not sure why I'm so overrun with emotions at the sight of them singing, yet, here I am, wiping away a stray tear. Reznor doesn't note the tear. Instead, he holds me closer while they start the song again. When it ends, guests start exchanging presents and sipping a warm drink that's sweet like peppermint but mixed with heavy cream. We chatter with our court and family, but the joy only lasts so long.

Reznor's eyes glaze over a moment before he rips himself from my arms and darts off into the woods behind the trees with Emanuel and Charles. Tatiana gapes with her mouth hanging open in shock. "What is going on?" she asks as we peer into the heavily wooded area they just ran through.

"I have no idea." I take her arm, moving further into the crowd and away from the tree line. I catch a passing guard. "What's going on?"

"There's been an attack, Your Majesty," he says lowly as his eyes scan the guests, other guards are working their way through the sea of people.

Rez, what do you want me to do with all of these people?

Get them back to the manor! I jump to action ordering the guards to usher the guests back to the manor. No one objects, all seeming rather thrilled to go back and open their presents; they're oblivious to the threat. Just as I'm about to leave the tree a small figure catches my eye. Bundled beneath the tree is Star.

"Star?" I call out, but she doesn't move. I beckon her again. "Star, it's me Liara, can you come out?" She slowly crawls out from beneath the tree. "Why are you crying?" I scoop the little girl into my arms and cradle her against my chest.

"I was looking for my mommy," she sniffles and hastily wipes her nose, "And when I found her, she was bleeding and wouldn't move." My attention drops to her, blood covering her hands, face, and dress.

"Oh, honey," Tatiana gasps out as she takes in the frail girl's appearance.

Wrapping my cloak around us, I hide her away from the cold wind. "Take us back to the manor now." The guards create a formation around Tatiana and I as we hurry toward the manor. I draw up a shield around us. I'm prepared for an ambush, so when it comes, I'm not surprised, but what does shock me is who is at the forefront of the attack.

Chapter Forty-Two: Crimson On The White Snow

I'd been so focused on getting Star away from the forest that I hadn't been paying attention to the path before us. But now, with my mother out of the woodwork and with thirty other soldiers surrounding us, I know I've made a mistake.

Maura has a sadistic grin on her face as she steps into the clearing. "I'm presuming that one isn't yours," she teases as she points to the sobbing little girl in my arms.

I set my jaw. "No, she is not, but you won't harm a hair on her head, or I'll end all of you," I warn while clinging tighter to the frail girl.

Maura starts circling us. She's scrutinizing the formation my guards have created around us. My six to her thirty are no match, including my powers. Although my powers are now stronger, I need space to yield them, and in these tight quarters, I might cause more harm than good.

Continuing to circle us, Maura starts another spiel. "You know, I would have saved myself a lot of trouble had I just drowned you in the bathtub all those years ago."

I cackle along, "I suppose you would have saved everyone a lot of trouble had you done that, but you didn't, and now here we are. Me a queen and you, nothing." My words anger my mother so much she falters a step.

She sneers with wild eyes. "We'll see how long you're a queen for."

Rez, I'm going to need some backup, I send down the bond while simultaneously continuing the conversation with my mother.

"Oh, well, I'll have been a queen longer than you ever have..." I give a conceding grin, "oh wait, you've never been a queen." This invokes another round of hateful words from her mouth.

Where? Where are you? Worry taints his voice as he asks the question quickly.

We're near the solstice tree. We haven't gotten very far. We're surrounded by thirty guards... I wait a moment before adding, *and my mother.*

"Not so tough, are you now?" Maura cackles again, drawing my attention back to the conversation.

Carefully, I pass Star to Tatiana along with my cloak securing the fabric around the shivering child. "I'm plenty tough. You just haven't gotten to witness my powers yet, have you, mother?" The winds blow around us as lightning flashes across the sky, "Care to see?" I wiggle my fingers as my eyes turn to their smokey grey.

The smile on her face fades. "We'll see about that. Why not give me a little show?"

The wind picks up around us, branches thudding against each other, snow blowing against us, my dress flapping in the wind. I'm furious. Yet again she's come to my home, my lands. Maura, or one of her men murdered the mother of an innocent child. Much to

Maura's dismay, I don't give her an elaborate show. I'm only stalling until Reznor can get here. He can use his powers in tight spaces. I cannot. The most I can muster is a shield that has been around us since the moment she stepped out of the clearing.

"Is that all?" Maura snarks with a cocky grin.

"No, that's not all. I can turn you to ash if you'd like."

Maura's face pinches up in question for a second, and only for a brief second do I see the fear in those crazed eyes. She retreats back from the circle. "Go ahead and turn one of them to ash then," she urges, waving a hand to any of her guards.

I turn toward the perimeter of the formation that's protecting us. Just as I'm about to reach forward to grab one of her soldiers, Reznor comes barreling through the forest. The soldiers leap to attack Reznor just as Emanuel and Charles burst from the woods behind him. The guards, however, don't move an inch. They're frozen in place by my powers. Reznor's purple mist shoots from his fingers, killing all the guards instantly.

Maura, too focused on Reznor, overlooks the invisible bonds that grip her until I force her to the ground with my powers. The snow crunches behind me.

Reznor steps next to me, crouching on the ground before my mother. "So, you've come to try and kill my wife again?" Reznor's eyes flare red while mine remain grey. We're too mad for our vision to return to normal.

"You know, she said that if she had drowned me in the bathtub all those years ago, she could have saved us all a lot of problems."

Reznor looks at me with bewilderment, then his eyes turn back to blue a moment later as amusement contorts his face. "Well, I guess it's a good thing she didn't drown you in the bathtub all those years ago," he teases, "but maybe we should drown her in the bathtub now."

It's awful to say, but I must admit, I contemplate his offer. I'm not proud of considering the recommendation of killing my mother. After all, she did care for me once. She took care of me in the mortal world and gave me the gift of life. Still, she treated me more like a pet than a daughter. She's one of my only blood relatives but letting her go unpunished for what she's done just isn't right.

Contemplating her punishment, an idea blossoms in my head. "What if we siphoned her powers and sent her back to the mortal world?"

Reznor casts me a sinister grin. "I have always liked your dark sided mind."

There's no use in hiding the slow blush that fills my cheeks, but it's outshined by the devious grin that I return to Reznor. I want revenge on my mother for everything she's done, but more importantly, we need information out of her first.

Reznor, reading my thoughts, nods his head as he rises from the ground. "I'll make you a deal Maura, I won't kill you if you tell me what you know. Maybe then we can work out an agreement on whether or not you live in this world, or the mortal world."

Maura cackles, "We all know that you're not going to let me live in this world. But you seem to forget, I don't want to live in this world, I just want *her* dead."

Reznor calmly tucks his hands behind his back. "We both know I'm never going to allow you to kill her." He flashes Maura a million-dollar smile, something that makes all women go weak in the knees. He's doing it on purpose. He knows how my mother feels about him. It disgusts me that she still cares that way for him. I do know that this time I can't blame my anger on the bond. It's because of my *actual* feelings for him that I'm so infuriated.

"Are you baboons too stupid to figure out what's happening? It's a shame because that information will help fill in a lot of the puzzle," Maura mocks.

Reznor's smile doesn't falter as he circles her kneeling position in the snow. The only sound to be heard is his soft crunching steps, and the slow blowing wind until Reznor's amused voice fills the air. "Oh, I'm sure I could figure it out if I wanted to give the time, or the thought. However, I don't. I want you to tell me because it's a bore." Reznor smiles brightly again. "You see, I don't care. I'll kill whoever I have to." He stops, standing behind Maura, gripping a fistful of her hair and yanking her head back. "Whether you're alive or dead does not matter to me." He forcibly let's go of her head before taking a step back.

Everything's suddenly funny to me, all of it. Her hallucinations over the years, her strictness, the fighting, the hitting, and all of it was to prevent me from getting here. Yet here I am, thriving in a world she never intended me to see. Everything she didn't want to happen, has happened, and now I'm a queen. The thing she hates more than that is the fact I'm with Reznor, the man she loves.

"So, Maura." I make sure to call her by her name instead of 'mother,' but it only earns a smirk from her. "What brings you to our lands on the winter solstice? Other than an attempt to kill me, of course. Did you come to join the party?" I batt my eyelashes, all the while making my way to Reznor.

Maura watches me advance toward Reznor with a hateful glare. "Oh dear, you know I only ever come to visit with the hopes of killing you."

Tilting my head to the side, I give a small shrug. Reznor's three steps away now. "That may be true, but this is the last time because you will either give us our information, or I'll have your powers siphoned and send you back to the mortal world. You can live the rest of your days a miserable, aging hag in the human lands." I wrap an arm around Reznor, leaning into his side. "Killing you would be too easy."

Maura scuffs. "You can't siphon my powers."

I pin her with a single look, while exuding as much power and strength as I can muster. "No, I can't, but I know someone who can." The wind rustles around us as I allow it to pick up, snow hitting us at a harder pace than before. Just for a moment, I wish I could see how I look through her eyes, to see if I appear as powerful as I feel.

Do you know someone who can siphon her powers?

I shoot Reznor a glare. *No, but she doesn't need to know that.*

He chuckles. It's *a good thing I know someone who can, and even better, they are at the manor right now.*

"So, what's it going to be? You give us the information willingly, and we won't ruin your life, or we have fun, and we do it my way." Reznor wraps his arm around my waist, caressing my side, both of us knowing it'll infuriate Maura.

"I'll tell you, but only because it's not going to change anything. You'll lose this war, and then you'll be dead, and Reznor will be miserable and alone. I'd rather he be alone than be with you. This information doesn't matter much either way."

Reznor's claws start to extend as he breaks his calm demeanor. "Suddenly, I'm not feeling very generous."

I place a hand on his chest while batting my eyelashes once again. "It's a good thing we aren't kind people, isn't it?" Reznor and I have discussed the darkness that lurks in me, but he has yet to ask why and where it came from. Many times, I've told him that I had a troubled childhood, but I never elaborated on it because I knew it would have only enraged him further. The darkness that lurked in me ever since I was little has grown over the years. Now, I'm starting to realize the darkness has been inside me all along. It's not a darkness involved with hate. It's what comes from my Nightlighter abilities. Tapping into that well of power, the glowing lanterns start to be snuffed out by a lurking darkness that creeps through the trees. "Last chance Maura, this is it. I'm done playing your games. I will no longer be a piece in your puzzle, and neither will Reznor. I'm done with you after today, whether you live or die. I don't care. You've ruined part of my life, and I'm not going to dwell on it further. You made my life hell for a long time, but now I'm happier than I have ever been. I'm not going to let you ruin it. So, what is it going to be?"

Maura's silent a long while, and just as I'm about to snap, she speaks up. "What do you wish to know?"

Reznor takes the lead. "Who is working with Whitehorn?"

Maura tenses visibly for a second. That fear she showed earlier is now back. "Lord Nostics and Whitehorn are working together. They both have a mutual problem. Of course, King Bellamy is also supporting them both."

"And why would King Nostics want to work with Whitehorn?"

Maura flashes him a toothy grin. "Again, a mutual problem, and that mutual problem is her."

"Where do you fit into all of this?" I ask as I try to absorb the information.

"Ah, we also have a mutual problem we want to resolve. Whereas they want Reznor's end, I want yours. I want you dead, and they both agreed, because with you dead, you wouldn't have been able to give Reznor his powers. But, seeing as that time has passed, we moved to a different approach. It still ends with you dead, so I stayed with their alliance."

"Oh?"

"Yes, although I highly doubt this war will end with you two winning it, so, that information is useless."

Reznor gleams at Maura again. If I didn't know it was a show, I would have been fooled by his act. "Why am I such a problem to Lord Nostics?"

"It's not so much that you're the problem. You see, he simply wants to avenge his daughter's death. Which was, of course, brought on by Liara."

I scuff loudly, "She was a whore who tried to kill me. How is her death my fault?"

Maura cackles, "If you never came, then she would have never been killed. Reznor wouldn't have defended your honor." I can see her point, but it still seems rather ambiguous. "That, however, is not King Bellamy's point. In the scrolls and earliest texts in this world, it talks about the two destined to be—the two yielding mass power and what would happen if they were together. One of the most repeated things is what would happen if there was an heir between you. That's what everyone is really trying to prevent. Imagine if you two had a child, what power that child would hold. No one wants a child to be born from you two, whether out of selfish reasons like control, or hate or fear. It's an agreement; no one wants you two having an offspring."

I stare at my mother, blankly. I hadn't even thought about children with Reznor. Other than bickering with Tatiana, of course, I genuinely hadn't thought about it. Judging by the look on Reznor's face, the thought hadn't crossed his mind either.

"This war is over a hypothetical child that isn't even here yet?"

Reznor matches my annoyance. "Who says Liara, and I even want kids?" Ah, he isn't sure if he wants kids either. A weight is suddenly lifted off my shoulders, along with a breath escaping my lungs.

"Whether the child is here or not, it does not matter. It's the premise that it could happen that is such a threat. Not to mention you're supposed to be King of All one day. These people who support you now, they may not support you later. Keep that in mind, *honey*." I chomp on my cheek as she addresses Rez with a pet name. Yet again, I'm disgusted by her words, but her attention turns from Reznor to me. "You know things could have been a lot worse for you."

I nod in agreement. "That's true, but not much."

Maura grins. "Oh, I imagine being dead is worse than being alive."

Reznor addresses her before I can. "Liara will not be dying."

Stop. You're giving her what she wants. Let's just get what we need and get out of here.

Reznor ignores my words. "If you or anyone tries to harm her, whoever tries will die a slow, painful death." He's smiling, but his words hold such venom, "And if there ever is a child, and someone tries to harm it or its mother, I will kill every person who tries, even if it's this whole damn planet."

Cutting off the topic of unborn children, or rather hypothetical babies, I ask, "Anything else Maura, before we decide what to do with you?"

"Nope, enjoy that title a little while you have it. You won't be a queen for long."

"Still longer than you've ever been one, oh wait, you've never been one. I could have sworn we covered this already."

Maura sulks. "Piss off. I gave you life, I can take it away too."

"We're done with this conversation." Reznor leans down, picking up Maura, only to launch her in the guard's direction. "Take her to the dungeon." The guards waste no time, wrapping her in chains while Reznor turns to me. "I'll have someone siphon her powers. She's returning to the mortal world as a human." I nod but step away from Reznor as I hear faint sniffles. I'd forgotten all about Tatiana and Star. I take Star into my arms. The moment she lays her head against my chest, she starts sobbing again. Tatiana places my cloak around us, fastening it around my neck as I soothe the little girl.

"It'll be okay. I know it doesn't make sense right now, but you'll be okay," I tell Star while I head for the manor without waiting for the guards.

This earns a protest from Reznor as he hurries to my side. "Wait, take the guards with you. You can't go off alone. We don't know if there is anyone else."

"Oh please, you killed all of the men," I emphasize to the dead bodies. "I need to get her to the manor!"

"That's fine, but you're not going alone. We neutralized a threat, not thee threat."

I sigh dramatically. "Let's go then. We can't have her freezing to death."

"Well, that was quite a show," Tatiana comments as we head to the manor, the six guards surrounding us again.

"Well, you know how it is."

"Why didn't you use your powers against her in the very beginning?"

"I did, but I can't use them in close quarters without risking hurting those closest to me in the process."

She nods her head knowingly. "Ah, so you need space to fling people around?"

I chuckled again, "Yes, I need space to throw people around."

"You showed her." I smile at Tatiana's words, but not out of joy. The instant we enter the manor, I ask Kora to get clothes for Star while Tatiana and I take her upstairs into an empty bedroom running a warm bath. We fill the water with pink soap in an attempt to brighten the girl's mood, but it doesn't even get a reaction. Star holds my hand the entire time as we wash her. I almost start to cry when the bath turns a darker shade of pink as we cleanse away the dried blood. Draining the water quickly, we wrap the towel around her just as Kora arrives with clothes. We remain in silence until Star turns to me with a tearful face. "Thank you."

"Anything for you." Her small arms loop around my neck. "Do you want to go find your dad?" She gives a slow nod.

Out in the hall, Reznor, Charles, and Emanuel talk in hushed voices, but they stop immediately the moment we exit the room. Reznor's face is ridden with guilt and sadness as tears leak down Star's face again. I know Reznor will feel guilty about this forever, as will I.

"Your dad is waiting in my study. Would you like to see him?" he asks Star. She nods her head without removing it from my chest. We go down the hallway in silence, Reznor staying close to my side while Emanuel and Charles linger a few paces behind us.

When Reznor opens the door to the study, the concerned eyes of the nobleman pass over Star. He has questions in his eyes, yet no tears. Little does he know a piece of his life has just been torn away. Reznor sits with the man while I take Star to the window.

Star reaches up, touching my hair, "You protected me."

"Of course."

"That woman back there, she's your mommy?" she asks, her small mind trying to grasp the situation.

"Yes, but she was a bad mommy."

Her face falls. "My mommy was a good mommy." Her voice cracks along with a piece of my heart.

"I'm sorry about what happened to your mom. If I could bring her back, I would."

Star sniffles, swiping at her nose. "Your mommy was wrong to want to hurt you. You're the nicest person I know. You're not mean."

"Sometimes, we have to act differently to certain people to protect the ones you love," I explain, hugging her tightly.

She jerks back. "My mommy loved the dress you got me. She didn't get to tell you."

Tears sting my eyes. "I'm glad she liked it." I try to keep my voice even, but it falters, betraying me.

"I'm sorry, I didn't mean to make you sad." Star wipes a tear from my face.

"You did nothing wrong." I crush her to my chest for the millionth time today.

"Why don't you go give your dad a hug?" I suggest, placing her on the floor. Star leaps into her dad's arms. After a few minutes, they exit the study leaving Reznor and me in silence. He sits on the chair facing his desk, staring blankly at his hands.

I rest a hand on his shoulder. "Rez, it wasn't your fault."

He reaches up, gripping my hand. "I know it isn't my fault, but now that child lost her mom, and that man lost his wife because of us." I don't have words to console him because he was right. It's our fault.

"Yes, it is because of us, but so many people are supporting us and want us to succeed because they want us to be together. They know you aren't a monster, and neither am I. They know we're good. I know it's awful, what happened to Arnold and Anisa or Star's mom. We can't change it. We lived when they died and for what? They would want us to live a long, happy life, to fight for our Nightsend and all of Dwimmér. All we can do now is move forward and try to make sure it doesn't happen again."

"I want to watch them all burn." He has such hate in his voice as he stands abruptly.

"And so, you shall."

After Reznor leaves the study, I stare at the closed door. He said those hateful words, then just left. He meant every single word. He wants to see them pay for the wrongdoing done upon us, and I want the same thing.

Knowing we still have a crowd lingering downstairs, and as much as I don't want to, I force myself to rejoin the party. People are smiling, cheering, glistening in the winter solstice joy as they pass presents, sing, dance, and eat. I can't bring myself to smile with the same gleam that I had in my eyes earlier; it's too forced. It's my obligation and duty to appear as if everything will be okay, to ensure them not to worry…though I'm not sure that's the case anymore.

    The truth is, with more people dying at the hand of our enemies, I'm becoming more and more skeptical about these people fighting for us. Of course, I know there is more to this than just Reznor and I being together. It isn't the point of this war. It's the power that comes from us that caused this.

    I mingle and mingle and mingle. Reznor doesn't make another appearance at the party. I figure he's somewhere with Charles or Emanuel. I haven't laid an eye on any of my boys since I returned to the party.

    After the last guest leaves the manor, I turn abruptly and head back inside to begin seeking out my husband. It's odd to call him that. At first, it was just a name, but now it holds meaning. Husband isn't just a word. He's a person, it's Reznor. I look high and low in that damned manor, but it seems he doesn't want to be found. I search everywhere but I don't dare call out to him through the bond. Yet again, Reznor wants to go through something alone, and I'm going to let him.

    Our solstice tree darkens my mood further. That beautiful ornament is meant to remind us of a cherished day when things were simpler. When I married Reznor, it was meant to be a new beginning for us, not a sentence to a life of loss. Yet here we are, newlyweds trying to fight a war while still trying to find footing in our marriage. They've always said newlyweds struggle, but I never pictured anything like this. I'm so focused on the bulb when a knock on the door startles me, I jump at the sound. Quickly crossing to the door, I open it to see Charles waiting there with his hands behind his back. "Reznor sent me to collect you," he says without meeting my eye.

"Now, Charles, if you're avoiding my eyes, it leads me to believe that I'm not going to like what you have to say."

He grins up at me. "No, I'm afraid you're not going to like my reaction to what's about to happen. Frankly, I think what's about to happen isn't painful enough."

"What's about to happen?" I lean against the doorframe.

"We're about to strip your mother of her powers. Reznor wasn't sure if you would want to be present or not."

Do I want to watch this? The woman who birthed me, who raised me. She's about to go through something tragic, yet I can't process how to feel or what to think. With a grim realization, I know I want to see if she will say anything to me.

"I'll come," I say at last.

Maura is strapped to a metal table. A bald man with the blue-purple eyes of a warlock stands near her head. It's a guest from the party, one I've met many times, named Victor. He's one of the few warlocks who live in our lands. He came to Reznor the moment he learned his mother had died.

"Queen Liara, how are you this evening?" he asks, causing all eyes in the room to shift to me, including my gagged mother.

"I've had better days."

Victor sighs, "That's understandable," before quickly smiling up at me, "I can make this fast or slow."

I tilt my head in Reznor's direction, who still hasn't torn his eyes from me. "Let him choose."

His eyes flash with confusion for a moment, then it turns to anger. "Make it slow."

At one point in time, I craved my mother's attention. I wanted her love, but now I don't feel anything. Maybe I'll feel guilty about it later. I might feel awful later in life, or it might set in when I write to my Grandma to inform her of what's happened to her daughter. But, for now, all I can think about is Star standing over her dead mother, along with the thought of Maura one-day harming Reznor.

I stand at the end of the table that my mother's strapped to. Her eyes never so much as flicker to me. She only peers up at Reznor. She truly has been in love with him, and she's heartbroken enough to ruin his life. She used me to condemn him to a lifetime of misery. After today she won't have that power anymore. I'm not entirely convinced that Reznor will let her live in the mortal world. She's manipulated my life for twenty-one years, but she's manipulated Reznor's life for hundreds.

Here I am, witnessing the man that I've grown so fond of glaring at woman who gave me life. Reznor peers at her with hate, and yet Maura still gawks up at him with love. Suddenly, I feel like I don't belong in this room.

As Victor lays his hand on Maura's head, muffled cries of agony and pain erupt from her throat as she thrashes against the restraints. She's trying to find any form of relief, along with straining to get away from his hand. Maura's magic starts floating from her body toward Victor's hand. The essence of her magic is beautiful, a baby blue, like the sky on a perfect day. Guilt starts to bubble up in my chest as the mist moves slow like molasses toward Victor's hand.

All eyes are on Maura except for Reznor. He's studying me while Maura watches him. He's gauging my reaction, looking for a protest from me or something else.

It's okay. I caress his cheek through the bond. *In thirty seconds, I'm going to walk out that door. It's not because I'm upset. It's not for satisfaction. It's for the fact that my being here will give her the idea that it'll haunt me later. I truly don't care. What I care about is you and this, right here. It's for you. So, I'm going to turn, and I'm going to leave. If you need me, you know how to find me.* With a final caress against his cheek, I start for the stairs. With my back to him, his gaze is like a physical weight till I disappear around the corner.

He's upset, hurt, angry, confused, a whirlpool of emotions, and in the mix of all that in the very center of it all, he's focused on me. Knowing this makes me just as sad, but sad for him. The truth is I've been focused on him; it's been like this all day. In the woods, when I was cradling Star in my arms, I was thinking about Reznor in the back of mind. Still, even after she told me about her mom. I'm concerned for Star, I care for her, but my fear for Reznor is greater. It grows every day.

It's past midnight. I'm still awake in our bedroom, nestled into the couch with a good book. I've read this page at least a hundred times, but the words aren't registering in my brain. My thoughts are still running wild. I'm so focused on my thoughts of Maura, Reznor, Star, the people, Tatiana, and what the war's pressing arrival means, that I don't notice Reznor enter the room. I didn't notice him cross the room only to gaze at the Solstice tree. "It's beautiful," he murmurs, causing my head to snap up. He places the ornament back on the tree. "I've been so busy these last few days that I haven't even gotten the chance to give you your present." He pulls a silver box from his pocket.

"You didn't have to get me anything. In fact, we agreed on no presents."

Reznor crosses the room, sitting on the couch, dragging my feet across his lap. "I know, but I wanted to get you something."

I eye him a moment before opening the box to find a silver wrist band with an engraving of *RN*. Reznor Nighterious, his initials. I place the band onto my wrist. "It's beautiful, thank you."

"This isn't me staking a claim." He lifts his sleeve to show a matching band on his right wrist. On the top of the band, the letters LN are engraved—Liara Nighterious. "It's a talisman," he explains, tapping the band twice to reveal an image of me, right now in this moment. I mimic his action tapping the band on my wrist, displaying a picture of him in a small circular orb above the band. "It will show whatever we are doing when you tap the band."

"What is this?"

He smiles. "I know the bond allows me to feel you and talk to you, to understand what you're feeling…" he rotates his wedding ring, "but sometimes just feeling you isn't enough. I want to be able to see you," he explains. "If you tap this band, it will show you me, and vice versa. Sometimes I just need to be able to see you. You've been seeing a side of me lately I'm not proud of. I'm sorry about that. A lot of old vendettas are being settled now. A lot of things haven't been explained to you that are causing havoc in your life right now. When this war is done, I will explain to you everything that happened and why what happened with your mother had to happen this way."

He still wouldn't meet my eye, but I speak anyways. "Rez, I'm not upset about what happened with my mother. You realize down there all she did was stare at you. That's all she wanted. I was a ploy in part of her games. I know that. I'm not upset with you if you think that's what's wrong."

Reznor finally brings his gaze to mine, and for the first time, I think I see tears building there. "Liara, I can feel your emotions. I know what you feel."

I shuffle closer, resting my head against his. "Read my emotions then, really read them. I'll open my mind up fully to you, read it." All I'm worried about is you, I say in my head, not down the bond and not aloud.

Reznor's hands dart out to cup my face while slanting his mouth across mine. It's slow and sweet, and that says more than either of us have dared to say in the past. Our mouths and bodies move as one. It allows me to stop thinking about my feelings—those emotions for Reznor that are growing past caring, blossoming into something else. Instead, I lose myself in him, and he into me.

Chapter Forty-Three: War Is Coming

It's been a month since the incident at the solstice. We've since held the passage ceremony for Star's mother The irony of her mother's name being "sun" caught my attention. The sun and the stars are never seen at the same time.

The day of the passage ceremony was filled with great sadness. I had met her mother once or twice, but tons of people flocked to the ceremony. They talked about how Sun lit up so many people's lives, and how she held a bright light in her heart.

Star clung to her father, but if she wasn't sticking to her father's leg, she was nestled in my arms, bouncing back and forth throughout the entire ceremony. The child refused to speak to anyone but her father, Reznor, and me. She had chuckled when Charles tried to crack a joke, but even his witty charm wasn't enough to bring the young girl to smile. No one could blame her for being sad. I pressed down my own guilt and sadness in an attempt to help the little girl through her grief, but nothing I did helped. I hadn't seen her since her father had taken her to visit with his parents.

With the ceremony now passed, I'm trying to get back to normal. I resume my training with Charles and Emanuel while Reznor and Maximus continue to plan the war. Today, however, I'm being summoned along for their meetings. At first, I protested, but one look from Reznor shut me up. It's that look that has me sitting in the back of the SUV with Charles and Emanuel as we head for town.

Outside there's melting snow and slush from the last snowfall. It's still winter, just a bit warmer than the frigid temperatures of last week. I used to love snow, but ever since the magic induced blizzard, I've come to realize I don't love it as much as I thought.

Charles snaps me out of my trance. "I don't know why he asked you to come if he's just going to talk to him the entire time." He gestures to Reznor and Maximus, who are talking in soft voices.

"Is he having an affair with Maximus?" Emanuel adds as he leans over the middle seat.

Laughter bursts from my lips as Reznor whips his head around and glares at the three of us. "I asked her to come for a reason, Charles," he says with annoyance. He completely ignores Emanuel's comment.

"Of course," Charles says in a formal voice, trying to cover up his grin with a severe expression, although failing miserably. Reznor glares at us a moment more before returning his gaze to the road. The moment he does, the three of us erupt into laughter again.

I pat Charles' arm. "Thank you, that's the most fun I've had in a while."

Charles is quick to add another joke. "That's even more pathetic. Maybe he is sleeping with Maximus!" Reznor turns around quickly with wild red eyes. Charles holds his hands up in defense. Much more of this, Reznor is going to wreck the car by focusing on us rather than the road.

"Just because I like men, doesn't mean Reznor does," Max adds which doesn't help the situation in the slightest.

"Gods, why do I bring this on myself?" Reznor groans, dragging a hand down his face.

Charles' comment, however, is correct. Reznor hasn't touched me in that way since the solstice. All I've done is train while he deals with Maximus. I see Reznor for two hours total out of the entire day, and that includes our dining times. We aren't even sleeping at the same times because he's usually coming to bed as I'm leaving. When we are in the same room together, our conversations often are about the war, or we're too tired to speak at all. As much as Charles is right, he's also wrong. We're both busy with things, and that means our *other* activities are being put on hold. It seems our lack of personal time together is bothering the staff more than us. We understand we're busy, but then again, they could be waiting for the blow up that follows whenever Reznor and I are apart for too long. I'm shocked the bond hasn't protested more, but maybe it's because we've developed such a sense of ease with each other.

As we get further into the town, the people wave as they catch a glimpse of me in the backseat of the car. The people have always been kind toward me, but ever since the snowstorm, their admiration has become more abundant. The people smile, wave, and even cheer as we pass. It makes me feel a little out of place. I'm not sure how to handle praise like this.

Reznor stops the car outside of an apothecary shop. All of us linger just before the shop's doors.

"What are we doing here?" I ask, gesturing to the hanging sign above the door that pictures a basket of flowers next to a cauldron with a purple liquid brewing inside.

"The woman who owns this shop is a seer. She is like a psychic in your world," Reznor explains as he steps toward the door.

"You dragged me out of the house to see a psychic?" I've never had much faith in psychics. I'm not a believer or non-believer. Just indifferent.

"Yes." Reznor opens the door disappearing into the store.

I follow the boys into the shop that smells of damp wood and sage. The room is filled with dried herbs, cauldrons, candles, even some brooms hang from the walls. The shop itself is dimly lit by a crystal chandelier. A frail, old lady creeps out from behind the glass counter. She has silver hair that poofs, stray strands moving in all directions. She wears a worn black dress that pools at her feet, but what captivates me is her eyes. She has the purple eyes of a witch, along with the chalked trident like marking that Queen Allegra had at the fall harvest; they even resembled one another.

The woman bypasses the greeting from Reznor, swivels around Maximus, then shoves Charles and Emanuel out of the way before standing in front of me. I unintentionally threw up a shield around me when she pushed the boys. I only notice it because as reaches out to grip my wrist she's stopped by my invisible shield.

"My apologies, my queen, I didn't mean to frighten you," she says softly.

A blush seeps to my cheeks. "It's alright, I'm sorry. It's a force of habit. We've had a rough couple of months." I drop the shield, allowing her to take my hand. Her purple eyes turn black as she holds my hands, gasping only loud enough for her and me to hear.

She releases my hand, a mischievous grin stretching over her features. "I want to speak to her alone before you all leave," she says as she turns around, directing her statement to Reznor.

Charles and Emanuel are the first to object. "No, she must be guarded at all times," they say in unison, earning a slap from the frail lady as she passes them.

"Oh, hush you fools, I'm not going to hurt the queen. I just want to give her a late solstice present."

Surprisingly, no one else protests. Instead, we gather at a table in the back of the shop. The circular table holds a crystal ball that gleams from the center. Each of us take a seat at the table: Charles sits at my left with Reznor on my right, then Emanuel, next the witch, and lastly Maximus.

Reznor's the first to start the conversation. "Why did you ask us here?" His hand reaches for mine underneath the table. I allow him to intertwine our fingers, but I can't help but think he's doing it because of the comments made in the car.

Liara, he warns. His hand tensing on mine.

What? I ask innocently. Our fun is ruined by the words that come out of the witch's mouth.

"War is coming," she says blankly while staring at Reznor.

Reznor nods his head. "Yes, it is, but we already knew that. There have been battles for weeks now."

She has a strained smile as she glances at the crystal ball. "I mean, the war is coming to an end soon."

"How do you know?" Maximus asks.

The woman circles her hand over the orb. "The spirits have told me." The crystal ball starts to mix with black, and grey, the opaque colors swirling around until the ball flashes bright red. With a snap of her fingers, the blood red color vanishes. "You'll know what I mean before the day is up, but the final battle is coming. This war will be over soon."

Charles asks the question the rest of us don't dare to ask, "Will we win?"

"I know a lot, but that is unforeseen. The spirits are keeping a rather tight hold on the outcome of the war." She points the finger at Reznor and me. "I'm assuming it has something to do with these two. Their connection has awoken a lot of spirits in the dark world. Some of them want to see the young couple succeed while others want to see their demise." She sighs deeply, "Therefore, they aren't very fruitful when it comes to giving me answers."

A chill creeps over my shoulders, and suddenly, I feel like someone's watching me. I cast a nervous glance over my shoulder, catching the glimpse of a white dress but the witch draws me back in. "You can feel them?"

"I don't know what you're talking about." Now I'm not sure I saw anything at all, perhaps it's just the chill that has me on edge.

"No, you feel them, that chill rising up over your shoulder. That's the spirits." I suddenly feel like I've been drenched with cold water. "They won't hurt you," the witch breaks my thoughts, "I ordered them not to, and if they do, they'll have hell to pay when I die and come to their world." She smiles at me. "Witches will protect the last Nightlighter at all costs, in this world and the next."

The conversation between Allegra and I resurfaces in my mind. She mentioned she's been waiting a long time to meet me. She's fighting only because I am the last Nightlighter. "Why?"

"Because your power is what gives power to us. Nightlighters were created by the gods to work hand in hand with the witches. We are meant to serve you because you are our one true leader. Your powers are strengthened by us as ours are by you. We all knew when you were born. We all felt it."

A wave of emotion rushes through Reznor as he grips my hand. He's having a flashback to when I was first born. He too had known the moment I was born. His emotions range from hope to sadness, then anger. Still, all those thoughts wash away as Maximus directs the attention back to the war.

"What do you suggest we do?"

The witch peers at us all. "I suggest you get your men in order and keep an ear to the ground." She ushers the boys out. "Now leave us. I must speak with the queen."

Do you want me to stay? He's very uneasy about leaving me with the witch.

No, I'll be okay. If she tries to hurt me, I'll scream, and trust me, you'll be able to hear it. Reznor laughs out loud at my words instead of down the bond causing questioning glances to come our way. Reluctantly, the four men step out of the shop, leaving me alone with the witch. She rises from the table, walking to the far wall, gathering three jars: a jar of a lilac-colored liquid, a jar of charcoal grey dust, a bushel of a dried blue plant. She also grabs a cauldron and a candle along with a wooden spoon before sitting back down before me.

"I meant to attend the solstice but didn't have the chance. The spirits were rowdy that night," she explains as she measures out her ingredients, then pours them into the cauldron. "That is not the reason I kept you. There is something I must tell you. The spirits have been harassing me about getting this information to you."

"Okay." I nod, trying to seem optimistic. "What do they want me to know?"

"There are three things I am going to tell you, although they will not be specific, two of the things you can tell Reznor, but the one, you cannot." She pauses as she pours in the liquid. "One, a blonde-haired snake and a silver haired demon are going to work their way into your life. I cannot tell you if they are, he or she, but I warn you if they are successful, it will be the downfall to your love with Reznor." I'm instantly alarmed not only by her words but by the specifics of what they look like. We've met many people with that color of hair. "Two, when it comes to the future, keep an open mind on a choice that Reznor will have to make. You may not see it now, but hardships will come into your life that will make you question everything you knew before in regard to your love." I'm stunned at her words. She speaks of a feeling and word that I steer clear of at all costs, *love*. I never put a label on what I feel for Reznor.

The witch gives me a warm smile. "I've been alive a long time. Some of his choices in the future, you are not going to like. You will resent him for it, but he does everything because he loves you. Even if you two aren't at that point now, you will be when these things occur." Her words settle my worrying heart, but it's short-lived as she continues. "The third thing is what you cannot tell Reznor. One of you will die on the battlefield."

"This battle?" I ask frantically.

"I cannot tell you when, or who, but one of you will die. Do not be concerned because you already know how to bring each other back. The one that will die will cross into the spirit world for two minutes, and twenty-four seconds. Keep in mind that if you trigger that part of the prophecy, other things will come." She lights the cauldron on fire, an orange blaze lighting up her face. "I don't mean to frighten you with these three truths, especially the one with death for one of you."

"You say all of this acting like there will be a future for Reznor and me."

The witch grins. "I cannot tell you if you will win the war or not, but I can tell you that you both will live long beyond this war. It will not be an easy one for either side. Many will be lost." The witch extinguishes the blaze of the cauldron. "You'll come to see me again, not soon, but you will return. The next time you see me, I will have better information for you. However, do not seek me out too soon, for I will have no answers for you then. You'll know when it's time, and you'll know *why* you'll need to see me. As for now, my queen, I bless you with protection."

"Thank you." I move to rise from the chair, but she stops me.

"Do not tell Reznor about the death between you two," she warns.

"Why can't I tell him?" I ask, curiosity getting the best of me.

"Because he will ensure that you never die, and if you are the one that needs to die, then it needs to be allowed to happen."

"You don't think I'll protect him?" A fury builds up in my chest at the thought.

"No, you will protect him, but you also know when something is too late to be saved physically, and something that needs to be saved by magic. The spirits made the request, not me." She leans over to me, taking my hand. "Trust the spirits. They know his troubles best. Waiting for you this long has put a hardness into his soul, one that only you can heal. He can't face the thought of one of you dying without that hardness worsening. Don't give up on him. He'll love you more than you'll ever know." Her eyes flash toward the door. "I'm afraid if you don't leave soon, Reznor is going to come back in. I suggest you make a speedy exit."

I stop at the door, lingering with my hand on the brass doorknob. "Do you take requests?"

She smirks. "I would suggest waiting till later to seek the answer to that question."

"Have a good day." Just as I'm about to walk through the door, Reznor attempts to come back in, causing me to collide with his chest.

He scans me over with worried eyes that turn to puzzlement as he takes me out of the shop door, keeping his arm around me. "What did she say?"

With a shake of my head, I reply, "I'll tell you at home."

He still gazes down at me with uneasy eyes. "Fine," he huffs as I pull myself out of his arms.

"Always so serious, Rezzie," I tease. Laughter erupts around me as the men cackle. I wink at Reznor as I stroll toward the car. Reznor's shocked, his jaw hangs open slightly. Climbing into the back of the SUV, we resume our earlier positions. I'm giving off a playful front, but beneath the facade, I'm petrified about what the witch told me.

Arriving back at the manor, I'm the last one out of the car, taking my time as I leisurely stroll up the stairs, lurking behind the group of tall men. Even in my heeled boots, I'm short as I trail behind them. My heels clicking against the concrete is the only sound to be heard. I study at the shoes, trying to focus on their leather rather than my thoughts. I've been out of it since I left the witch's shop. The darkness I always feel in my chest swells harder today. Reznor waits at the top of the steps when I tear my eyes from the concrete.

I hope he isn't reading my mind; I learned a trick of sorts when it comes to keeping Reznor out of my head. If I think about something else while more pressing thoughts linger in the back of mind, then Reznor won't know my real thoughts. With this information, I'm not sure I'm doing a good enough job to keep my thoughts from him.

"You're quiet today," he notes when I'm in arm's reach. He wraps an arm around my waist, guiding me to his chest.

"No quieter than usual."

Reznor laughs loudly. "Please, a couple months ago, you were talking all parts of the day, laughing, telling jokes, yelling at me. Now, you hardly talk, what's wrong?"

"Nothing's wrong. We're at war. It seems like a bad time to be cracking jokes. Plus, people keep dying for us, and it's not even here yet."

"The war has been here, but few battles have been near." Reznor caresses my sides. "I felt like that when I fought in my first war. I was young, sending people off to die when I didn't truly understand what we were fighting for. You'll learn and understand as we go. We have people willing to fight with us. It helps."

"Is it even worth it anymore?" Those words might not have been the best choice as I registered Reznor's expression. His brows bunch up, a slight grimace forms on his lips.

He grips my sides tighter. "If I have to lose every single soldier, I have in order to protect you, it'll be worth it."

"But it shouldn't be that way," I protest. "You shouldn't choose me over thousands of lives."

"This war isn't about us. It's about the power we have. We don't have to like it, but it's what we have to deal with. This war can't be avoided, and like it or not, thousands of people are willing to die for you and us." Reznor's words anger me, pulling me out of his grasp as the guilt crawls up my back again.

"Maybe they shouldn't be," I mutter under my breath. I know I'm upset about what the witch said, but these feelings aren't just because of her words. I've been feeling guilty more and more as time passes, as the war worsens. The witch's words are just the icing on the cake. I've been thinking about everyone dying since I consoled Reznor after what happened to Sun. Maybe it's the survivor's guilt, or perhaps it's her words but either way, I need to focus on the good versus the bad. I can't focus on the fact that they died while I survived, but I can keep them in my memory and heart as I go on.

After my run in with Reznor, I spend the rest of the day hiding in the sunroom. I don't want to let the thoughts capture my mind, but in the end, they win as I stare out the window blankly for hours. I survey the dead winter scenery through the window, not moving from my spot on the couch. The only reason I even take my eyes from the winter landscape is because Emanuel sits down next to me.

"Maximus asked me to come fetch you," he says, copying my actions and gazing out window with me.

I sigh deeply. "Oh joy, I do warn you if things get too boring, I'm leaving."

Emanuel laughs. "How is staring out the window more thrilling than talking about a war?" he asks as he grins wildly.

"That is a valid point, Mr. Emanuel." He links his arm with mine. We walk silently to the study, creating a calmness that eases my earlier state of worry. When I step inside the study, those feelings vanish.

Reznor's sitting behind his desk with a rather large glass of whisky in his hand. Based on the bottle, he's been drinking for some time. With a glance around the room, Maximus and Charles both have glasses holding hefty amounts of liquor.

"That can't be good," I mutter under my breath to Emanuel before entering the room.

Reznor's face is a mix of emotions, most noticeably are his eyes flashing to red, then back to their stunning blue. His brows are tugged up in worry, but it's mostly concealed by his pressing anger. He has an intense stare to the maps before him. He doesn't even glance in my direction when I ease into the room.

Come here, Reznor mumbles down the bond as he uncrosses his legs and adjusts his seat. I hesitate briefly before crossing the room and taking a seat across his lap. He loops an arm around my waist while the other grips onto the glass. Keeping a blank stare as he continues to focus on the maps.

Bad day? I ask.

Reznor tilts his glass back, swallowing a large heap of the brown liquor before bringing his eyes to me. *It just keeps getting worse.*

Maximus stands near the desk with a letter in one hand and a glass in the other. "The witch was right."

Snapping my head in his direction, I ask, "What do you mean?" I had forgotten entirely about her words to us other than her warnings to me. One peek at Reznor tells me he and the others find the news is a burden. It seems I'm the only one shocked.

"One of my spies contacted me. He intercepted the path in which Whitehorn will be moving all his forces. His target is the witches' land. It's the middle ground between our alliances and theirs," Maximus says, sighing.

"We need to figure out where we can intercept," Charles says before taking a drink.

"They have a lot of warriors, and they're moving fast. The final battle will be upon us shortly," Maximus tells stiffly.

I snatch the glass from Reznor's hand, taking a swig of the burning liquor before handing it back to him. On a typical day, he would have laughed; he would have smiled and teased me because he knows I hate Lycan whisky. But today, he understands why I drink the foul liquid. "What do we do?" I ask while trying not to shudder from the liquor's warmth. Their alcohol is *strong* here.

Reznor shakes his head. "We get ready for battle. It's about the only thing we can do." Although the war has been coming for some time, this all seems fast and abrupt. How has it come time to fight already? It seems like just yesterday I had arrived in this magical world. "There's nothing we can do tonight. Tomorrow, we'll meet with the others and start a plan of action." Reznor takes another gulp from his glass, finishing the drink, "but for now, we need to take your mother back to the mortal world."

I scoff, "Oh, no, no, no, I'm not being a part of that."

Reznor's shoulders shake with his laughter, rising from the chair while lifting me in his arms. "Oh

The Magic Stolen

love, if I have to go, you have to go. We're a matching set," he teases as he heads for the door of the study.

"What? Why do I have to go?" I ask, trying not to flail about too much in his arms.

"Because she is your mother," he insists as we ignore the snickers of the men following behind us.

"She's your long-time enemy!" I counter.

"That's not the point—we're doing this together," he says, growing flustered.

"Fine, but can you put me down?" I swat his chest playfully.

"No," he teases, "I rather like to carry you." He purrs, a smirk on his face, "Plus, you haven't let me toss you around lately."

I openly gawk at Reznor, mortified by his boldness as the boy's snicker and cackle behind us.

"Reznor!" I exclaim, swatting his chest again, earning another round of laughter from the boys. This is going to be a long trip, but it turns out traveling through portals is very speedy.

After gathering Maura from the dungeons, Reznor opens a portal to a forest and bright green field. He takes us just outside of a port to the mortal world. Here, it's spring. The colors and life make me miss the heat and warmth of summer days. Back home, it's winter slush, but here, it's blossoms and greenery. I hum, soaking in the sun, resting my head against Reznor's chest for a moment.

Reznor finally puts me on the ground. I'm gracious as I wander into the tall grass. I'm not sure if he had held me to annoy Maura, or for his own amusement but either way, he's now cheery. Maura, however, is not. She fights against Emanuel and Charles as they unshackle her restraints.

"You can't send me back this way! It's on the opposite side of the planet. All of my stuff is in the United States!" She argues resisting against them as they try to shove her into the gaping hole in a tree that shimmers like silver dust.

"That's not my problem, Maura, walk through the portal, or I can throw you through it. Your choice," he states as he clasps his hands behind his back.

"She might like that too much," Charles mumbles from behind her.

"You're probably right," I snicker as Reznor glares at me, but behind his expression, there's amusement in his eyes.

"I refuse to enter here," Maura says, stomping her foot.

"Throwing it is." Reznor tries to grab her.

"No, no." She slaps Reznor's hands away. "I'll walk." She takes another step before turning to glare at me. "I never loved you." Her words sting more than I led on as I keep a neutral face. "When you lose this war, and your marriage crumbles, I hope you think of me." She turns her attention to Reznor with tears in her eyes. "I always loved you, and I always will love you. If you ever want to see me—" She doesn't get to finish her last words to Reznor as I force her through the portal, using my powers to send her flying through the hole in the tree.

"She talks too much," I snap through gritted teeth. My anger only earns laughter from the group.

"Are you jealous, darling?" Reznor teases, hugging my waist.

"No, I won." I shrug with a pointed expression.

"That you did," he smirks before kissing the top of my head.

Reznor drags me back to our bedroom the second we return to the manor. He insists we're going to talk about the war and strategies to intercept them. That doesn't happen, instead, we comfort each other with our bodies. Between sessions, we talk about anything and everything, but the war. We're like this all night. Laying with my head against his chest, his hand strokes my hair while I grip his sides. I tell him about the witch's words, and he's as puzzled as I am.

"I hate open- ended answers to questions I wasn't asking," he mumbles against my head.

"I think it's because you're so impatient."

Rez starts to protest but stops. "You might be right." He leans down, pressing a soft kiss to my shoulder. "The sun will be up soon." he husks against my shoulder before biting it playfully.

"I don't want to sleep. Waking up will only make things harder."

Reznor flips us over quickly. "Then let's start today off right."

Chapter Forty-Four: Interception

Reznor and I are reluctant to leave our room this morning. We're dressed and ready to face the cold winter weather, but yet we don't make an effort to move. After procrastinating a few more moments, we leave the room in a sea of black clothing from head to toe. We hadn't intended to match, but here we are. Our sweaters even seem to mimic each other along with our black jeans; we're like a perfect set. It's as if our clothes are predicting the mood for the day. We both have an inkling today will be a good one.

Maximus sent word early this morning informing us he discovered the point of interception for our forces against Whitehorn's army. Reznor and I wait in the study for his appearance, although he's running late for the first time since I've met him. When Max finally arrives, he bursts through the door looking rather disheveled with half of his shirt tucked into his pants, one sock up high, the other drooping at his ankles; he's a complete and utter mess. What's most startling of all is the lack of his other shoe. He appears flustered as he flails his arms about marching into the study.

Reznor and I exchange alarmed looks. *What happened to him?*

Reznor chuckles lightly. *I'm not sure, I can't tell if he's been attacked, or if he did the attacking*. He pauses. *If there even was an attack,* he muses as he mocks his friend through the secrecy of our bond.

"Sorry," Maximus says as he adjusts his shirt, tucking it into his pants. "I fell asleep shortly after I sent you that letter, then I completely dismissed my rising call and well—" Maximus suddenly stops speaking as he stares down at his feet. "Well damn it, I lost my other boot!" he exclaims as he reaches down, taking off his remaining boot, tossing it aside with a loud thud.

Reznor eyes Maximus wearily. "We can discuss this later if you like."

"No, no, no, I've found a point of interception. We must check it out immediately. Their forces will be moving quickly." He hurries over to the maps. "There is only one point that we can intercept his armies and have an advantage.

"Where?" Reznor asks as we lean over the maps.

Maximus points to a patch of mountains. "Right here, the Belivok mountains."

Reznor instantly starts shooting down the idea. "Those mountains are treacherous. How could we even navigate an attack?"

Maximus tosses his hands up in the air. "That's why we have to go and *look*." he motions to our clothing. "Why do you think I asked you to dress like this? We must go soon!"

I place a calming hand on Maximus's shoulder. "We can go, but you're not equipped to travel like this. Like you said, you only have one boot." Maximus starts to protest, but I stop him as I grip his shoulder tighter. "How about we take Emanuel and Charles, while you start picking out whose armies we should move first," I suggest, attempting to make him feel important, but also not be a danger to himself, or us on the steep mountainside.

Max nods his head. "That's a good plan, but I think I'll take a quick nap first." Without another word, he strides from the room, leaving his single boot on the floor of the study. Sleep is his main priority, and that's something I can respect.

Reznor starts laughing as soon as Max shuts the door, "You and I were up all night, and we don't look like that."

I grimace, pinching the bridge of my nose. "Reznor!" I hiss.

"What?" He shrugs his shoulders. "No one's in here."

"That's not the point."

"I feel that my argument is valid; no one heard, no one can judge."

"Oh, shut up."

Reznor's lips tug upward. "Ah, there's my girl." He beckons me with a curl of his finger.

Hesitantly, I cross to stand before him, then deposit myself onto the desk in front of him. "Just because you and I are used to staying up all night doesn't mean everyone else is." I'm unable to keep my amusement out of my voice. I've been up over twenty-four hours. I should be exhausted, but sitting here with Reznor, I'm not even tired.

He bites his lip, shaking his head softly. "We're going to have to get this out of our system before we go to war."

Once his words register in my brain, I jump off the desk, trying to get away from him. My advances to create distance is ruined by two strong arms. "Can't run away from me that fast." His voice is hot against my ear, earning a tremor from my traitorous body.

"You're impossible sometimes."

He grins down at me with a twinkle in his eyes. "Well, I guess you're just going to have to get used to it."

I drape my arms over his shoulder. "I think I already am." We both lean in for a kiss, but our lips don't meet as Charles and Emanuel enter the room.

Charles makes a noise of disgust. "I hate when Mom and Dad kiss." He hunches over acting as if he's going to vomit onto the rug.

Reznor sets his jaw. "Stop referring to yourself as our child; that's disrespectful to our good genes."

"I think it's kind of cute," I tease, "although I see you both as brother figures rather than my children."

Reznor's face contorts in mortification, his brows furrowed, mouth scowling. "Don't encourage this." he motions a finger between the two men, then us. "You can claim him as a child, but he certainly won't be getting any claims from me."

"Please, I act like all of your mother's half of the time. I truly don't know how you all have remained friends this long. I swear I stop you guys from killing one another every day." I say, reflecting back on the many near arguments I've stopped between the three men.

They're all silent for a moment until Charles starts cackling, holding his stomach. "Well, you might be the mommy of the group, but we all know who the daddy of the group is."

My jaw falls open. If it could have tumbled to the floor, then it probably would have. Glancing at Reznor whose expression mirrors my own.

Reznor attempts to get a grasp on his shock, running his palm down his forehead. "Did you just call me daddy?" he asks Charles with a straight face.

"Wait, isn't Liara supposed to be calling him daddy?" Emanuel questions, his words shocking us all again. A choking sound clogs my throat as I try and fail to speak.

"Emanuel!" The three of us say in union, but he slightly laughs, clearly enjoying himself.

"We are done with this conversation!" I snap as heat spreads its way across my cheeks. I attempt to hide it, scurrying off the desk.

Reznor is fascinated by my reaction to the topic. *Oh, do I sense daddy issues?*

I whirl around, glaring at him fiercely. *We are not having this conversation right now, Reznor Silas Nighterious,* I hiss down the bond.

Reznor runs his tongue along the top row of his teeth provocatively. *That's fine, we can talk about it later. I'm sure you'll be calling me daddy then.*

"Reznor!" I screech, horrified by the assumption...but also feeling something *else*.

After the boys collectively harass me a little while longer, we all fetch our coats then go through Reznor's portal, stepping through to the clearing before the Belivok mountains. They're massive white-capped mountains with rough, jagged edges with unforgiving pointed cave openings amongst the steep slopes. I don't understand how Maximus thought this would be a good battleground if the summits are this daunting from the ground. The bodies of stone are split by a valley running through the heart of the mountains. The peak is broad and wide, with a long trench that stretches on for miles all through the center of the canyon. Then, just before the entrance on our side is a large open snowy field.

Reznor's silent as he studies to the opening midway between the mountains. Opening another portal, we follow him through. Appearing high up on the side of a peak, it allows us to see the expanse of the broad valley below. On either side of the ridges, there's large snowy fields just before the entrance and exit of the canyon valley.

Reznor points to the far end of the mountain. "They're going to bring their men right down this valley. It's the fastest way through. Going around is another four-day trip each way."

"We could have a division at the front, then have a second division move in from the back to compress their forces. Make it harder for them to fight. Although it'll be risky in the confined space," I suggest, analyzing the ground below. The weight of their stares takes my attention from the harsh walls. "Think about it. We could even have some of our archers hiding up here and shoot down into the fight," I add quickly, hoping my idea won't be shot down.

Reznor seems proud. "That's a great idea," he says with a grin toying on his lips.

I'm giddy between the expression in his eyes and his words. I've gotten something right in the war for once. I just think the plan is common sense. If we can trap and weaken them, why wouldn't we?

Emanuel nods farther down. "That is a great idea, especially if we can divide the forces. They would never suspect our soldiers to be hiding in the cave mouths and nooks in the mountainside."

"It also would be easier for you both to use your powers from up here because then you can spread your magic out further. Use it as more of a blunt force to separate the large mass of soldiers. You could actually see who you're hitting," Charles suggests.

I nod in agreement. "Plus, I don't know how much use my powers will be in a tight space like that. Although it's long, it's not that wide, and I don't want to hurt our soldiers."

"It's larger than it looks." Reznor opens a portal to the valley below, and we all step through. "As much as I like the idea of having you safe and tucked away up there, I can't help but think your powers will be of more use down here." he wades across the snow, deeper into the trench.

"How far away are Whitehorn's soldiers?" Emanuel asks as he moves to stand next to Reznor.

"I'm not sure. Closer than we would like, and they're moving quickly." Reznor tugs through his hair, his nervous tick.

"We need to find out. This thing will be pointless if we don't get our soldiers here in time to fight them," Charles adds, joining them to inspect the area.

"We may need to slow them down." Reznor's eyes light up as an idea springs to his head. "You could make a storm," he says to me.

"What?" I ask confused.

"You could make a storm to slow them down."

"Even if I could, I would need to be near their location to do it. I'm not even sure how long it would hold."

Reznor regards the trench. "We'll need to get the path of their movement from Maximus and decide when, and where we can get you close enough and still be safe."

"If we conjure up a storm each day they move and let it gradually build, they won't think anything of it," Charles adds.

"Even if I could, couldn't they just diminish it anyway? They have hundreds of warlocks fighting with them."

Emanuel crosses his arms. "No, your powers are stronger; therefore, it trumps any of their abilities. Nothing they could conjure could outweigh the Nightlighter powers; the most they could do is a gradual defense to ward it off."

"We could get the witches to help. If I can't conjure one, then maybe I can use my power to strengthen theirs to create the storms."

"Or their powers could fuel yours," Reznor tilts his head back, having momentary relief. "Before we bring this idea to the Queen of Witches, we need to select the best places to move and hide our men."

For the next four hours, we trudge through the snow and mountains as we mark the places where our men will be placed. We also plan some escape routes if we need them, which hopefully we won't. We mark everything down onto a map we created, including every detail about our plans. The map contains every little detail, from the crests in the mountains where our men will hide to small caves in the valley and hide deep into the forests. We've chosen the battleground, using the mass advantage of it. This is an ideal attack zone; Maximus is right.

Once we're done marking and scavenging the woods, we go back to the manor to collect Maximus before visiting Queen Allegra. Reznor, thinking he's a comedian, opens a portal directly into his bedroom. Max startles awake as we all exit the portal and into his warm room in the manor.

He flails in the bed, covering himself with the blanket as he pulls it to his chest. "What in the Gods' names are you doing in here?" he asks bewildered.

Reznor ignores his question. "You were right about the mountains. It's a great idea."

Maximus beams brightly. "Of course, I was! Tell me about it all. What's the plan?" he asks with excitement, moving to a sitting position in bed.

Reznor rolls his eyes. "Why don't you get dressed and meet us in my study?"

Maximus stands from the bed abruptly. "No time to change, tell me now. Time is of the essence!"

Laughter bursts from my mouth. "You need to at least get dressed. You can't meet the Queen of Witches looking like that." I point to his nakedness.

Reznor, now realizing his friend's nudity, steps in front of me quickly, blocking my eyes from viewing Maximus. He growls lightly down the bond, *Liara.*

I didn't do anything, Reznor, I tease. *Why would I want that scrawny man when I have you?* My words only ease some of his tension, but not all of it.

"Meet us in the study once you're decent," Reznor says coolly. He continues to block Maximus from my view (even though I'm not looking) as we leave the room and head for the study. Reznor scowls at our laughter with his lingering anger. He stops, turning to face all of us. "It's not funny. You know how the mating bond affects men when it comes to other men and their mates," he hisses. I think Reznor's embarrassed at how mad he's become so quickly.

"Reznor, we don't have mates. We don't know," Charles taunts between his laughter, which doesn't improve Reznor's anger.

"You've been around other mates other than Liara and me! You know how they act, don't play stupid. Liara would have done the same thing if it had been a woman." His words set my blood boiling as the thought enters my mind...maybe he has a point. We don't address the matter again as the study door comes into view. Reznor sits behind his desk, annoyance flowing off of him in waves.

I sit across his lap, hoping to calm him down with my touch. *It's not a big deal*, I whisper down the bond while stroking the side of his face, brushing back a strand of his un-styled hair. He's been wearing it naturally lately. "I like your hair," I say in an attempt to calm him down further by changing the subject.

This gets me a hearty chuckle from him. "I've had more important things to do than style my hair."

"Just take the compliment."

He grabs my hand, kissing the palm that had been toying with his hair. "Thank you."

"You're welcome! Now was that so hard?"

Emanuel and Charles start snickering from their spots on the couch. "You two are something else," Charles muses, "And to think she hasn't been around this entire time."

"I feel like I've known her forever," Emanuel admits.

"Ditto," Charles chimes in, seeming pleased as ever, a toothy grin on his face.

"Don't worry, you'll grow tired of me eventually," I taunt with a wink.

Never, Reznor angles my chin down.

A blush tints my cheeks as I tear my gaze away from his intense blue eyes that regard me so fiercely it embarrasses me. It's like he's looking into my soul whenever he does that, and it scares me every time.

I roll the hem of my sweater between my fingers. "Do we need to change before we visit Queen Allegra? I feel like we're underdressed."

"It's time for war. You don't have to wear gowns anymore," Charles says while poking Emanuel in the ear, who quickly slaps him.

"That means I don't have to wear heels any time soon!" It's the little things in life.

"Oh, just you wait, when the war's over, and we've won, there is going to be a massive ball. You'll need to wear a gorgeous dress, and heels," Reznor taunts.

"Is that for your enjoyment or theirs?" Charles prods, earning a promise of violence from Reznor's eyes.

"You all love to push my buttons, don't you?" he grips my ass rather boldly, "But let's not be coy. It's for our image as king and queen, although I do plan on enjoying it."

"Why do our conversations always end up like this?" I ask, grimacing at my mate's pleased satisfaction.

"Please, you act like we can't hear you. We must have some sort of payback." Charles says too casually. That startles both Reznor and me as we exchange nervous glances.

"The scary part is I don't know if you're lying or not," I say, while trying to analyze their expressions. Usually, I can tell when they're lying, but not this time.

They smirk at each other. "I guess you'll never know," Emanuel says.

Reznor takes on a cocky expression, running his hand up my hip, squeezing it. "That just lets you know I'm doing a good job."

Oh, Gods could this get any worse?

"Or maybe Liara is doing a good job," Charles taunts Reznor. Ah, I guess it can get worse.

"Alright, we're going to stop this conversation now; we don't need a fight breaking out today. We have too much going on. Save it for after the war." I place a soft hand against Reznor's tense shoulders. He's been doing so well with his temper, but the bond can bring out the worst in him.

Charles thumps his head to the back of the couch. "Mom and Dad are always so serious," he mocks in a condescending voice.

Luckily, Maximus enters not a moment too soon, letting the previous conversation die away.

"Alright, what's the plan?" he demands now that he's fully clothed. Reznor begins to relay the information as he pushes forward the map we made of the mountains. Max soaks it all up like a sponge as he thoughtfully inspects our plan and locations we've selected for our soldiers. Next, Rez dives into the plan of the storms and why we need to go see Queen Allegra.

"Perfect, let's go! Whitehorn's forces are about six days away. We need to be ready in five, so we can move in on the sixth. If Liara's storms can slow them down just one day, it'll be perfect," Max says with confidence as he outlines their path, showing where and how Whitehorn was moving.

Stepping through the portal to the Witch's kingdom, a chill creeps over my shoulder, an eerie feeling setting in. A dark, daunting castle waits before us, but something about it is strange, and the energy surrounding it seems *off*. The windows are grey stained glass along with high towers and a sharp-pointed roof. Even the brick of the castle is darkened, yet it's still magnificent.

"Beautiful," I murmur. I've always liked darker colors and spooky things in the mortal world. This place is right up my alley. Well, it would have been if I didn't have the urge to flee. We stride to the pointed iron gate, the guards letting us in immediately as if they're expecting our presence.

Inside the castle, it mirrors its exterior of a cold dark appearance with high ceilings and bare walls. It mimics something out of the renaissance. There are flaming torches in holders against the stone wall. Reznor reading my mind, he leans down till his mouth is directly by my ear. "This is one of the kingdoms that choose not to use the advances in technology. They prefer to live as natural as they can," he says, his voice just barely a whisper.

We're guided by a servant in a black gown with a hood hanging over her face. She takes us to a large open room with a long wooden table. The only light of the room is coming from the roaring fireplace. The flame's green, emitting more of a glow than a normal fire would.

Queen Allegra enters, dressed in a black gown that falls to the floor with slivers of a shimmering black intertwined with matte black material. She still has the symbol painted across her forehead in silver.

"King Reznor, Queen Liara, I'm assuming my sister was in contact with you?" Her eyes scrutinize me as I shuffle closer to Reznor.

"Your sister?" I ask.

"The witch in the apothecary shop in your town; she's my sister." The three things the witch told me are seared into my mind: forgive Reznor, don't allow the blonde snake and silver devils to ruin our bond, and that one of us will pass into the shadow world for two minutes and twenty-four seconds.

"Yes, she did contact us," Reznor speaks, his voice cool and calm. "We've come to tell you the final battle in the war will be happening soon, but I've also come to ask a favor."

Allegra motions to the couches, inviting us to sit. "And what might that be?" she asks, settling down in the leather chair. Reznor and I sit against a scaled forest green couch. I'm trying not to think about what kind of animal it had once been.

"Liara needs to conjure up a storm for the next six days, including one today. I'm wondering if your witches could help her. We don't want the storms to weaken her before the war."

"Of course, I would love to help. I will help her with the first storm today, and we will add on more witches the more intense the storm gets." Allegra's smile is directed at me. "I've wanted to see your powers in action for quite some time."

"You have?"

"Yes, I have. I've been waiting a long time for the last Nightlighter to come back to us. However, I'm assuming King Reznor is more anxious than myself." Allegra winks at Reznor, who's been peering down at me tentatively. He nods his head but doesn't speak. Instead, he just focuses on me, watching my reaction.

"Let's get going then." Maximus's lack of patience is a saving grace. All that attention is making sweat grow on my palms, a clammy sensation starting in my stomach.

Reznor opens a portal, the men going through first with Allegra and me following. We arrive in a heavily wooded area. The men scout the site before working through the underbrush of trees. Off in the distance of the forest, the sounds of stomping boots and shouts of men are heard, along with the soft glow of lights.

"This is far enough," Reznor states, focusing on the moving men.

Allegra turns to me, taking my hands. "Do you know how to conjure a storm on your own?"

"I've only ever done it with my emotions, but I've had some practice. I think I have an idea on how to start it."

Her eyes flare as her lips tug up. "Then you start, and I'll assist."

Closing my eyes, I start to think of a storm. A light snow, like a picture-perfect Christmas, cold enough to let the snow fall, but a chill that can be warmed by the ones you love.

The wind starts to blow softly, snowflakes falling from the sky, kissing my hair and skin with their presence. When I open my eyes, Allegra starts to chant while I focus on the sky, watching the snow fall around us at a slow, steady pace. Marveling in how it feels, but my bliss is cut short as her chanting stops.

"You conjured that storm with such ease; I hardly had to do a thing. You're stronger than I thought," Allegra beams, releasing our hands. "I'll have the list made. Just visit me over the next five days, and I'll go with you to conjure the storms."

After Reznor opens the portal back to the manor, Allegra sends the boys through the portal but stops Reznor and me from doing the same.

"I wanted to warn you about my sister's words, but I never got the chance. I do wish to let you know that I will do everything I can to help with the war."

"Thank you," Reznor says as I lean into his side.

"I hope you two know I intend for you to have a long, happy life," she pauses, scanning the area. "We will have to finish this conversation another time." She rushes through the portal before it seals shut. Reznor does the same, taking me by the hand as we go through our portal home.

Back in his study, Reznor sits at his desk while I lounge on the couch, studying him as he scans the documents and maps in front of him. "We have to visit each of the kingdoms tomorrow and tell them to prepare for the battle." He stands, slowly making his way to me. "It's time for us to get ready for war."

Chapter Forty-Five: Seeing The Kingdoms

The morning comes fast as Reznor and I silently dress. Our backs are to each other as we both dress on our sides of the closet. A cold, saddened feeling has crept into our bedroom, setting me on edge as it crawls up my back. I pull the black blouse down my body, tight at my navel but flows till it reaches my waist. The fabric crosses over my chest, the sleeves flowing until they cuff at my wrist.

As I slip on the heeled boots, I risk taking a glimpse at Reznor and find him placing the cuff links on his black dress shirt. His face is blank, but his eyes are full of emotions: anger, confusion, anxiety. I rip my gaze from him and zip up the other boot. I have to force myself to leave him in the closet. Whatever he's thinking, he's doing it silently, and for some reason, I think he needs a minute alone. I can hear him heave a deep sigh, but I keep rooted to my spot by the fire, waiting until he emerges from the closet.

"Ready?" he asks, stuffing his hands deep in his pocket.

"Mhm." I stride for the door, but Reznor's grasp on my forearm halts my steps.

"Wait," he says quietly, his eyes not able to meet mine. He focuses on the raging fire, the flame matching his wild emotions.

"What?" I take a step closer to him. Reaching up, tilting his head till he looks at me, his stare is pensive.

"I just need a minute…" He stops, his hand pulling me closer to him by my waist. "I just need a minute with you before we go, and all hell breaks loose. I need one last minute where everything is fine, with just you and me."

I wrap my arms around his waist, resting my head against his chest, clinging to him. I can't speak. I don't trust my voice, or the right words to find their way to my tongue. Reznor holds onto me tightly as he nestles his head against my throat, breathing in deeply at the base of my neck. After holding me a while longer, he releases me then takes my hand in his. We stride out the door and set off to the kingdoms to inform them that the final battle is upon us.

The first kingdom we arrive at is the Kingdom of Demons. The king and queen again mirror each other in every action as we enter the large grey castle. Everything about the castle is grey and dark but not as fearful as the Kingdom of the Witches.

The king and queen sit across from us at a table in their dining hall. "What brings you here?" asks the queen just as Maximus's father and stepmother enter. The King and Queen of the Faeries take their seats next to the demon royals.

"It's time for battle. We've found an interception point of Whitehorn's forces. In five days, I will be back and have a portal open to move your soldiers into my grounds for temporary housing. We'll spend the last night before the battle at my manor, then move in the morning where we will brief each quadrant of soldiers and place them where they're needed.

"We'll also be hosting a feast in their thanks the night you all arrive, but the time has come to fight." Reznor declares every word with authority, his tone radiating power. He is always in his element when acting as king. He never falters.

Cheri, the Queen of the Faeries, smiles brightly as she hurries from the table. "I'll gather my soldiers," she gushes before scurrying out of the room with a pep in her step.

A low chuckle from Typhore, her husband. "She's always loved going to war. We'll see you in five days." Typhore bows his head to us, then clears out of the room, leaving us with the Demon Royals.

The queen nods her head to us, then bids us farewell. Just like that Reznor and I are off again. We visit Allegra next. Surprisingly, she's waiting outside for us with six other witches wearing black hooded dresses.

"Nightlighter, these are the witches that will be casting the spell with us tonight." She motions to the other witches. None of them meet my eye. They all form a circle around Reznor and I, before they all fall to their knees and bow their heads to us.

"We are at your service," they say in unison.

Allegra also bows to me, but she does not fall to her knees like the other witches. "Perhaps you should be Queen of the Witches." Her tone is undesirable, but she doesn't seem malicious.

I grip onto Reznor's arm. "No, I found my place. It's with him in our lands."

Allegra's smile only widens. "As you wish, rise my lovelies." The witches rise without a word, and Reznor opens a portal once they're on their feet again. We enter another densely wooded forest Where the snow is still falling from yesterday. I step away from Reznor, and the witches encircle me again, joining hands with Allegra.

"Whenever you're ready." Allegra casts a knowing grin as she stands with her witches.

Closing my eyes like I did the first time, I summon the second storm—the type of storm that causes snow to stick to the ground. A storm that is enough to be an annoyance, but not a danger. The wind picks up, and a chill sets in. Then the witches start chanting, my eyes opening as the snow starts to fall a little bit harder than it was before.

I seek out Reznor, who watches me admiringly. He leans casually against a tree. A feather light caress skims my cheek from the bond. Y*ou always amaze me*. His words warm my heart in the cooling temperature.

The witches cease chanting, unlinking their hands, and they follow Reznor back through the portal, but Allegra stops me from following suit. "I want you to know that my witches are under orders to protect you at all costs, and no, your mate didn't ask me to do so. These are my orders. Liara, I want you to have a long, happy life. My people have waited too long to meet the Nightlighter, and now we must protect her." I'm about to protest when she dismisses me, stepping through the portal, leaving me alone. I hurry through after them before Reznor freaks out. I don't utter a word to him about Allegra's orders to keep me alive, though. Not because I'm worried, but more so because Allegra's words make me concerned we might not win this war.

Upon returning to the manor, Reznor calls for a car to be ready in twenty minutes. My confusion matches Charles and Emanuel as they both glance my way, but it's Maximus who actually voices his concern.

"What are you taking a car for?" Maximus demands as he studies a map.

A deep sigh slips from Reznor. "I'm taking a car to go see Tatiana."

"Why? That wastes time we could use to plan!" Maximus argues.

"It's none of your business."

"But—"

"Rez, the car is ready," I lie, grabbing his hand, hauling him from his chair, and out the study door before an argument erupts between Max and Reznor.

Luckily for us, the car is actually ready. Reznor speeds out of Nightsend as we head for Greensboro. Thinking we're going to be riding in a comfortable silence, Reznor surprises me as he talks about random things: the type of trees we're passing, how he absolutely hates the color yellow, that the cars in this world run off magic, and the first car ever invented was made here. Still, the young demon who crafted the vehicle, took the idea to the mortal world where he became rich. We discuss whatever little minor and non-important things we can. By the time we get to Greensboro, we're a mess from laughing so hard for the last hour.

Tatiana narrows her eyes, casting us strange looks as she watches us settle in the sitting room of her castle. "What is going on with you two?"

"Nothing." Reznor coughs to hide his chuckle before quickly gaining his composure and relaying the information about the war to Tatiana.

"I'll have my soldiers ready, but I must ask why you drove here to tell me?" She has a hint of teasing in her voice.

"No reason."

Tatiana rolls her eyes. "Do you two want to stay for dinner?"

"No, we've got some planning to do when we get back, and we can't waste any more time," Reznor says as he pulls me up from the chair. We scurry back to the car, cackling as we clamber back into the vehicle.

The ride home is filled with the same banter. It's a joyous time that I'm savoring because before we know it, the final battle will be here, then things won't be this joyful. I want… no, need to savor moments that are easy like this before things get too bad.

Chapter Forty-Six: The Final Feast

The five days leading up to the final feast pass in a blur. Over those five days everything happens quickly. Our home becomes a camp for the soldiers. The beautiful land is hardly recognized due to the large tents and unlit bonfires prepared for the arriving armies. The open fields and lands surrounding our manor aren't the only things that are busy.

The armory is a madhouse with weapons being pulled, sharpened, others assembled as our soldiers prepare for war. I avoid that part of the manor at all costs. The last time I was there, I was instantly bombarded by soldiers and their weapons as they argued over who got what.

I hope today doesn't share the same chaos as the past few days because today, Reznor will open four portals to move the armies into our lands. We've been preparing not only for the move-in day, but also for the feast we will be hosting tonight. It's a final thank you, a wish of good luck, and a farewell to some. No matter how good of a location we chose and how much of an advantage we have, we are still going to lose people on the battlefield tomorrow.

With great reluctance, this morning, Reznor and I part ways. He goes to open the portals and start bringing in the soldiers while I head off to town to visit Morana. She sent word yesterday, asking for Reznor or I to come by and pick something up from her. I promised to return quickly and help with the soldiers who would be moving in any second now.

Oddly enough, this is only the second time I visit our town without Reznor, but both times he's been the reason for my visit. One day, once this war is over, I'm going to spend all day wandering through the town.

I admire the shops that come into view as we pull through the main road, but my eyes quickly find Morana's inn and the woman sitting on her porch despite the cold. The moment the car stops, she hurries from the porch and envelopes me in a hug the second I'm out of the vehicle.

"I was hoping he would send you!" She coos, clutching me tightly. "I've been wanting to speak to you."

"Oh, what about?"

Morana glances around the busy streets. "Let's talk inside."

I follow her into her office. Just as I'm about to take a seat, she strolls over to her wall of bookshelves, pulls back a book, then suddenly, the bookshelf becomes a door. She pushes it open and waves for me to follow her. I force down my amazement, following her through the door. Inside is another office of sorts. It looks more like a library; the small room is surrounded by old books with symbols on the spines that I can't even begin to understand. I really need to learn some of these new languages.

In the center of the room, there's an old purple couch atop of a tattered rug that has constellations woven into the fabric. I sit on the sofa as Morana moves to the wall of books, pulling a sword down from the top that is sheathed in a black case.

The Magic Stolen

Morana gazes longingly at the blade in her hands. "I need you to give this to Reznor." She passes the sword to me.

"What is this?" Pulling open the sheath, Nighterious is carved into the blade.

"This was his father's sword. He gave it to me shortly before he died. He told me to save it for when Reznor would need it."

"Does Reznor know this is what you sent me to get?" I ask as I re-sheath the sword.

"When he receives this, there are going to be some emotions that are going to bubble up. You're going to need to be there for him." She smiles at me and squeezes my hand. "But I have no doubt in my mind you know how to handle him and what he needs.

"I want to talk with you because I knew you've never experienced anything like this in the mortal world. This will be different than anything you've ever seen before; it will make the attack on the manor look like child's play. I just want to make sure you're prepared for what will come tomorrow." She peers at me with sad eyes, cupping my hand with both of hers.

I'm silent, processing what I wanted to say. Still, the words start falling from my tongue before I'm ready. "I know tomorrow is going to be full of violence, blood, and one full of loss, but I'm prepared to fight for our lands and for our future."

Morana's eyes gleam. "When Reznor's father met his mother, he knew they were mates instantly. She had been visiting from another village, and when he laid eyes on her, he said that's when his world disappeared. All he could see was her. Their happiness was put on hold as the war came, and she was strong and fearless, while he had been powerful and dominated the field." She snorts. "Much like you are. You and Reznor remind me so much of his parents. It's startling." Her laughter slowly fades as she turns somber. "Reznor reminds me so much of his father. Both have short temperaments and fluctuating emotions. They both can make you feel so little with just a narrowing of their eyes, yet they can also make you feel so loved.

"And then there's you, who is so similar to his mother. You have those caring and nurturing characteristics, but yet you're not afraid to get your hands dirty or put someone in their place, and you'll do anything to protect the ones you *love*.

"You'll do anything to protect Reznor, so it makes my next words sound foolish. Please try and ensure he comes home. He is like my son, and that makes you like my daughter. I want both of you to come out of this in one piece."

"I promise I will do everything I can to make sure he comes home." I hope she truly understands that I mean every single word. I'm praying whatever Gods are looking down on us that they will make sure he comes home.

"I know you and Reznor have come a long way from when you first came to my inn almost seven months ago. You've been here a short time, and I already see the changes in you both. I love watching you two not only grow as individuals but grow together. At every problem and every bad turn, you two have grown for the better. I want to see the rest of your story unfold, and what your future will be with him by your side.

"Reznor has lost a lot in his life. He had a light in his eyes that dimmed when his parents died, and then it went out completely when a woman broke his heart many years later." Morana stops, swallowing thickly, "Then you came and the light that had been dead for so many years was a raging fire again, because of you."

I'm at a loss for words and unsure of what to do. Luckily, she continues, "Reznor's family is gone except for Tatiana, Emanuel, and Charles. Those are the people who he chose to be his family, and now *you*. He could have rejected you, he didn't have to find you, but he chose to." She gives a smile that she only ever uses when she speaks about Reznor. "He chose *you* to be his family."

My heart warms at the words, but she forgets something. "Morana, that may be true, but you're also our family. You're the mother figure that raised him after his mom died, don't forget how important you are to him!"

Morana hastily wipes a tear from her eyes. "This isn't about me," she insists. "He has never looked or *loved* someone the way he *loves* you." Her words touch my heart and strikes a fear deep in my gut at the same time. The worrying part is the ember, a faint flame that sparks in my chest.

"Morana, you have to understand you aren't replaceable. You're important. We come to you for a lot; we love you. You're just as much a part of his family as the rest of us. Hell, even Max, who is a pain in my ass, isn't replaceable when it comes to our little family. I want to thank you for all the kind words and all the help you've given me since I've arrived. I don't think Reznor and I would be where we are without you. I don't know much about being a queen, and I don't know much about war or problems between kingdoms. But I do know that I would do anything to protect you, Reznor, and every single person in these lands."

"That's a lesson that can't be taught, and that's why you're such a great queen and an even better wife. You want to protect everyone you love and care about, and nobody has to tell you to do it. You fell in love with these people. You haven't even gotten to know them yet or see all of Reznor's lands. You've hardly had any time to learn the ways, but you're already a queen that will be remembered for years to come.

"Look at all the lives you've touched already, little Star for example. If you hadn't been here to comfort her when her mom died or been someone for her to look up to, she could have processed her death very differently. She would have been lost without you, but she isn't because you were here. Even in this war, you know part of you is fighting to win this war for her, so she can have a future."

I grimace slightly. "I know it's selfish because I feel like this war is being fought just so Reznor and I can be together. A large part of me is indeed fighting so Reznor and I can have a future," I smile shyly, "but a larger part is fighting for everyone, the townspeople, Star, you. My few run-ins with Whitehorn are the reason that I'm fighting so hard because I know that I need to keep him from winning. After all, if he does… everything will be ruined. No one will have a future if he wins, and that's the biggest reason that I'm fighting."

Morana pales. "Another thing you have gotten right, my dear. Luckily your and Reznor's power dies with you, and Whitehorn will never be able to take that from you." Morana stands from the couch, starting for the door only to stop again. "Be careful, my dear, watch out for yourself and watch out for Reznor. I expect both of you to come home."

"Trust me, I'm hoping the same."

"You should tell him, you know."

"I'm unsure of what you mean." I know exactly what she means, but I don't want to acknowledge it.

"The thing you're leaving unspoken. I understand why you haven't, why you both haven't, but you're going to war soon. You don't want to wait, and it be too late to say what you want to. You should head back; the manor is probably a mess." She exits through the secret backroom before she closes the door and replaces the book, sealing the entrance shut.

"Once this war is done and over, you tell Reznor to hold on to that. His father told me to save it for when he would need it, and now, he needs it."

"Are you sure you don't want to come along and give it to him yourself?"

"No, I think the best person to give it to him is you." She embraces me tightly. "Take care of my boy."

"Trust me, I am going to do everything in my power to make sure he stays safe."

"I know you will. I can see it in your aura when you talk about it and him. It lights up, especially when you two are in a room together. You both are almost too much to handle."

"You can see auras?" I utter shocked.

She snickers, "Oh yes, it's one of my gifts, but it's rare for a Lycan of my type. I've been able to see them ever since I was a little girl. That's how I knew when I met you that you were, without a doubt, meant for each other. Your auras almost match."

"What do you mean?"

She falters for a moment. "The colors. You both have the same darkness that lingers in your auras with a hint of light. They light up brightly in a beautiful gold when you two are together, or if you talk about one another." She takes my hand. "I know what makes Reznor's aura so dark, but yours, I was surprised to find. Your past is your business. You don't have to dwell on it. Just know that Reznor will always be able to understand your past just like you've always been able to understand his."

A slow burn seeps to my cheeks. "Thank you for the advice. I will keep that in mind."

After our little talk, she embraces me once more then sends me on my way. I don't leave with the cheerfulness that I had earlier after being reminded of my dark past I keep to myself most of the time.

The manor's drive doesn't come into view a moment too soon, a sigh of relief escaping my lips as I practically leap from the car once it comes to a halt. I hurry to find Reznor after I safely tuck the sword in our room. Now isn't the time to be giving him that. Using the bond, I locate him in the back of the manor standing with Tatiana talking, four large portals off to the side of them. Each portal shows each kingdom with the soldiers piling through one after another in lines of six across. It takes me a few minutes to work through the sea of soldiers to get to them.

Reznor, seeming to catch my scent, turns his head in the direction I'm coming from. He opens his arm to me, instantly pressing me to his side. "How was Morana?"

A wave of emotions course through my mind, but I choose to ignore them. "It was good. She's good." He studies me warily.

Tatiana, however, voices her suspicions. "That's a load of crap, but I trust I'm not meant to be part of this conversation. I'll take my cue and exit stage left," she teases, patting my shoulder as she passes.

"Are you alright?" He brushes my hair back over my shoulder. "Your mind is reeling, and the bond is sending me too many emotions to pick which one is the most pressing."

I lean into his touch, resting my head against his shoulder. "I'm fine, Rez, I promise. What can I do to help?"

He sighs profoundly and releases his grasp. "You can direct them to the camps." He smooches me on the cheek. "Are you sure you're okay?"

I playfully push away from his chest as he reaches for me again. "Yes, Rez, I'm sure." I wink at him over my shoulder as I hurry through the camps, trying my best to shove down the resurfacing feelings and thoughts. I need to focus on the bigger issue. War.

The rest of the day passes in a blur as body after body comes through the portals. The grounds fill up quickly along with the camps. Once the sun sets, we're full of soldiers. With everyone here, the kings and queens from each kingdom stand on the stairs before the many surrounding soldiers that line the back garden.

We're gathering to bless them before the feast. Reznor and I stand next to each other in the center in the pairs of royals. He wastes no time as he dives into his speech. It seems as if even the fires crackling grow silent to listen to the king's words.

"This feast has been prepared for you all as a thanks for your service and for your willingness to fight for us tomorrow. Know that this cause is something we all equally believe needs to be fought for. Whitehorn has been troubling these lands for years. Now it's time it comes to an end. All of us that stand before you will stand on the battlefield with you tomorrow. We might not all walk off the field, but our thoughts and prayers are with you. This is one way to show our thanks before we go into battle.

"Tonight, you should enjoy yourselves because tomorrow we fight, and some of us may not return. Just know we are fighting with you, and no matter what happens, your willingness to fight has not gone unnoticed. May the Gods bless us all tomorrow before we move into battle. Amen."

A battle cry erupts from the soldiers. "Whoo, whoo, whoo," they chant in response before turning to the feast. Off in the distance, music starts playing while the royals turn back to the manor. We all sit at the lavish dining table, all of us underdressed. Everyone wears sweaters, blouses, pants, not a single woman in a dress and not a single man in a suit. Tonight, we're equals right now as we sit at this table, and for the first time since my arrival, the generals and second in commands join us also.

I sit between Reznor and Emanuel while Charles dines with the soldiers outside, although Reznor had agreed to let him dine with us. Emanuel remains silent throughout most of the meal, which leads me to nudge him lightly. "What's up? You're not talking," I say quietly.

"You're not talking much either," he points out as he takes a bite out of his steak.

I start to protest but think better of it. "Valid point. I rather dread dinners like this; I feel out of my element."

Emanuel tries to muffle his laughter. "I think we both are out of our element then."

A shrill laugh erupts from Tatiana as Cheri tells her another joke. Emanuel and I exchange knowing looks. "At least she stopped shamelessly flirting with you."

"Thank the Gods. She was making me really uncomfortable."

My laughter comes a bit louder than it should. "I think it was making everyone feel uncomfortable."

"Maybe if you keep talking to me, she'll leave me alone," he suggests.

"Nothing can stop Tatiana from flirting," Reznor amuses as he inserts himself into the conversation. His hand moves to grip my inner thigh, his movements hidden by the tablecloth. "Don't worry, you won't need to deal with this much longer. The dinner is almost over."

As if on cue, Tatiana shifts her attention back to Emanuel. "So handsome, are you busy later?"

Emanuel doesn't falter a moment. "Yes."

"Hmm, such a shame, especially when—"

Reznor cuts her off, "I want to thank you all for fighting with us, for bringing your forces to stand with ours. I know that this war has been a long time coming, but I'm still thankful for everything you all have done. Tomorrow will not be easy, and we only have a slight advantage. His soldiers will be ready to fight. We are going to have to give it our all tomorrow. With that in mind, tomorrow, you're going to witness some things you've never seen before. I can't elaborate on it now because the only explanation will come from your own eyes. Just know I won't walk off that field till Whitehorn is dead, and the threat has been neutralized." Reznor grips my thigh tighter as he speaks, grounding himself to me to keep his anger from rising to the surface. "Enjoy tonight and do as you please, because tomorrow, blood will be shed." Everyone in the room lifts their glasses to Reznor in salute before we each take sip.

Shortly after his speech, Reznor ushers me from the room, and somehow, we end up back in my old bedroom, gazing out across the balcony at our land that is littered with soldiers. Their figures glow softly in the light of the fire. Laughter, music, and multiple voices are heard, the soldiers enjoying their final carefree night. Some of them will die tomorrow. It isn't a question. The question is how many?

No matter if it is just one, it will still be too many over a war for power. Whitehorn is a threat to everyone, and if he doesn't die, it all will have been for nothing. My biggest fear is how eager Reznor is to stay on the battlefield. How he is willing to make whatever drastic measures it takes to secure *our* future, *their* future, *my* future.

"Stop thinking about tomorrow. Just focus on the now," Reznor soothes, resting his head atop mine, holding me from behind.

"You're not supposed to be reading my mind, Reznor," I snip as the figures below start dancing around the fire.

"I never agreed to that, Liara." He moves his head to the crook of my neck. "I like to read your mind because I still need to figure you out."

A chuckle rumbles in my chest. "Reading my mind won't help you figure me out. Hell, I can't figure me out."

"I figure you out more and more each day. Just wait, I'm going to know everything one day, then things will be easier."

"That sounds invasive."

"Can you tell me one thing?" he asks against my neck.

I'm silent as I process whether I want to answer a dark, looming question tonight, especially with a battle happening tomorrow. "Fine, one thing." I say at last.

He tenses. "What happened with Morana today that had you so upset and confused when you got back?" It's then I sense his nervousness. He's wondering what I *know*. I rethink our entire conversation over in my head, but the only thing that sticks out is the part about my past.

"She pointed out that she could tell how dark my past is because of my aura, and that you and I had the same amount of darkness in our lives. It just startled me that the darkness from my past is permanently engraved into what people see in me," I say, choosing to tell the truth while focusing on the soldiers frolicking.

Reznor lightly grasps my chin, turning it up to face him. "Your past isn't something that defines you. It only helps shape you. That's all," he says, as he gazes into my eyes. I can't help but smile up at him. Adoration must be etched into my face because that's what I feel. I peck his lips lightly before shifting in his arms to face him.

"We need to go back to our room so I can give you Morana's gift."

With shaking hands, I grab the sword from the closet and give it to Reznor. His face pales, his jaw tensing as he unsheathes the sword. "I thought this was lost for years. Where did she get it?" He examines the blade.

"She said that your father gave it to her shortly before he died. He said to give it to you only when the time was right, and you needed it…Morana thought that now was the time. I don't know why she didn't give it to you, but she said it was better if I did and—"

"No, Morana was right. It only makes sense that you gave it to me because my dad received this very same blade from his mate. The last time I saw this was three days before he died."

"What?"

He sheathes the sword. "He knew one day I would need it, one day I would need it to fight for you," he says the words so quietly that it sends chills across my skin. "You just gave me the other thing that I've been searching for years." He humorlessly laughs as he sets the sword next to the bed. "It always comes back to you."

Reznor moves fast, quickly pulling me to him by the waist. His lips claim mine with ease, moving together leisurely as he tugs me closer, although I doubt that's possible. We're chest to chest, our bodies molded together. He cradles me like I'm porcelain, deepening the kiss with a swipe of his tongue into my mouth. We shuffle to the bed, Reznor popping each button off my blouse at a painfully slow rate. He tugs it off my shoulders, not once taking his lips off mine.

Even when my knees touch the back of the bed we clamber down onto the mattress, but we never part. I tug at the fabric of his shirt, pushing it up his body. He allows me to pull the shirt over his head only to attach his lips to mine again. "Slow," he murmurs against my lips. "I want to do this slowly if it's our las—" I cut him off with a searing kiss, not wanting to hear talk like that, but I slow down my movements.

I tug at his hair, pulling him down. He crushes me into the sheets, but it's a welcomed weight. I move slowly, memorizing the feel of his hair in between my fingers. I don't dare break the kiss as he drags his hand across my sides. I'm afraid if we stop kissing, then he'll talk, then I'll cry, and I don't want that. We both must think the same thing as we continue to take breaths through our noses, but as Reznor reaches for my pants, he tears his face from mine.

He nibbles down my neck and across my shoulder as he unzips my pants. Easing back, he slips my shoes from my feet, then slowly pulls my pants down my legs. He kisses from my ankle, up to my thigh, across my hips before dragging my underwear down. His head dips between my legs, his tongue making a long swipe before circling my clit. His leisure strokes are just enough to make me desperate. Shifting my hips, he sinks two fingers into my core, curling and pumping them slowly. He picks up his pace with his tongue only to slow with his fingers. He switches back and forth, driving me absolutely insane.

He sucks hard, my back arching off the mattress as I grip his hair.

"Rez..."

He nips at my thigh. "No, we're going slow."

He swipes my core one last time before sucking his fingers clean. I fumble with his belt as he leans over me, crashing his lips to mine. I can taste myself on his lips as he delves his tongue into my mouth.

"Pants, off," I demand, pushing at his chest.

He shucks off his pants and shoes before climbing back on top. Reaching out, he works my hair out of its braid, running his fingers through the waves and kinks. "You're beautiful," he whispers quietly as he admires my body.

With his head hanging over mine, I memorize his broad shoulders and the smoke tattoo across them. I reach out, tracing the path of smoke up and across his shoulder. When I come to the end of the tendril, I find he's been watching me the entire time. "And you say

I'm the confusing one." My voice is barely a whisper as I look into his eyes that hold all his emotions ranging from sadness to anger, lust, admiration…and something else. I close the distance between us and envelope his lips in another slow kiss. I don't want to think right now; it would just ruin things.

Reznor's hands shift to my back, unclasping my bra with one hand before discarding it. I moan into the kiss as his hands find my breasts, kneading the flesh in his warm, calloused hand. I grip onto his shoulders, looping my arms at his sides. Pulling him down against me, his erection collides with my thigh. Reznor gives a hearty groan that starts deep in his throat.

I drag his underwear down, wanting him inside me. But he's in no rush as he hovers above me, nibbling on my neck, leaving open-mouthed kisses across my mark. He sucks on it lightly before he positions himself between my folds and pushes inside slowly. Our moans mix as he seats himself as far as he can. Kissing my shoulder, his thrusts start slow, moving at a bittersweet pace.

His hips rocks against mine, and as I crane my head to the side, my eyes shut, enjoying the simple bliss of joining with Reznor. He grips underneath my shoulders, pulling me down. Growling lowly, "No." A hiss falls from his lips. "Look at me, Liara," he says, his grip on my shoulder not loosening as he continues to thrust, ever so slowly.

I force myself to meet his eye. The need to kiss him is urgent and pressing. I lean up and kiss him, trying to convey my feelings through my lips. He does the same as it quickly turns into a passionate one.

Though things are moving slowly, the buildup in my stomach tells me I'm close, and from the tensing in his shoulders, so is he.

My eyes start to flutter shut again as he starts to thrust harder, but as his grip tightens on my shoulder, I pry them open. We gaze into each other's eyes as we come undone, our limbs a tangled mess around each other. But not once do our eyes leave each other's until our lips meet again. We kiss, and kiss, and kiss. When we finally tear our bodies apart, it's short, and instead of trying to sleep, we go again and again. Each time we come together, it's slower than the first, and every time, a small part of me breaks with the fear of what might happen today on the field.

The one thing I know, as the sun starts to rise, is how I feel about the man that's clinging to me like I'm his anchor in a storm. We both hold to each other so tight in dead silence, so that when the knock on the door comes to wake us up, I startle and grip him closer. He's the first to leave the bed and move for the closet. I only follow after I hastily wipe a tear from my cheek. Today we go to battle, and today the war with Whitehorn will end.

Chapter Forty-Seven: Blue Lights in The Distance

The clothes I wear are more like armor. The leather pants sheath knives in various places along my thighs and tucked inside my boots that lace up my leg. I wear Reznor's mother's leather jacket with a strap of knives across my chest, but unlike last time, I now have a chest plate that covers from my breasts to just above my hips. It forms to my chest, a subtle shield, a matching one at my back to protect my vital organs. I braid my hair in a single sleek braid down my back. Reznor appears in the mirror behind me.

He wears a version of the same outfit except his armor is lined with symbols, but the one that catches my eye is my Nightlighter crest seated across his heart. His sword is resting at the center of his back. A single black band with a small divot in a 'v' formation rest on his head, the v in the middle of his forehead. A matching band sits in his hand, which he secures to my head, ensuring it fits snuggly. When he's pleased that it won't move, he takes his hands away from my head.

"Still need to show you're a queen even on the battlefield."

"How long do we have?" I ask as I peer into his eyes, again there is that lingering anger. I grasp the sides of his hips. "Save it for the battlefield."

"We have ten minutes before we have to be down there." His eyes briefly close, trying to calm the red that keeps flashing there.

"I'm going to stand here and hold you for the next ten minutes." I don't wait for him to respond or give him a chance to. I wrap my arms around him, and a few seconds later, he does the same. We hold each other for ten minutes in our bathroom, not uttering a word, but then when the time is up, we move. We leave our room behind, then march down to the field. I hate swords, but I'm given one anyway, along with a gun strapped to my thigh. We meet with the other royals, and from there, Reznor starts to give orders. It all happens quickly because he rattles off the plan, and then we move in. Four large portals open to four separate parts of the mountain.

One at the front of the mountains, where a large portion of our forces will go, then two quadrants of archers are moving through the second and third portal. The fourth portal leads to the back, where they will hide off to the side until Whitehorn's forces move through the mountains.

I step through the portal with my shadows for the day, Charles, and Maximus. The soldiers here are already getting into position. The leaders in this sector will be Reznor; he will be the one to give the go-ahead. Along the tops of the mountains, the demon royals are waiting for Reznor's signal. All the archers are blending into the mountainside. At the back and hiding on the sides are the royals of the faeries and Tatiana. The Queen of the Witches will be with us at the main fighting point. Her only request was to be near me. Even as I cross toward the lingering men, I feel the eyes of Allegra's personal soldiers on me. One of them even tagging along, moving into formation with Maximus and Charles.

Reznor is at the very front of the mountains, directing the soldiers. My steps toward him make him glance at me quickly, although he continues to instruct his men.

"Open me a portal to the top. I need to do the last storm so it can cover us until the rest of the forces get through."

Reznor set his jaw and hesitates for a moment; already, he doesn't want me out of sight. Reluctantly he opens a portal to the top far end of the mountains. I go first, although the boys jump through immediately after me. I walk to the edge of the mountain, and at first, I don't see anything but a massive forest, but then a moving, glowing object distracts me. I quickly realize they're lights on vehicles, and a lot of them. Whitehorn's men are closer than we anticipated.

Rez, they are closer than we thought. My words are barely down the bond before a portal opens, and Reznor leaps through.

"Shit!" he curses. "Conjure the storm and try to slow them down. Call out to me when you're done, I need to get back down there and get those soldiers moving faster." Reznor is back through the portal the moment he finishes speaking.

I turn to the male guard of Allegra's. "Are you a witch?" He nods his head but doesn't say a word. "Can you do the spell with me?" Again, another nod of his head. I stick my hand out, and he grasps it before he starts chanting. I close my eyes and think of a massive storm, one that's hazardous on the roads, a storm that is a blanket of white, one that will last just long enough to get all the soldiers into position. My storm begins when I open my eyes, the wind blowing hard. The snow falls quickly, the wind shifting in the direction of Whitehorn's men. I drop the witch's hand once he ceases the foreign chanting, but as we study the storm, it seems to stop as it reaches his forces.

"What's happening?" Maximus asks as he inspects the blue light rising from the position of Whitehorn's men.

"Oh, they want to play. They're blocking my storm with their magic." I glance over my shoulder at the portals still open, allowing archers access far across the mountain top.

"We can do one of two things; I can use more power and try and slow them down, or we can go down and help Reznor."

"You're the queen, your choice," Charles says with a knowing look.

"I say we play." I conjure my powers, feeling my eyes turning grey. "You might want to take a step back or hold on to something. It's about to get windy." Charles, Maximus, and the guard crouch into a nearby cave as I summon a stifling wind and freezing chill, along with as much snow and sleet as I can muster. I launch the wind at the blue light, the breeze rattling around me, the cold nipping my ears.

I hammer them with the storm until the blue light fades. Then, the storm falls full force against his forces. Only then do I stop my assault with the weather allowing my original storm to continue. *I'm done*, I call slightly out of breath. A portal opens a second later. I pass through, the men following behind me. Reznor looks skyward as I approach him.

"You put on a nice show," he compliments though his voice is tense.

"I had to. They were using a blue shield-like spell to block my powers from their forces. They might know we're here now."

Reznor shrugs his shoulders. "If they knew to use the shield, then they could be on to us. Everyone's almost in place. We'll be fine. All we have to do is wait."

Waiting is the worst part. We have set the trap, but now as they start to move through the mountains, I feel this is worse. All our forces are in place; they alert us that the first of Whitehorn's parties are moving into the mountains. Reznor has me with him as we stand with Allegra.

"Do you want her up there with you or back here with me," Allegra asks, and I instantly want to protest, but Reznor's words stop me.

"She stays with me. We're weak if we're separated, so everyone's jobs in our personal guard is to keep us together."

"I'll have my guards come up there with you. The witches will lend their powers to her when they can."

Reznor's arm finds its way around my waist. "Thank you."

Allegra nods. "You're welcome. Now the one thing you both can do for me is live."

I chuckle in light of the situation. "Don't worry, we'll try our best."

A low whistle screeches; all our heads turn toward the mountains. Reznor and I step up to the front. Our guards, new and old, circle around us. It's odd to be surrounded by thirty people knowing their one job in this war is to solely protect us and keep us together. We're strongest together, a weapon when we combine our powers. Today, we will operate as one, and if we're separated, that's when the problems will begin.

Reznor and I stand next to each other as we look into the valley between the mountains. I can feel eyes on us from all angles. They're not only watching Reznor, but they're also watching *me*. These people have heard the legends of Reznor and what his mate will bring. But now that they see me, his mate, and that we are bringing on a change in history…it's something everyone wants to see. The eyes only shift off us as Whitehorn's men come into view, but they know we're here. They knew our plan because the second they see us, they start firing guns, arrows, magic, anything, and everything they can.

"Now!" bellows Reznor, and the moment he says the word, we join hands, and the Battle of Belivok begins.

Chapter Forty-Eight: The Battle of Belivok

Reznor and I shoot his purple mist combined with my powers and send the first batch of soldiers tumbling to the ground, their screams erupting from their throats in pain as our powers tear through them. It takes only a moment of shock on their part before the battle truly begins. It's silent for three seconds.

One,

two,

three.

Then, all hell breaks loose. Each side charges the other. The soldiers surge around us, plunging into the clearing of the mountain. The burst of colors and the clash of weapons echo immediately, followed by the sounds of bullets ricocheting off the walls of the mountain, like bee-bees hitting a tin can. The screams echo as we all advance further into the mountains. Whether it's theirs or ours, I can't tell as we pass through the walls. Reznor and I need to be here because of our powers. Still, I quickly realize it's a bad idea as the area becomes crammed with bodies and the spilling of powers on both sides.

The warriors and Whitehorn's hideous creatures are tearing each other apart in any way they can, whether it's by magic or steel. Reznor and I are being submerged into the madness as the first of Whitehorn's men breach our line. A cluster of them wind up before us. The guards don't get a chance to act as Reznor draws his sword, and I do the same. We strike two down instantly. All the training over the last few months has paid off as we're able to fight together with ease. A large man is coming full force at me with a double blade, but I swing low, slicing his leg while avoiding a lethal blow meant for my chest. The man yells and jumps to strike me again, but he doesn't get a chance; my blade pierces his chest as I rise quickly. His body drops when I withdraw my sword.

I hurry to help Reznor as three circle him, knowing he's the stronger between the two of us. The creature doesn't see me coming from behind it; I slice its head off with ease as it goes to strike Reznor. The window of surprise is short-lived as one of the men come at me next. He punches me in the face causing me to stagger back a step.

I smile as I spit blood to the ground. "Didn't mommy ever tell you you're not supposed to hit girls?" I sneer before sparring with the soldier. He swings hard, trying to move me away from Reznor. He so focused on me, he doesn't see Reznor come from behind as he stabs him through the back and cuts his spinal cord in half. He takes my hand, then we move further through the mess of bodies, our guards encircling us again. A sea of arrows starts falling from the sky like rain as the archers move into position.

More shouts and screams echo through the canyon. That's our indicator that our forces from the back are now moving in. But our relief is short-lived as a cluster of Whitehorn's men charge our way. As I feel my eyes turn grey, Reznor's turn red, and we obliterate the wave of men in seconds as our powers flow like a purple smoke turning all the soldiers to ash. The men didn't even get a chance to scream. They're dead in seconds. Reznor and I killed at least a hundred men in literal seconds.

Our guards even seem to take a step back as they witness the raw power we share. Gasps escape from a few of our soldiers and Whitehorn's as they witness the ash falling to the ground around us. We press forward, hand in hand as we continue our attack. Soldiers try to attack us from all angles. Our guards kill off who they can, but some still manage to weave past their formation, then Reznor and I defeat them ourselves.

We have to protect each other often, as more break through our guards' defense. I've gone through four of my daggers now as I had to take on more than one attacker at a time. I'm guessing Whitehorn realizes Reznor and I need to be separated because that's what his soldiers are doing. When they broke our guards' line, they try to drive us away from each other. It works but only for a moment as I send the seven men surrounding me in different directions. I hurry for Reznor, daggering a man in the neck before stabbing a creature in the chest with the same blade. I need to get closer to Reznor, or things will just get worse.

Just as I'm pulling my knife out of another man's back, I'm tackled to the ground by a Lycan with blood dripping from his forehead. We struggle on the ground as I attempt to throw him off. He has my hands pinned on either side of my head, but my legs aren't as secure. I use all my weight to drive my knee up into his groin, kicking harshly. The man howls and rolls over as I narrowly miss a scrape of his claws. I straddle him as I drive my dagger into his heart.

I pant a moment before I withdraw my knife. As I rise from the man, I'm suddenly hauled upward by Charles. "Stay with me!" he seethes as he keeps me at his side. The only person I've fought with more than Reznor, is Charles. Charles and I work together, striking down as many as possible, creating a system where we use each other to defeat our attackers. We angle our attackers so that we can finish them off quickly as we continue to move, trying to gain ground toward Reznor as the others keep driving him away from us. Two creatures charge us at once, fighting by using magic.

The creature throws a fire orb at me that I deflect. Anger flares across its hideous face as I continue to deflect their magical attacks until I stumble on a root that starts to grow around my ankle. I use my sword to hack it off before jumping onto the creature. I tackle it to the ground as the beast starts throwing punches, and once again, I'm forced onto my back. The creature isn't prepared for the gush of wind that shoots out of my hands, sending it flying against the mountainside.

I clamber back to my feet and grab the creature off Charles by its neck, snapping it. Charles is shocked for a moment before telling me to duck. He swings his sword to stop one that was aiming for my head. In all the commotion, I don't notice someone coming up on my backside, until I'm hauled against their chest and away from Charles's fight. I spin, sword drawn, ready to fight when I recognize Max. "Oh, thank god," I breathe, letting him take me with him. We circle the large man fighting Charles. Max strikes him down quickly, then I'm placed between the two, along with a number of our men forming a protective stance around me again.

"Liara!" Allegra shouts. She and a group of her witches are fifty feet away from me, surrounded by men on all sides.

"Get down!" I shout. My men and the witches drop to the ground. Whitehorn's guards aren't as smart; I throw them against the mountain. They bathe the wall in blood, their bodies breaking as they crash into the unforgiving rock. The next instant my guards are back on their feet again, getting closer to me along with Allegra and her witches as they form an extensive formation around me.

I seize Charles by the arm. "Where is Reznor?" I shout, panic starting to erupt now that I can't see him.

"They took him further into the clearing. We need to get you to him!" he shouts back over the roars of the battle.

Red hot anger rises in me as I turn to Allegra. "Have your witches lend me their power," I shout before storming through my group of soldiers. My eyes turn grey as I allow the darkness that I usually keep buried to rise. Like boiling water, it starts exploding through my veins, and then suddenly, the walls of the mountain starts to shake as I walk through the valley.

I fling body after body against the wall as they try to approach me, never getting close enough to actually touch me. The ground shakes under my power; each step I take through the canyon feels like an earthquake. The sky fills with lightning and roars with thunder. People began fleeing in terror as I cross the ground. I just catch a glimpse of Reznor's purple mist in the distance when the grey in my eyes dissipates. Whitehorn's forces are running in the other direction as I lead *my* soldiers further into battle.

We go quickly. I strike down every soldier that dares attack me in my pursuit toward my husband, toward my *mate*. No one is going to stop me from getting to him. Charles and Maximus fall into step beside me, protecting me. However, I think they do it more to make themselves feel better. Hurrying, the further we get the more creatures come, but now I can see Reznor fighting along Emanuel and some of our guards. I can *see* him. My body sags with relief, but it doesn't last long as a figure slams down from the sky in front of me.

Whitehorn stands before me, anger seared into his features, but he isn't alone; another man slams to the ground with him. I take one look into his eyes and know who it is instantly. I'm looking into the eyes of Serena's father, the daughter that died because she attempted to kill me.

Chapter Forty-Nine: Seeing Red

I don't get to cast Reznor a final look because it takes all of thirty seconds for Whitehorn and Lord Nostics to team up on me. Even with Charles and Maximus, we're struggling against the two. Their soldiers are doing their job, keeping our forces away from us, and as more soldiers move toward the boys. I realize this is a fight between Whitehorn, Nostics, and me.

Maximus and Charles are being driven away from me; I do what I can to protect them by throwing a shield up over them. It's the only thing I can do as I fight the two men. They circle me, Nostics and Whitehorn prowling around me like I'm their prey. But I've never been a fan of hunting. I use my powers to throw Nostics into a wall just as Whitehorn moves to strike me. I have to use both hands to stop his powerful swing as he slams it down upon me. I grit my teeth and use all my weight to push up against the sword.

It works to my advantage because Whitehorn stumbles *one* step. Then another until he's backed away enough for me to send him flying into the same wall that I sent Nostics into. However, Nostics has recovered quickly and is raging.

"So, you're the woman who's behind all this?" He spits as he swings hard. I jump back, avoiding the blow, but he is quick and cuts a slice across my thigh.

The blood flow is instant, but I ignore it and the pain as I throw a dagger at his thigh.

He howls in pain as he yanks it free. Whitehorn returns, bearing a bloody smile as he spits at my feet. "You're a talented little thing, aren't you?" He slowly circles me again, both men mimicking the other. "Maybe I'll keep you as a pet, turn you into a plaything," he taunts as Nostics makes a move to grab me, but I deflect and land a long gash against his arm with my sword.

"I'm not yours to touch," I snarl.

"I can do anything I want, and Reznor would just hate it if I turned you into my plaything." His smile tints red. It makes him that much more daunting, but yet again, I push down the disgust and fear.

"No, she dies, Whitehorn," Nostics says, swiping for me again. I use my powers to push him to the ground. He hadn't expected that, and neither did Whitehorn. They're even more surprised when I pull the gun from my thigh and shoot Nostics in the back of the head, his blood splattering up against my leg and body. Then I raise the gun to Whitehorn.

I know it's a slim chance that the gun will have any effect on Whitehorn, but I empty the clip into his chest anyways. This action has more than one intention. Yes, if it hurts Whitehorn, that is an added bonus, but my real intention is to capture the attention of Reznor. It works. I chance a glimpse in his direction, our eyes meeting for a split moment. In that single second, his eyes turn red. A roar echoes through the mountains so hard that snow falls from the tops. I know what the cry means and so do all of our soldiers. That's an order to get to their queen and for Whitehorn to get the hell away from his mate.

I smile as I toss the gun to the ground and shift my sword back into my dominant hand. "I'm not what you expected?" I guess, hoping to stall him in any way.

"No, you're not, but it doesn't matter what I think. You'll be dead before any of them can get to you."

"I'm okay with that, but just know you're dying with me," I sneer before sending him flying to the wall. I quickly follow, striking his back as he falls to the ground. He's on his feet again in seconds, the slice on his back not hindering his attack in the slightest. He swings to strike me. I quickly block it, but he hits again and again. Over and over, hard and fast.

I roll away from him, coming back up on my feet; his sword digs into the ground where my body had just been. "I'm getting really tired of your shit," I sneer as I throw a dagger into his shoulder.

"What do you mean?" he asks with a devilish grin, pulling the blade from his shoulder, not flinching from the pain.

"Who decided you could play God?" I ask, jumping away from another blow from his sword. He's trying to wear me down, and it's working. I'm growing tired. His heavy blows make my muscles ache and scream in protest.

"No one decided I could play God because I am a God," he seethes. He makes a move to drive his sword into my heart, but I swipe at the last second, and he ends up slicing my shoulder.

"That statement alone proves why you're not a God." I dare another look at Reznor. He has only moved maybe another ten feet; he's hardly any closer than before.

"He isn't going to save you," Whitehorn taunts as he swipes and lashes at me, making me leap back. I'm getting too close to the wall behind me. "He got what he wanted out of you, his powers; you're nothing now."

I know he's lying, but the darkness inside of me devours the words. Lightning strikes down into the mountains, dismantling a group of vicious creatures. "One, you're wrong," I say, throwing him backward with my powers. "Two, you'll never get my powers or his because you're not *worthy*." I take a step toward him, shoving him back further. "Reznor already has the power that's been stolen from him, and not you or anyone else will ever take them again."

This triggers Whitehorn. He rapidly approaches, swinging hard and irrationally. He isn't thinking, he's just striking whatever he can, and wherever he can. "You know nothing, girl," he sneers with a feral voice.

"Please, why do you think he has so much power? His father knew he was *worthy*. The God that gave him the power knew he was *worthy*!" I pause to deflect a blow from his sword. "They knew he was meant to be king!" I strike back, slicing at his face and neck. "He knew that Reznor was destined for greatness when you're destined for nothing but death by my hand!" I'm screaming now; more lightning comes down from the sky, and the wind is picking up quickly.

Once again, I call out to the darkness that resonates so deep inside me, the part that enjoys every blow that I've made today. That part of me that craves darkness and destruction, the part of me that craves war. This part of me is alive for the first time, and it's hungry, and I'm more than willing to feed it.

The wind rages harder. An evil smile creeps onto my face as I conjure up my powers, using them to slam my sword against his. Whitehorn flies back, landing with a groan, the first sound of pain he has allowed to slip since we've started fighting. I want to kill Whitehorn, but not just to satisfy that dark side of me. No. I want to kill him for several reasons.

He is the reason for Reznor's mother's death, and in a way, he is responsible for his father's also. He's the reason Anisa died because of his crazed plan with Lord Nostics. He's the reason Arnold was murdered. He's the reason Star's mother was murdered. Whitehorn is the reason for all this carnage and death that litters the ground around us. He needs to die.

I advance on his weakened state, and I swing down hard again, but I swung too hard, and my sword shatters. The ends of the blade, once smooth, are now broken into razor-sharp edges. It matches Whitehorn's blade that also cracked under the pressure.

"Not possible," he mutters as he rises from the ground, moving to pull a dagger from his belt. I should have assessed him earlier. He has weapons in his boots and against his waist. He has a lot more weapons than me. I'm down to four daggers, my powers, and years of pent of up rage. "How did you do that?" he demands as he pulls a second knife.

"You should investigate into your enemy more before you fight them," I snap; the grey in my eyes hasn't left. The power howls in my veins. It hasn't been used to its full potential. I suppose that's good because I need every ounce of my power to defeat Whitehorn. Even then, I'm not sure if I *can* win.

"You won't be my enemy once you're dead. The time for play is over," he hisses, moving to strike me. I use my shield to block the blow from his second blade as I use my own knife to stop his first from connecting with my side. He strikes again and again, ruthlessly attacking. I struggle to keep up. Using and dropping my powers like this makes it hard to focus while also deflecting a knife. I make a fatal mistake and fumble my step, and it's that single step that allows him to sink the dagger into my side. He slips the blade through the opening in my armor, and it hurts like nothing I've ever felt before. My warm blood starts pooling down my sides.

I won't give him the satisfaction of crying out in pain. I use the proximity to stab him in the thigh. I penetrate the knife so deep that it slams into his bone. He hisses in pain and wrenches his dagger from my side. This time I can't stop the cry that slips past my lips as the blade is torn from my flesh. I distantly hear my name being called, but I can't focus on it as I try to put space between me and Whitehorn.

He's approaching too quickly, swiping hard. I block the best I can, but I know I'm losing this battle. Blood is seeping out of me in various places, and I'm growing dizzy. I can't avoid his next blow as he punches me in the face, sending me staggering. It's all he needs to sink his dagger through my armor and into my stomach. With a smile on his face, he twists the blade. But he has made a grave mistake without knowing. I'm able to *touch* him now.

I summon all my magic and think of turning him to tar, his blood in his body turning black, freezing his blood, and neglecting his body of oxygen. Whitehorn only falters at first, but then he starts grasping to me as he falls at my knees. The black tar seeping out of his mouth, ears, eyes. He's spitting it out.

"I told you." Blood's running out of my mouth now. "If I die, you die too," I say before shoving him away from me. The action jerks the dagger in my stomach. My name is called yet again, and now I know who said it.

"Rez," It's barely a whisper as I find him still fighting off the enemy soldiers. *Rez,* I call down the bond as I began stumbling to my knees.

"Liara!" he screams across the field. Hearing him over everything else, his sweet voice is music to my ears. Our eyes find each other as I use my last bit of strength to call down the bond. He needs to hear me say it—just one time.

Rez, I struggle to talk even down the bond. *I never got to say it.* I choke on my blood as I fall to my side, the dagger moving deeper inside my stomach.

"Liara, hold on!" he begs, aloud or down the bond, I'm not really sure at this point.

I love you, Reznor. I'm barely able to get the words down the bond, but once I do, my eyes start fluttering, begging to shut. Before I give in to the cold darkness, I see red and feel a smothering heat, but the last thing I hear is a mighty roar before it all goes black.

Reznor

The moment I'm separated from Liara, a panic creeps down my spine, slow heat rising quickly. That panic is nothing compared to the terror I have while battling Whitehorn's men, while Liara fights Nostics and Whitehorn *alone*. I'm slaughtering men left and right, hacking and chopping, all in the hope I can get to her, or at the very least help her. The enemy just keeps coming. I'm totally surrounded by screaming, howling creatures, and armored men, most of whom are against me.

Their goal had been to separate us all along and Whitehorn chose Liara for a reason. He knows what I value most in this world. It's the woman who is fighting fearlessly, wielding a sword like she's done it all her life, not months. If I open a portal now, I can get to her, but the men I'm battling will make it through the portal with me. I can't risk any more people in a fight with those already deadly men. So, I fight harder, I swing harder; my magic is already working simultaneously to strike down as many soldiers as I can. It still isn't enough.

I continue watching her, searching down the bond, ensuring she's still alive, but it's when she fires her gun at Whitehorn that I feel a part of me fracture apart. She stands beautifully, even covered in blood, as she empties her entire clip into Whitehorn's chest. Her eyes find mine, and I know she's done it on purpose. Liara knows she's losing, and it's her only way to seek help. It's then that I can't control the rage.

My *wolf's* roar erupts through my throat as my eyes turn red. I shout down the mind link to my warriors, "Get to her now!" Liara is fine for now, but how long can she last? I can't focus on that. No, I need to focus on getting to her. If I hadn't been butchering men before then, I am certainly slaughtering them now. Killing soldiers with one blow, trying to lessen the numbers, but it still isn't working.

I sense Emanuel's same panic. Both of us often glance in Liara's direction, only to see her hacking away at Whitehorn. A sudden rage goes through her; then, lightning shoots down from the sky. I need to hurry. My frequent glances in her direction cost me time, but I need to know she's alright. With each passing moment, she's losing the fight and more soldiers are pressing in like the tide.

It's when her sword shatters against his that the fear starts building up, the panic engulfs me as I see how little she's armed with. Yet even though she's at the disadvantage, Liara doesn't stop. I *need* to get to her. Turning back to the soldiers before me, I slice them down with ease. I can *feel* her pain down the bond; that's when he stabs her in the side.

"Liara!" I scream frantically, but she doesn't look my way. I start shoving my way through the men, not caring if they injure me. I make little progress towards her, but I'm trying. Forcing my mind back to the fight, I try to strategize a plan to cut across the field. Yet, it all stops when I *hear* her cry of pain, and my attention is snagged to her again. He's going after her again.

I bellow her name again as he plunges the knife into her stomach. My blood starts boiling as Whitehorn smiles with satisfaction, while crimson pools down her front. I cut down soldier after soldier as I part through them like water.

"Liara!" I scream again as she shoves Whitehorn's lifeless body away from her. Her lips move, but I can't hear what she says, so I scream her name again.

Rez, she calls down the bond using the nickname she's given me. It has my heart shattering as she starts to stumble. Her words are forced as she continues, *I never got to say it.*

"Liara, hold on!" I roar, cutting down the soldiers between us; there are just too many.

I love you, Reznor, she mutters those words down the bond. My world stops completely. She said the words I'd been too scared to tell her all this time.

"Liara!" I wail as she falls to the ground. The fear turns to red hot rage as I start to feel myself burning from the inside. The smoke tattoos on my hand turn red as fire erupts over my skin. I roar in rage, in sadness, in loss and love. The world around me turns to red as I seek to burn every last one of Whitehorn's men. I disregard the screams of pain and fear around me as I step across burning bodies, solely focusing on the woman lying on the ground with a dagger in her stomach.

I don't care what happens anymore as I race for her. The fire goes out on my body as I fall to my knees beside her. Dragging her body into my arms, I pull the dagger from her stomach. I can't lose her. Not *her*. Anyone but her, not when she finally makes me feel whole. Not after years and years of feeling alone. Not now, when I finally feel like I have someone. Not when I've spent so long not loving a soul the way I *love* her. I can't lose her. I won't lose her.

Laying my head to her chest, I find that her heart is still beating. She's still *alive*. Placing my palm over the gushing wound in her stomach, I call upon my healing powers. I have to save her. I need her. The magic flows from my fingers in the same grey glow that hers does. It waifs from my hand down her body, her wounds healing before my eyes. I sag with relief as the light returns to her cheeks as my powers heal her.

Peering down at her closed eyes, she takes even breaths, her breathing no longer slow and shallow. Cradling her head, I work through her braid, trying to rid the blood from her hair. "Wake up, Liara." I beg, fussing with her hair, then pulling her body closer to mine.

I swipe a tear from the side of her face, kissing her forehead as tears build up behind my own eyes, begging to fall as I longingly gaze at her. "Liara, please wake up." She shifts, her head nestling into my hand.

Those blue eyes flutter open and find mine instantly. "Rez," she cries as she reaches for me. I lose it, yanking her to my chest, burying my head in her neck. Liara is *alive*.

Chapter Fifty: Going Home

"Wake up, Liara," Reznor's voice is strained as he pulls me closer to him, his hands moving through my braid. "Liara, please wake up." His voice is what I cling to, begging my eyes to open so I can see him. I move slightly, nestling my head against his hand.

"Rez," I mumble as my eyes finally open, blessing me with the sight of Reznor. Relief washes over his face before he hoists me into his arms, burying his head against my neck. I drape my arm around his shoulder, trying to pull him to me. His body starts to shake, his shoulder trembling. He releases me abruptly and crashes our lips together. He kisses me hard and passionately, a kiss full of *love*.

He jerks back, cupping a hand on either side of my face. "You can't do that to me." Tears stream down his cheeks. He pulls me into his embrace again. "You don't get to make me *love* you, then go and get yourself almost killed!" His words make me freeze. He loves me back. It's stupid, like some little girl, I feel giddy, but I just hold him tightly. "You don't get to do that," he says again, quieter this time as his hand fists my hair.

"I'm sorry." My voice breaks. Once again, he's saved me. He brought me back to him. I thought for sure that I was going to die. He doesn't release me till we hear footsteps. It was only then that he lets go, drawing his sword, ready to kill anyone that gets too close to me. He freezes when he realizes it's Charles and Maximus. Helping me to my feet, I take in the damage that Reznor inflicted after I blacked out. Everything has been destroyed around him. Hundreds of soldiers in both directions are dead on the ground, engulfed in flames. He kept to his word and let them all burn. The only people left standing are our soldiers, and all of them are shocked.

Then, a slow clap starts erupting from all around us. Maximus and Charles fall to their knees, then Emanuel, then everyone else amid the mountain. I don't know what to do, I don't know what to say, so I just lean into Reznor's side. Scared to let go as if this all will become a dream, and I'll be lying on the ground half dead. Reznor raises a hand, and they all began to rise back to their feet.

"Let's go home," he says to everyone, but I know those words are meant for me. He holds me tightly as we lead our forces out of the mountains and back through our portal to the manor. For the next eight hours, we collect our dead and treat our injured before everyone returns to their kingdoms, to celebrate the win and mourn their losses in their own way. I haven't left Reznor's side Part of that is because he hasn't released my hand, but the other part of me never wants to let him go again. He's even hesitant to let Tatiana hug me goodbye, but he can't stop her. Nor could he stop Emanuel, Charles, and even Maximus from taking their turns from embracing me tightly. I'm most surprised by Maximus. "You are so good for him; thank you for being what he needs," Maximus whispers in my ear before returning me to Reznor's arms.

Allegra doesn't dare to take me away from him. Instead, she envelopes us both and says she wants us all to have dinner sometime once we all recover from the war and the final battle at the Belivok mountains. We agree, but neither of us are in a hurry to be around anyone other than each other. Especially after today, I just want to be alone with him.

I don't protest when Reznor drags me upstairs; I'm more than glad to fall into bed with him, where he makes love to me. He asks me over and over to say it again. So, I do. I tell him I love him as we hold and mend each other in our own way. He tells me he loves me each time. It must have been the only thing that falls from our lips most of the night. I lay my head against his chest, feeling a tiredness settle into my skin.

"I love you, Liara, more than you'll ever know," he murmurs against my ear, leaning down and kissing me softly. Reznor opens his mouth to speak again but is stopped by a knock against the door.

I want to know what's happening, but I'm just *so* tired. I'm vaguely aware of Emanuel waiting outside the door.

"Somethings wrong," is the last thing I hear before the exhaustion overtakes me.

I wake up naked, in a bed that isn't ours. I'm in Tatiana's castle. She's sitting next to the bed, one look in her eyes, and a sickening feeling strikes my gut.

"Where is Reznor?" I ask, gripping the sheets tighter to my chest.

"He left you here..." she hurriedly adds, "he said he was coming back to get you; I just don't know when."

Read on for a look into book two of The Nightlight Series:

The Power Brewing Within Her

I watch the events unfold from the top of the mountain peak. I had to take care of the six guards, but that's an easy task. I'm merely watching, unable to act due to orders that have been in place since this war began.

The young queen battles my father, and I'm shocked she won as she ends him with her powers. She has a rage in her eyes that I've seen in few before, I must admit even covered in my father's blood she's the most beautiful woman I've ever seen. No wonder the King is so transfixed on her, but he won't have her long. I'll make sure of that, because watching them now, I see the danger that they hold. The raw power that surges between them, that kind of power cannot go unchecked.

I take note of the way he prowls across the fields, as he steps over body after body. He only has eyes for her. He ignores his flames as he kneels to his fallen wife. I'm hoping she's dead. I leave my body, possessing a demon on the field. With heightened hearing, her heart beats faintly. The king takes her into his arms, placing a hand on her chest until it starts to glow. The king heals his queen with little thought, and that's when I realize the backup plan has failed. I only stay long enough to watch them rise. Returning to my body only to vanish from the mountains. I need to figure out who messed up, and why those royals are still breathing…for now. But there is more than one day to bring a couple to their knees.

Acknowledgements

When it came to thinking of people to thank and acknowledge for this book, I struggled at first. Not for the reasons most would think, but because I have so many people to thank.

There are a few specific people and places that helped inspire this book, and it seems only right to thank them. To the ones whom I shaped Charles and Emanuel after, thank you for being such great friends and immaculate role models for my life. Thank you for letting me bring anything and everything to you without fear of being judged or mislead. Thank you for joking with me when times were hard and making me laugh when I felt like there wasn't a thing in the world that could make me laugh on certain days. Thank you for being like the big brothers I never had.

To my writing space down A- hallway, thank you for the peace and serenity you offered my mind. To my little blue haired friend, thank you for allowing me to care for you. Thank you for helping me brainstorm ideas. I hope you never lose your passion for writing, and someday I hope you get to publish your book. I'll be rooting for you.

To my friends who helped brainstorm ideas and put up with my constant bantering and complaining when attempting to perfect this book. But this book isn't perfect; it's flawed and completely unique on its own, just like me.

To my best friend, and intern for the help and putting up with my frantic thoughts. The amount of texts, calls and conversations we've had over this book doesn't even scratch the surface for the amount of work we've put into it. Thank you for being my sound board and always telling me when I'm taking it just a bit too far. She knows what I'm talking about, so I'll leave it at that. I can't thank you enough but giving you your own character is a good start!

To my mom, thanks for supporting me when I veered off my original career path. I know you had certain hopes and goals for me but thank you for supporting this one for it makes me the happiest. I hope someday you finish your first novel and love it as much as I love this one.

To the readers, I hope you love this book as much as I loved writing it. I hope their story touches you the way it touched my heart as I wrote it. Thank you all.

Love,

Skylar A. Blevins

Made in the USA
Middletown, DE
23 August 2024

59068345R00390